Waiting for April

WAITING FOR APRIL

a novel

SCOTT M. MORRIS

ALGONQUIN BOOKS OF CHAPEL HILL

2003

Published by
ALGONQUIN BOOKS OF CHAPEL HILL
Post Office Box 2225
Chapel Hill, North Carolina 27515-2225

a division of
Workman Publishing
708 Broadway
New York, New York 10003

Printed in the United States of America.
Published simultaneously in Canada
by Thomas Allen & Son Limited.
Design by Anne Winslow.

LIBRARY OF CONGRESS CATALOGING-IN-PUBLICATION DATA
Morris, Scott M., 1966–
Waiting for April : a novel / by Scott M. Morris.—1st ed.
p. cm.
ISBN 1-56512-370-0
1. Middle-aged men—Fiction. 2. Fathers and sons—Fiction.
3. Florida—Fiction. I. Title.
PS3563.O2439 W35 2003
813'.54—dc21 2002038600

10 9 8 7 6 5 4 3 2 1
First Edition

For Mama and Daddy and Julianne

Whan that April with his showres soote
The droughte of March hath perced to the roote,
And bathed every veine in swich licour,
Of which vertu engendred is the flowr; . . .
—Geoffrey Chaucer

There is the world dimensional for those untwisted
by the love of things irreconcilable. . . .
—Hart Crane

Waiting for April

PROLOGUE

My father first appeared in Citrus on Christmas Eve of 1965. He arrived on foot, wearing tailored wool trousers, a black mohair jacket, an Egyptian-cotton button-down with French cuffs, a charcoal-gray ankle-length cashmere coat and wing tips said to resemble the hue of some poor animal's blood. His cuff links were sterling silver and bore the monogram SRC, as did his signet ring, his handkerchief and his calfskin satchel. Hidden inside the amber folds of that satchel—tucked into a pocket, which had been sewn shut—was the Bronze Star he'd earned in Vietnam and a letter of commendation from the president.

He would later explain that he'd been making his way across the panhandle of Florida when bad weather forced him to look for shelter. There were two storms that afternoon, as a matter of fact. A cold front had descended from the north, while the remains of an exhausted tropical storm that had been gamboling about the Gulf of Mexico suddenly moved inland. They met and prepared to fight over Citrus—the brash freezing air on one side and the warm outraged winds on the other—just as my father came walking up Main Street.

Mother was on the square that day, as were my aunt and uncle and James Henderson. They were only teenagers at the time, except for Henderson, who was in his early thirties and just coming to realize that his marriage was a colossal failure. The holidays were something of a relief for him, however, largely because his wife, Heddy, could be persuaded to wear seasonal lingerie and admit to minor enthusiasm for what Henderson would later describe as their "loveless ruttings." Henderson was standing in front of the courthouse contemplating such prospects when he noticed my mother and my aunt, June and April Lanier, walking toward Ligget's Drugstore.

As soon as Henderson saw April he felt a thumping ache of recognition in his heart, the second-most unruly organ in his frame. Henderson took his heart seriously, and it had lately begun to take April Lanier seriously. Given his bent toward nostalgia—something that was intensified by his veneration of youth and his neurotic conviction that he was already becoming an old man—it was not surprising that April Lanier generated an invincible case of nympholepsy in him.

She was only fourteen at the time. In the parlance of romance and certain romans à clef she was coltish, though never skittish in any genre. In the flustered mind's eye she fluttered the mind's eyelashes, a revelation of soft burnished flesh with supple russet highlights in the form of lips, cheeks, the rivers and rivulets of her balmy palms and every hundredth strand of hair. In plainer terms—which Henderson eschewed—she was simply a stunning and original beauty gifted with the kind of features that would in later years make her even more exceptional. Everyone who saw her realized as much, and she had a way about her that made people not only realize it but become constantly aware of it.

My, she is lovely, Henderson was thinking, already musing in the grandiloquent manner of a man who was sixty or better while fingering a gold pocket watch. Presently he opened his little ticking oyster, his life, his world, the ages, and drummed a glassy sky that protected a pearly ocean floor marked by Roman numerals around which silently scuttled a stout half-arm, a healthy whole one and a nervous emaciated one. Henderson made motions over all these things. He searched for magic casements on the foams of his perilous seas. He conjured and sank and surfaced and chanted to himself, at last dropping anchor on a shoal of borrowed poetry: . . . *but April is the fairest of them all, and the cruellest, breeding lilacs out of a dead heart, mixing memory and desire, stirring dull roots (and lifeless limbs) with spring rain in dead winter.* . . .

Leonard Collins, who was to eventually marry April and so become my uncle, leaned against the Confederate monument in front of the courthouse and grew irritated with Henderson. He could not have known that Henderson was just then creating ridiculous tributes to the girl Leonard loved most in the world, nor could he have picked Eliot—or any other poet, for that matter—out of a lineup of iambs or thugs, but his instincts were sound, and Henderson had the look of a person thinking something pompous and soggy about April.

"I said Merry Christmas," Leonard repeated.

"Oh, I'm sorry. I didn't hear you. Yes. Merry Christmas."

It was Leonard who first saw my father. He often applied his wide back to the base of the Confederate monument while peering impatiently down the street, as if steeling himself to repel an invasion. Weighing well over two hundred pounds, Leonard could have done quite a lot of repelling, and he always seemed to believe he might one day be required to do something along those lines. In fact, what might be called a posture of aggressive defensiveness had been natural to him since boyhood. He had in various ways and at various times squared up against enemies real and imagined, no matter the cost, a practice that served him particularly well on the football field. As a result, the townspeople of Citrus were used to seeing Leonard hulking around and watching over things, but it was not until that Christmas Eve that he actually encountered someone worthy of his attentions: namely, a man of unknown origin and possibly sinister intent. Having spotted my father freshly turned up with the foul weather, Leonard was instantly suspicious.

As well he might have been! The sky was so deeply overcast that streetlights had come on all over town. Violent gusts of wind caused Christmas decorations to bang out frantic protests against storefront windows. Roads emptied as alleys and cats wailed under the assault of increasingly harsh gales. The false snow that had been sprayed onto the sills of the hardware store sloughed off and made false flurries. An innocent red bow tore free from a mailbox and tumbled helplessly across the square. Santa, sleigh, and reindeer were assailed and scattered from the roof of Citrus Cinema. Three wise men who had been bivouacking on the courthouse lawn were kicked out of town; a bevy of shepherds and sheep were sent packing; two very proud parents were pushed over and pummeled; a discount inn was dismantled. Camels, hay, horses and a spare donkey were shoved off-stage and sent begging through backyards. Even Baby Jesus went M.I.A. And beyond all that chaos, a stranger smoked a cigarette while walking up Main toward the courthouse.

Right off, Leonard noticed that the stranger wore what he would describe as "prissy" clothes. He further noticed that the stranger walked with a confidence that bordered on insolence, as if trailing somewhere behind him were a limousine and chauffeur and he had condescended to stroll into town to make a game of his arrival. Leonard Collins was incredulous. "Where in the hell did he come from?"

Henderson looked over then. "I don't know, Leonard," he said. "Blown in from the storm, I reckon."

Stopping perhaps fifty feet away from them, my father placed his satchel on the ground, reached into his back pocket, retrieved his handkerchief and began to wipe his neck and forehead as if it were a hot day and he'd been sweating. This alarmed Leonard, who took it to be a sign of flagrant nuttiness. "It ain't right to be traveling around on Christmas Eve," he announced. "It ain't Christian."

"Well, Mary and Joseph did it," Henderson reminded. "He may be hard up."

"He don't act or look hard up to me."

"Oh, *that's* the spirit of the season."

The first burst of hail covered about half the square, light and unthreatening, the unhurried work of a farmer tossing corn across the yard for his chickens. Another round fell in the same manner. There was thunder in the distance.

"He's a kook." Leonard rubbed his mouth angrily. "It's about to come down hard. I'm getting April and June and calling Mama and Daddy to come get us."

"Hold on," Henderson told him, still eyeing my father, who seemed impervious to the calamitous weather. "Let's go on over to Ligget's. I'll call Heddy and she'll come and carry us all home."

They walked over in the gloaming sheen that had enveloped the town as tiny particles of ice and water drifted down in windblown patterns, shimmering like silverfish shaken loose from old books in God's library. Leonard stopped suddenly and peered back over his shoulder, but my father was gone.

MOTHER AND APRIL were looking out the window, watching the square darken, while Henderson called his wife, who could not come right away for some reason. After hanging up the telephone, he rolled his eyes. "This is what I get for taking a nice little walk into town," he said.

Mr. Ligget smiled and brought out a bottle of bourbon. "Care to join me? Christmas gift."

Although Ligget's would one day be converted into an aerobics studio and its fine counter and grill pressed into the service of healthy shakes and tasteless sandwiches, on that dark afternoon it was something of a lighthouse for Mother and April and Leonard and Henderson. A well-appointed lighthouse at that, where a man could have a drink if the circumstances required it.

"Me, too!" Yes, and a woman, too, like Mother.

Even then, I suppose, she must have been more woman than girl. Though just a senior in high school, she had been the head of the Lanier family for several years. My grandmother had been killed in a car accident —though a titan of a woman, she was no match for a wobbly tractor— after which my grandfather became so depressed he grew sickly and suffered a series of increasingly debilitating strokes that confined him to the house. It was left to Mother to care for everything and everyone, and that gave her the right to adult privileges now and again so far as the townspeople were concerned.

"Who's that, James?" Mother asked, pointing outside.

Henderson wasn't listening. He was concerned with April and the way she was just then toying with her plump bottom lip. He began to drown himself in another blend of poetry, something that was to become a lifelong habit. *April, April, with cruel sweet showers thou hath pierced to the roote, hast washed the droughte of a broken heart, flooding it till it . . .*

"James?" Mother pointed again. "James, who's that man?"

. . . bursts.

There was a vicious crash of thunder then, and after that a profound and ringing silence. Henderson turned to the window. Staring back at him was my father.

"EXCEPT HE WASN'T staring at *me,* Roy. No sir. He was staring at *you-know-who,*" Henderson would tell me, shaking his head. "I'll never forget it. I'm sorry to have to keep going back to that moment so often. I know it must bore you. You'd probably rather get on to the more salacious parts of the story. To the killing and whatnot."

I was in college when we first began to have these conversations about my father. Henderson was entering the final years of a long and distinguished career as a congressman, and I had gone to Washington during the summer before my senior year to stay with him at Mother's request. For various reasons, Henderson and I were already somewhat resentful of each other at that point, but we were also good and ready to once and for all confess everything we knew about what had happened, and so my presence released a flood of recollection from him. He referred to these discussions as our capital chats.

"But I just can't help it. I can't ever seem to get that moment out of my mind. The moment *before* we saw him. When he might have turned away or wandered down a side street and gone to another town. It's *that* moment that won't leave me alone. There were so many things we could have done with our lives. So many possibilities. And then it was too late. Your father had arrived."

He would look at me as if there were something I could have done about it.

"Walked right in. And that was that."

There are different versions of my father walking into Ligget's, but they all have this much in common: When my father, whose arrival was heralded by what was later considered to be an all-out battle between a blizzard and a hurricane, who appeared with all the mystery and purpose of an archangel—Lucifer or Michael, as no less a celestial being would do—when this stranger, who would proudly announce that his name was Sanders Royce Collier, first laid eyes on April Lanier, "He had some kind of a damned meltdown!" Or so Henderson described it.

My habit in those days was to roll my eyes at what I took to be Henderson's extravagance. He was, I tried to believe, putting us—himself, my family and my town—into a seedy saga with purple intonations. I could almost hear the mawkish accompaniment of a harpsichord, the stabbed keys and bleeding notes, as Henderson went on with our pet gothic tale while behind us the luminous bone-gray dome of the U.S. Capitol looked eerily like the mired skull of some gigantic monster.

"It's true and you know it!" Henderson would insist. "Oh, you know it very well!" he'd cry.

At any rate, I had good cause for rankling Henderson.

"Yes, it's the damned truth. And I'll tell you, I think he lost it right then and there. He was almost bashful. And I thought, *Boy, he's nothing like he looks.* Even Leonard warmed to him. Somewhat. If he'd known your father was going to stay on, it would have been a whole different story. In that case he would have given in to his almost instinctive hatred of your father from the start. But, like I've told you before, at first they could almost tolerate one another."

"Because of the war," I'd say to help him along.

"Yes. That's right. Leonard was enlisting and your father had already been over there. As you know, your father was one of those so-called advisers, the ones that were in Vietnam before it was ever publicly acknowledged as a real conflict. He was awfully fierce, I'll tell you that. The thing about him—and I learned of it far too late—was that he possessed a terrifying capacity for cruelty. Of course, he was awfully brave, too. As for Leonard, well, he went over there and got injured."

"His lung, right?"

"You have an unpleasant way of lingering with words as if you're implying something, did you know that?"

"I'm just asking."

"You must have inherited it."

"Must have. I didn't mean to interrupt. Go on."

Henderson would grunt, after which he'd straighten himself and continue.

"As I was saying, he came off as a sensitive sort of person. Very charming. Looked like he came from money. I did notice his accent wasn't quite right. A monied South Carolina accent was still a highly particular concoction in those days, and his wasn't mixed as smoothly as it should have been. So I asked whereabouts in South Carolina he'd come from and he told us he'd rather not talk about where he was from. 'I reject where I'm from,' he said. We all looked over, completely stunned. Who in the world has ever said 'I reject where I'm from'? The choice of words alone should have warned us of something. 'You what?' June said. 'What do you mean you *reject* where you're from?' That's when he reached into that fantastic coat of his and pulled out his handkerchief. We all became quiet and he wiped at his mouth and composed himself. 'It's because of my father,' he said. He looked down sadly. 'Because of my father I've had to reject where I'm from.' Give him this much—he could tell a story."

"I guess he was just telling the truth, in a way."

Henderson sometimes stared at me oddly, as if he were a little confused, and early on I had the feeling I knew some things he didn't know about my father.

"He certainly didn't have many options." Henderson grinned. "You don't miss a trick, do you?"

"Tricks are my specialty."

"Like father like son."

"Touché. That's what I'm to say, right? Touché?"

"Very nice, Roy."

"So he rejected where he was from."

"Yes. He rejected where he was from. And we listened like little children to every word that came out of his mouth." Henderson would close his eyes and shake his head. "How I remember it, Roy. The hail was really coming down by then. Your father even jerked back once or twice because of all the racket. I suppose it did sound as if we were being bombarded. Ligget's was the only place that was still open on the square. All the other storefronts were dark. We were sealed off from the rest of the world, the rest of the South, the rest of Florida, and even the rest of Citrus. The courthouse looked like the mainsail of an old ship, Columbus's ship, lurching in the storm. You could hardly see it, but every now and then it would be there beyond the window, Columbus trying to get to us, and it seemed certain he wouldn't make it, that we were the New World and we were going to remain undiscovered. Freshen me up, Roy, if you would."

I'd take his glass and pour him another drink. If he wanted to smoke, I'd lean forward to light his cigar.

"I really didn't know what to make of his story, to tell the truth. It was clear something had gone disastrously wrong. As we were to learn, he was not one to walk away from a confrontation. He may have come across as calm and cool and collected, but the fact of the matter was, he liked to be calm and cool and collected in the middle of all hell breaking loose. And he was not above breaking it loose all by himself if it happened to come to that, as you very well know."

"Yes, sir."

"But I liked him. Damned fine-looking specimen. Had a nice edge to him. His most distinguishing physical characteristic was his eyes, of course. He was right friendly and quiet, except for his eyes. And that is why he wasn't shy." Here Henderson would raise his long right forefinger as if he were on the House floor and the cameras were rolling. "Because he could make a lot of noise just with the way he would look at you."

Everyone who ever spoke of my father agreed with Henderson about his eyes. They were bright blue, spoked with shards the color of burning sulfur, yet there was no heat or warmth to his stare. Sometimes it seemed as if the work of those eyes, the very inversion of light into images, was visible to those who looked his way, as if he were drawing them in so that they might watch what he was making of them as he turned them and their world upside down.

"But it was more than his eyes. He captured the most peculiar quality of the Southern male."

"A special languorousness," I would say.

"Yes, that's right. An almost defiant languorousness that is spared from arrogance by carefully observed manners." Henderson would circle his fingers on the surface of the table as if he were polishing. "That seems to have been groomed and bred into the kind of man in whom the male principle is so strong that it can't be tampered with. Your father had learned it. Note I said *learned* it. I saw that much, believe me. He was a good student. Imagine the nation's beloved all-American boy and then turn a hundred and eighty degrees and you will see your father, lounging against a street light."

Henderson would sometimes crash his fist down then. Having built up the languorousness, he would crash judgment upon it. He'd describe the storm and the drugstore and my father with great pleasure and suddenly turn against all that he'd said. It often seemed that in doing so he was turning against me.

"I don't have to tell you what that does to a woman. And if the girl is young and innocent it's just unfair."

"Yes, sir. But which girl are you talking about?"

"Both of them, goddamnit. Don't be such a calloused smart-ass. You sound just like him. I'm talking about both of them, by god, and I reckon you of all people damn well know it."

He'd turn away then, already sorry he'd attacked me. To make him feel better I'd pour him some more bourbon.

"Forgive me, Roy," he'd say softly. "Forgive me. I reckon you know about it better than anybody."

PART ONE

ONE

While it is true I eventually came to know a great deal about what transpired between Mother and April and Leonard and my father, when I was growing up it often seemed life had dealt me a hand of cards I wasn't permitted to examine. As I became older and the stakes became higher, I was left with no choice but to play my hand blindly. Not surprisingly, I played it badly. During my teen years such ignorance proved especially costly, particularly where April was concerned. Yet even as a child I could sense that my world was governed by events and forces that had been carefully concealed from me and that maneuvering in such a world would never be easy.

After Mother and my father were married they lived with my grandfather and April. As I would later learn, this was a rather precarious situation, to put it mildly, and it didn't last long. My grandfather did his part to ease tensions by dying shortly after the wedding. I did my part by being born a few months later. And April did her part by marrying Leonard and going to live with him.

She did not go far. They lived less than a quarter of a mile away, just around the bend in the white sand road that passed in front of our house. Leonard pulled up one day with an enormous double-wide trailer just before he and April were married. The gleaming smokestacks of his eighteen-wheeler hissed and puffed as he came to a stop, the brakes groaning under the pressure of the load. When Mother and April and my father came out to see what the ruckus was about, Leonard put the truck in gear and drove on toward the line he'd paid the surveyors to make, the trailer rocking and jiggling behind him.

The five hundred acres my grandfather had accumulated were evenly divided between Mother and April. Leonard had gone to the trouble of having that division clearly marked, something Mother and April would never have done on their own, but then drawing that line was a gesture between Leonard and my father. Leonard parked just past the bright orange ribbon that had been wound around the stakes by the surveyors and placed the trailer so that he could sit on his front steps and watch the line.

Because Mother married first, and no doubt because she was the oldest and had taken care of everyone for so long, she was given the old house, a spacious country dwelling with high ceilings, thick walls, a tin roof and wide porches, built by my grandfather and his friends and neighbors from lumber cut and planed right on the property. There were four large bedrooms, each with its own fireplace. A canning shed stood out back, as well as a smokehouse and a large barn. My grandfather had made a decent living as a grocer and a farmer and eventually owned better than fifty head of cattle.

After he died Mother sold the cattle and filled the house with antique furniture. Once she'd driven the chickens over to April and Leonard's trailer and had given away the hogs, she tidied and sculpted the backyard. She placed old-timey wind chimes of delicate painted glass on the porches to keep the house company when no one was around. She converted one of the bedrooms into a library with rolling ladders and floor-to-ceiling bookshelves. She lined all of the closets with cedar. She bought a telescope, too, and a globe, which was black as tar but glowed a preternatural blue when its heart-lamp was turned on, a seemingly miraculous event so compelling that in no time I learned the nations of the earth and returned to them regularly with awe. Eventually Mother transformed the entire house into something quite remarkable, an exceedingly comfortable showplace that would merit inclusion in *Southern Living* or a ritzy interior-design magazine.

But as a child, the deluxe trailer appealed to me more. Its advantages, I believed, were obvious. For one thing, it could be moved around. It wasn't moved around, of course, but it could have been. April and Leonard could have taken the trailer down to Lake Julep and fished from its roof, for instance, or into the middle of the woods and used it as a deer stand. They could have taken it into town and sold lemonade, an idea I'd press upon them with considerable energy whenever I hoped to earn pocket change. There wasn't any reason to take it anywhere, but I was mightily impressed with the fact that it was possible. Peculiar feats of mobility within the safe confines of home are the very stuff of dreams to a child, after all. A tyke's first and most rewarding flight is from the foot of the bed to the landing light of the doorknob, compared to which a trek up Everest is but the somnambulant shuffling of an old man's feet. How unsurprising that the trailer was for me a portable playground of delights.

Mother, on the other hand, was not very impressed with the trailer. Perhaps it would be more accurate to say it horrified her, though it is also true that she took no small amount of pleasure in the fact that she found its existence to be defining. Simply put, April and Leonard were the sort of people to live in a trailer, while she and my father were not, making the trailer the encapsulation of a certain aesthetic that throughout my life she urged me to avoid. For Mother, there was such a thing as the metaphysics of trailers. To her, a trailer meant something dark and spiritual in the dark and spiritual scheme of things.

Yet Mother wasn't the only person to place such importance on the trailer. As Leonard very well knew, my father did, as well. Actually, what bothered my father wasn't so much the trailer as where it sat. It sat just a few feet from the line, a line that, as had been made perfectly clear to my father, was not to be crossed. For someone who had taken up a life of wandering, a life that knew few boundaries, the situation was difficult for my father to take.

I don't remember many things about my father from those volatile days, but the few things I do remember remain indelible, and my impressions of him have always been vivid. Very early on Mother worked hard to make certain my memory was agile, about my father and everything else. I was reading quite well by five, and by six I was memorizing poems and enjoying the practice of adult conversation. Each Thursday morning when the *Citrus Sentinel* was delivered to our big tin mailbox, I ran out to fetch it so Mother and I could peruse its fourteen pages and have a long discussion about local events and world gossip. On my seventh birthday I was presented with a honey-dipped ukelele, which I fiddled with daily, and the year after, a violin, against which I committed countless atrocities. The only instrument I ever became proficient with was the piano. My grandmother's upright had toothsome ivory tusks and shiny blunt black stubs, sharply contrasting keys that seemed like a marvelous field of play.

Aside from all that, though, I have no doubt I would have been able to recall things about my father with great clarity even if Mother had been content to let my mind rot in front of a television, principally because my memories seemed so at odds with the stories she would later tell me about him. Sorting out such discrepancies forced me to think about my young life more rigorously than I otherwise would have. Mother described my father as gallant and gentlemanly, for example, while I recalled that he was frequently surly and uncouth. Of course, that would not have contradicted what I was told about him—that he had been forced to leave his family and to turn his back on his heritage and therefore had come almost to despise it.

Though Mother taught me to revere him, she herself often appeared anxious and out of sorts with him. Whenever I left the house it seemed like an escape, and I sometimes felt badly because Mother had been left behind. Yet the truth of the matter was Mother seemed to want me to leave the house and even encouraged it.

Sometimes I believed my presence prevented them from enjoying a secret and better life that was possible only after I'd gone out the door. Sometimes I just thought they wanted to argue. And sometimes I sensed I was in some strange way a reminder of something they regretted, which, of course, is exactly how children feel about themselves when there is turmoil between mothers and fathers.

The fact is, I occasionally suspected that my father used me against Mother, as if my existence were a reproach to her. Sundays were always the worst. Mother would be laboring in the kitchen, her face dried of color from a night of drinking. My father would be slumped in a chair, ashen and bitter, waiting on breakfast. He usually wore a suit, though he never went to church. As often as not he'd busy himself with some task of cleanliness, such as clipping his nails.

"That's rude at the table," Mother would tell him.

"Don't be prosaic," he'd reply.

"That's not the right word."

"Yes it is."

"No, it's not what you meant."

"Sorry. I forgot you read minds. She reads minds, Roy. Hey, June, maybe Roy'll inherit that from you. Maybe he'll be able to read your mind one day. Wouldn't that be something?"

"It would be something more than what he'll inherit from you, that's for sure."

Such a statement was the very kind of thing to shake my father up, but then my father was the very kind of person who thrived when shaken up. And so he'd look at me and flash a smile and perhaps wink. The only time he paid much attention to me was when he needed an ally. On such occasions he would fuss with me pleasantly. I'd walk in with my tie crooked, and he'd straighten it for me, motioning for me to come over and wiggling the clip until it was properly in place. "There's my boy," he'd say. He'd check my shoes to see that they were tied, and if he was not too hungover, he might go so far as to tug at my socks. But he'd never kiss me or take me into his arms if he could help it.

One thing that later struck me as odd, and would continue to do so for many years, was his interest in Mother's, or anyone else's, attempts to better me. Whenever she'd tell him of my reading prowess or of some other accomplishment, he'd eye me seriously and tell me he expected great things of me. He even supported my going to church as often as I did, telling me to pay close attention to my Sunday school teacher and to be the best in my class. He took enormous satisfaction when he heard me reciting scripture verses and the like. I say this was odd because his interest in me was otherwise, as I've pointed out, largely tactical and superficial.

"Have you had breakfast?"

"Yes, sir."

"He came in this morning and ate a banana all by himself," Mother would proudly report. "And poured himself a glass of milk like a big boy while Mama and Daddy were still in bed, isn't that right?"

"And I had a cup of coffee."

"Oh, come on. You did no such thing," my father would protest.

I'd stare into those terrible eyes of his and try not to turn away. "Yes, sir, I did," I'd tell him.

"He's advanced, June," he'd remark, staring at me critically but approvingly. "Already drinking coffee."

As a matter of fact, I *was* drinking coffee. Of a sort, at any rate. My desire to grow up and make sense of things had already become so strong that I'd pour a cup of milk from the carton that was kept on the bottommost shelf so I could reach it, and then fetch the coffee can, also placed on that same helpful lower shelf, and spoon in a small serving of grounds. Though I could never stomach finishing off the grounds, it seemed like a sensible first step toward manhood to at least have them in the cup. Manhood being the thing foremost on my mind at the time, I went directly to the kitchen each morning for my coffee, something I supposed every man-of-the-house, not to mention every man-about-town, required.

"Sure wish I could get a cup of coffee," my father would say.

"Just hold your horses, Sanders."

"That's right, Roy. I have to hold my horses on Sunday mornings, but on Saturday nights everybody wants to ride."

"Do you mind with him around?"

"I don't really mind one way or the other."

They were too exhausted to argue with any vibrancy on Sunday mornings and would merely fillip each other with chatter. I'd creep away as soon as I could and take a seat on the front porch to wait for April. Soon enough she'd pull up, and I'd run full tilt into her arms.

While Mother and my father were stale and spent and reeking of alcohol, April was fresh and sweet-smelling. And while they were sometimes lacking in physical affection toward me, April could hardly be in the same room without bringing me near and taking me into her arms. She showered me with attention and tenderness and carried me off to the trailer to spend my days—and very often my nights—with her.

Mother appeared to be in favor of this arrangement. She and my father occasionally went to the Gulf Coast or New Orleans, and April would take care of me while they were gone. Leonard was sometimes around, though every other week he'd be out on the road, hauling loads. My father left town frequently, too, something Mother said he had to do in order to keep an eye on his investments. Mother herself worked as an assistant to Henderson, and once his political career was launched she began traveling a fair amount as well. April, on the other hand, was almost always home. She sometimes worked at the church day-care center, but usually she worked out of the trailer, in a bedroom converted into a workroom, where she took on projects as a seamstress. In either case, it was possible for her to look after me morning, noon and night, and that is just what she ended up doing.

It was April who carried me to church and taught me to dance and took care of me when I was sick. It was she who sat by my crib and sang me lullabies and told me stories from the Bible and taught me to pray and to give my heart to Jesus. While I did not have any experience to contradict it, even as a child I recognized my situation to be beyond the normal scheme of things. Then again, it was the only scheme of things available to me, and I liked it. It never troubled or confused me because I never once thought of April as my mother or even as a substitute mother. Nor, in fact, did I think of her as my aunt. Far from it. I instead thought of her as an exotic and beautiful woman into whose hands I had fallen by some marvelous twist of fate, like little Moses, adrift in his straw basket among the reeds of the Nile, found by Pharaoh's lovely daughter.

April also sensed that our relationship wasn't destined to be traditional. As I grew older she'd sometimes refer to herself as my "old aunt April" and the like, but as soon as such words came out of her mouth we'd both begin laughing because they seemed so ludicrous. What a delightful secret we were! Great buddies, mad confidants, we were linked by eternal golden braids fastened to the thick of our souls. My life at that tender toddling age was divided into exactly two states of existence: waiting for April and being with April. There was no third.

As I WAS EXPLAINING, Sunday mornings were always the most troubling periods of anticipation. Mother usually kept to the kitchen when it was time for April to come for me, but my father, if he was around, would often wander out to the front porch and plant himself in one of the rockers to await April's arrival, a practice that unnerved me.

My father would sit with his legs crossed neatly, inhaling from an unfiltered cigarette, usually a Lucky Strike, I think, though such an evocative brand may simply derive from the romantic imperatives of memory. What is more certain is that he had the gift of never appearing ordinary. It always seemed he'd just arrived from some important destination and might be gone to another at any moment. All his movements were highly stylized. He gestured with his hands in an almost feminine manner, halting these motions to gently toy with the flesh atop his knuckles. His nose was aquiline and his lips a little too red. He kept his hair, which was the color of cola, well trimmed. He never did anything in a hurry, though if he wanted to he could become very aggressive and in a matter of seconds change his demeanor into something capable and dangerous.

I recall once when Leonard challenged him to a contest of marksmanship, and I was given a glimpse of how serious a man my father could be. He and Leonard each placed a tin can on a fence post. Leonard had backed away about fifty yards when he noticed my father apparently didn't think much of that distance.

"Not far enough for you?" Leonard asked.

"Suit yourself," my father told him.

Leonard took aim and blasted his can into the pasture. When he handed my father the rifle, my father looked it over as if he had never seen one before, actually holding it away from his body like an amateur. Then he smiled, winked at me, and began to walk down the road. After he'd gone another fifty yards, he turned around.

"Cute," Leonard said.

But my father had changed. His face was suddenly grave and hard, and he handled the rifle as if it were simply an extension of his body. He peered down the barrel and drew a bead and fired without thinking much about it, knocking the remaining can from the neighboring post.

"Pulls a little," my father said.

"Very funny," Leonard said.

My father produced a cigarette from somewhere—I never saw him with an actual packet of cigarettes and later in life would wonder if he believed packets were too vulgar for him to handle—and began to draw from it with visible pleasure.

"Maybe it's just me," he said. "It's been a while. I'm probably a little rusty."

I watched his eyes catch cold fire from behind a veil of smoke and shuddered in the jumpsuit April had made for me, while an ironed-on swordfish leaped across my chest trying to throw a hook.

I REMEMBER A SUNDAY morning when he sat clicking his signet ring against his teeth, staring pensively into the yard while a rooster crowed in the distance. I knew something had gone wrong the previous night because I'd heard him and Mother arguing in their bedroom. I left the porch and headed down the little brick trail, which was overgrown with patches of soft fern, to search for a pecan under one of the two large pecan trees that rose at the end of the walkway. Ordinarily my father would have had some comment or other to make to me, something to tease me about, but this time he said nothing. When I turned back, I discovered that his eye had been blackened.

"What happened to your eye?"

"I had an argument last night."

"With Mama?"

"No, no," he chuckled. "With your uncle."

"Uncle Leonard hit you?"

"We both did some hitting. It's all right."

When April drove up, my father was trying to smoke in his usual casual manner, but it was obvious even to me that his nonchalance was forced. April hardly looked at him and seemed not to notice his condition, and I could tell this aggravated him.

Her hair was pinned up. She wore heels and a little black dress. It wasn't a church dress at all but something daring that she could have worn to a cocktail party. She rarely had the opportunity to go to such parties, and by way of making up for this Leonard bought her nice clothes when he could, outfits he would get James Henderson to pick out in Washington. April would often wear these outfits to church.

April was a favorite of the old ladies who ran the Citrus Hills Church of God, and although her attire was frequently risqué by their standards, her devotion to the church and her tireless enthusiasm for their enthusiasms, for their shoes and recipes and new Bibles, removed her from any possibility of censure. Having many times seen the affect of her boldly walking into the sanctuary in some modish big-city getup, I might add that these ladies, not to mention their husbands, were unabashed admirers of April's beauty, which they believed, not without reason, somehow lent their lives a little glamour. They would move in close and huddle around her, pinching their lips and telling her she looked like an angel.

All the old stories about the beauty of the Lanier women are true, by the way, but the generations seemed to have been building toward something that amounted to April. Like Mother, she had long chestnut hair, though hers was a little darker and the red tint less pronounced. Where Mother's was straight, April's was rambunctious. Mother's face was the more rounded, of the sort that painters prefer, while April's was sharper and almost handsome with strength. The contrast of her plump, sweetheart lips with her strong jaw created a ferocious sensuality. And while Mother and April were both gifted with wonderfully long legs, April's were the more shapely, probably because she spent so much time walking through the woods and because she'd taken ballet from kindergarten right up through high school.

Not that April was perfect. I shall never forget the shock of discovering that the prescription dandruff shampoo I had always assumed belonged to scruffy Leonard was in fact dewy April's. She was an inveterate nail biter as well and had terrible toes. I could go on, but as anyone who has had any experience with a woman who is not only beautiful but also lively and tenderhearted knows, such details take on their own peculiar charm, so what's the use?

At any rate, it was my father who taught me to notice April in a way that a child would not otherwise have noticed her. When she got out of Leonard's truck, for instance (always a Chevy, usually with thirty-three-inch tires and a six-inch lift), her little black dress would often slide up before she could get it back down. I would notice this because I could feel the hot stare of my father's eyes over my shoulder.

There was a palpable tension whenever they were together. My father often appeared vulnerable around April, if not a bit afraid, something that was unusual for him. He tried hard to combat this with sarcasm. I hated it whenever they encountered each other, and as I was soon to discover, I had good reason to wish that they might remain apart.

Whenever my father stared at her as he did that Sunday morning after his fight with Leonard, watching her dress ride up her thighs nearly to the white of her panties, I stared hard, too, wanting to see everything he was seeing and hating tremendously that he was seeing it. As a boy I appreciated that she was tanned and soft-skinned and that her waist was firm. I loved to knock my ears against her hipbones when we stood side by side. But such innocent pleasures were ruined whenever my father was around. When April talked, my father watched her mouth carefully, and so I did the same, searching out her full lips and anticipating the darting of her tongue after an ever wayward wisp of hair. She'd show me how to make a muscle, and I'd be very impressed with her slender arms and the two pale blue veins that ran to the crook of them, with her little horseshoe triceps and the slight rise of skin over her biceps, but when I caught my father spying on our muscle-making I believed we must never flex in public again. If she carried me on her hip, allowing my head to rest against her breasts, I would find that my father's attention was riven there, as well. And whenever she'd squat down to tie my shoes or zip up my pants, I'd see him gawking and would quickly turn to examine her, finding a delectable bouquet of cleavage that I knew very well he shouldn't be seeing.

I even remember the terrible feeling he caused me one day as I played my favorite game of running up to April and hitching my fingers into the back pockets of her jeans and swinging my body against the backs of her legs with my own spread wide about her. My father saw this and began to chew his lip. I became so highly agitated that I tried to claw my way up April's back and succeeded in pulling her jeans down just far enough to make everyone—Mother was there as well—extremely uncomfortable. April was then in the habit of wearing loose jeans, a weary post-hippie fad that had finally foundered in Citrus for a few years after no telling how many detours and pit stops in its cross-country journey from California. When we were alone my hitching a ride with her and jerking her jeans down was great fun. But, as I say, my father changed all that.

It was after the jeans incident that I first thought to ask April how old she was.

"Almost twenty-two," she told me.

"Are you too old for me to marry?"

"I'm already married, baby."

"But if you weren't."

"Well, when you're fifteen, I'll be thirty, an old lady," she said.

"No you won't. You'll be pretty."

"When you're twenty, Roy, I'll be thirty-five. Can you imagine a twenty-year-old boy and some thirty-five-year-old woman?"

Had someone announced with incontrovertible certainty that there was no God, I would not have been as disturbed. Though I fought hard against it, I was shortly convulsed with tears.

"Hey, don't be sad, baby," she said when she realized she'd devastated me. "I was just being flirtatious with you." She tugged the bottom of my shirt and rubbed my stomach. "I was just playing, just fishing for a compliment. Come here. Listen, I'll always love you. Do you hear me? I know one thing—you're going to be so handsome. You'll have all the girls."

"No! I want you!" I insisted.

"You've got me, darling. Don't you ever worry about that. Look here. Look right here into my eyes. You'll always have me."

One thing my father could never do was make me feel guilty about staring into April's eyes. A rich dark hazel, they were always a touch glassed-over, sparkling with life and compassion. Perhaps the most distinctive quality about them, however, was that they were so arrestingly honest. The only way I know how to put it is that they seemed as if they were somehow *undressed*. Because of this her stare was quickening and warm, and if she chose it could reach a temperature that was impossible to resist, whereas to look into my father's eyes, which were studied and cold, was to fear being frozen to death.

On that particular Sunday morning, however, the only thing I noticed about my father's eyes was that one of them had been blackened.

"Well, good morning," he said as April straightened her dress.

"Rise and shine," April said curtly.

"Oh, very witty. How's Leonard, by the way?"

"Just fine. Why do you ask?"

"I'm on a new kick. Trying to be neighborly."

April stared at him, but only for a second. "Come on, Roy. We're going to be late for Sunday school."

"Is Leonard going?" my father asked.

"Leonard's watching Billy Graham on television."

"Good for him."

"Stop looking at me."

"Excuse me?"

"You heard me."

"I'm not to look at you? Is that right?"

"Not like that. Not unless you want another one of those."

"Your aunt is threatening me, Roy."

As we started toward the truck I turned my head for a last look and caught Mother staring out the window and realized she'd been listening. When I came home that afternoon my father was gone.

"Daddy's gone for a walk," Mother said.

"Why'd Uncle Leonard hit him?"

"Because your uncle is a bully. Whenever he encounters something better than himself he tries to destroy it."

"But he's got April."

Mother stopped what she was doing and leveled her eyes at me. "One day, Roy, you'll grow up and you'll learn what it means to play second fiddle and you'll realize that's exactly what your uncle is doing."

The situation deteriorated rapidly after that. Once my father's eye had been blackened he began to take risks around April. He couldn't tolerate anyone believing he'd been bettered and wanted to prove he hadn't put much stock in the outcome of the fight. He toyed with April, as if he were mocking the idea that he could ever be interested in her. He would wink at her or comment on her figure and say, "Don't go tell Leonard, now."

He often did these things when Mother was around, and they would laugh about it, as if April were a naive little girl who couldn't distinguish teasing from something more serious. "April's looking awfully good in her shorts, June," my father would call out. "Better get in here quick before somebody loses control." By the time Mother wandered in he'd be laughing and telling April not to take him the wrong way, that he was just trying to have a little fun.

He once went so far as to smack April on the behind. In response, she slapped him hard enough to knock him over my grandfather's old recliner. Mother came out then, and April reprimanded both of them, saying it wasn't right the way they carried on and that it had gone too far.

"Oh, April, you think everyone's on the make," Mother said. "You always have. And you'd especially love to think it was true of Sanders."

This led to a terrible argument between Mother and April. I was sent to my room, and my father went outside to smoke a cigarette. When he walked past my window he saw me and smiled. "Get used to it, little man," he said.

He and Mother liked to giggle about April and Leonard and what they thought of as their country-bred simplicity and lack of sophistication. They would put on a Thelonius Monk album, the insider's choice for those who believed Charlie Parker had become too popular, and smoke and have cocktails and cut up about what might be going on over in the trailer.

"They're probably praying for our worldly souls," Mother often remarked.

When they talked against April like that they seemed to get along better for a while, though it never lasted. They would laugh only so long before a deathly silence set in, after which they could hardly bear to look at each other.

Because of all this I almost came to despise my father. My childhood daydreams consisted not of vanquishing dragons and winning the hand of some maiden in a foreign land, but of taking care of my father and doing it in a way that would make April recognize me as a hero. When Mother wasn't in the room, my father would look at April with such desire that it terrified me, and I always tried to place myself in front of her in order to defend her. One of the last memories I have of him, as a matter of fact, concerns an incident that required me to do exactly that.

April had brought me home one day after church and put me to bed for a nap. Mother had gone into town, and by the time April left my room my father had shown up. I crept to the door listening as he began saying the usual things, but then I heard April tell him to let go of her arm. He told her he was sorry and that he needed to explain something to her. I remember being chilled by the sound of his voice. It was weak and tender, and I realized he was begging April to hear him out. She wasn't interested in doing that, however, and jerked free of his grip. I'd cracked the door at that point, just in time to see him lunge for her as she began to leave the house. I ran out and began flailing my arms into the small of his back, crying wildly and hitting him as hard as I could until he released April's arm.

My father looked at me and tried to laugh. "Oh, Roy," he said. His voice was low and trembling. "April and daddy are just playing. We're just wrestling around. But you did good. I'm proud of you. You handled that just like a man."

LESS THAN A YEAR later my father was dead. It happened in May. I'd gone to the Wednesday night service at Citrus Hills with April, but afterward she'd taken me back to the house because she was going to pray. It was her practice to walk through the woods and pray in those days. Sometimes I went with her, though more often she went alone. Mother and I sat on the back porch as she left. I remember Mother wished her luck, which caused us all to laugh. "You know what I mean," Mother said.

Not long after this my father came home. He'd been drinking. Presently he and Mother got into an argument, and he stormed from the house. Even though it wasn't cold out, Mother built a fire for some reason, and we sat in front of it listening to music. I had just fallen asleep on the couch when the telephone rang. It was Leonard. He wanted to know if Mother had seen April. She told him that she hadn't seen her for over an hour. When she hung up she seemed nervous. Later that night the telephone rang again. It was the sheriff.

We got into our old Mercury and raced down the dirt road into the night, heading toward town. Mother cried and banged the steering wheel and wouldn't tell me what was wrong. When we got to the hospital, which was not much more than an emergency clinic, really, I sat in the waiting room with Leonard. I asked where April was. He told me she was busy and that I had to be a good boy for her. After a few more minutes I asked about April again.

"She's with an old friend of ours," Leonard stated. He was sweating and wiped his eyes. "Everything's going to be fine. She's with one of our good buddies."

I began to cry then. "Who? Who is it? Who's she with?"

"Hey, now. Don't you start boo-hooing."

"But who?"

"She's with a fellow named Sterns Reel. Isn't that a funny name? Old Sterns Reel. I just came from over there. Now you have to be quiet. Everything's going to be fine."

Just then Mother rushed from one of the rooms, crying out my father's name. Leonard went over to her, but she attacked him and screamed at him, asking where he'd been all night and what he'd been up to, demanding to know what the sheriff was going to do about things. After some nurses led her back down the hall, Leonard reached down and patted my shoulder.

"I'm going to have to go, Royce," he said. His cheek was red. Mother had hit him. "Your mama will be out in a minute. You be a good boy until she comes back out, all right? These nurses will help you if you need anything."

"Are you going to that man's to get April?"

"That's right. That's where I'm going."

"Can I go with you?"

"No, you'd better wait right here on your mama."

That night I was told my father had died while hunting. I never felt comfortable asking Mother—or anyone else, for that matter—more about it. The little scraps of information I came upon were few, most of them variations on a theme: He was hunting alone and the gun misfired; he was hunting with friends and was shot mistakenly; he was hunting alone and shot by another hunter by accident. All of which would have occurred at night.

It wasn't uncommon for men to hunt at night in that part of the country, but my father was never much of a hunter, by day or night. It was hard for me to imagine him prowling around after dark with a gun and a flashlight.

As I grew older Mother often spoke of my father's poetic nature and boundless passions. She told me that many people believed he'd committed suicide, that his deeply romantic inclinations had made him a stranger in this world and that in the end he couldn't endure the suffering. She made a strong case for this, for why he might take his own life and how there would be dignity in such a course of action; yet when I asked if it was true, if that was what had happened, she said she didn't think so.

Many years later, after a very bad argument, I again asked Mother about his death. I asked pointedly, insisting that I wasn't interested in complicated stories or theories. It was her duty to tell me the truth, I said. I didn't for one minute think she'd tell me anything after that, but I knew it would at least hurt her feelings, something that was foremost on my mind at the time.

"You're normally not cruel, Roy," she said. "Don't get that way. It's hard to stop once you start."

She frowned, but then told me that my father had been shot to death. She said it coldly, without warning.

"Hunting?" I asked.

"Whatever you like to call it."

IF HIS DEATH was mysterious, his funeral was disappointing. When I asked Mother where his South Carolina people were, she explained they'd disowned him so thoroughly that they wouldn't even come to the service. Thank goodness James Henderson was there. He was a great help to Mother, and she clung to him throughout the service while I stood between her and April. Someone draped a flag over my father's casket, but no guns were fired in his honor. He was dressed beautifully, something I remember not only because dressing beautifully was his custom but because I myself didn't have anything respectable to wear, just a white secondhand three-piece polyester suit with a broad navy blue clip-on tie and white vinyl shoes with big gold-plated buckles.

My father was buried in our family plot, where my grandfather was buried and where his father, the first Lanier to arrive in Citrus, was buried, as well. This wasn't the town cemetery but a country cemetery about ten miles out, which at the time consisted of a scattering of twenty or so wafer-thin tablets carved with names, dates and verses of scripture, standing in various states of disrepair, some leaning, some straight, some fallen, bringing to mind a collection of snaggled teeth rudely plunged into the stark sunburnt hill that emerged on the other side of a hammock of cypress and live oak. He was pale and spent and ready for such a place, I suppose, though his dark hair appeared raffish against his powdered skin and he possessed the fraudulent smile of the dead.

Those in attendance noticed that I lingered by the open casket and had to be led away. Some no doubt attributed this to grief or to the morbid curiosity of children. But the truth was, I remained there watching him for so long because at last I could look at him without flinching, without fear, for his sockets were sunken and dry, and his lids were pressed once and for all over his remarkable eyes, eyes the likes of which no one would see again for years to come.

TWO

One evening not long after the funeral there was a meeting between Mother, April and Leonard, and Sheriff Lolly Porter. After Mother brought a serving tray of iced tea into the living room, I was told to go outside with Skipper Chiles, the sheriff's deputy, who promised we could have a look inside the patrol car. He seemed certain we'd have a grand time of it in there, but shortly we fell prey to an anxious silence punctuated by the angry shouts that escaped the living room and gained the front seat of the patrol car and piled there.

Soon the shouts became loud and frequent enough to stop the crickets' and katydids' shrill keening, and Skipper Chiles nervously began to tell me about playing football for the University of Florida, where his fraternity had actually branded him—he pulled up his sleeve and revealed the terrific scar that welted his enormous brown arm—and about his three years in professional football before he hurt his shoulder. His hero, I learned while we waited out that meeting, was none other than my uncle, Leonard Collins.

But not long after he began to tell me about Leonard the front door flew open, and Leonard himself walked onto the porch. We stared at him, waiting for some hint of what we might expect next. Leonard stood over six feet tall, and his build was thick and square and powerful. As if to emphasize this, he kept his hair cropped short. His nose flared, and his thin lips often appeared bloodless and tight. That night as he stood on the porch he had the aspect of a bull that had been tormented into a state of supreme agitation and looked as if he might turn around and begin tearing the house down.

Sheriff Porter eventually came out, followed by April and Mother. Mother was hollering at April. Her accusations were so fierce, Sheriff Porter tried to calm her down, which caused Mother to claim he was playing favorites and not fulfilling his duty. She threatened to call James Henderson and have an investigation launched. She threatened to have Sheriff Porter fired and everyone sent to jail.

"You're all just jealous!" she cried. "That's exactly what you are. And you hated him. Because he was better than all of you put together. Because he came from a prominent family and that intimidated you, all of you. You hated him. Admit it! You did! And you wanted him dead!"

She saw me peering over the dashboard of the patrol car and called to me. When I stood in front of her, she burst into tears and took me into her arms. "At least I've got Roy. At least I've got my baby." I knew that when she said this she was staring directly at April. Because I so deeply resented being used to hurt April in this way, I began to fidget and squirm, but Mother wouldn't let me down. Suddenly I jerked back into one of those perfectly heedless swoons that children enact as if they couldn't care less should they topple to the floor and bust their heads open. Poor Mother had to lunge to keep hold of me as a consequence. After that she cried even harder as she clung to her now tarnished trophy of a boy.

When I later recalled that evening I felt ashamed for having struggled to get away from Mother in her hour of need. Of course, when I eventually learned the whole of the story, I returned to a composure of resentment. It would be many years before I would ever be able to look back on that scene with enough detachment and maturity to realize—and to genuinely feel—that what was called for was nothing more or less than pity. But following my father's death, pity was a sentiment in rather short supply.

As WOULD SO OFTEN be the case, James Henderson came to our rescue. He showed up a few days after the confrontation to announce that he was taking Mother on a vacation. They traveled to Miami Beach and then spent a week in Key Largo and yet another in Key West, reading Hemingway and drinking daiquiris, they said. When they returned, Mother was completely and marvelously changed. Sun-kissed and bright-eyed, she seemed buoyant and steady and happier than I'd ever seen her.

Over the next few months I realized things were going to be much better for all of us with my father gone, just as I'd suspected from the start. Every month Henderson would send Mother a crate of expensive wines and a box of new books and albums. Heddy had recently divorced him and won a good settlement and moved to Colorado, a place I have ever since associated with venal ex-wives rather than ski slopes and resort cabins. By way of explaining the newfound closeness of her relationship with Henderson, Mother said he was lonely and needed her comfort.

Mother proved to be a stupendous comforter, as it turned out. I am to this day filled with pride whenever I recall eavesdropping on telephone conversations between her and Henderson. I never went so far as to pick up another receiver and listen in, but instead overheard Mother's side of things from a hiding place behind an overstuffed rocking chair. And what I heard! She'd discuss complicated political topics with Henderson for hours at a time. Having read up on this or that point of policy, when he next called she'd be ready to act as his trusted adviser. How often I watched Mother poring over books, a pencil behind her ear, another in her mouth and yet a third in hand for underlining.

Though careful with research and strongly analytical, Mother's strongest suit, as became clear, was strategy. She possessed a comprehensive and ruthless knowledge of what would and wouldn't work with people. It wasn't long before Henderson trusted his career to her judgment. Questions of political principle aside, it was Mother who, very early on, saw the handwriting on the wall for Southern Democrats and urged Henderson to flip to the Republicans. Had he done so, I have no doubt he would have gone on to become a senator, something he very much wanted to do for a while.

Mother began to read novels again, too, something she'd quit doing with my father around. She even acquired a few well-known pen pals, authors that she made me promise never to tell anyone about, and so I won't tell of them even now. "It's common to boast of uncommon acquaintances," Mother explained. Whenever a letter arrived from New York or New Orleans or Mississippi or Europe, she'd uncork a bottle of wine and settle into her reading chair.

My grandmother's bedrom, the bedroom that had been converted into a library, slowly filled with photographs of various writers whose rather dramatic poses always struck me as far more fantastic than any story they could have hoped to write. One of these writers actually came by for a visit. He showed up wearing a tennis outfit, military-issue pilot's sunglasses and a pistol, which he referred to as his "friendly pistola" before handing it over to Mother as an impromptu gift. Mother in turn declared the fellow to be "talented beyond reason." He asserted that she was right, but could he have, rather instantly, some or perhaps maybe all of the whisky on the premises to stay the constant pain of his orphan's heart? I can still recall the wild gesticulations he made with sentences as hellish bats swarmed round his belfry that night.

Mother made certain he was amply provided for, of course, and at some point I was degraded by being forced to run pass patterns throughout our living room against a defensive backfield of defenseless couches and chairs (the poor things couldn't lift their arms) so that he might prove to us that he had once been a quarterback of the first rank. This tickled Mother until several expensive vases were shattered. I crept to the couch greatly relieved that our game had ended when suddenly Mother and I heard what the taxonomy of a gentler age designated as a "blood-curdling" scream. It seems the writer mistook his own reflection in the hallway mirror for a murderous spook (no, it was not my father; *his* shade was busy with certain other preparations), after which he fled Citrus for his life. He never returned that I know of, but when I later came to treasure his work I was gratified to discover that each time he published a book he sent Mother an autographed first edition.

That Mother should be a party to such extraordinary incidents didn't seem strange in the least. Bold, intelligent, commanding, driven and good-looking, she'd always been adept at getting whatever she wanted. She was also making up for lost time and opportunities. Both my grandfather and my grandmother had completed college and had expected their daughters to do so, as well. Neither Mother nor April were able to follow that path, but Mother intended, with my father out of the way, to compensate for it. Furthermore, she had Henderson with all his pull and prestige to help her. Small wonder she was acquainted with writers and presidents—those two made quite a team. I would one day learn that they entertained extravagantly in Washington and were extremely popular socially. Her duties required her to be in that city frequently, she said. She and Henderson were often together in New York, as well, and on several occasions they even traveled to Europe. She returned from such trips with new clothes for me and souvenirs. Sometimes Henderson would return with her, and he and I would make like adults and discuss politics and literature. At night Mother would prepare a gourmet meal, and we'd sit together and catch up.

"Your future is going to be so bright," she'd tell me, beaming.

"I'm going to be a professional football player and a pro bass fisherman and a preacher," I used to respond, but when I got a little older, and I realized that this had the effect of slapping her across the face, I would simply say, "I hope so."

"Oh, you will," she'd promise. "It's your destiny."

ALL THAT TRAVELING made Mother very happy, but it made me even more happy, because so long as Mother dined at Taillevent in

Paris or sipped coffee and clotted cream at Demel in Vienna or plotted and gossiped at the Palm in D.C., I was free to stay with April and Leonard in their deluxe double-wide trailer, an adventure which included, to name only a few enchantments, plenty of hunting and fishing and dips in the Jacuzzi that had been installed on the back deck, watching April shake Jiffy Pop over the orange eye of the stove, arts and crafts expositions galore, not to mention such ne plus ultra pleasures as gobbling piggies-in-the-blanket, collard greens and pole beans fresh from the garden, cathead biscuits slathered in butter and topped with homemade mayhaw jelly and sometimes even taking a swallow from a can of High Life, which remains, after all, the Champagne of Beers.

April and Leonard had always spoiled me, but their efforts redoubled after my father died, another benefit of his passing. Though I was supposed to sleep in the smaller bedroom that April used for a workroom, I was often allowed to crawl into their king-size bed in the master suite at the end of the trailer. If I had a nightmare, they would rush in to check on me, and when I told them that I'd dreamed about my father getting shot they'd immediately whisk me away to sleep between them.

I must admit I sometimes fibbed about these nightmares. I always felt guilty afterward because whenever they believed I'd been troubled by my father's death it set them spinning with activity and concern. They'd rub my back and assure me everything would be all right, but later in the night I'd hear April walk down the hallway with Leonard following her, and eventually I'd hear her crying. I'd bury my face into her pillow and promise God I would never tell lies about nightmares again, but within a few weeks I'd find myself on the little bed in April's workroom, alone, concentrating on what might have happened to my father the night he was killed. I'd squeeze my eyes until my head ached, trying to force myself into a nightmare so that my escape to the king-size bed would be legitimate.

As I grew older these efforts began to produce terrifying results. My imagination, by nature and circumstance quite overdeveloped already, was empowered even more, and soon enough my visions were lush with detail. I'd lie in bed and practice certain scenes until I had perfected them and almost made them real.

For a short while I tried to imagine that Leonard killed my father. I'd stage-manage a cruel confrontation between them in which Leonard stabbed my father with a serrated hunting knife. But then I'd remind myself that my father had been shot, forcing me to reshoot the scene, so to speak, with a hastily amended script—sorry Father, yet another bloody tumble for you—that placed a gun into Leonard's angry hands before I cried *Action*. I always regretted thinking up such things. I felt I had been unfair to Leonard by making him kill my father, and after the killing had taken place, I would think of the seriousness of my father's death and would feel guilty for making myself a participant in it. But there were other things I imagined that were even more disturbing than that.

Sometimes I'd see myself walking through my house when suddenly I'd hear the sound of a struggle in the kitchen. As I crept through the living room on dreamtoes, I'd picture every piece of furniture, every photograph on the mantle, the worn places in the wooden floor, the ticking of my grandfather's grandfather clock, even Mother's discarded slippers pitched on their sides as if frozen in a state of shock. Peeking around the corner, I'd discover April, bound to a chair. And there was my father, lording over her with a terrible smile. She was usually in her nightgown —the same nightgown she wore when she placed me into bed each night, a silky slip with thin straps, though when I imagined her in the kitchen, tied to the chair, the nightgown was torn and pawed and sheer. When she saw me she cried for help, which prompted my father to relieve himself of a hideous laugh. "*Roy?* Help *you?*" He'd look my way and wink. "Roy's on *my* side."

Because of my traumas April allowed me to stay up late and watch television with Leonard, which inaugurated a lifelong habit of insomnia. We often sat up until midnight, watching the evangelical Christian programs. Leonard enjoyed the preachers, though not uncritically. He was, in fact, something of a connoisseur.

"He don't know homiletics, Royce. That's Greek for preaching. Bet your mama don't know that."

Bathed in the pulsing translucent glow of the television, I'd sit beside him, sipping milk or juice while he sipped High Life or Jim Beam. We'd watch a western awhile, then flip over to see who was preaching and size up his talent. "Nothing finer in this world than to be a preacher, Roy," Leonard would tell me seriously.

"Why ain't Brother Glenn on tee-vee?"

"Don't say 'ain't' so much. You'll get me in trouble. And being on tee-vee ain't got nothing to do with it. Sometimes the ones on the tee-vee got rejected from their actual church bodies and are sorta like bums having to hustle from strangers. I don't mean all of 'em, now. I don't mean the greats like Rex Humbard or Oral Roberts or old Billy Graham. Brother Glenn don't have to be on tee-vee is all I'm saying. He's got Citrus Hills."

"I ain't never leaving Citrus Hills. I ain't going on tee-vee neither."

"Good. And don't say 'ain't' so much. Space it out."

I should explain that our church, Citrus Hills Church of God, was a decidedly out-of-town affair, a point of geographic, cultural and theological consequence. Far from Citrus proper and the picturesque A.M.E., Methodist, First and Second Baptist, Presbyterian and Episcopal sanctuaries—even the dumpy little Catholic "cathedral" was just a short walk from the courthouse—Citrus Hills met in a rather ugly white cinder-block building with crude but brightly stained glass windows designed by a hare-lipped non-representional impressionist craftsman who favored harlot reds and Popsicle purples. The pews were upholstered with plush royal blue cushions, while the shaggy carpet was of another blue color I have never been able to identify. At some point we came by a second-thought, secondhand, slightly charred steeple, thanks to the charitable folks at A.M.E. and a bolt of lightning.

Several miles from town, down a long chalky gravel driveway that sent up wisps of holy smoke behind each arriving car, Citrus Hills was a burly, outrageous, happy roar of window-unit air conditioners, Pastor

Glenn (whom everyone referred to as Brother Glenn) and his loyal congregants. The evening services sometimes lasted until midnight or later, especially during the summer, when there were any number of revivals for any number of reasons. April would take a quilt and some blankets, and after it became late she'd make a pallet for me under the pew and allow me to sleep or to work on my Bible Heroes coloring book, a piece of revisionist claptrap in which slick old Abraham was cast as a muscle-bound hermit with stern lips and dynamic Jesus became an effete flat-faced farce with slightly crossed eyes. Praise God indeed for the more brutal and truthful Bible itself, to which I would turn as soon as I'd become bored with breaking crayons and rubbing their nubs to colorful coins.

Inflation has ravaged that currency but not the rainbow residue of its memory, and to this day, whenever I spot a solitary child in a mostly adult sanctuary, I'm reminded of my reading and minting and calculating exchange rates, and of how I'd lay my head sideways to spy out the trunkish legs of the older women, some of whom still wore beehive hairdos that towered like ziggurats, as they stomped their flat feet to the music. When April slipped off her shoes, I'd tickle her toes until she shot me a look and told me God was watching. Chastened, I watched back for a while.

One more curious thing about Citrus Hills Church of God was that Leonard never went. It was clear he missed attending the services, because he always listened excitedly to whatever news we had about them. He liked to hear of the "rousements." If Brother Glenn had become heated up and had taken to "running the aisles," Leonard would smile and nod when we told him about it. "Sounds like y'all had church down there," he'd remark pleasantly. Whenever April sang solos, she'd return with a tape recording for him. "They're still praying for you, Leonard," she'd sometimes tell him, her voice gone sad. "I know, darling," he'd say. "And I appreciate it."

"Why doesn't Uncle Leonard go to church?" I once asked April as we were driving home from a Sunday night service.

"Leonard?" She sighed. "Well, that's a long story."

"Tell me it."

"Not tonight, honey," she said. "It's too late. I'll tell you some other time."

"He said he was going to be a preacher."

"Oh, he was. He would have been a great preacher."

"But why didn't he?"

She stared out the window of the truck, trying to decide if she'd heard me.

"Why?" I repeated.

"It's part of that same long story," April said.

She motioned for me then. I scooted toward her, and she began to run her fingers through my hair.

"I *want* Uncle Leonard to be a preacher," I continued. "It's not fair."

"I know it's not, Roy. I wish he was a preacher, too."

THOUGH APRIL DIDN'T always answer the questions I put to her, it's worth noting she rarely made use of the cloying condescension of baby talk where little *Le Roi* was concerned. Instead, she addressed me as the man I so powerfully longed to be. Much like Mother, she never really worried about talking over my head. She always shared her thoughts with me, even when they were substantial.

Our best talks occurred whenever we went for long walks into the woods. We went out almost every day, often wandering for hours at a time. April savored the woods, the freer and wilder the terrain the better, a predilection she passed along to me. We'd wade out into a creek and wriggle our toes into the sand, feeling the pressure of the water against our ankles and the sweet suck of the creek bed as our feet sank. "See that dragonfly?" April would take my head and steer it. "Sitting on that elephant ear? See?" I'd nod between her palms. "You have to learn to be perceptive, Roy. Don't just blunder through life."

Her tastes tended toward the mysterious rather than the magisterial. Butterflies were beautiful, but lightning bugs were better. A canyon?

Grand. But a cypressy bayou at misty daybreak was grander. She believed God was simply too creative and powerful to be guarded and mannered in His best productions. Which was why the earth, she explained, was teeming and fecund and almost decadent. Her response to evolution, about which she never gave much thought until I began pestering her with Darwinian minutiae imported from the schoolhouse, was that perhaps it was good as far as it went but that it hardly went far enough. The intricacy, the conceits, the sheer bravado of nature struck her as more than was necessary for the fittest to survive, an idea that was, I'd later learn, similar to the beliefs advanced by that most hard-nosed of scientists, the great Russian lepidopterist V. Sirin.

Making such connections was to become a lifelong habit, by the way. As I grew older I would frequently run into April's ideas in the works of various thinkers. This was partly because of her prescience, and partly, I will concede, because of my persistence in looking for some bit of April everywhere. But how could I not? My little experiences with her when I was growing up, the sort that most people would discount as mere child's play or fancy, were for me the wet clay of my slowly setting world. How lucky I'd been to walk the woods with her, searching after the strange and curious: speckled eggs, magnolia petals turned buttery by the sun, the smell of rain, the glimpse of a fox's smile, the flash of minnows racing beneath a momentary burst of sunshine that had pierced a sky crowded with flocks of sheepy cloudlets, the strutting, reared-back flight of a chesty hummingbird. . . .

A hopkins here, a hopkins there, everywhere a hopkins, is how I came to think of it. I well remember rushing that splendid word home to April after having thought it up during a tedious English exam in high school. My vocabularly list for that week—portmanteau, instress, inscape, individuation—had apparently inspired me. I proudly explained that a hopkins *wasn't* a *portmanteau* with parts that could be peeled away but instead an indestructable coinage that paid homage to the pied poet of *instress* and *inscape* and *individuation*. When April asked if hopkins was plural or singular, I realized I hadn't the slightest idea.

"Maybe its like grits," she finally said.

And so it was from then on—hopkins, a dizzy little conundrum possessed with singular and plural mobility, which we used to describe anything that struck our senses as a sui generis marvel demanding detailed investigation. "Oop, there's a hopkins," April would say. She always found them first.

April hunted hard for hopkins. In fact, she allowed beautiful things to saturate and exhaust her. It sometimes felt as if we were soaking up too much, walking too many miles, spotting too many animals and colors and observing the finer points of too many twilight skies. Because the result of all this, which I felt even as a small boy, was a deep, aching longing from being in hot pursuit of the world and always just missing some best part of it. Of the many things I learned that would help me deal with the difficulties that were soon to overtake my life, this was the most important: April and I had long had paradise in our hearts, and yet we'd been learning it could not be found entire in this life. Our duty was to keep looking for it nonetheless.

April's devotion to nature was never merely contemplative, however. She liked to roll up her sleeves and make her mark. While she wasn't much on hunting, she was a savvy tree climber and fort builder. Though Mother was the better equestrian, April enjoyed horses more. Speaking of horses, she hated snakes. When she found one near the trailer she'd grip my wrist and we'd creep into the living room, where she'd get the twelve gauge. Once back outside, I'd lean against her hip with my fingers in my ears while she fired. "You sombitch," she'd whisper.

She'd been a *National Geographic* subscriber since girlhood. When we weren't out doing what might fairly be called fieldwork, we were often looking through those sturdy periodicals. Sometimes April would make me do written reports on what we'd read. When Mother was in town, she also handed me various assignments. It must be remembered that the Lanier girls were the daughters of a very dedicated schoolteacher who made them both into indefatigable assigners. My grandmother had always kept them busy with assignments, and when she died, Mother and

April had continued the tradition with each other and later with me. Mother was a *New Yorker* reader, and as a boy I was frequently sent over to the trailer with some article that Mother had assigned for April to read. In turn, I might be sent back home several hours later with a *National Geographic* story that April would expect Mother to acquaint herself with.

I was a beast of burden for books, as well, but the assignments I'm talking about weren't always concerned with reading. Mother and April were both very competitive gardeners, for instance, though not of the secretive variety. Whenever one of them discovered some beneficial technique or potential risk, they'd promptly tell the other. They might assign each other to grow Big Boy tomatoes or to find a new flower to cultivate. And there was always the steady rush of my little feet as I delivered difficult recipes from trailer to house to trailer to house and so on and so forth. Mother had the great advantage here, since her kitchen was state-of-the-art and spacious, while April's lacked certain amenities and was altogether a tight fit. But that didn't make April concede so much as a soufflé. April lived for the lopsided contest anyway. Overcoming less than adequate circumstances was for her the very spice of life.

April was also addicted—as Mother would tellingly put it—to surprises and dares and excitement. As a girl, April had been the one who had to be called in to supper after dark because she was still chasing piglets out in the pen after my grandfather had promised her a nickel each time she caught one. It was April who jumped off the roof of the barn into a pile of hay when Mother said it couldn't be done. April was the last to emerge from Lake Julep during breath-holding contests, and she routinely swam beyond view underwater in order to make everyone believe she'd drowned.

Adult April was no different. She and Mother and I sometimes played poker together, and during these matches Mother's cunning and April's daring were vividly displayed. On one harrowing occasion April claimed Mother was cheating and suddenly pulled a forty-five from her purse and smacked it down on the table.

"I aim to put a stop to that cheating," she stated with a straight face.

Mother was flush, furious. "Is that thing loaded?"

"Of course not, June. Recover yourself."

"You little bitch," Mother said.

I had fallen out of my chair laughing because of the look of terror on Mother's face but then saw that no one else was joining me. Mother and April were staring at the forty-five, neither of them saying a word. Finally April removed it from the table.

The really strange thing was that Mother didn't mention my father and what had happened to him. Later that evening, when Mother had gone to get us something to eat from the kitchen, April looked at me and whispered, "That probably wasn't such a good idea."

While on the subject of gunplay, I should add that even though April was a capable marksman, she was a better fisherman. Fishing, in fact, was her forte. Some of my fondest memories are of her teaching me to fish. We started with shiny cane poles and earthworms dug from the black muck near Lake Julep's edge, but before long I was casting with a spinning rod and wanting to use shiners in order to go for the truly big bass which April referred to as lunkers and Leonard called sow bellies or hogs. That kind of serious fishing required a trip to Reel Bait and Tackle, whose proprietor was the eccentric—and for me the profoundly unsettling—Sterns Reel.

STERNS WAS A BACHELOR, though not by choice. The man was simply too fat to marry. Depending on the angle and lighting, he presented from two to three chins. If he wasn't in the mood for formal grooming, his dark hair became slick and greasy. Sprouting as it did atop his pale, gargantuan body, the look was distinctly lascivious. He alleged there'd been several women nearly his size who had fallen under his spell, but he envisioned something dainty and delectable.

"Always wanted a skinny librarian," he told me once. "Some wild-ass thing with a whole lot of attitude and those cat glasses them old ladies wear. Make her take 'em off for me. *Slowly*."

The first time I met Sterns I didn't care for him at all. I remembered his name from the night my father was killed and that April had been at his house and that I didn't like it. As it turned out, Sterns Reel didn't care for me, either. He looked me over sourly and made me feel I'd spoiled an otherwise pleasant afternoon.

"Roy, this is our good friend Mister Sterns." April gave me a hug as I held out my hand. "And this is Roy."

"I see," Sterns said. "Good to meet you."

"We're going to try out some shiners. It's Roy's first time with shiners," April told him.

"Sure. What size you want?"

"How about medium?"

"They last. Had any luck lately?"

"Hadn't been out much. Leonard says he gets depressed when he goes fishing. It's a new ailment. And he's starting to go out on the road more."

"So you got you a new fishing buddy."

"I'm going to teach him how. Royce is sweet."

"He comes from good stock, all right."

"Sterns," April said.

He shrugged and walked over and began dipping shiners from the live well into the Styrofoam bucket we'd brought with us. April ordered a dozen, but Sterns scooped fifteen or more and shoveled in some ice. When April went to pay, Sterns wouldn't take her money. "You know better," he said.

"Oh, Sterns."

Sterns blushed. He seemed keenly aware of his toes and awkward, like an elephant preparing to pirouette. Something inside him was twisting in a demure way, from the look of his eyes.

"Tell Leonard I got me an eyeful of his wife and she's something else. You tell him."

"You tell him yourself."

"Pleased to meet you, son," Sterns said. "You're in good company. There's never been anything she can't catch, I'll tell you that."

On the way out Sterns's voice suddenly rose over the ringing of the little bell that hung from the door handle to announce customers. He was following us. "Hey, son. Your uncle is a bona fide hero. Anybody ever tell you that?"

"He's too young for all that, Sterns. Leonard'll tell him when he's ready," April said.

Sterns continued walking over. "Here, I got something for you." He handed April an envelope.

"One of your little love notes?"

"You know the rules. Wait until you're all the way down the road."

April gave Sterns a hug while I scowled. I hadn't heard anything about Leonard's heroics at that point, but I knew Sterns Reel meant something about my father by mentioning it. I was not at all pleased that he'd given April an envelope, either, nor that she'd referred to whatever was inside it as a love note. As soon as we drove away, I told April I didn't care for Sterns. I said I thought he was fat and probably a bad person. To be certain she understood the extent of my distaste, I called him Mr. Reel. Where I grew up, there were exactly two acceptable appellations children and young people could use with adults. The more formal of these was the traditional "Mister," "Missus" or "Miss" followed by the adult's family name. But as a sign of affection one could say "Mister" or "Miss" followed by the adult's Christian name. Most of the adults in Citrus were Mister or Miss this, that and the other, except for Mr. Haney, who was Mr. Haney to everybody except his grandchildren. So when I called Sterns Mr. Reel instead of Mr. Sterns it was an unmistakable abandonment of cordiality, and April knew it.

"Baby, you don't even know him. Don't judge people until you learn more about them. Sterns has had a hard life."

It was true. There was a story that used to circulate about how Sterns wanted to be a movie star but couldn't make it because by the time he'd turned eighteen he'd acquired almost three hundred pounds of weight without a single visible muscle. After three years at Vanderbilt, studying literature and drama and history, he came to the conclusion that school wasn't right for him in spite of his having made excellent grades and being just shy of graduating with honors. He was, he maintained, an adventurer. So he bussed himself out to Los Angeles, was hooted at his first twenty auditions and consequently began to harbor ill feelings toward the entertainment industry. He remained there for two years.

"Only the whores were any good to me, Roy," he explained. "For a couple hundred bucks you had you a quality best friend, a centerfold bunny and a damned good time. They laughed at all my jokes. You know I'm just pulling your leg now."

On a park bench on Sunset and Vine he sought to teach the industry a lesson by reading most of Aquinas's *Summa Theologica* over the course of three furious months, thus kicking the system squarely in the gonads, or at least that was how he saw it. Of course, who else in the world has ever read Aquinas on that despicable corner?

When he completed the last page, a tear fell, or so the story went, at which point it was suddenly clear to Sterns that he needed to be monkish and neglected. He was big like Aquinas and brainy to boot. He further noted that his bald spot had grown into something of a tonsure. What he needed was beautiful countryside and a monastery, minus monks, prayer bells and mundane tasks. Reel Bait and Tackle was born.

After he returned to Citrus he moved back into his childhood home. His father, who'd been only modestly corpulent but had found exercise as repellent an activity as his son did, had died of a heart attack back when Sterns was in junior high school. He'd been very wealthy and was well prepared for his exit. Financially speaking, Sterns and his mother were set for life. Soon after his father's death, his mother no longer wanted to be in the old house, though, and when Sterns went out West she purchased a home in New Orleans. She'd been much younger than her husband—she was in her mid-twenties, whereas he was in his early sixties when they met—and Sterns begged her to leave Citrus and try life again, which she did, successfully, eventually marrying and starting another family. She left the sizeable old house for Sterns.

"Doctor said I'd be retarded," Sterns frequently declared, commenting on the age of his father. "But turns out I'm just borderline dumb-ass."

The original family home was massive. Sterns converted the upstairs into his living quarters and the downstairs into a bait shop. The only remnant of the former glory of the downstairs was a Steinway baby grand piano that sat in what had become a storage room stacked with lures, beer, nets, hooks, bobbers and booze. (Unofficially, Reel Bait and Tackle also served as a package store.) Aside from the piano, which Sterns kept polished and tuned, the place possessed the dusty charm of an old bar or hunting camp. Sterns believed it shouldn't be too tidy.

In addition to his new business venture, Sterns subscribed to the Great Books Club. He also began writing a novel on the sly, something that meant so much to him he usually refused to talk about it. Before becoming a novelist he'd tried his hand at painting. He wasn't without talent by any means, but in every painting there was a dark, brooding face peering from a window or walking down a back road. "Why is that man always in there, Sterns?" people would ask.

The figure that Sterns kept painting caused people to dislike his paintings intensely. After a while, Sterns agreed with them and gave up. "That fucker," he would call the man he seemed to have to paint, the man who had finally forced him to stop painting altogether. "That undeniable fucker."

The more I learned about Sterns over the years, the more I came to admire him, but in the beginning, as I've pointed out, I found him to be sinister. So sinister, in fact, that my fear of him ruined that first serious fishing trip. I'd hoped to catch a record bass to make April proud of me, but my skills completely destructed because I continued to think about the night my father died and to wonder why April would have been with Sterns Reel at Reel Bait and Tackle.

"What did he give you?" I asked.

"Oh, I almost forgot." She pulled the envelope out of her pocket and opened it. "He gives me little messages. Just little things he's written."

"What does it say?"

"Let's see. . . ." She laughed. "Oh, Sterns. You're crazy."

"Tell me."

"It says: 'Strange stormy weather sets my tipsy heart spinning.'"

"That's dumb."

"It's interesting, Roy. It makes you think. I bet strange stormy weather sets your tipsy heart spinning."

"No, it doesn't," I said. I frowned and cast especially hard. "I messed up again."

She attended to the tangle, a nasty knot the size of an apricot. To make matters worse, my amateur casting, a rough whipping motion, had ripped the shiner from the hook and sent it flying over the water before it landed with a smack and swam away.

"Let's learn how to hook again," April said.

She squatted and retrieved a shiner from our bucket, holding it firmly in her hands. Its tail wiggled and its eyes bulged, but she took the hook and carefully punctured the meat just below the dorsal fin.

"You get it right below his backbone so it sticks, see?"

"Does it hurt?"

"Not very much. I've felt worse."

She laughed and gently cast the shiner past a patch of lily pads. When the bobber submerged a few minutes later, I yelped with delight. "Let him take line," April said. I could see the bobber waffling just under the surface of the water, gaining speed, a wobbly orange streak spooning into darker water. My heart pounded. "Not yet, let him run, let him run, easy, easy. Okay, now! *Now!*" April shouted. "There! Come back. Hard. *Hard!* You've got him. You've got him, Roy!"

"He's big! Hold me, hold me, he'll pull me in!"

She crossed behind me and brought me close. We fought, but the fish was strong and heavy, and the drag had been set too tightly. When the bass made a final charge, the line snapped.

"Lord, Roy. He must have been incredible. You hooked one of the big ones." I leaned against her and felt something tearing inside me. "Hey," she said. "Don't cry. There's plenty more where that one came from. Don't cry."

"Did you fish with Daddy?" I asked.

"No," she said. She kissed my cheek. "Of course not."

"Why not?"

"Your daddy didn't like to fish."

"You promise?"

"He wasn't a fisherman, Roy. He hated fishing. He wasn't built that way."

"I am," I told her. "I'm built that way."

THREE

And so I built myself that way. By the time I was ten I'd become so accomplished a fisherman I could always catch something, even on a cold or blustery day. April gave me a subscription to *Bassmaster* magazine, each issue of which I read repeatedly, cover to cover, studying the advertisements as well as the articles, dreaming of shiny bass boats and expensive graphite rods and taking trips to all the famous lakes, especially the fantastically exotic Yahoa nestled in the mountains of Honduras between Tegucigalpa and San Pedro Sula. *Bassmaster* said that an entire prehistoric city lay miles beneath Yahoa's surface. Monkeys screeched from the trees and panthers cried during the night and, best of all, record numbers of large-mouth lunkers awaited adventurous anglers.

In response, Mother foisted the *New Yorker* on me. Venerable as that magazine was, she quickly realized it couldn't compete for a boy's attention against the likes of Lake Yahoa, so she put in a word to Henderson. Next time I saw him he handed me a copy of *The Old Man and the Sea*, which I'd already read, and a leatherbound edition of *The Compleat Angler* by Izaak Walton that I found was fun to flip through. At last he presented me with a gold-embossed hardback of *Moby-Dick*, which I took to diligently but gave up on after a hundred pages, beaching it on my bedside table beside my alarm clock and a sepia-tone stack of good intentions. If only that blubbery white whale had been a big beautiful bass, Melville couldn't have written enough pages to satisfy me.

I wasn't unenthusiastic about such fishy literature, but there was simply nothing quite as satisfying as curling into my grandfather's old recliner and scouring *Bassmaster* for the latest developments in plastic worm technology, reading up on the new juices, secret scents and seductive rattlers plied into the supersoft plastic, the glitter chips imbedded into the curlicue tails, the patented designs, the freakish colors: shadlike quicksilvers and charming chartreuses, salamander pinks and froggy greens, various vermillions and enough shades of indigo to sate a morose master's pallette. Where other teens copped the illicit thrill of sweatily thumbing through *Hot Rod* magazine for ample cleavage, lean thighs and swelling hips—*Playboys* were harder to find in Citrus than unicorns—my rebellion took the form of idolatrous readings about spinning rigs and trolling motors and crank baits. The names and faces of those lures remain real cockle burners: Heddon's Bayou Boogie, Arbogast's classic Jitterbug. Sputterbuzz and Hula Popper. Frenzy Popper. Wounded Spook. Chugger Spook, Super Spook and coy Super Spook, Jr., to round out the Spook family. The fortuitous little Lucky 13. And who could deny the charm of Tiny Crazy Crawler, a silver bullet of a bumble bee with metallic wings that stalked across the top of the water? Speaking of bees, I still smile whenever I see those friendly, diving Bagley Balsa Bs and Honey Bs with their blushing profiles, wide, smiling eyes and merry barrel chests—tender bent teardrops, exuberant paisleys of delight, each one a perfect little hopkins. See them dive! Feel them wobble deep!

I could go on and will.

Rebel! Roustabout! Rapala! A revolutionary roll call of enticements!

With such pleasing accessories I naturally fished all the big-time bass tournaments in my head and won a great many of them. There was even a horrible period when I—a fifth-generation Floridian, no less—considered going to the University of Tennessee simply because the famous television angler Bill Dance was an alumnus of that institution and seemed to me the freshest of fisherman in his garish Day-Glo tangerine U of T cap.

Mercifully I outgrew that phase, though I never outgrew fishing, and so the struggle over my soul continued apace. For my twelfth birthday, April and Leonard bought me a twelve-gauge shotgun and a twelve-tray tackle box big enough to house a spaniel. The battle was capably joined when Mother produced a fancy edition of Faulkner's *The Big Woods* and a collection of Hemingway's short stories with all of the hunting narratives checked off in the table of contents. She also had Henderson purchase a Barbour hunting jacket for me.

"But you'll have to stop lifting weights so much or you'll grow out of it before the fall," Mother warned. "And those protein drinks, too. I hate those things. They're tacky."

I HAD JUST BEGUN to lift weights in what Mother, perhaps rightly, considered a neurotic manner, which is to say I never failed to clock in five workouts a week per Leonard's instructions, becoming so exhausted I would collapse on the bed with my body in the grip of a satisfying fever. Many of the athletic boys my age had weight sets as well, but they were comprised of toy barbells and dumbells onto which they would fasten plastic concrete-filled pretend plates. My equipment, on the other hand, was all iron and steel; and unlike my peers, who gathered together to curl and press but mostly to tease and taunt and have some fun, my workouts were serious and rigorous.

Leonard had added a carport to the trailer, and he and Sterns pulled up one day with a weight bench, a squat rack, a barbell, dumbells and hundreds of pounds of plates.

"Sterns has gone and bought you a present," Leonard said.

"We don't want you to end up being no sissy," Sterns told me.

Once everything had been set up, Sterns loaded two forty-five-pound plates on the barbell and lay on the bench, stretching and groaning as if he were about to attempt a world record.

Leonard spat tobacco juice and chuckled. "Need a spot?"

"For this? Shit, this ain't nothing. My head weighs more than this."

Sterns pressed the weight twice, then stopped abruptly, placing the barbell back on the rack. We watched him. He didn't move. His arms hung limply by his sides.

"Roy?" he called.

"Yeah?"

"Always remember the importance of warming up."

"Lord, Sterns. You hurt your teats?" Leonard called.

"I believe I've paralyzed 'em."

Leonard helped Sterns up. "Come on, Roy. Let your old uncle show you how it's done. This here's how *I* warm up."

He loaded another forty-five-pound plate on each side and plopped down on the bench and began pressing the weight as if we were on the moon. "This is fun," he said. He looked over at me and smiled. The ease with which he lofted the barbell made it appear as if he were participating in a comic skit. "I could do this all day." He started humming.

Sterns shook his head respectfully. "You're looking at the original hoss, there," he told me.

I watched intently, and as Leonard continued, at last breaking into a sweat and truly working, I became unnerved. The sort of power he possessed seemed critical to me, and I committed that I would do whatever it took to gain that kind of raw strength, a kind of strength that I believed could break any restraint or shoulder any burden. I simply had to have it.

Which is why, aside from working out, I never failed to consume my daily protein drinks, one every morning, noon and night, made according to Leonard's recipe, which consisted of two scoops of vanilla protein powder, a tablespoon of peanut butter, honey to taste and whole milk. Though it is true Mother despised the sound of the blender, it's also true that she willingly boiled down piles of turnip and collard greens for me and scrambled eggs and made chicken and tuna salad until her arms ached. Sometimes she would even go so far as to walk over to the trailer to have a look.

Leonard would be standing over me, yelling: "One more! One more rep, Roy!" and there Mother would be before we knew it. These appearances were rare, and they always spooked us a little.

"Hey, June."

"How's the"—she'd make a curling motion with her arms—"whatever going?"

"Going fine. Roy's tearing it up."

"I wish he'd learn to wear a shirt. Can't he make muscles with a shirt on?"

Leonard would smile. "He don't mind me."

"Well, don't y'all stop on my account."

She'd watch for a while, and for all her protestations I believe she was occasionally somewhat amused.

Of course, we couldn't train with much ferocity with her around—I couldn't be cursed at, nor could I growl—and it wasn't long before all three of us were bored. By then April would have wandered out.

"Hey, June." They'd hug, and April would look at me. "Roy, put a shirt on."

"I wish he would." Mother would say, frowning.

"Now!" April barked. "This instant!"

I'd stare at the strange alliance of Lanier eyes and quickly cover myself.

"Come see what I'm making, June."

"Don't hurt yourself, Roy," Mother would say before walking into the trailer.

"I'm watching out for him," Leonard always promised.

Though still trucking a fair amount in those days, Leonard nonetheless managed to supervise my training pretty regularly. Whenever he returned from hauling a load he'd inquire about my weight lifting and ask how many sprints I'd run since he'd been gone. He'd feel my shoulders and make me tell him about what I'd been eating. He insisted I not participate in Pop Warner football, claiming it would ruin me, and he furthermore insisted I not attempt to play my first year in junior high for the same reason. It was better, he advised, to wait until the eighth grade, just as he had done. In the meantime, he and he alone would be the one to prepare me for my debut. Since Mother didn't care about my playing football anyway, and since I trusted Leonard with my future completely and wanted to follow in his footsteps, I didn't lament this decision in the least.

So while other boys of my age were practicing with the Pee Wee and junior-high teams of Citrus, I stood at attention as Leonard pulled a chair out to the dirt road and told me to go take my mark. After a sip of High Life he'd hold up the stopwatch and call "Ready, set, go." He'd time me and immediately send me out again. We'd repeat this until he'd finished his beer, something that required about ten minutes, after which he'd go into the trailer to grab another while I lay on the ground fighting for breath.

"All right. On your mark, get set—"

"Wait, wait a second."

"Wait a second nothing. You wanting to play football or be a cheerleader? On your mark! Get set—get set, there, now that's a stance, lean and mean—all right, mark, get set, go!"

He bought a big red blocking dummy for me, as well, and when I was good and tired and he was good and drunk, he'd stand behind it and tell me to "hit and spin." I'd hunker into a three-point stance about five yards away, waiting for him to call "Hut," which was my cue to rocket from my stance and hit the dummy with my shoulder and then spin away.

"You got to hit it quick and hard, but you've got to be light about it, you've got to be gone," he'd tell me. "You hear me, Roy? I mean gone!"

Because my training schedule was dictated by Leonard's drinking habits I trained almost continually when he was home. We might go out on a hot afternoon and work through a six-pack for the better part of an hour, then later that night, sitting in front of the television, he'd tip his pint to his ear and look at me. "You hear that?" he'd say. "Old Jimmy Beam's talking to me. Hold on. Well, hell, Royce, he says we've got to go back out there again."

It wasn't long before I was running Leonard out of beer on a regular basis. Eventually my advances in conditioning and his advances in alcohol consumption led him to issue a challenge.

"Know how to become the best damned running back in the whole country? Well, I'm gonna tell ya. You'll be the best damned running back in this whole country the day we come out here and you run until your old Uncle Leonard passes out drunk and you have to carry him into the damned trailer without even breaking a sweat. All two hundred and fifty pounds of me. That means you better keep at them weights and running and eating all the time. Speaking of which, you hungry?"

"Yes, sir."

"Me, too. You've exhausted me. Let's go to town and get something to eat."

WE'D USUALLY GO TO SONIC. April always ordered a chili pie, while Leonard ordered a triple with cheese, two chili pies *and* tater tots. Not to be outdone, I'd order the same. We'd eat in the truck, sharing the bench seat, watching the cars pass and waving.

When I was in high school Mr. Little, Citrus's resident storefront entrepreneur, opened Beachy Breezes Tanning Salon across the street from Sonic, which made that end of the street more respectable, but before Beachy Breezes blew into Citrus with its sunny tingling *z* the only thing sitting across the street was a run-down convenience store and Rough Riders Last Resort, which sold BMX bicycles, motorcycles and, it was rumored, cannabis. "I better never catch you in there," Leonard said to me once.

"Where?"

"You know where," April said.

"Ain't nothing but *high*cycles in there."

April swatted my arm. "Where'd you learn that?"

"*High cycles?*" Leonard chuckled. "Son, I ever catch you in there with one of them *high*cycles I'll shove my size twelve so *high* up your ass, you won't taste nothing but shit and shoe laces, you got that?"

"Oh, very charming, Leonard." April rolled her eyes. "You're so discreet."

"I'll discreet you if you don't watch it."

April gave him the finger. "Discreet this."

"Yeah. Discreet *that*," I said.

After Sonic Leonard usually wanted some more whisky, and so we'd be off to Sterns's place, where he could get a pint of bourbon. It was about this time that Citizens Band radios became popular. Because of Leonard's work he'd always been familiar with them and had had one in his pickup as long I could remember. But now April had one in her arctic blue 1966 convertible Mustang, and Sterns had one at the Bait and Tackle. Even Mother became fascinated with the trend and set one up in her kitchen. Leonard's handle was Main Man. April's—why, I can't remember—was Star Bear. Mother took Chief Squaw as her moniker, though for the most part she just listened in. I was Junior, and Sterns, the Bull Shipper.

"Breaker one-nine for the Bull Shipper," Leonard would call into the microphone whenever we were headed Sterns's way. We'd giggle and wait. "Bull Shipper you read?"

"You got the mighty B.S. What's your ten-twenty, Double M?"

We'd take turns talking to Sterns until we pulled up into his yard. Sometimes Mother would catch us before we got there.

"The Chief Squaw wants to know who's driving."

"Star Bear'll be driving, breaker."

The breaker stuff really cracked Mother up. "Don't be out late, *breaker*."

Once we arrived at Sterns's we'd visit for a while, but eventually Leonard would be ready to drive again. He routinely begged Sterns to join us, but Sterns never would. Occasionally they'd become angry at each other, something that was very unusual.

"We're going by Mama and Daddy's. Go with us."

"I better stay put. Might have a customer."

"Aw, come on, Sternsy."

"That old place scares me. You know that."

April once even had to take Leonard's arm and pull him toward the door. "If it scares him it scares him, Leonard," she said. "Let's go."

"Get over that shit, Sterns."

"You get over it."

"Y'all stop it," April, said. She looked at me and motioned for me to walk out the door. "Roy," she said.

"I'm over it," Leonard was saying. "Hell, that business never bothered me one bit."

"Leonard, shut up," April said. "Roy, go."

"Sorry. I didn't know everybody was so sensitive." Leonard slung the door open. "It's my goddamned place anyhow. I reckon I can decide if it's scary or not."

I suppose it could be a somewhat scary place, especially at night, though sitting between Leonard and April it often seemed something more than scary—it seemed terribly sad. Leonard's mother and father passed away a few years after he and April were married and left Leonard their house and all the property. He kept most of the land but sold the house. He gave some of the money to Henderson, who invested it for him and kept a portion at the bank just in case. Mr. Jenkins, the man who bought the house from Leonard, had said he was going to tear it down, but he'd never gotten around to it, and it had become dilapidated. The porches sagged, and much of it had been overcome with wisteria. The melancholy thing about the old house was that it seemed somehow to still be just barely alive. When we'd pull up it would stir pitifully in the wind and attempt to open a jammed door of welcome, but all it could ever really manage was to stare back at us with a grateful though pained expression.

Hoot owls nested in the rooms, and every now and then we'd hear their eerie taunts. If the moon was full, Leonard would get out and throw Chiclets into the air so I could watch fruit bats appear out of the darkness to swipe at them. Usually, though, we'd just sit quietly, listening to Leonard sip bourbon.

"Nobody ever played football like Leonard," April would say after a while. She'd say it proudly, but her voice always sounded lost and girlish. "He got scholarships to all the big schools. Nobody could stop him. I wish you could have seen him, Roy," she'd continue in dreamy tones. "When he was a little boy, he used to run through the woods and practice against the trees. Can you believe it? Against trees. He did. That's how he got so good. He was used to playing against trees. He'd take off and run right into them. Leonard wasn't afraid of anything."

"I wasn't afraid of much, I don't believe," Leonard would admit. "Hell, couldn't nobody bring me down in them days."

WHEN I LOOK BACK on those days—those days of *my* youth, not Leonard's—it's clear to me that I trained as hard as I did because I wanted to emulate Leonard and become a football star, but it is also clear that I trained so hard because I knew my father, who was a gifted athlete, had not liked sports at all. As I have already revealed, this same motivation, to be as unlike my father as possible, was something I consciously had in mind when I began to fish, too. But of the two, fishing and football, football was by far the more visceral renunciation. I couldn't for the life of me picture my father running intervals or doing one-arm curls or hitting and spinning with a red blocking dummy. Consequently I did such things relentlessly.

"Your father would never drink those protein drinks," Mother would sometimes tell me when she saw me firing up the blender.

"They have all the essential amino acids," I'd quip, but what I wanted to say was, "Exactly. He'd never drink a protein drink in a million years."

Though Mother tried to be supportive of my athletic endeavors, she remained worried that I would become a dullard because she believed athletes were dullards. What she really feared was that Leonard would turn me into a simpleton and that April would finish me off by transforming me into a teetotaling Pentecostal. Given Leonard's method of conditioning—challenging me to cause him to drink himself unconscious—it is ironic that she saw things this way; but that is not to say it was surprising, for Mother could never make up her mind about Leonard. Sometimes she thought of him as a bore, while on other occasions she thought of him as a beast. When it came to my preparations for football, however, she was reasonably sure they would lead me to become a prude and a square, and she was increasingly concerned about what she began to refer to as "Shriner tendencies."

"Alexander the Great," she'd announce. "Very smart. Not a Shriner. Julius Caesar, smart—not a Shriner. Napoleon, genius, but not a Shriner. Writers—*writers,* oh, let me tell you, young man—not Shriners. Robert E. Lee, there's a real gentleman. Robert E. Lee would *never* join the Shriners."

"I'll never be a Shriner, Mother. Give me a break."

She frowned. "I'm so afraid you'll end up doing *something* like that and taking it very seriously, driving around in one of those little go-carts with a fez on your head and wearing pantaloons. Please don't end up like that, Roy. Boosterism and all types of puritanism are to be avoided. I know I'm giving you the speech I said I wouldn't give you for the thousandth time, but I'm your mother, it's my job."

"I'm not a geek, Mother. It's just not in me to be one. Take it easy."

"Well, you need to know. And the nuances are important. Back to the war. Sherman, for instance, was a plain out-and-out bastard, vicious and uncouth. Anyone can be a jackass, Roy; pardon my French, but it doesn't take much talent. That's not what I'm talking about. Just don't become too Goody Two-shoes, that's all I'm saying. Have honor and character and loyalty, obviously, but don't be a prig. This is the kind of thing a young man learns naturally from watching his father, but we do the best we can, don't we?" She looked at me anxiously. Then, suddenly, she snapped her fingers and said something I will never forget: "Wait, I've got it! Be the kind of man that would only be elected president if there were a national crisis." To this day that continues to strike me as exceptional advice.

Along those lines, I never joined the glee club or the chess team or anything else of that nature. When I entered the eighth grade I became a member of the quiz bowl team at Mother's request but was kicked off when I refused to stop dipping during the tournaments. I'd pop the buzzer, spit tobacco juice into a Dixie cup and say "Theodore Dreiser" or "Jeremy Bentham," but Mother worried nonetheless.

April was herself keen to make a man of me, no less than Mother and Leonard, but where Mother's approach was theoretical and Leonard's centered on physical conditioning, April's consisted of going directly for the jugular. When she once caught me placing bream into the frying pan in an effete manner, she informed me that simply wasn't the way a man operated. "Oh, Roy, please! Just throw them in there, for heaven's sake. Be a man!"

I worried that the grease might splatter my arms and told her so. Her response was impeccable: "You *should* be worried about grease splattering *my* arms. You shouldn't be worried about your arms at all."

There were many lessons like that, and I sometimes believed April was letting me in on all the best secrets about women and that I was gaining an unfair advantage in that regard, one I was only too happy to have, though as I was to learn, such wisdom was not without its costs.

Sitting before her sewing machine, or walking along one of our favorite trails through the woods or across a pasture, April would stop and turn on me with her eyes to remind me of these lessons. She'd pull her hair back from her face and twist and fold it into a loose tapestry of curls held in place by a favorite plastic clip that was manufactured to look like an alligator's mouth. This procedure required her to extend her arms above her head and stretch her torso in a fashion that disturbed me enormously. I'd cast about with my eyes, but I could never find anything to hold my attention away from April for very long.

For all her boyishness, everything about her drew a clear and unmistakable contrast between what it meant to be a man and what it meant to be a woman, which made her lessons about manhood all the more effective. Even when she participated in so-called manly activities, her aptitude never disguised her warmth and softness nor a finely tuned tenderness and sense of play that overwhelmed her work and made watching her a delight and made watching her for very long an invitation to become besotted with the desire to win her affection.

As I ENTERED junior high school April became something more than an inspiration, however. She became overpowering. What in the world had happened to our old innocent walks through the woods? Where once—it seemed only yesterday, and now today *both* sets of yesterdays seem only yesterday—our journeys had consisted of theological musings and the heady intoxications of nature, everything had suddenly changed forever. When she would tell me to "snap out of it" and to "get my act together" with a kind of tough swagger, her arms crooked atop her head, I was left diseased with confusion.

This condition was permanently aggravated one summer morning after my first year of junior high when I had gone too long without a haircut and arrived at the trailer looking older and woolier than Leonard cared for. My appearance, in fact, seemed to alarm him.

He was sitting on the couch watching a talk show. "Man shot himself with a damn derringer. Like a big fat dumb ass. Bullet didn't even get through his skull. Just spun around his head twice and lodged right up above his ear. Called the police on himself. Can you believe that shit?" He looked at me. "Look at you. You look like a damned criminal yourself."

I was reaching for the OUR DAILY BREAD container that sat on the breakfast table, a little plastic loaf filled with tiny strips of cardboard of various colors, which had verses of scripture printed on them. Every Sunday after church April made me pick one out and memorize it. At any given moment during the week she'd say, "What's your daily bread?" and I'd fire the verse back at her.

"Your hair's atrocious, if you don't mind my saying so," Leonard continued. "April, come in here. Roy looks like a rat's been nesting in his hair. Tell me he don't need a haircut."

"Billings butchers me," I said defensively.

Normally I went into town, where Vernon Billings, a palsied old barber with horrific breath, terrified me with scissors for the better part of an hour. I'd leave the shop and walk over to the courthouse lawn, sitting on a bench, feeling my neck and ears for nicks.

"I hate the way Billings does his hair," April said. "Maybe he ought to go to Ilene's with me. She does a nice job."

"To the beauty parlor?" Leonard was shaking his head. "Not to the beauty parlor."

"Billings's got the shakes," I protested.

"Well, somebody better cut it," Leonard said. "And I sure wouldn't carry him to no beauty parlor. Tryouts are a couple of months away and I don't want him acting like no pansy here at the last minute."

Leonard lorded over his few channels of television like a demagogue, working the remote control (still something of a spacy wonder in those days) with triumphant flair. Sometimes he'd issue a judgment, then switch channels for emphasis. If he believed his pronouncement to be significant enough, he'd lower the volume, speak softly, then blast the volume back before anyone could respond, which is what he did on this occasion.

"Turn that idiot box down so I can hear myself think." April hollered.

"I can't hear you. Television's too loud."

"Don't be cute," April said.

Leonard turned the television off and looked at me again. He smiled, but I could tell he was growing irritated. "What's everybody getting all excited for? It ain't no big deal. Hell, April, why don't *you* cut it," he said. "April cuts mine, Royce. Look how pretty I am."

"Hang on a minute," April said. She walked over and began studying my hair. "Maybe that's not such a bad idea." She boxed the side of my head. "Come on, Roy."

"Better ask his mama before you do anything specific. She might have a particular style in mind."

"Oh, hush," April told him.

"I'm going out to see Sterns," Leonard said. "Give Royce a military cut. He could use some discipline. Matter a fact, might be best to just cut his whole damned head off. He'd look better. Probably think better, too."

"Take Howl with you. I don't want him bothering us."

Howl was Leonard's dog, an unreliable mixture of Labrador retriever and chow. He was just over a year old. Leonard had found him on the side of the road when he was still a puppy, barking at what Leonard jokingly referred to as an "invisible phenomenon." He slept under the trailer and during the warmer months walked around in what looked to be a state of crisis, flashing his stout blue tongue and charging bumble bees when he had the energy.

"Don't worry. I'll fix you up," April said to me. "Go out back and I'll get everything."

Leonard had built a large deck behind the trailer, where he could sit and watch the sun set, barbecue, drink whisky or occasionally take a pair of tongs and flip hot pieces of charcoal at the chickens, a thoroughly malicious bit of behavior from which I confess to have always taken a great deal of pleasure and even practiced myself whenever I had the opportunity. I went and sat in one of the folding chairs, and April walked out with shampoo and conditioner, Leonard's electric razor, several towels, a hand mirror and a pair of scissors and placed everything on the lid of the grill. She brought the garden hose over and told me take my shirt off and proceeded to wet me down.

"Damnit to hell it's cold," I said.

"Don't be a baby," April said.

"Shit," I said.

"Watch your mouth. You're not too big for me to whup."

"I'd like to see you try."

We'd only recently fallen into the habit of taunting each other this way. I could usually persuade April to play football with me, and she'd never miss an opportunity to throw the ball at my head as soon as I wasn't looking. When mulberries were in season I'd pick a few to eat, then a few more to pitch against her cheek. There were endless chases and countless contests of all kinds. April seemed frustrated by my size and refused to believe I had become stronger and faster than she. For a while, in fact, it seemed as if everything we did was to some extent competitive.

She gave my head a jerk. "I'll try you if you're not careful."

"I'd like to see you try," I repeated.

A stream of icy water splattered my face. I snatched the hose away and returned fire.

This proved to be a supreme miscalculation, for what began as a perfectly childish exercise in revenge, a trick that any boy would understand, suddenly became serious, a kind of seriousness a boy would not understand at all. As April screamed and darted about to avoid getting wet, I began to watch her with a level of interest that bordered on outrage. She was trying to take the hose from me, and I was getting angry about it and about the fact that her flimsy white cotton T-shirt was soaked through. I found I had no serviceable vocabulary for what I saw, no language at all.

In my stupor, she prevailed and yanked the hose from my hand, ordering me to set the chair aright and plant myself in it. "You're dead, Roy," she said. "I mean dead. You couldn't be any more dead if you tried. You're going to learn a lesson, buddy. You're going to learn a lesson you'll never forget."

That proved to be what might safely be called a cosmic understatement. For the fact of the matter was, I had arrived at a turning point in my life, and that turning point had the effect of turning my life upside down.

But still she kept on: "Do you hear me, Roy Collier? Huh? You're not so tough now, are you? Just keep your ass in that chair, buster." She fisted my hair and shook my head. She tongued her top lip furiously. "And I'm going to get a cattle prod. Whenever you sass me, that's what you'll get. A shock to your system."

I intended to respond to this but found I couldn't speak. She began fidgeting with my bangs and then rubbing my sideburns between her thumb and forefinger. Her silence roared about me while I was turned to hot mush. The most startling thing was that she had become gentle with me. She said, softly, "Okay, baby. You ready?"

As I have pointed out, former beauty transactions were arid and geriatric, if not a little brutal. I'd never before surrendered my neck to a female's care, never dreamed of April coddling my head and keeping me close and clicking and purring about my ears. Even now when I linger at this humble country boy's crossroads it seems so easy to let the intervening years wash over me and to sit back and feel my head lighten and my resolve weaken as hair and time slowly fall away. . . .

Her first move was decisive: She placed one hand upon my nape and another beneath my chin and began to twist and angle my head, looking just past my eyes with an intense expression, as if my soul had vanished and all that was left was my body, something for her to perfect and work on without regard to my feelings or wishes. She spoke in a low intimate whisper that was at the same time distant, like a sculptor carefully searching out the limbs and lines of his final design beyond a rough and rocky exterior. Her voice was careful and near: "Close your eyes, darling."

Standing behind me, she began humming an old Presley number: "It's Now or Never," I believe it was. She squirted shampoo—the only ugly interruption of that choral morning—then brought my head back against her stomach, against the wet cotton already warm from the skin of her belly. "Keep them closed," she said. Her fingers were insistent and patient. I felt weak and sleepy. Plump sunlight against my face, red and purple blotches roamed the tormented horizon of my eyelids as I sank further and further down. When she warned that the water was coming, it was nothing to me anymore, and as she rinsed sparkling suds from my hair I swallowed clumps of electric air.

"Wake up, Roy," she said. She looked me over tenderly, taking a moment to thumb my brows. "You have such pretty eyes," she told me, her voice lush with force. "Such-pretty-eyes, such-pretty-hair," she chanted.

The bottom blade of the scissors drew a cool line across my forehead as she clipped my bangs. She'd come in close to do it. Her mouth opened slightly and made a pained little sigh as her warm breath fell lightly across the bridge of my nose, a silken garland of sound. My cheeks flushed and ached. But she noticed nothing, and I could not resist taking her in again as she moved behind me, whispering, "There, that's nice," against my lobes while working the scissors around. The pressure against my scalp and the rush of her mouth raked me head to toe—the wedging of the blades, the hot seep of her breath, her nearness . . .

"One more thing." She clicked on the electric razor to groom the edges, work that brought her between my legs.

"You're not a little boy anymore," she remarked, brushing hair away from my eyes. "You're so lovely."

"You are," I said.

She took the towel and scrubbed my head roughly. "No, you are," she said right back.

"You really are," I said.

It bothered me that she wouldn't take my compliment seriously, and suddenly I began to feel as if I might burst into tears. I almost certainly would have done so, in fact, had she not at that exact moment held up the hand mirror for me to examine myself. I didn't like what I saw one bit. More accurately, I was greatly disturbed by myself. I had been changed too abruptly. Billings's rule was to do as little as possible, but April had really involved herself in ridding me of hair. Here was a whole new face. Though it was somehow familiar, it didn't particularly remind me of myself. I thought I looked older and yet . . . no, was I perhaps just different? Had I never really seen myself before? This wasn't good at all. What exactly was wrong with me? I kept looking, growing more irritated, then finally pushed the mirror away.

"I'm hideous."

April giggled. "Hideous? You're so handsome it's ridiculous."

Her saying this about the new and obviously wretched me truly annoyed me, though I could not just then say why.

LATER THAT SAME SUMMER I had my chance to carry Leonard into the trailer. He'd come out to train me with a six-pack and a half pint. He went through the beer pretty quickly, and after the bourbon, which he drained with great anger, he slumped over in his chair. I wrapped my arms around him and struggled to get him up, but we tottered and crashed to the ground heavily. He shoved me away and blamed me for our fall, claiming I'd tripped him. "Just like a fucking Collier," he said. I offered him my hand, but he slapped it away. "Get the fuck off me. Just get the fuck away." After slowly getting to his feet, he sidestepped a few yards, then staggered into the trailer, where he sat on the couch and stared at me.

"Guess you ain't as big and tough as you thought you was," he said. He could barely keep his head up. "Thought you was all growed up, ain't that right? You probably think you're going to waltz out on that football field in a few weeks and just kick everybody's ass. Well, I've got some news for you—thanks to *me* you *might*." I thought maybe he was finished with me, but he suddenly seized a pillow and threw it just past my head. "And you know what?"

"No, sir."

"You look just like your daddy, is what."

"No, sir, I don't."

"Goddamned right you do. Ask April. Shit, she knows it. Might even like it."

"I'm going home," I told him.

"Not till I'm finished you're not. Come over here, you little shit. You look goddamned identical to him. I mean, goddamn, Roy, what in hell are we going to do about it?"

"I don't know."

"Well, I don't, either," he said. "But we got to do something."

FOUR

By the time I entered my final year of junior high school I was nearly six feet tall. In the kitchen of both Mother's house and the trailer were walls where my various heights had been penciled along with their corresponding dates. At some point I'd taken a black felt-tip pen to draw a line at six feet, knowing my father would have just come up to that line but no farther. I suppose Leonard had his line and now I had mine. So many lines were drawn—and crossed—where my father was concerned.

Of course, as soon as this line was established, every time I entered either one of those kitchens I would have to place my back against the wall in the hope that at last I had surpassed that taunting black mark. Naturally it seemed to me that I would never make it—that I would be doomed to live out my life as an under-six-footer, a man who was shorter than my father, thus *truly* falling short of the mark, something that was intolerable to me.

All of which affected my posture in a most beneficial way. Since Mother and April were also fanatical about posture and quick to correct me if I slouched, I learned to stand proudly, shoulders back, as if I'd been born into another century entirely. Leonard's training procedures, combined with my maniacal intake of protein milk shakes and other supplements, had caused my frame, which was by nature lanky, to thicken and take on muscle. My nose was becoming narrow like my father's, but my lips were full like April's. My father had small, almost elfin ears, and I had them, too, though unlike him, but like the Laniers, my skin was tawny and burnished the year round. My unruly dark brown hair, tinged with rusty highlights, was strictly Lanier. The lines of my jaw and chin and cheekbones, on the other hand, were becoming sharp and prominent, which could have been the fault of either side of my family.

Yet for obvious reasons, reasons having nothing to do with acne or baby fat, both of which I was spared, my face troubled me. After brushing my teeth, a quick glance in the by now dreaded mirror sometimes revealed a harsh expression, even if I felt relatively happy. Walking the square, I would occasionally startle myself when I caught my reflection in a storefront window. Although I hadn't been brooding, my eyes and brows seemed severe, and my mouth had been drawn into a tight pout. How could this be? I was not Salingeresque, damnit—I played football! I was far too quick to be caught in the rye and far too clever to be running toward that cliff unawares in the first place. I just wasn't cynical, hip or world-weary. My world was invigorating April, salutary Citrus, finger-licking-good fried chicken fresh from Mother's skillet, and a very fast forty. Hell, *I* was all heart. And all of my heart beat the following morse code: Four dots, a dot and a dash, five dots, five more dots, two dots, a space and two final dashes. Translated into telegramese, I was H.A.P.P.Y. Stop. The End. To continue, I would often whisper, "You have a friendly face, Roy." I'd smile and sometimes even make myself laugh to evince this friendliness. "You're friendly," I'd remind myself. "You're very friendly." If I was on one of my extended reading binges I might put it like this: "My, but how friendly you are, Royce!"

To my chagrin, I began to discover that my classmates considered me pensive and somewhat unapproachable. I contended that I was awkward and shy, not conceited or aloof. I didn't understand how others could be so misinformed about me or how they could be so cruel as to find traces of my father in me when it was perfectly clear that I was nothing at all like him.

These classmates didn't know much about my father—just the tidy town legend of his suicide or murder in the dark of night—but their assertions, which I picked up on here and there, seemed in my more irrational moments to be part of some growing conspiracy to link me to my father. And of course I couldn't forget the comments that Leonard had begun to make to me when he'd had too much to drink, nor the way Mother and April would every now and then stare at me as if my appearance had put their nerves on edge. When I caught them fixed on me like that, they'd apologize for "drifting away" and then make some remark about how much I was growing.

If it weren't for football I might never have persuaded my peers that I wasn't haughty and that I didn't think I was too good to fraternize with them. It wasn't that football caused me to blossom as a social being so much as the fact that success in football caused everyone to believe that the very aspects of my personality that had formerly been considered flaws were instead to be thought of as winning attributes. Once I'd earned a starting position at halfback and began running touchdowns, and once our football team began shellacking opponents, it was decided by some secret ballot that I was "quiet and cute" and that my eyes were "intriguing," assessments that were more to my liking. These decisions were arrived at by female classmates, of course, but it was those same female classmates, much more than the principal or parents or teachers, who ran Citrus Junior High School.

Yet if football won me friends and brought me into closer contact with my peers and made me feel like a person who was the very antithesis of my father, it also caused me to become more fully aware of the fact that my feelings for April were complicated, to say the least. In grade school it was easy enough to while away my days without serious relationships or conversations. So long as I did well in kick ball, no one asked much more of me than that. But in junior high I discovered that girls were no longer satisfied with peanut-butter-and-jelly sandwich halves and pumpkin-seed bracelets and furthermore that friendships of any variety demanded a threatening level of intimacy.

"You don't get close to nobody," Clancy Teagues would often tell me. Clancy was our quarterback. Possessed of handsome café au lait skin, girlish eyelashes and a sleek frame, he walked beautifully, feet hardly touching the ground. I thought a great deal of him, and he was always right in complaining that I never allowed anyone to get very close to me.

"I'm close to *you,*" I'd remind him. "And don't like it."

"I don't even know why I waste my time on you."

"Friendship has its costs, Clance."

"You're a fucking nasty-ass cracker is what you are."

Because so much of my family's history continued to perplex me, a stubborn privacy defended me from questions for which I had no ready answers, such as *How did your father die?* and *Why did your mother allow your aunt to rear you?* What's more, while most of my peers thought my connection to April was overly intense, they also believed my family was overly intense generally. Just for starters, my father had been killed and the circumstances of his death were mysterious. Mother traveled to distant cities to meet up with our congressman, James Henderson. April and Leonard lived in a trailer instead of a house and had no children of their own. All the grandparents had died, a very conspicuous fact, since most of my friends' grandparents were alive and well and living in Citrus.

I later came to realize that many of the older people in town viewed Leonard and April and Mother as overgrown children. The feeling was that they were almost like orphans who had been left out in the country to fend for themselves and so had developed strange habits and peculiar ideas. As a matter of fact, that was something of the truth. To be around the trailer or the house was to sense a want of authority, as if things had gone amuck and we were all waiting on Granddaddy or Grandmama or perhaps Leonard's mother or father to show up and straighten everything out.

For such reasons we were considered "characters," but we were well regarded for the most part because everyone knew Mother was very intelligent and admired Leonard and believed April to be beyond criticism of any kind. Looking back, it is clear to me that we were in many ways coddled and treated with kid gloves no matter what happened. As my football playing began to garner attention, there were many townspeople who took that as proof that things couldn't be too terribly wrong for us.

I, ON THE OTHER HAND, was not so sure. Having given myself the impossible task of denying that April was a supremely sexual creation, I would from time to time try to assure myself I was all right by making rather desperate romantic sorties. On star-strewn evenings after away games I'd ride back on the team bus while my blood grew hot and demanding. My face lifted toward the night sky, I'd pray for God to take away my devious energy and rogue thoughts. Yet by the time we entered the school parking lot I was already imagining talking April into a wrestling match and making vile advances under that time-honored ruse.

I recall a night when my thoughts about April became so fully realized in my mind that I decided I had to take action. When we arrived back home after an away game there would be scores of family members and fans and students waiting to greet us. The dance corps girls would be waiting there, too, and of course the cheerleaders. On the night in question, I walked by a cheerleader named Lee Johnson, whose reputation was sturdy, and offered to walk home the sumptuous Lorri-Anne Harris, whose reputation was less than sturdy according to my own groundless estimations. It was rumored that I had eyes for Lorri-Anne. It was also rumored that she had started that rumor. She was certainly capable, and I certainly didn't mind. Hidden away inside myself as I was, a girl like Lorri-Anne offered the possibility of sweet release.

A bundle of curves and curls and lashes, Lorri-Anne had meticulously-cultivated silken skin that made my mad fingers sing. Woven through her laughing green eyes were quiet halos of gold. She had a blunt drawl without a hint of vulgarity. The wet corners of her mouth giggled and whispered and tenderly conspired. A sensual fidget, her ankles crossed and uncrossed, her knees knocked and unknocked, her fingers tapped her lobes, chin, lips, oh, a thousand times a day, and I should know. She could lick her nose and had long dextrous fingers and pretty toes with which to pinch the hairs of my nape. Her thighs retained a soft blond down, the swirls of which in bright sunshine drowned me. She took karate; I rather liked the way she kicked. She read a book on yoga; I watched her stretch in all the ancient ways. Her hair was a fiery honey-blend. She kept her nails clean, her breath minty, her locks berry, her skin fruity, her teeth shiny, her heart near and dear, though when she was crossed she became very nasty. A lost game of chess could cause her to topple the board and charge out of the room. Anything less than an A made her pissy. She actually—repeatedly—tried to outrun me.

Swaybacked, without fear or false modesty, she drove the boys crazy. She once even roughly collared my neck with her arm at a party and pushed her tongue into my mouth! Every now and again she'd call me her boyfriend and wink. More unsettling still, she stole my navy blue Future Farmers of America jacket and wore it with the collar up in the broad beams of daylight.

Additionally, Lorri-Anne was, well, a little *weird.* "I want you to refer to me as Miss Harris," I remember her informing me. We were juniors in high school at that point, solid steadies. "Just occasionally. 'Miss Harris, may I kiss you,' that sort of thing."

"*Miss Harris?* Are you *serious?*"

"If you want me to pay you any attention. *Serious* attention."

"What if we're, like, totally naked?"

"Especially if we're that."

"So when we're like that I can *sexually harris* you?"

"Sometimes I worry you're stupid, Roy."

"Sometimes I worry you're a nut case."

I suffered greatly for that one.

We had very few actual dates over the course of my ninth-grade year, the year we realized we were fond of one another. On our first her granddaddy drove us to the hardware store to purchase a doghouse for her new black Labrador retriever. The Harrises were out for the afternoon, and once we returned home Lorri-Anne waved her magic wand—she had a flawless one—and her granddaddy instantly fell asleep on the couch. We, meanwhile, repaired to the backyard to set up the doghouse. Having done so, *Miss* Harris insisted we make sure it was safe for her puppy. Said inspection required the better part of an hour.

Our second date was more traditional. We cruised Main Street and circled the square seven or eight times in the backseat of one of Lorri-Anne's girlfriends' cars; she was already in high school and so could legally drive and had agreed to chauffeur us around that night as an excuse to spy on an ex-boyfriend. After cruising, we pulled over to talk to classmates we'd been with all week for most every waking hour, though on weekend nights on the square a miracle of amnesia occurred and everyone greeted everyone else as if seeing them for the first time in years. Eventually we got hungry and went to Sonic and then were dropped off at Lorri-Anne's house by twelve, where we chatted with Mr. and Mrs. Harris before going out to the porch to engage in ten minutes of conversation and twice as many minutes of hand holding and that variety of hard kissing which leaves one's jaws sore and crooked the next morning.

Lorri-Anne and I did not, however, walk hand in hand on that post-game night when I made my initial advances. Instead we took steps that placed us hip to hip, pushing and shoving our way home. Before turning down her street we became crazed and seized each other under a mulberry bush, where I'm sure I remember she assisted me in opening her blouse.

Dishabilled in the moonlight, to verb it up a bit just as it was then, her breasts were lovely, what little I could see of them, anyway, behind the sturdy lace of her bra, but they did not prevent me from thinking of April, which left me with no choice but to place my hand between Miss

Harris's thighs. This bit didn't do the trick, either, and I was frightened to go any further. That and the fact that she promptly removed my hand.

"You're darling," Lorri-Anne whispered. "The strong and silent type. They make movies about men like you." Being an honor-roll student and a leading thespian, Lorri-Anne was known to deliver comments like that.

"Silent movies," I said.

"My gosh, Roy. You actually said something. You can run *and* talk! This is a terrific development!"

I smacked her fanny before we walked into her yard. "Oh, you!" she said, like an actress from one of those old movies she loved.

After she disappeared into her two-story house on Jefferson Street, I looked up and waited for the light to come on in her window. When it did, she walked over and waved and blew me kisses before drawing the curtains. And I, sadly, regretfully, inevitably, turned away feeling certain that I'd been unfaithful to April somehow, making my way through the now spent streets of Citrus under increasingly intricate layers of guilt: I felt guilty for having betrayed April; I felt guilty for having thought up a scheme to fool around with a girl instead of praying for a solution as Brother Glenn would have wanted; I felt guilty for feeling guilty about betraying April and all that such guilt implied.

I BEGAN THE LONG WALK home at a brisk and frustrated pace. We lived a little more than a mile from town, and it was a point of pride, if not honor, for me to walk wherever I went until I was old enough to drive a car, though even then I would frequently continue to take off on foot. By adding another pleasant mile to my journey I could visit Sterns, something I was beginning to grow fond of doing. Whenever I felt ashamed, something about his profane grumpiness liberated me. I also appreciated his unusual concern for us; for me and April and Leonard, that is—Mother and Sterns avoided each other completely. They were too much alike to be around each other, I supposed. They were both dominating presences, extremely bright and dogmatic about life. Sterns's loopy affection for April and Leonard didn't sit well with Mother, either.

He was forever buying things for April and Leonard, and quite often these gifts were expensive. Whenever I'd come home with news about some exotic purchase he had brought over, Mother would glare at me. "Oh, of course. That'll fit in perfectly at the trailer."

Many of Sterns's gifts *did* look ridiculous in the trailer. April and Leonard may have had the only double-wide in the country with a fancy leather couch, club chair, ottoman and recliner from an exclusive furniture manufacturer in Thomasville, North Carolina. And that is to say nothing of the framed artsy photographs, or the set of Wüsthof kitchen knives.

Because of all this, my trips out to Sterns's were somewhat of a secret. To put it more accurately, I simply never told Mother about them, since she did not seem to care for the information in the first place. As for Sterns, he always spoke highly of Mother and defended her any time I'd issue some gripe against her, something I did rarely and in the mildest terms. He became angry whenever I tried to talk about things that had happened between Mother and April. Very often such a discussion resulted in my getting blamed for causing whatever had happened.

"You oughta cut your mother some fucking slack sometimes," he said once. When he looked over he saw that he'd intimidated me. "I mean, you ever considered that you're just a terrible pain in the ass?" This was meant to comfort me.

But his gruffness never concealed the fact that Sterns liked me. He gave me packets of plastic worms and sometimes beer, though usually he'd present me with a bottle of RC cola.

"You want an RC?" He would already be giggling.

"Sure." I would already be feigning boredom.

"A *Royal Collier* cola?"

"Yeah."

"How 'bout a *Roy Crown?*"

"Sounds nice."

"That's some kinda fancy name you got."

"Well, it suits me."

Whenever I asked him to he would go into great detail about Citrus's history and the history of my family and his own. His knowledge about these things was considerable. It was from Sterns that I learned that Mr. Lawrence's father had come up with the term Citrusvillians, "Citrusites" sounding like something that infested orange groves and "Citrusonians" making a terrible mess for the mouth. "Underneath, we're all just Citrus-*villains*," Sterns liked to point out. I also learned how Citrus came to be called Citrus. Old man Haney's father and one of the Alexanders had planted some groves as a joint venture. At the time our town was called Water Town, which no one really liked, so they came up with Citrus. The name was put to a vote and approved. Problem was, Citrus was located several hundred miles north of the critical freeze line, beyond which the winters are too harsh for sensitive ruby red grapefruits, ponderosa lemons and navel oranges, as Mr. Haney and Mr. Alexander soon found out. Within a few years a single cold night destroyed hundreds of acres of seedlings and the business went bust, but everyone agreed the name Citrus was too good to give up, accurate or not, so it stuck.

Not that our winters were severe. It rarely actually snowed in Citrus, and even when it did it was always an extremely mild affair that had the unconvincing aspect of a frosty toupee applied to the head of the town. During one of those rare snows Sterns came up with the title to his novel: *The Snows of Citrus Past,* though he often referred to it as *Buried Beneath the Snows of Citrus Past.*

Sterns had developed a complex and wonderfully nuanced take on Citrus's social fabric and could locate the standing of each family with precision. On the wall behind the counter hung a large tricounty map. He knew each plot of land, roads that remained uncharted, backwoods shacks that had escaped notice and creeks that had eluded the mapmakers. Whenever April and I discovered something interesting, we'd tell Sterns about it. There were many hunters and fishermen who did the same. Sales of property were reported to Sterns as well. He'd take a collapsible graphite fishing rod and use it as a pointer and tell me of the latest news.

Sterns would also go over old stories about April and Leonard and Mother, stories I most wanted to hear, exclamating each utterance by slicing the baited air of Reel Bait and Tackle with his collapsible rod, though eventually he'd hit upon something that made him sad.

"April and Leonard never really had much of a chance, if you ask me," he'd sometimes say. He'd wander into one of the back rooms at that point without saying good-bye.

By the time I'd completed the mile hike out to Sterns's place I'd begun to wonder why the hell I hadn't stayed with Lorri-Anne beneath that mullberry bush. I must have appeared furrowed and browbeaten when I walked in.

"What's wrong now?"

I shrugged. "Nothing."

"You got a pimple on your chin, by the way."

"It's from my chin strap. It's not a pimple."

"For a football player, you're as glum as they come."

"I am not."

Sterns was sitting in a rotten-looking tweedy chair with a book in his lap. When he stood, the crumpled chair made an exasperated noise. "You shut up," Sterns told it.

We walked back into the storage room. Sterns grabbed a beer and sat before the piano. He played a few bars of the "Moonlight Sonata." "You need you a sweetheart," he said.

"I'm working on it."

"Working on it, huh?" He sighed, plunking a grouchy minor chord. "If I'd ever once looked like you in my entire life I'd have ruined myself with women. I'd never have stopped. Maybe that's why come I never got crushed out on April like everybody else did. We were at two totally opposite ends of the spectrum. I was the standard-bearer for ugly and she was the ideal beauty. We had our jobs to do and just respected one another."

"Aw, Sterns."

"You, on the other hand, are right up her alley."

He had been looking at me when he said this, and the embarrassment that came over both of us was such that we couldn't break away. Finally he grunted and used the back of his shirtsleeve to wipe his forehead.

"Well, runs in the family, I reckon." He got up. "Here, sit your ass down and play me some of that jazz your mama's spent hundreds of dollars trying to teach you."

WHEN I GOT HOME Mother had the stereo going and danced over to give me a hug. "Four touchdowns, Roy! Four! Coach Crawford told me people are talking about you all over Florida and you're not even in high school yet!"

"I had a pretty good night," I said.

"You had a *great* night, honey. I've got some Champagne to celebrate. Don't worry. It has all the essential amino acids."

Though Mother hadn't really wanted me play football, once it was clear I'd be playing anyway she began to read up on gridiron rules and strategies. She arranged her schedule so that she was in town for all the home games. After the games, we'd often enjoy a late supper together. She'd fry chicken or prepare shrimp and grits, and there was always an exceptional bottle of wine, of which she allowed me only a single glass until I reached high school, at which point it became share and share alike. It would be years before I realized the quality of wine I was given. At the time I assumed there were only two kinds, Mad Dog 20/20, which one drank with one's peers to get sloshed, and then Mother's magical elixirs that made the world tender and vibrant.

The house would be awash with warm candlelight. Mother referred to herself as my "late date," and for the first hour or so our conversations were always charmed. But soon enough she'd catch me looking at my watch, something that would cause her to put her napkin down and frown. "Oh, Roy. Please be careful over there tonight," she'd tell me. "I worry about your being over there this late."

When she was tight, she could be more direct. "I wish you wouldn't go over there," she'd say. "You should have seen him at the game. He was completely smashed. He takes bourbon and pours it into his Coke right there in the stands. He hardly even hides it anymore." If we began to fight or the evening turned dry and quiet, she could work herself up to a full denunciation: "Leonard's dangerous, Roy. I'm not going to beat around the bush with you about it. I don't know why I can't get you to understand that. He was sloppy by halftime. And I know where it goes from there. Believe you me. I know exactly where it goes. I've seen it. At first he's all smiles, sure, but then he turns the corner. I don't want to start an argument, but he's turned that corner more than once. And I'm not just worried about you, Roy. I'm worried about April, too."

"April? April's fine, Mother."

"You just can't see it. You're too close to her. But his behavior is taking a toll on her. I can see it. I can see it in her eyes. And I hate your being over there late at night when he's been drinking. It worries me. Your being over there just makes things worse because he's jealous of you just like he was jealous of your father. It worries me sick, Roy. Why do you have to go? Why?"

If I hadn't already seen Leonard turn the corner—and I hadn't by a long shot, as I was to discover—I had at least watched him approach it. Not only had I helped him into the house on more than one occasion, he would sometimes show up at the practice field during the week swilling bourbon from a pint bottle tucked into a brown paper bag, that most obvious of disguises. On the way home he'd become critical of me, saying that I wasn't hitting the hole fast enough, that I wasn't trying hard enough, that I needed to be far more aggressive.

"Are you listening to me?"

"Yes sir."

"You damn well better be. I don't come out here for my health."

Our relationship had become a tricky proposition for both of us. He liked that I was growing bigger and was becoming a formidable football player, especially since he had to a large extent engineered these accomplishments, but these accomplishments also brought out something bitter in him. He could—and usually did—praise me to high heavens, yet if April complimented me he sometimes threw out a remark that took me down a notch or two. When he'd had a lot to drink I'd often find him staring at me with a puzzled expression, and on some occasions his expression would be closer to contempt. "I hate that shirt," he'd say of a shirt that he'd approved of only a week before. "You're tracking dirt all over the damned carpet," he'd announce, though we'd been inside for an hour, and I had, in fact, taken off my shoes. "Roy might make a decent football player if he'd just listen to me once in a while," he'd comment, knowing full well that I never deviated from his instructions.

As I had already realized, the truth of the matter was that Leonard was onto something. Having been brought up in a family of farmers, he knew to take the claims of blood quite seriously. Only a person far removed from the source of his sustenance can believe that people spring up willy-nilly and grow into anything they please with no regard to the sort of seed that gave them life or to the kind of ground in which they were nurtured. Leonard was far too wise for such thinking, and he understood all too clearly that he and April and Mother weren't the only ones who were having a hand in rearing me. My father was also having a say in the matter. And it was my father's say that troubled Leonard, for he began to fear that it would be decisive.

He knew I was becoming too fond of April. It isn't stretching the point to suggest that he must have been worried all along that certain of my father's predilections would manifest themselves in me. Though he tried to be supportive, the prospect of my looking more like my father as I approached manhood and feeling so strongly about April at the same time did not sit well with him.

"Damned fine running," he'd say when I walked over to the trailer after a game.

"You run so beautifully," April would tell me.

Leonard would roll his eyes. "Don't go giving Royce the big head. He can't hardly fit into his helmet as it is."

Leonard gave his evaluations of my performance from his fancy recliner, his socked feet crossed, a High Life resting on his belly. He enjoyed providing these post-game commentaries, though after a while his cheer wore thin. At some point he'd stand and insist on showing me certain maneuvers, becoming so physical with me that it caused April to jump from the couch and tell us to stop. "Y'all are gonna tear the trailer apart," she'd say.

Leonard would be staring at me, panting, "You see I've still got it in me."

Eventually he'd become entranced by the television and fall asleep. His snoring was ferocious, and April and I would giggle and creep out the door. "Don't mind Leonard," she'd tell me. "He's so proud of you. He just wants you to have all the opportunities he didn't have."

We were always too excited to call it a night at that point, and so we'd leave the trailer and head out to Lake Julep. Night fishing was the best and most adventurous kind of fishing as far as April and I were concerned, and it was especially fun to go after a big game.

The sky was vast and beautiful over the water. Because we were hundreds of miles from a city of any size, the stars were bright and throbbing. I felt pleasantly isolated from my friends, football, school, Leonard, Mother and the rest of world. At that time there were only a few houses on Lake Julep, and even they were far from the part of the lake we frequented. Mr. Haney, one of Citrus's wealthiest citizens, owned most of the property surrounding the area we preferred. He'd built a simple dock with several gas lamps and a boathouse in which he kept an old wooden powerboat, though as far as I knew April and I were the only people who ever spent any time there. When Leonard bought a johnboat one Christmas, Mr. Haney told him he could keep it down at the dock. It was fourteen feet and came with a live well and two plastic high-backed fishing seats, one in the front, one in back. We equipped it with a sleek black fourteen-horsepower Mercury and a five-speed trolling motor with a weed guard. From this craft, all that we ever wanted was attainable.

Lake Julep was undoubtedly the perfect place for April and me. It snaked like the letter *S* and was eerily beautiful in every regard. In holding to April's beloved primordial aesthetic, it was overblown with life.

There were catfish and bream, gar and mud fish and bass and specks, wild shiners and minnows, not to mention tadpoles, frogs, alligators, various breeds of turtles, turkeys, egrets and owls, all manner of birds and insects—mosquitoes, too, I'm afraid—plus feral hogs, deer, otters, eagles, quail, bobcats and April and me beneath a sky hot with stars.

We released most of the bass we caught, though we had Mr. Edwards, the taxidermist, mount a few of our largest conquests for the walls of the trailer. When we were hungry for fish to eat we usually went after specks or bream, which were tastier than bass anyway. After we'd come back to the dock I'd watch April clean our catch, her arms and legs slick with sweat, the fish scales glistening on her brown skin. If we'd had a good night, she'd become feisty.

"What are you looking at? You better get over here and help me instead of standing there and watching." She'd cock her hip craftily, pointing at me with the knife. "You know that Elvis song, Roy? Like a one-eyed cat, peeping in a seafood store."

"A one-eyed cat? It says that? Dear me, April."

"When I was growing up I used to sing that all the time until Leonard explained it to me. I was horrified."

"What's a one-eyed cat, anyway?"

"You hush."

She'd squat down and continue her work, sending scales flying in all directions. If it wasn't too cool, she wore a T-shirt and cutoffs. Neither of us wore shoes unless it was cold.

"Get to work," I can hear her saying. "Get to work right now this instant!"

I don't recall when it first occurred to me to strip down and dive into the water, but from the first time I risked it I was hooked. I'd wait until April was busy with the fish and sneak to the end of the dock, where I'd quietly remove my shirt and shorts and boxers and then holler her name and dive into the water just as she turned around.

"You just wait," she'd cry.

"For what?"

"For the trouble you're in."

After a few minutes she'd come over and sit on the edge of the dock while I swam.

"Do you remember how I used to bathe you when you were little?" she once asked. "You were just a baby. I took you out in the yard and put you in that old washtub."

When she said this I felt the first tremors from the shifting and unsettling of deep memory. Beyond anything I could visualize was the feel of soapy water and the squawking of chickens and then me and the water being pulled into sunlight.

"I used No More Tears so it wouldn't hurt your eyes. I couldn't stand it when you cried. It upset me so much. But you didn't cry very often. You were so cute. I always made you a little crown with the bubbles. Little crowns of No More Tears."

I swam beneath her, resting against the wooden ladder while she kicked her legs.

"Stay where you are," she warned.

"Forever?"

"Yes."

"I can't stay like this forever."

FIVE

I didn't hear the story my father told in Ligget's Drugstore until I was sixteen years of age. I learned of it because Mother had grown increasingly concerned about my affection for April and because she believed April and Leonard had become far too important to me, not to mention that she feared Leonard would one day attack me during a drunken rage. The story became part of a long-running commentary about good breeding and my good name, about trashy people and decent people and even about people of the highest rank, which meant my father and his South Carolina people and by extension Mother and me, though not Leonard, and because of Leonard, not April.

And so I learned of my heritage and my responsibility to it much as a young aristocrat who has fallen for his chambermaid would be informed of his position in life and the unseemliness of carrying on further with a woman who was beneath his privilege. Mother never mentioned the obvious things, such as the fact that April was my aunt and that she was married and that our relationship must heed those important boundaries. Nor did she console me by explaining that it is not altogether uncommon for a young man to have a crush on a cousin or an aunt and that in time such feelings usually mellow.

"April has to live with the decisions she's made," Mother had lately begun to remark as she sat on the front porch, looking toward the bend in the road. "Nobody forced her to marry Leonard. She could have gone somewhere else and met someone else. She didn't have to stay here."

When she said hard things like that, she'd stare hard, too, peering down the road as if trying to develop a type of vision that would allow her to gain difficult places and make them clear.

But eventually her eyes would soften, and she'd turn to me and say, "I don't mean to be unkind. There are just differences between April and me, and that means there are differences between April and you. That's all I'm saying. I'm not saying we're better. I'm just saying you have to understand the differences."

I couldn't look at her when she said these things, and for that reason I suppose she believed she had to keep saying them.

"We're Episcopal and they're Pentecostal, for one thing," she'd continue. "We go to church every now and then, and they go all the time . . . because it's their crutch."

"Leonard doesn't go to church," I'd remind her.

"That's right. And I'll get to that later. But just remember this: He wanted to be a preacher. There's a lot about Leonard and April you don't understand, Roy. There's no kinder person than April in all the world. You know how much I love her. I'm not being ugly, I'm just explaining things to you. You're spending too much time over at that trailer. You should be with your friends more. You should come with me to Washington and New York and New Orleans and learn about the world. We could even plan a trip to Europe, Roy. We could do a lot of things. But your whole life is football and April and Leonard, and that's not a life."

When Mother at last realized that all her lessons and attempts to marshal artistic genius had not changed my attitude and behavior in the way that she wanted, she turned to something altogether more powerful. That altogether more powerful something was my father.

The time had come to summon Sanders Royce Collier, who in my mind, much like the velvet-suited man with the cane and untamed locks in Caspar David Friedrich's *Wanderer Above the Sea Fog,* stood atop the highest hill of Citrus, staring down at me. The spell he cast was indeed that disturbing. It must be remembered that before his death I was forced to keep a watch on him because of April when I'd just as soon have run from him. And that after his death I continued to have to be on the prowl for his presence, as he would from time to time pop up in order to wreak havoc. Worse, as I've revealed, he was of late attempting to somehow emerge *within my very own body,* forcing himself into the features of *my* face to make it *his* face and taking my for the most part *innocent* thoughts and twisting them into his own *unseemly* ones!

I remember very well the night Mother first told me the story my father had told in Ligget's. I'd returned from football practice one mild October evening during my sophomore year of high school, and Mother had followed me into my bedroom, nervously weaving two strands of hair. As I removed my shirt, her eyes filled with what I thought of as imitation tears. "You're beginning to look more and more like your father," she said. "Oh, you look so much like him. I'm so proud of you." She clucked her tongue. Something purporting to be a splash of something wet and heartfelt spilled onto the floor at Mother's feet while I cringed at her comments. "Just look at you. I don't even know when you started shaving. When was it?"

"About a year ago," I told her, stepping back, trying to remain dry.

"That long? How could it be that long? I hadn't even noticed."

After I showered Mother called me out to the back porch. She'd already poured glasses of wine for us. She placed a bucket of pole beans on the floor next to a paper bag of tips and announced that she had something important to tell me.

The night had graciously complied with her request for the proper atmosphere for her story. A rusty harvest moon hovered over the barn, sending twilight tenderly to bed. The wind chimes tangled eerily, the sounds of tinkling glass as lulling as a heavy narcotic. The gourds that hung from the eaves of the smokehouse began to knock against one another, too, sending out the hollow, lonesome music of tiki drums. All about us there seemed to be a sweet unraveling.

"This is serious business, Roy," Mother said sharply. "But now that you're becoming a man, it's time you knew." She looked at me and reached for my hand. "I know I should have told you all of this a long time ago. I'm sorry I didn't. It's just that some of these old memories are so painful. I don't like thinking about some of the things I'm going to tell you, and sometimes I even try to forget some of them. But we've reached a boiling point. With Leonard, I mean. And the only way to get you to listen is to explain why he acts the way he acts. And that means I have to tell you about your father and what happened when he came into town."

She released my hand then and took a deep breath and began to tell me my father's story, the one that had so impressed her in the drugstore all those years ago.

"Your father was a gentleman and wouldn't tell us everything at once, especially not with two young girls present. He told us what you might call a polite version."

"What do you mean a polite version?"

"I'm going to tell you in a minute. I just wish you could have heard him tell it, though. What a voice he had. Oh, Roy, he was so eloquent. And deadly handsome. He just arrived that Christmas Eve, just showed up in town, standing there with those terrible storms coming on. It really was something. I mean, being brought up the way we were, it looked like the kind of sky you would see before Jesus comes. If we'd heard trumpets it would have scared us to our knees. You wouldn't have recognized your mother in those days. I was so naive."

She smiled, but when she saw I wasn't smiling she quickly looked away to cast her smile toward the barn, squinting a little as if the moonlight were too bright. "There's the old pump," she whispered. She enjoyed taking a gourd down to the pump in the backyard to have a drink. She'd often remind me of how my grandfather dug the well and how important it was to keep the pump primed, but on this night she was far too anxious for that.

"Well, surprise," she said softly, still looking away. "It wasn't Christ coming that Christmas. It was your father. And right off I thought, *No, not Jesus, but at least an angel,* because he was so lovely and unexpected. What a beautiful accent. He had a very dignified Southern accent. I believe the South Carolina accent is the most beautiful. Everybody noticed his accent and—"

As the sort of cruel luck of that long night would have it, someone suddenly knocked at the front door.

"Oh, shit," Mother hissed. "I mean shoot. I ordered a pizza."

We were too small a town to have a pizza chain, but an enterprising young man had returned from Pensacola having learned to bake pizzas and had hired a crew of high schoolers and delinquents to deliver anywhere in the county. When Mother returned she had a quilt slung over her shoulder. She handed me a paper towel.

"So what about father?" I pressed.

"I was just thinking about his vocabulary."

Mother took a bite of pizza, chewing it in a petite and precious way that instantly riled me. I could have jumped up and down and all around that porch like a frenzied professional wrestler going on a tirade.

"It doesn't shame me to admit I wasn't educated to that level at that time," she continued. "I was always a reader, but not like your father or James. One day you're going to have to take time out of your busy schedule to go to Washington to spend time with James, it's as simple as that. We'll see the monuments and the White House and see Congress while it's in session. But remember one thing: If you ask James about your father, he would think you were being rude by going outside the family to learn about the family—and he would be right—so I hope you won't ever do that."

"No ma'am," I said. "I won't."

"That's important. Propriety's important, Roy."

"I know," I said.

"Anyway, we wanted to know why your father had come into town, of course. The way your father explained it that night, he and your grandfather Collier had gotten into a terrible fight because of your father's high school sweetheart. Your grandfather didn't want them to be married."

Mother rolled her eyes and shrugged dramatically within her quilt, bringing her knees up and planting her feet on the seat of the rocker like a young girl.

"Why didn't he want them to get married?"

"Well, it wasn't about them, really. It was really about a conflict between a father and a son and about your grandfather Collier asserting his authority. You see, your father was not the kind to be ruled over. It wasn't rebellion, it was simply his nature. It was a clash of two fierce wills that just happened to come down to that girl. Because to tell you the truth, from what he later told me, he didn't even love that girl all that much. He said he wanted to marry her because your grandfather was testing him. He did not like to be told what he could or couldn't do. That's the one thing he couldn't tolerate. Even if things became dangerous he . . ." Mother stared at me. "Well, your father just didn't like being told what to do is all I'm saying."

She put her pizza down and took a sip of wine. "He told us they had a fight," she said. "Over the girl. And afterwards your grandfather became terribly sick. Your father's brothers and sister blamed him for it and things grew tense. Nobody was backing down, and your father was afraid that your grandfather, who was getting on up in years, would get hurt one way or the other. Or else he would just walk over one day and shoot somebody for saying the wrong thing. Because the girl's family was firing back their own bad opinions of your father's family. It was just a matter of time."

"This is what he said in Ligget's?"

"Not quite that much. But I'll tell you one thing, he didn't tell us anything too personal. That's something he would never do, no matter what else you may have been told."

"Nobody's ever told me anything, Mother."

"April may have said a few things. Not that I blame her, but I sure wouldn't put it past her."

"Not about this she hasn't. I've asked her. Over and over again. Just like I've asked you about a million times. But nobody ever tells me anything."

"Or Sterns. Good heavens. What a talker."

"Sterns? What would Sterns have to say?"

"Sterns is writing a novel, after all. Listen, I think Sterns is brilliant. But he's a gossip. And he likes to tell stories."

"What's wrong with that?"

"Nothing. Unless it invades someone's privacy."

"Sterns doesn't do that, Mother. Its not like I hang out with him all the time."

"Well, I'm just saying. And don't act like I'm against Sterns like you act like I'm against everyone else. I used to defend Sterns when we were kids, for your information. Me and Leonard and April. All three of us." Mother sighed. "I don't want to fight tonight."

"I just want to hear the story."

"Don't be impudent."

"I'm just saying."

"Let's stick to the story," Mother said.

"Fine with me."

"Then don't interrupt."

I made a motion that sealed my lips and tossed their key through the screen door and into the yard.

"Where was I? Oh, right, your father told us he had to promise not to marry the girl for your grandfather's sake. I guess that's the main point. And it broke the girl's heart, especially since he didn't blame it on your grandfather, which he wouldn't have. Anyway, after that, he went off to Vietnam. And when he returned from the war, your grandfather had died, and the family blamed him to some extent. That was what caused him to start wandering around the country. He was on his way to New Orleans when he saw those storms coming."

"But that's not exactly what really happened."

Mother looked at me carefully. "No. Like I told you, what really happened was personal, and he couldn't have told us that. I mean, he didn't even know who we were. But later, after we began seeing one another, he told me the truth. I guess I'm the only one who knows, besides James. He told James."

"Why did he tell Mr. Henderson?" (There was never a *Mister James* as far as I was concerned.)

"Well, James and your father became great friends. This may be going a little too far, but I think James may have even aspired to be like your father. He was crazy about Sanders. James introduced him to all the best people in town. They started going to all the parties."

"Father knew the Haneys?"

"Of course. And the Alexanders. And the Thompsons. He became a part of their circle. Listen, I know you think Citrus is the center of the earth, and you should, it's your home, but the Haneys and Alexanders and all the rest of them are small fry compared to someone like your father. Your father was the real thing, Roy. Your grandfather Collier was a very wealthy farmer and a member of Charleston society. All those Citrus families were quite proud to be entertaining someone like your father. Did you know your father lived in James's back-house until we got married?"

Mother smiled and nodded and began to tie her hair up. She'd kept it long while most of the other mothers had gone in for shorter, more practical cuts. Mother didn't believe in that sort of practicality, however, something I admired about her. She approached the most trivial details of life with a winning romantic attitude. When she wasn't wearing a smart new outfit, she went in for old jeans or khakis and bulky sweaters. Perching her glasses on the end of her nose, her cheeks flush before a fire, I often wondered if the pleasant look on her face was because of the novel she was reading or because she knew she appeared bookish in a fetching way. Unlike April, Mother was the kind of woman who was always aware of how she looked, which was not necessarily a bad thing.

"James and your father. What a pair." Mother frowned. "Of course, by the time you came along those days were long gone. Leonard made sure of that." She sipped her wine and began to shake her head. "What you don't realize is that Leonard caused a lot of problems for me and your father. He caused problems while we were dating, and he caused problems after we were married. Just look at where they live. I mean, think about it. Leonard can afford a house. He has money hidden away. James has told me. But he had to buy that godawful trailer and set it just on the other side of the property line. Just to be provocative. He caused the whole town to turn against your father."

"What did he do to cause the town to turn against him?"

"What *didn't* he do? That's the question. He ran your father down all over Citrus. But I don't want to get into all that yet. I haven't told you what really happened that made your father come here in the first place. I have to tell you that because I'm afraid if I don't someone else might and whatever they'd tell you would be a lie. I'm the only one who knows, besides James. A lot of people have tried to hurt me by spreading rumors and commenting on things they know nothing about. But it's nobody else's business. Do you understand?"

"Yes, ma'am."

"Because this is important."

I managed to nod and then looked away.

"You remember how I've told you your grandfather Collier could be old-fashioned, even difficult. Well, what really happened with that South Carolina girl was a far cry from what your father told us that night in Ligget's."

"I'll bet."

Mother gave me a look, which I ducked by reaching for another slice of pizza.

"Anyway, your father told us he backed down because he didn't want a confrontation to develop between your grandfather and the other girl's parents, but the truth is your father wasn't in the least willing to back down and he didn't leave town right away, either. He told your grandfather he was going to marry the girl come hell or high water, as a matter of fact, and your grandfather said he'd better prepare for both if he did. The part about the two families feuding was true. The girl's father was naturally pretty upset. But the real conflict was between your father and your grandfather. And it got ugly. It got very ugly."

"So he didn't go to Vietnam right away."

"No. Not right away." Her eyes searched mine as if she were seeking permission for something. "Oh, Roy," she whispered. "But I have to tell you."

"Tell me what?"

"What your father told me. What he said happened."

"Yes, ma'am. I want to know."

"Of course you do. It's what he would have told you if he were alive. I have to honor that," she pointed out, though her tone was questioning.

"Yes, ma'am. Tell me."

A whippoorwill cooed in the darkness, and Mother tilted her head and listened. She smiled awkwardly, to herself. When she began again her voice was soft and distant and even.

"One night your Grandfather Collier couldn't find your father anywhere. He checked all over town, one place after another. Then he saw the car. Your father had checked in under a false name, I don't remember what it was, Will or Bill or something, something stupid and obvious. . . ."

"They were in a hotel?"

"A motel," Mother corrected. "But boy were they in for a surprise. To begin with, your grandfather decided he wouldn't knock on the door to the room. Oh, no. He decided he'd burst in on them and catch them in the act. He wanted to shame them and break the relationship up for good. So he got a crowbar from his trunk and walked over to the room and pried the door open. It was a cheap room with those thin plywood doors, and the door popped open as easily as a pill box." She winced as if she could hear the plywood cracking. "He stormed in waving that crowbar, hollering. They weren't fully dressed. Or they weren't dressed at all—I don't know and I've never wanted to know, frankly."

Mother was still staring into the yard, her face braced and determined. "It gets worse," she said, her voice a little lost. "It just gets worse. Your grandfather Collier started pounding the foot of the bed with the crowbar. He shattered the bedside lamp. In the state he was in, he could've really hurt somebody . . . so your father grabbed him by the arms and shook him, trying to get the crowbar loose. They struggled and fell over a chair. The girl was screaming for your father to stop, but your father had one thing on his mind—getting that crowbar. And he did. But when he did a terrible feeling came over him. The girl ran over and cupped your grandfather's head into her arms. 'Call an ambulance, Sanders! Call one now!' But your father didn't move. He just looked down and started to cry." Mother exhaled sadly. "The autopsy revealed that your grandfather had had a heart attack."

"He died in the motel?"

"Yes. Right in the motel. Your father told the girl to go home, and then he waited on the ambulance. He called his family and told everyone that he'd gone to the motel to be alone but that your grandfather had found him and broken into the room and that they'd argued and so on."

"And they didn't believe him."

"Some did, some didn't. The stories started flying. And not only did he have to deal with the fact that he had, in his eyes, killed his own father, he also had to deal with the fact that he'd killed him with a half-naked teenage girl in bed behind him. She wasn't much older than you. Your father wasn't too much older than you, for that matter."

"So he had to leave town."

"Things just got too serious after that. The rumors were terrible, and I know something about rumors. Rumors about him and the girl and about what they were doing in the motel. And about what your grandfather had seen—had caught them doing—and how that was what actually killed the old man. Everywhere he went people would whisper or give him looks. The girl was heartbroken and wanted to be with him, except now he couldn't stand the sight of her. His mother accepted Sanders's version of the story and never voiced any doubts. But his brothers and sister couldn't accept it. So he went overseas. It was the only honorable way to get out of town.

"He was very brave, Roy. His mother died while he was over there, and even after he'd served his time he didn't want to come back home. Finally he did, though. Except that home was the last place he wanted to go. He spent a few days in South Carolina, and then he drew down on his trust and headed out of town. That was the year he showed up in Citrus."

Mother looked at me and smiled a smile that infuriated me—it was the sheepish smile of a martyr, and it did not come naturally to her. "Wait here. There's something I want to show you," she said.

When she returned she had my father's leather satchel and a tiny skeleton key. She scooted her rocking chair closer to mine. "It's time for you to have some things that belonged to your father," she told me. She worked the little key until the lock clicked. I'd known about his satchel for a long time. It sat on the highest shelf of her closet, a closet that she kept locked. "Here we are," she said.

She produced my father's signet ring and his handkerchief and his sterling silver cuff links, the very ones he'd been wearing the Christmas Eve of his arrival. The ring had been polished recently, and the letters seemed regal and fitting. The handkerchief had also been well taken care of, and its silken SRC stood out brilliantly against the soft white cotton. But best of all were the cuff links, which I imagined Lorri-Anne would find tantalizing.

"I want you to have them now," Mother said. "You're becoming a man, and I want you to have these so you'll be reminded of exactly what kind of a man you are to become."

"They're beautiful," I said.

"Your father had taste, that's for sure. Just don't wear that ring while you're playing football. And don't wipe football sweat off with that handkerchief. You have to take care of nice things."

"I'm going to keep them in my room," I told her.

"Look at these clothes. Oh, my, Roy, so many memories. These are the very clothes he wore that day." She held up his shirt, thumbing the French cuffs for me to see. "You're probably too big for it already. You keep drinking those awful protein drinks."

I took the shirt from her. Holding it up to the porch light, I noted with satisfaction that it *was* already too small for me.

"Maybe you could fit into these," Mother said, offering me the wool pants, which were also too small. She moved on. "Now look at this!" She presented the mohair jacket but as quickly brought it down. Obviously too small! She frowned, then looked back into the satchel. "Now *this*. Surely *this* will fit."

It was my father's charcoal gray, ankle-length cashmere coat. She urged me to try it on. Though it was a little tight, I could get into it. It was terribly elegant, especially to a teenager, and even if it had belonged to my father I nevertheless wanted very much to be able to show up somewhere with it on.

"How handsome you look," Mother said. She bit her bottom lip and tugged at the sleeves. "The arms are a little short, but it's still very lovely. Just don't button it. You're too big in the shoulders. You shouldn't want to look like Leonard, like a big piece of meat. You should want to be sleek like your father."

"I want to play football, Mother, not look like Leonard. And I don't have an ounce of fat on me."

"Of course not. I'm not saying that. I'm just saying you're getting too many muscles. I'm just saying watch it. I'm not criticizing. Nobody in the world could be any more proud of you than I am."

"What about the satchel?"

She looked at the satchel and withdrew a little. "Oh, the satchel. . . ."

"Can I look at it?"

"Let your mother keep it a little longer," she said. She began to pack up the clothes that didn't fit me. "But you can wear the coat to the Christmas dance. Won't you be something? You'll be the best-looking man there! Oh, my!" She laughed and then looked playfully cross. "You'd better wear it while you can, at the rate you're growing."

Mother patted my knee and went to get some more wine. She took the satchel with her, and I could hear her walk to her bedroom to lock it back in the closet. I shook my father's cuff links in my hand as if they were dice, contemplating Grandfather Collier and his salacious demise. It seemed exactly like *my* father to have killed *his* father while in the nude with an also nude teenage girl in bed behind him. The story hit just the spot. And then him leaving town to go get into *another* fight—indeed, to get into a *war*—how perfectly SRC!

That is not to suggest I wasn't touched by what I'd heard, because I did empathize with the loss and bitter shame that my father must have endured. In fact, after hearing the story, I actually felt a grudging respect for my father and his plight, if only momentarily.

Mother had wanted a much more radical transformation than that, however, and it was pretty clear that she believed she would get one. With me proudly posing in that charcoal gray, ankle-length coat and greedily scooping up my father's signet ring and handkerchief and cuff links, how could she not believe it? Though this irritated me a little, I was glad to see Mother pleased. After all, I did want my father's things, and if wanting them made her happy, so much the better.

I could never have guessed what was coming and that our evening was already spoiled. I would later realize that whenever someone divulges anything of consequence, feelings of panic and resentment are almost certain to follow. I was to learn that when it came to Mother and stories about my father, the panic and resentment were especially keen, and no matter how hard I might try to avoid it the conversation would eventually turn to April.

What ruined it that night was a last comment made as we were on our way to bed. It seemed almost accidental, a careless mistake, but such things happen at the last possible moment for a reason.

"And remember one other thing," Mother said.

"Yes, ma'am."

"In addition to the things about your father and who you are, remember not to ever talk about any of this with April. Do you promise?"

"Yes, ma'am, but—"

"Do you promise?" she interrupted. "Because if you can't promise and if you can't keep your word, I'll have to take all of it back. And I'll never tell you another thing again as long as I live. Do you understand?"

"No, ma'am, but I promise."

"Don't be clever with me. You know why, too."

"No, ma'am, I don't."

"Oh, yes you do. Oh, yes you most certainly do. And we're not going to talk about it tonight, not after we've had such a good time and been able to act like mothers and sons should act, for once. Or do you want to take even that away from me?"

"I said I promise."

"You're just going to have to decide where your allegiance lies, Roy. I'm sorry, but it's come down to that."

"I know where it lies, Mother."

"Do you? I hope so. Because things have gotten out of hand as far as I'm concerned. You don't even refer to her as your aunt. You never have. But she *is* your aunt. It's not your fault. It's not even *her* fault. If it's anyone's fault it's *my* fault. But you're the one who's going to have to do some thinking, Roy. Some thinking about character and honor and about doing what's right and behaving with dignity."

A FEW MONTHS LATER I was elected a sophomore class favorite of Citrus High and stood on the Christmas float, waving and throwing candy canes into the crowd during the parade. Later that night at the dance (Lorri-Anne and I were on the outs) my date had gotten sick and had to go home, so I called April from the principal's office. We went for a ride into neighboring towns to look at decorations. We drove for hours in the Mustang, talking on the C.B., wishing truckers Merry Christmas and inquiring about their destinations. We drove to Chipley and Bonifay and even as far as De Funiak Springs.

By the time we came home Mother had found out where I'd been. She'd gone up to the dance. She was just so proud of me, she said, that she wanted to see me in all my glory and maybe even share a dance with me.

I found her in the kitchen. She was crying and wouldn't look at me.

"You can be so cruel, Roy. You do just what you please, no matter who it hurts."

"But I didn't know you were coming up there," I said. "Please. I'm sorry."

"You're cruel, Roy! You're cruel to your mother!"

I tried to touch her, but she slapped my hand away.

"When you were a little boy you were sweet. But now you're selfish." She looked at me then, her eyes fierce and cold. "And I'll tell you another thing. Another thing that makes you cruel. April isn't doing well and you're not helping matters."

I stared at her in disbelief.

"Don't look at me that way. It's the truth."

When I started to say something, she cut me off.

"I don't want to hear it. I'm not manipulating you. I'm not the wicked witch trying to ruin your fun. I'm telling you the truth, because if you care about her, things have to change. Leonard is getting out of control with his drinking, and he's not above hurting her or you, or both of you, for that matter. I blame him for a lot of this. He never would leave her alone. Ever since we were children he followed her around and kept pushing and pushing and pushing about marriage. But what's done is done. You've got to realize what I'm saying, Roy. Do you hear me? Do you? Or do I have to beg you? Because April is losing herself, do you understand?"

"That's not true," I insisted.

"It most certainly is."

"No it's not. It's ridiculous."

She stood, and fresh tears gathered in her eyes. "I've been too lenient with you. I've allowed you too much. For her sake. It was all for her sake. And now it's backfired."

"Mother, please—"

"No, you listen to me, damnit!" she shouted. "You don't know what you're talking about! You don't know anything about anything! Your whole world revolves around her. Just think how hurt and embarrassed I was, traipsing up there to have a dance with you and being told by Mrs. Harlan that you'd run off with April. *Run off with her!* Don't think people don't notice things like that, either, Roy. Because they do. And then to hear the two of you cavorting all over the place on the damned radio. Oh, people have noticed a lot of things for a long time. And I won't go through all that again. I won't. Take that damned coat off! I can't bear to see you wear it! I said take it off! Take it off right now!"

When I removed the coat she grabbed it, clutching it to her chest and sobbing over it. But after a moment the coat itself seemed to make her angry, and she threw it to the floor.

SIX

After our argument, I lay awake most of the night, fearing that come morning Mother would initiate a campaign to separate me from April and Leonard and that all our lives would be thrown into irrevocable turmoil. Rather than concerning myself with certain telling details of our conversation that would have proved helpful down the road, I leaped headlong into black and invigorating fantasies, imagining that Mother had stayed up the entire night developing an itinerary that included shipping me off to some loathsome boarding school in Washington or Virginia. There had always been talk, between her and Henderson, that is, about sending me to St. Albans, which I took to calling St. Albatross, talk that I had never taken seriously. Now it seemed a distinct possibility, and I tossed and turned and beat my pillow as if to make it confess some secret about Mother's doings down the hall.

In no time I was picturing with great clarity my principled refusal to leave Citrus, and even an improbable but highly detailed chase scene in which I was beset by slaverous bloodhounds and snide officers of the law all across the panhandle. After days of effort, Sheriff Porter had to break the news to Mother: "Your son's just too quick, Mrs. Collier. We can't catch him." All of which I heard from a perch in a nearby chinaberry tree, having doubled back to Citrus to enjoy my triumph.

But the next morning there was no talk of St. Albatross or April. And instead of having to escape through the hills of Citrus I merely had to sit down to a breakfast of eggs sunny-side up, bacon, grits, biscuits and honey and fresh orange juice.

"I talked to James early this morning," Mother said. "I'm afraid I have some bad news. Things aren't going well for him and I'm going to have to go back to Washington sooner than I expected. I may have to stay longer, too. I'll probably miss your last game. I'm sorry, Roy, but I promise to be back for the playoffs."

Though her face was expressionless, her eyes remained nervous and wanting, and it was something of a shock to come down from the crazed heights of my volatile night to witness such genuine pain. I was instantly ashamed and could not stop staring at Mother. It looked almost as if she'd placed a mask over her real face, which I imagined to be sacked with panic, and that her eyes, peering through the eye holes of that mask, were giving away her true condition—a state of crippling anxiety. When she took a sip of coffee the cup actually shook in her hand. I wanted to go to her and tell her how much I loved her. It was what she needed most in the world, and I knew it.

"Are you all right?" I asked.

"Oh, I'll make it. I'm just tired. I wish I didn't have to go to Washington. The timing couldn't have been worse."

She began sopping her eggs with a pinch of biscuit. She worked intently, as if trying to scrub the plate clean, and when the biscuit had crumbled she dabbed at the yolk with her fingers, slowly dotting *I*s and crossing *T*s.

"I'm really sorry about last night," she said softly. "I was upset. But I shouldn't have taken it out on you. I don't want you to worry. We're going to be fine."

A few days later I drove her to the airport in Pensacola. I stood and watched the little twin-engine airplane as it taxied down the runway, bound for Atlanta, where Mother would switch to a proper jet for the rest of the trip to Washington, and cried without restraint with my forehead pressed against the pane of the window. I cried all the way home and went into my room, and still I couldn't stop crying. I felt that an unbearable fissure had opened between us. I felt that I had failed Mother. And I felt that, just like my father, I'd left her stranded and alone.

To MY SURPRISE, when she returned in a few weeks she was refreshed and poised. Though I didn't make the connection at the time, this was just how she'd returned from vacationing with Henderson after my father's death. She was so cheerful, in fact, that she steered us through the holidays without incident, no mean feat, considering. She cooked Christmas dinner for us and even got along nicely with Leonard. It didn't seem she was going to do anything about me and April. It didn't seem that she and I were across a divide anymore, either. What seemed quite obvious was that I had overreacted due to the common throes of teen angst.

I began to feel silly about that night, that "exaggerated night," as I came to think of it thereafter. I also felt silly about my day of crying. By way of proving that I'd created the entire affair in my head, I began hugging Mother all the time. And she hugged right back! It was as easy as that.

It was far from as easy as that for James Henderson, however, and early in the new year, Mother was back in Washington once again. "Poor James," she kept saying as she packed. "He's too good for them. *All* of them."

Though a yellow-dog Democrat, Henderson saw that his party was heading in a direction he found more and more difficult to follow. Some of his closest allies were thinking of switching to the other side, which, as I stated earlier, was exactly what Mother strongly urged him to do. Still others were forming a coalition that would one day be called the blue-dog Democrats. James wasn't particular about the color of dog, really; it was the Democratic party in general that was troubling him, and the fact that it was moving far away from his north Florida constituency at the very time he was contemplating a run for the Senate.

Henderson was in a jam. He believed it would be ignoble for a man of his age and standing to suddenly switch parties and, furthermore, that it would be feckless to surrender his own party without a fight. He agonized about his situation, and his agony began to require Mother's constant attention.

"Obviously somebody's got to set those people straight," Mother told me as she prepared for another stay in Washington.

"Give 'em hell," I said.

"Oh, don't you worry. I'll give them worse than that."

I did not think the Democrats and Republicans had a chance in the world against Mother, as a matter of fact, and they were very fortunate that her true intentions were for the most part apolitical. She merely wanted to fortify Henderson, something she was very capable of doing, for Mother was the kind of determined person who lived for the opportunity to exhibit loyalty in the teeth of difficult circumstances. She also enjoyed a good fight, and I can well imagine those two occupying a corner table at one of Washington's elite dives (there are such places, of course), knocking back cocktails and damning the barbarians to oblivion.

At any rate, the impact of Henderson's political troubles were for me beneficial, because Mother's energy had found a fitting outlet, or so I supposed. We never mentioned our fight again, and as time passed it began to seem as if it had never happened. Our relationship actually improved. I'd ferry Mother to the airport, where she'd hug and kiss me and tell me she wouldn't leave if it weren't absolutely necessary, and when she'd return we'd stay up half the night talking about her activities and gossiping about various politicians. Having recently taken up smoking, she'd fret with her cigarette, rolling it between her fingers nervously before lighting it, as if the future of the republic were resting on her shoulders.

"There's no honor anymore, Roy. That's the problem. It's win at all costs. When politics becomes that important to people, the country suffers, believe me. I'll tell you what would help dramatically," she'd say, pointing the cigarette at me. "If we brought back dueling. I'm serious. Make people pay for their remarks. Oh, boy, would I get some satisfaction out of some of those people. *Satisfaction!* That's what they called it when they fought a duel. They were demanding *satisfaction.* By the way, do you know why we quit dueling? It certainly wasn't because we became more sophisticated or humane. We gave it up because we became cowards. Plain and simple. People lost the nerve to defend their honor, and then they lost their honor. That's how it happens. Don't ever let me catch you being a coward, Roy."

"I'd be afraid to be a coward around you, Mother."

"Very funny. But you know what I mean. Sit up straight."

She'd look me over with mock severity, and then we'd break into a fit of laughter over her tough talk.

Given the circumstances in Washington, bedeviled and bedraggled Henderson began coming into town more often than usual to nurse his supporters and no doubt himself. I'd never felt comfortable around him, but it was at this point that we began to truly annoy each other.

"You got a girlfriend, a steady?" he asked me once.

We were standing out by the barn, tapping our toes against the wooden rails of my grandfather's hog pen.

"No, sir."

"Oh? Why not?"

"I'm too busy."

"Too busy doing what?"

"Playing football, studying, hunting, fishing, whatever," I said.

"I see."

A gust of wind whipped his thin white hair out of shape. Henderson patted it down and removed a cigar form his coat pocket and smiled without pleasure. All his life he'd had to endure a mediocre physique—"medium build, medium height" is how he would be described to a stranger—but in his later years he'd somehow thinned out, making him seem taller and more supple. He was the kind of man who had become more handsome as he'd grown older but felt that all the prizes had been lost in his youth. Now that he possessed the wisdom and looks and money and fearlessness to win them, it was too late.

The press fondly referred to him as a gallant and eloquent Southerner, but he would be the first to point out that these compliments issued from the mouths of those conditioned by an age noteworthy for its lack of eloquence and gallantry, that indeed had come to view such attributes as undemocratic. In fact, to put it that way, to engage in a kind of humility that at the same time raked various cultural blights over the coals, would be a decidedly Hendersonesque trick. In truth, he was simply a polite person, blessed with enough charm and dignity and eccentricity to seem courtly, a man of some education—again, by the going rate it would seem he was highly educated—and some means, but such was apparently enough to distinguish him. That and the fact that he was a Democrat who considered the Republican party to be the last bastion of classical liberalism—"that arrogant spawn of a godless enlightenment," as he put it—and his own party to be, well, a spectacular, whining, pandering disgrace.

He was further cursed with the ability to appear cheerful no matter how he actually felt. His blue eyes twinkled even when he meant to cry, and he stood with congenial rectitude even as his heart sank.

"Too busy for a girlfriend, though," he remarked. "At your age. My. That's pretty busy." He lit his cigar and drew on it until he'd shrouded himself in smoke. "But you like girls, don't you?"

"Mostly I like older women," I said.

His eyes flashed before he could compose a look of disapproval. The one thing I liked about Henderson, even in those days, was that he was always a bit devious.

"Really? That's interesting. I go in for younger women myself. But then, I'm older than you." He smiled at me. "Do you know what you say to that, Roy?"

"What?"

"If you want to be a gentleman," he continued.

"Tell me."

"Touché," he said. "You say touché. You're going to have to learn these kinds of things now that you're getting older."

HENDERSON WAS RIGHT, of course. I was getting older. But more importantly, I was getting *taller.* That year I at last surpassed the longed-for six-foot mark. By summer, I'd surpassed it by better than two inches, in fact, and well remember measuring myself over and over again in Mother's and April's kitchens to be certain. It was deeply pleasurable to realize that if my father were by some monstrous trick to return from the grave, he would have to look up if he wished to meet me eye to eye, and that in turn, if I were to seek out his deadly gaze, I would have to look down on him.

Not only that, I weighed well over two hundred pounds—twenty-five pounds over, to be exact, a good forty pounds heavier than my father had ever been. When Leonard and I were in the trailer together if often seemed too small to hold us, and we were forced to shuffle around each other gracelessly, like two caged bears. It was also about this time that Leonard began to drink heavily. I'd supposed he was already drinking heavily, just as Mother had been continually pointing out, but now he started to drink an amount that made me realize he hadn't been drinking heavily at all. "You're growing like a damned weed," he'd say, spitting out "weed" belligerently, as if to suggest it might not be a bad idea to uproot me from his garden.

Everything depended on how much he'd had to drink. With a moderate amount of whisky in him his moods could be expansive, but when he'd had too much he became judgmental. That was nothing new, of course. What *was* new was that his level of intensity had become frightening. Our earlier training sessions, I was beginning to see, had been mild affairs in comparison. Even at their worst I cannot say I ever believed I was in danger. But as my junior year drew nearer, that began to change.

Leonard was careful to never show his dark tendencies around April, however, and for my part I never mentioned Leonard's behavior to her because I didn't want her to worry or to become angry with him. Strange to say, I believed I had to protect him. Of course, my greatest fear was that *Mother* would somehow find out about our encounters.

The one thing I might have been expected to worry about was my own safety, but I was sure I could handle any ordeal with Leonard. What's more, I quickly came to believe it was my *duty* to allow him to voice his hostility. Because of his tirades I was learning things about my father that made me feel sorry for Leonard and made me believe I owed him. His life had been one of frustrated ambitions, after all, and it seemed to me that my father had been responsible for much of his unhappiness. I'd learned, for instance, that my father had been the reason Leonard hadn't gone to seminary and become a preacher. Leonard didn't tell me *how* my father was responsible—it would be Mother who would tell me that story—but he was adamant that it had been my father's doing.

When he was sloppy from alcohol and unsettled in his heart, he'd frequently demand that I go with him to train. If I tried to refuse he'd become indignant. "What? You're too good for me now? Now that I've made you a big star?"

I couldn't endure such questions, and so I ended up doing pretty much what he asked of me, running countless sprints and drills and going out for passes when he was so drunk he could hardly hold the football in his hand in order to throw it. When it sailed away wildly and I didn't catch it, he'd accuse me of trying to make him look bad or of being a second-rate receiver. We didn't practice in front of the trailer anymore, largely because he didn't want April to hear him cursing and because he knew that if she saw him acting that way she'd stop him. Our new field of play sat directly behind his boyhood home, where I'd carry out his commands until he ran out of whisky, as was our custom.

WHEN TWO-A-DAYS started that summer, my workouts with Leonard necessarily came to an end, but not our trips out to the old house. He'd drop by to watch the end of the second session every afternoon, walking onto the field and keeping a sharp eye on me. Even though it was clear that he'd been drinking, the coaches were proud to have him around, and so was I. There was always talk about whether or not I was going to break his rushing records, talk the coaches promoted. If I insisted I couldn't, Leonard would insist that I could and that I'd better. The one time I teased him and said I *knew* I'd break his records, he smiled and announced: "Tell you what. If you do, I'll give you an hour to draw a crowd and kiss your ass."

After practice I'd get in his pickup and we'd go out to the old house to "work on a few things," as he put it. We'd arrive after dark, and he'd show me this or that, usually with impatience. Eventually he'd tire out and I'd have to listen to stories about his and April's life that were intended to intimidate me and make me uncomfortable.

Not all of his stories were antagonistic, though. As I've explained, very often his drinking would make him melancholy and gentle. He'd grab my neck affectionately as we sat on the rotting planks of wood and tell me I was going to be famous and that this would be my breakout year.

Even after school started he continued to show up at practice a couple of times a week to carry me out to the old house to talk. Things were going better for me than any of us expected, and he seemed driven to be as near my football playing as possible. Just as he foresaw, I'd grown enough and matured enough to become a formidable running back, though he thought I could be even better. He believed something was lacking, and I thought he was right, but I didn't know what.

We'd sit on the porch and he'd point into the thick woods and say: "Right out there is where I got *my* start." He'd say it as if it were a key that I needed in order to unlock my potential.

"Tell me again."

"You don't want to hear that old story."

"I'm never tired of that story," I'd tell him truthfully. I wanted so badly to please him, to be taken into his trust and to win his approval.

"A damned secondhand football. That's how hard up we were. Aw, shit, Roy, you already know all this. . . ."

But then, before I had the chance to plead for him to continue, he'd begin to tell me about how his father, Gaither Collins, had made him a present of a secondhand football for his twelfth birthday.

"Never drop the ball, is what he told me. Never drop the ball as if your life depended on it. Sleep with it to get good and used to it."

None of which pleased Leonard's mother. She didn't want Leonard to learn football or any other rough sport. Having fastened to his inclination toward tenderness, she longed for him to become a preacher. Leonard himself had only one dream: to grow up and marry April Lanier. But he worried that he stood in a long line that grew longer each time April met someone new, a line that included adults and perhaps even supernatural beings.

Part of the preparation his mother had devised for his future as a minister included a fairly advanced study of the Bible. Flipping through Genesis one evening, Leonard buckled with fear when he learned that after Adam and Eve had sinned, the Sons of God traversed the earth taking the daughters of Eve for sexual pleasure. No one, not his mother or father nor even his pastor, seemed sure exactly who the Sons of God were, but this much was certain: They were evil and much stronger than ordinary men. It was after this discovery that Leonard began to run through the woods and fields, throwing the ball high and a little ahead of himself, racing to get under it and to catch it, believing—just as I would soon come to believe—that if he were strong and fast enough he could prevent something wicked from happening.

"Think about that for a minute and you'll know how come I ended up running as good as I did," he would tell me.

"You ran against demons."

"You got that shit right. Twelve-year-old boy running up against demons."

• • •

Toward the end of the season we were sitting on the porch one night when I noticed he seemed more restless than usual.

"Y'all are gonna win the championship," he said. "I guarantee it."

"I hope so."

"You got to run harder, though. You're a top ten back this year, that's pretty damned good for a junior, but . . ."

"I'll run harder."

"You got to run with . . ." He looked at me and paused. "Fear," he finally said. "The kind of fear that makes you think them other players ain't shit. There's a kind of fear that pisses you off. Maybe it ain't fear. Maybe there ain't a word for it. I don't know. But I've felt it. That's what you gotta feel."

He'd become frustrated. I was nodding, but I knew it wasn't enough. He pushed me suddenly. "Look out at them trees." He motioned. He wanted me to really look. "Hell, go out there and see how long you last."

I did not want to go out there and suddenly felt he might make me. I searched for some question to occupy him. "Why is Sterns afraid of those woods?" I asked.

He turned his head to me. "What do you mean?"

"Sterns said he was afraid to go out there."

"Sterns is just feeding you shit. He's just lazy." Leonard took a long pull and nodded. "You want to know the truth about them woods?"

"Yes, sir."

He stared at me bluntly. "Fuck," he said. "Fuck, I'll tell you." But he seemed confused. He pointed again. "It's different out there. You think about a little boy being out there. Think about *anybody* being out there. You wouldn't want to be out there, especially at night."

"I can see why Sterns is scared."

This made him even angrier, for some reason. "I'll go out there right now." He started to get up but didn't. He grabbed my arm to get my attention. "Fuck, I'll go out there right now and beat the fuck out of anything that gets in my way. You better learn to do that, too, if you want to amount to anything. You hearing me? Just go the fuck out there. That's what I did. That's what made the difference."

I pulled my arm away. "I don't want to go out there."

"You're gonna have to."

"No, I'm not."

"At some point," he said softly. He took a sip of bourbon. "I'm just messing with you. I'll tell you."

He began to tell the story of how he had developed so odd a habit as running into trees. Previously he'd offered only sketches, but now he went into great detail; and where before he'd described his peculiar training methods with touches of humor, it was suddenly clear that Leonard's solitary practices were nothing at all to laugh about. As I was about to realize, the way Leonard learned football was nothing short of terrifying, and as he talked and the night thickened we saw that there was no way to hold that terror at bay or to coat it with chuckles or even to consign it to the past. We both knew very well that there was something about his old story that was, so to speak, still in play.

"Right out there," he kept saying, growing more frustrated, pointing into the darkness, trying to make me see.

Right out there was where he'd faced whole teams of horned spirits, ripping the ball from the sky and breaking past them and on toward April and Mother's house. Right out there was where he beat the demons mercilessly for April, beat them for hours and hours at a time, his lowered shoulders shattering demon bones, his legs striking like pistons and tearing demon cartilage. Alone, under the glare of a merciless summer sun, his neck and flanks glistening, his face agonized as tears of sweat streaked his cheeks and forehead; alone, threshing winds of winter in a tattered coat, his ears stiff and bright red and stinging, his hands numb but still worthy and still capable as he rushed through the chilled woods where he learned to confront the pain and to enjoy denying it. Leonard Collins became fierce in his understanding of the game.

At some point, he said, he began to believe the old live oaks themselves had been transformed into derisive spirits. It was not hard to understand how he could have come to such a conclusion, for there was indeed something rueful about those woods. Sterns wasn't the only one who thought so. Though I'd never admitted it, even I thought so, and I was the sort of young man who always longed to be out of doors. Whenever I had a bad dream, the badness resided *inside* a house or building, while my refuge lay just beyond the creepy, confining walls. The woods were a sanctuary for me.

But those particular woods were different. Whenever I walked through them I sensed that something was watching me or that I would presently stumble upon something better left alone, some horrible scene that would destroy me. All of the countryside was full of birdsong, but in those woods, I noticed, a deathly silence prevailed. And interestingly, of all the places that April and I wandered, we never once wandered there. We had often gone to some trouble to avoid that particular place, in fact, though I'd never asked why. I suppose I sensed the danger of the place instinctively. I furthermore sensed that not only were those woods to be left alone, they were not ever to be talked about, either.

Leonard's story confirmed my suspicion. I even began to wonder if he was hiding something from me and that for all his talk about what had happened in those woods, he in fact wanted to tell me something *else,* another story altogether. Because it seemed he was talking around and around and getting anxious and always just barely holding his tongue. This was rank speculation on my part, but I was coming to believe those horrible woods were deep and dark enough for *many* terrible stories.

"So you just started running into the trees?"

"What? Shit, no. Do I look crazy? First time it happened accidentally. I was just dodging those bastards and I tripped on a root and fell head first into one of 'em. The biggest goddamned tree out there. It's one of them great big old live oaks, but not the pretty kind. This fucker's evil."

I was more than prepared to believe this, though I didn't like to think of a live oak as being sinister. Live oaks were my favorite trees. I am well aware that there have been more than enough descriptions of them in literature already, not to mention the fact that they have appeared in countless coffee table books of photography, but in passing I might simply point out that I have always found these venerable giants to be by far the most beautiful—and, more important, the most *evocative*—trees on earth, compared to which the redwoods of northern California seem merely tall. To the ardent tree climber such as I was, live oaks were whole worlds of wonder. In the part of the country where I was from they were plentiful and grew to outrageous sizes. Their branches, which dipped and twisted and soared so energetically, were to me wonderful floating boulevards and side streets, each one with its own particular resting places and vantages. These live oaks were entire airborne kingdoms. And while they were magnificently stalwart, I could not help believing they were at the same time on the move, whole groves of them steadily advancing in some campaign with their dangling pinions of moss and their branches twisting in all directions, as if frantic to seize everything around them. Looking down from the top of one of those old live oaks, the earth seemed tremulous, and when I peered across the countryside I felt a little dizzy but also a little indomitable. For when the wind blew, and I bobbed and seesawed astride a high branch while Howl sniffed out trails far below, it seemed I was part of a vast army marching toward some momentous conflict. My heart beat for war and flight; the earth groaned; time was driven back and halted and the sun and moon stood still.

For such reasons I developed a lasting affection for the live oaks of Citrus. One could almost say that I came to know certain of them personally. I considered them to be my friends. Many of them had been friends of April's, too, and she had passed these friendships along to me, but I had made many new friendships myself. Right through high school I continued to climb them, and when I passed one of the trees that I knew, I would sometimes give it a kindly pat. And why not? These trees had often hidden me away from trouble and put me closer to God. They'd shielded me from rain. Whenever I was feeling sad they would become a little unhappy themselves and take me up from the ground into their sturdy arms. Only the cypresses out by Lake Julep ever meant as much to me.

Still, I knew Leonard was right—while certain live oaks were dependable and friendly and guardians of children, there were certain outlaw cousins that looked quite dangerous, certain *renegade* live oaks that seemed as if they would do terrible things to a boy if he wandered out and became lost. The old woods behind Leonard's house were full of such renegade live oaks. And that is why it was no wonder that Leonard believed one of them was after him, especially after it swatted him to the ground and knocked him nearly unconscious.

There Leonard lay, flat on his back, blood dripping from his forehead, completely disoriented. That was bad enough, but what was worse, he'd dropped the ball, the very thing his father had told him to never do. To make matters worse, he realized it rested before the live oak, clutched between two grasping roots.

Leonard was convinced that the live oak was watching him, waiting to see what he might do. There was no question in his mind that if he left the football and came back for it the next day, the oak would have devoured it. He was also fairly certain that if he ventured nearer to retrieve the football, the oak would *seize him and tear him*—here he tried to laugh—*limb from limb*. Still, as far as Leonard was concerned, leaving that football beneath that old oak was as good as leaving his soul there. He simply wouldn't do it. So he knelt and prayed and then stood and rushed to get the ball.

That is when something of consequence happened: After fetching up the football, instead of running away, he stared straight at the tree as the terror inside him revolted into anger. He yelled out, furious. He kicked the tree's trunk. He spit at one of its branches. It wasn't enough. So he backed away, tucked the ball tightly under his arm and charged into the old tree. It knocked him back but not down. "Nobody, nothing, brings *me* down!" he cried.

From then on he ran against the trees, becoming surefooted and fearless and powerful.

And when several years later he first stepped onto an actual football field and the crusty coach of Citrus County Junior High ordered him into uniform to see if he could hit and Leonard told him he wanted to play quarterback and throw himself the ball and Coach Crawford (who was still alive and coaching when I played) grinned and said, "You intend on being a one-man team, son?" and Leonard said he'd prefer it that way and Coach Crawford cursed under his breath and shook his head and tugged his cap and ordered Leonard to play halfback, it happened at last: At last the demons were not invisible and a million strong in an open field, or disguised and sheltered in a sepulcher of live oaks with tendrils of black and gray moss swathing the branches like unholy incense. No, at last they had taken human form and would know how serious he'd been those years in the fields and woods when he twisted and spun like a hulking lunatic rushing headlong across a vacant horizon.

The first boy he met he knocked out cold. The second had his shoulder dislocated. Then Leonard was past them.

He ran savagely, in a state of vicious panic, hurling his body forward, heedless of potential injury or of his own physical limitations, which were few. The fact of the matter was that football was never very much fun for Leonard. It was, he confessed to me that night, somewhat horrifying.

Yet it was not the trees alone that made football seem this way to Leonard. After all, he'd learned to best them. It turns out something else happened. That something else, not surprisingly, involved April and Mother. And it was galvanizing enough to cause Leonard to play with unmatched ferocity as a young man, which caused Citrus County Junior High to win the state championship twice and Citrus High to win it three years straight, which in turn led college coaches to actually send scouts to sit in junior high bleachers to observe junior high games and later to wait after high school games to pump Leonard's hand as if he were the president. What's more, it proved to be very much a part of how I came to play football so well. To its account one more junior high and two more high school championships may be added.

"You have to understand one thing," Leonard warned me before telling me of that fateful event. He took a long pull and wiped his mouth on his sleeve. "Your Mother was smart." He tapped the side of his head. "And *mean.* She teased me all the time back then. Teased me about April. From the time we were just little children on up through our marriage. I don't reckon she's never stopped."

I was always a little surprised to see that Mother's ridicule still wounded Leonard. I was also surprised to learn how thoroughly she dominated him and almost everyone else that came into her orbit. Not that such information clashed with what I knew about Mother; but it was hard to imagine Leonard allowing himself to be toyed with like that. It was also hard to imagine April, who was four years younger than either of them, as the one who protected Leonard from Mother, though that is often exactly what happened when they were growing up and Mother hatched a scheme against Leonard.

April and Mother were both, Leonard often explained to me, extremely dramatic little girls, full of mischief, free-spirited and almost without fear—country girls, in other words—and a favorite game of theirs was to stage weddings and funerals and coronations and to carry these productions as far as they could. Leonard enjoyed the weddings, since they involved him and April pairing up, though Mother usually insisted they divorce within a few hours. She would make them go into the barn, where she'd made a desk out of a bale of hay, and there she would present them with the divorce papers she'd drawn up and actually force Leonard to pay for them. Since he did not have his own money to pay for these unwanted divorces, he'd have to borrow from April herself.

The funerals, on the other hand, were not as much fun. Leonard was made to lie down while April and Mother tossed dirt over him, after which he had to remain completely still while they made long speeches in his honor. If Mother caught him moving or trying to wipe dirt from his face, she insisted they start over from the beginning.

I suppose coronations were the easiest. Mother would walk around wearing a blanket as a robe while Leonard and April were expected to genuflect before her and kiss her hands. Degrading, no doubt, but a small price to pay compared to the other games.

"Then one day she comes up with the bright idea to hold an execution." Leonard finished his pint and quietly set it between us. He sighed. "I shit you not. That's June, all right. Tried to execute April behind my back. And she damn near did it, too."

The original plan was for Leonard to be executed, but when he refused, Mother demanded that he go home. As soon as he left, Mother took the laundry cord, swung it over the branch of an oak tree—a friendly one, but what could it do?—near the canning shed, tied a slip knot and fashioned a noose.

"Are you willing to die in Leonard's place?" she asked April.

"I guess," April said.

"Do you love him or not?"

"I guess," she repeated.

"Then you must pay the price," Mother told her.

She prepared a written confession explaining that Leonard had committed treason against the state, the state being Mother. The Sun King had nothing on Mother. "Moreover" and "subsequently," she declared, "the named and guilty party" had foolishly attempted "with forethought and malice" to escape justice.

Leonard breathed heavily. "Shit, it's embarrassing. We was around thirteen, your mama and me, anyhow. But boy your mama liked them games. Never quit liking them."

April dutifully climbed onto the chair, stripped out of her dress—Mother convinced her that this was standard execution protocol—and allowed the noose to be slipped around her slender neck.

"Do you want to hang for a little while just to feel it?" Mother asked. "You can put your hands under your chin. It'll be just like swinging on a rope and we can pretend. I'll do it if you do it. You can execute me next."

As soon as April grabbed the noose and nudged her chin into it, Mother kicked the chair away. "Off with her head," she screamed, imagining the guillotine, I suppose. April began to cry instantly, holding to the rope for her life, while Mother danced around denouncing her crimes.

"It was a damned mess," Leonard explained. The whisky in him had begun a second fermentation, and he was speaking with great seriousness. "I'd gotten about halfway home when a bad feeling came over me. After the whole thing was all over with, April told me she'd just been hanging there praying I'd come back. I reckon her prayers were answered, 'cause I started thinking how June probably wasn't going to give up on the idea of executing somebody. With me out of the way, that left April. So I turned around and cut back through them woods there, throwing the football to myself as usual. I was pretending to just be playing along, but I was really throwing the ball and heading back toward y'all's house quick as I could. That terrible feeling that something had gone wrong just got worse and worse. Them old woods had never seemed so dark to me. It wasn't too long before I believed they were trying to hold me back and to keep me from getting to y'all's house. I ran like I'd never run before. But then it seemed like I was running up to trees I'd never seen in my life. I knew them woods like the back of my hand, but I'll be damned if I didn't get plumb lost. I ran one way and then another. Everything looked different. I was scared and worried to death about April. I kept asking God for help, but I got to where I believed them trees were swallowing my words up, and even though I knew better I got to thinking God couldn't hear me. Pretty soon I was crying. But I was still running. Running in a way that made all the running I ever did when I started playing football seem like a joke. The truth was, I was running for April's life. And I guess that meant I was running for my life, too."

He grunted then and looked away. "Anyhow, I reckon I wasn't lost, 'cause after a while I saw the barn. I come up behind it and looked into y'all's yard and shit." He tipped his cap back. "I damn near had heart failure right on the spot, I'll tell you that," he said.

"First off, April was naked except for her panties and socks. And I was at that age where it mattered. Mattered big time. All I ever cared about was playing football and being a preacher and April being my wife. I know I was young, but you know what they say about puppy love—it's damn sure real to the puppy. And there she was, kicking her legs up and screaming. I couldn't believe that shit."

I never learned exactly how long he waited there, crouched near the barn with his football. Given the circumstances, I am sure it must have seemed like a long time. However long it was, he told me he suddenly thought about the Sons of God and the fallen angels. April was literally hanging there, exposed, offered up like a sacrifice, and Leonard believed he was about to see something vile descend at any moment, something cloven-hooved and sharp-eared that would alight on goat's legs and move toward her with a bowlegged, beastly swagger. He'd never contemplated the sexual act in any detailed way before, but now it came to him grimly and at once.

When he finally broke from his hiding place and ran to April, Mother was outraged. "It's just a game," she said. "It's not real, you idiot. You jackass. Get away. Get away or you're dead. She's being executed because of you anyway."

Leonard paused for a moment in front of the naked flesh of his preacher-boy dreams. He had no choice but to wrap his arms around April if he was to save her. So his face pressed into her belly as his arms tangled around her legs. He twisted and staggered for a few cruel seconds until April finally got free of the noose.

After Leonard put April down she continued to cling to him. "Don't cry, Leonard. Please don't cry. You saved me," she said.

"I saw you," he wailed. "I saw you naked."

"Oh, that doesn't matter," April insisted.

She let him go and stooped to pick up her dress. After she put it on she turned to Mother and stomped her foot.

"You're next June. You kicked the chair away. You cheated. You're going to get executed for it."

"Get dressed, you pervert," Mother told her. "Sick. You're *both* perverts."

Leonard looked at me. "Everybody was always a pervert according to June. You'd do well to always keep that shit in mind."

THE FOLLOWING SPRING Clancy and I were the subject of a short write-up in a national sports magazine. DIXIE'S DYNAMIC DUO made much of the fact that Clancy was a black quarterback, while I was a white halfback, and I suspected even at the time that *that*, more than our achievements, was the reason for the article.

"It says you're white," Clancy remarked as we sat reading the article together.

"Well, I'll be damned." I looked where Clancy was pointing. "Guess you never know who you're dealing with."

Mother was out of town when the copies first arrived in Citrus, but April baked a red velvet cake with cream cheese icing to celebrate. Sterns came over, and we sat on the back deck while Leonard cooked steaks with Howl sitting reverently beside the grill, waiting for fallout. The sky was so clear, we could see the lunar lakes on the moon's surface.

When I cut the cake the knife struck something hard in the center of it.

"There's something in here," I said.

"In the damned cake? Are you sure?" Leonard asked.

"Maybe it's a skull," Sterns remarked.

"Please, Sterns," April said.

"It's a box or something," I said.

April clapped and pointed. "You better get it out of my cake right now."

Inside the moist red heart of that velvety cake was a cardboard box. And in that cardboard box was a new top-of-the-line Shakespeare bait casting reel. It was silver and shiny, with that most famous of fishing names engraved on its side in an eloquent cursive script. *Shakespeare.* It purred like a strummed kitten when I spun its arm.

"That takes the cake, don't it," Leonard said.

"I knew somebody was gonna have to say that." Sterns was genuinely tickled. "Better you than me."

Later that night Leonard made a sloppy but delicious batch of piña coladas. Sterns raised his glass for a toast. All he said was: "To Roy. To Leonard. And to April," but something made him break down. April went to him, and after he cried a little more he started laughing. "Why do I do that?" he asked.

"I wish you wouldn't," Leonard told him.

"You're looking at two people that've stood up for me more than you could ever know," Sterns said, drying his eyes. "I mean through some real bad times."

April hugged Sterns. "And vice versa," she said.

"I'd say we're pretty even," Leonard concluded. "'Cept you keep filling our trailer up with shit."

Sterns kissed the top of April's head. "This one here's nothing but guts and beauty," he said. "You know she came and got me out in California?"

"It was a vacation, Sterns."

"Bullshit. You weren't there but a couple of days."

"When?" I asked.

"You didn't even hardly count yet," Sterns said. "I guess my letters home were overly depressing and these two got worried. So April flew out and brought me back. I was ready to get the hell out of there but I'd sorta gotten stuck. It was a good feeling walking through that airport with her, I'll tell you that. She was the best-looking woman out there—*and leaving*."

April punched my shoulder. "Don't act so shocked, Roy."

"I'd just never heard that before."

"Maybe there's a lot you don't know about me," she teased.

Leonard chuckled. "Yeah. Anybody ever tell you she worked for the CIA?"

"You blew my cover, Leonard."

"I better run along before I hear something that'll get me killed off," Sterns said. He looked up at me then.

Talk of killing and murder never bothered me, but whenever anyone said something like that a nervous glance always followed, and I'd try to make a face or a comment to show I took no offense. Lorri-Anne once licked the problem solidly. A friend had brought up something about someone being shot and without missing a beat Miss Harris stated: "What a coincidence. Roy's daddy was shot, too!" She received a special treat for that one.

"Go get your forty-five," I said to April that night. "Sterns knows."

"Well, hold him down," she said. "He might try to make a run for it."

"Take your time. He ain't gonna get far," Leonard roared.

"Oh, fuck y'all." Sterns put his drink down and grumbled out of his chair. "Congratulations, Roy. You've turned into a fine young man. What a pleasant surprise." He walked over and put his arms around me. "You're a big son-of-a-bitch, I'll give you that."

After Sterns left Leonard blended one more round. It wasn't long before he'd fallen asleep in his chair with his drink resting comfortably on his belly. Suddenly I caught April staring at me.

"I wonder how tall you'll end up being," she said.

"I'm through."

"You're awfully tall," she said. Her voice had become a whisper. "What are you?"

"Six two and a half. How tall was my father?" I could not help asking this question, such was my satisfaction in having bettered him by two and a half inches. "As tall as me?"

"Oh, no. Six feet maybe. *Maybe.* I don't remember."

"Who was better-looking?"

She brought her silver cross necklace to her mouth and began to run it over her lips. She was wearing a cotton dress and a leather jacket. All night I'd watched her maneuvering to keep that dress down, but now she'd given up trying.

"Who was what?" she asked absently. She looked me over, then looked away. "I've already told you."

Leonard jerked in his sleep and dropped his piña colada, though it didn't wake him. April walked over and shook him and helped him up and guided him to bed. After a few minutes she returned and pulled her chair close to mine.

"Do you remember that time when I was little and I said I wanted to grow up and marry you?" I asked.

She laughed and touched my arm. "Of course. But it wasn't just one time."

"Do you remember what you told me? You said that by the time I grew up, you'd be an old lady and that I wouldn't want to marry you. Do you remember?"

"I said that?" She tilted her head back to check an unexpected tear, but it got past her and caught at her lips. "Oops. I guess I was wrong. I'm not an old lady yet, am I?"

PART TWO

SEVEN

April had taught me to observe intensely, to feel intensely, in short, to *live* intensely. She had fine-tuned my mind and my heart to pick up the subtlest of signals and had cultivated an ardent sensitivity in me. These were precious gifts, and I had always been grateful to her for them, but as I grew older I began to understand more clearly something that as a boy I had only been given bruised hints of—if having my senses stripped of all their dull, customary defenses made me more receptive, it also made me more vulnerable.

I have already pointed out the ache and longing she and I sometimes felt after our furious hopkins hunts. I would one day come to believe that such experiences might fairly be described as allergic reactions to life itself. After all, during the spring, when everything is so wonderfully renewed, people succumb to allergies because the world has become too potent for their senses. The very seeds of life, which fly and scatter through the air so heedlessly as the earth restores itself, overwhelm the body. With all of nature charging forth robustly, eyes swell and swelter and water. Ears tic, throats itch, noses run. In much the same way, the kind of feverish awareness April advocated would often lead to an allergic reaction of a spiritual and emotional nature, leaving one's soul reeling and unsteady.

Since most of my awareness was so often trained on April, it is little wonder that I eventually began to feel as if I were becoming allergic to her in the way I've been describing. I had always been delightfully dizzy because of her, and by my early teens I learned that such delight could quickly turn to dismay. Now I was beginning to suffer convulsions that were much more chaotic. For me, every day was April Fool's Day. Sometimes I was merely goofy and adoring and stupefied. Sometimes I was no different from any other nephew in the presence of a shockingly attractive young aunt. But as I approached my final year of high school I found myself in a state of agitation that grew increasingly more bewildering.

To make matters worse, April had started to regard my behavior with suspicion, something that thoroughly shattered what little acceptable comportment I could muster. This transformation occurred not long after I withdrew the shiny silver Shakespeare reel from that red velvet cake. It suddenly seemed as if she were evaluating me, evaluating *us,* to determine if anything was amiss. This naturally put me into a panic and forced me to conduct similar investigations. Not surprisingly, I very quickly had no idea how I ought to behave, for everything seemed tainted on one level or another. All our flirtations—the very wings that carried me merrily through my days—suddenly soured. Short of disappearing, it seemed there was absolutely nothing I could do that was acceptable.

From such a sorry state it was inevitable that I would become acquainted with that storied calculus of denial that dictates that the way to prove that what one has been doing isn't wrong is to do it even more zealously—so zealously it *does* become wrong, which is the point, because *this* wrong is clearly a *mock* wrong, a *pretend* wrong, and how could a person *truly* engaged in a wrong at the same time *feign* to be engaged in *that same wrong?*

I never professed to fully understand these and other similarly convoluted justifications, but that did not stop me from manufacturing them. And while these justifications caused me to behave idiotically, all such idiocy was for the most part harmless, though I admit it is severely embarrassing to recall just how ridiculous I was. I began to pour cold water on April's stomach when she was sunbathing and to make her dance with me whenever a catchy tune came on the radio. At church I would write her notes that asked her to check the yes or no box to determine if I was indeed the handsomest man alive. Or I'd toy with her ponytail until she batted my hand away. The amazing result of all this—aside from having turned myself into an appalling nuisance—was that it actually worked for a time. When I acted like that, it was impossible for April to take me seriously.

But this did not last very long. Because the thing about the diabolical calculus of denial I've been describing is that it is a swirling maw that can only be sated by more and more extreme forms of behavior, especially when some crisis arises that threatens to unhinge its mad logic. And shortly, there arose just such a crisis.

One afternoon just before my senior year I went over to the trailer to find that Leonard had gotten drunk early and broken a piece of china in the microwave, which put April into a comprehensively vicious mood. "Leonard broke one of Mama's dishes," she said. There were rings under her eyes. I could tell she'd been crying. "I've told him a million times not to put Mama's china in the microwave. A million times. But he just won't listen. And his drinking. June knows. She's all upset about it. She's all upset about a lot of things."

"What kind of things?" My voice had hardly risen to the level of a whisper. "What kind of things?" I repeated.

"Things, Roy. Nothing. She's just upset."

"Upset about what?"

"Please, Roy."

"Please, what?"

"She's tired of Leonard's drinking too much. She's been complaining to me about it."

"But that's not your fault."

"I don't know."

"I *said* it's not your fault."

"Well, that settles everything, doesn't it, Roy?" April sounded eerily like Mother. "Just because you say so. Just snap your fingers, right?"

Suddenly, of all things, I snatched the dish rag from April and popped her in the arm with it.

"See? This is what I mean," she said. "Why can't you act right?"

I was furious, and before I knew it I'd popped her again. It must have stung tremendously, because she cried out and struck me in the shoulder.

"I said stop, Roy. This is not the time to be playing around. Can't you understand that?"

I reached out and poked one of her ribs then, and she knocked my hand away.

"This is exactly what I'm talking about," she said. "I want to be alone."

"What do you mean, exactly what you're talking about? Talking about what?"

"Nothing. Just let me alone."

"Talking about what?"

"Nothing. Please go."

"Oh, so I can't tickle you anymore? There's something wrong with *tickling you?*"

That vile calculus demanded that I tickle her right there and then. There were no two ways about it. If I did not, it would mean that Mother was preparing to do something drastic. If I did not, it would mean that April feared our relationship troubled Mother. If I did not, it would mean that there was something wrong with tickling April and, more important, that there was something wrong with *us*.

Since I already had her cornered, I seized both her wrists and quickly transferred them to one hand and started to count her ribs. This was an old game for us. April couldn't bear to be tickled, and in the past her resistance had often become so violent it was comical. On this occasion, however, her struggling struck me as offensive, an outright accusation. It took several seconds to actually get control of her hands to begin with, and then I had to lean into her with all my weight to pin her against the counter. She kept trying to stomp my feet. There was no laughter. "Let go of me! Let go of me now!" Her voice was harsh, and even though I could scarcely credit it, somewhat fearful. "Stop it, Roy! Damn you! Let me go!"

I simply couldn't tolerate such a betrayal and became harsh right back.

"Stop what? Stop this?"

"Damnit, stop!"

"One," I began. She twisted wildly and nearly got away, but I held fast. "See, now we have to start over. One. Two—"

Before I got to three she broke free and slapped me. She slapped me so solidly everything went black for a few seconds. I had to grip the kitchen counter to keep my feet. When the room came back into view it was cluttered with brittle pinpoints of light. My ears rang loudly, and I could feel a fat version of April's palm throbbing on my cheek still.

"Get off me! Get off me!"

I was dizzy and about to cry and couldn't believe what I was hearing. "I'm not on you!" I tried to step toward her to tell her, but she swung at me again. "I'm not on you! April, I'm not on you! It's just a game."

"You bastard!" she cried. "Just a game! I've heard that before! Just get away! Just get away from me! I want you away from me!"

"I'm sorry—"

"Sorry's not good enough! Do you hear? You never listen! Why won't you listen? Sometimes I don't even know who you are anymore! Sometimes . . ."

DURING MELLOW AND nostalgic twilights I'd run into town, circle the square, and then take to the streets that fell away from the courthouse at random. It was always pleasurable to run, but whenever I'd disgraced myself it became necessary, and at such times I ran for miles and miles. The townspeople would wave and offer cheery greetings:

"How many miles today, Roy?" or "Looking good, son! Keep it up!" or "Run one for me, Roy, doctor says I could use the exercise!" At that time of day most of the porches were full of people and activity beneath large paddle fans. Children at play in the yards. The men drinking bourbon or beer; the women, vodka tonics or white wine.

My grandfather's grocery store had been bought out by a large chain when I was a child, but it had not satisfied their profit requirements, and so Mr. Lawrence, Citrus's most civic-minded citizen, bought it back and rechristened it Lanier's Grocery in my grandfather's honor. I always ran past it and past the firehouse and the police station and the jail, where our convicts (so mild a lot of criminals they were sent out to clean the streets of Citrus under very little, if any, supervision) would commend me on my diligence and request cigarettes as if I made a habit of running with a spare pack. I often ran down the winding street where my grandmother had had her fatal accident. When I ran through the quarters, some of the younger boys would stop their endless games of basketball —score 100,002 to 100,004—and watch for a moment: "Look—they go somebody after Roy!" one of them inevitably hollered. For some reason I often fell for it and looked back over my shoulder, which sent them into shivers of laughter.

In the spring there were always patches of sweet scents to run through, invisible swaths of honeysuckle or freshly cut grass or wisteria or the very earth itself. Steaks on a grill. Coming rain. Wet sidewalks. Clay or sand. The air was clean and bracing and easy on the lungs, and it was possible to run at high speeds for great lengths of time. Or to go slowly and feel the strength to run forever.

I usually ran instinctively, sprinting when I felt the call or easing around a corner to find Lorri-Anne face down on a lawn towel, sunning delinquently behind a white picket fence with a diet soda and a glamour magazine, her bikini top unmarshaled in a clump like discarded ribbon. "Haay-Roy. You running or sneaking around?" she'd call, curling a leg.

"Little of both."

"Come over in here."

"I've got to train."

"Train over in here."

Sometimes I would, especially if I'd gotten into trouble with April. None of the little negotiations of loving ever embarrassed Lorri-Anne or made her withdraw from me. I never had to say anything to her about my circumstances, either, and because of this I often told her far more than I would have believed I could share.

I had a favorite hilltop where I always finished my runs. It was in a pasture that belonged to Mr. Haney, stocked with gentle, white-faced Herefords that never minded my intrusions. From there, as evening settled over Citrus, I could see the lights of town and the water tank. I could see Sonic and Beachy Breezes Tanning Salon and Super Star Celebrity Video and the various stately churches and steeples. Farther on was the mall, which boasted a department store and fifteen other outlets that to us seemed quite enough, and a lovely junkyard. And beside it the quarters where some of the dwellings were mere shanties, some quite respectable, and some with homegrown works of art decorating their yards: a pyramid of assembled tires, a standing cross made of painted hubcaps, even a dinosaur fashioned from scrap metal. In the other direction lay the rolling countryside and Lake Julep and an occasional farmhouse. Nothing that I saw was alien to me. I knew the owner of almost every house in Citrus, just as I knew the name of almost every tree I saw and almost every plant and flower. I knew each little creek and sluice and pond and pasture. When it was windy the silvery undersides of bay leaves roared up in rasping waves, and in the late spring and summer lightning bugs sparked and careened in the twilight. The sunsets, especially in the warmer months, were thick as fruitcake, dripping like caramel, a swarming canvas of buzzing colors. An expert would point to the great humidity visited upon that part of the country, how the light refracts again and again through pale planets of water that catch flame and turn into a billion tiny palpable prisms, but I say it is nothing less than the exalted exhalations of angels.

I have read that these intense sunsets and especially the fervent aroma of the land and vegetation are what so stunned the early Portuguese and Spanish explorers. When they came within a few miles of the coastlines of the South they noticed a heavy succulence and marveled at the power of it. After my runs I would smell those same smells and watch those same skies and marvel and fret until weary. Sometimes I'd take a short nap, falling asleep under swirling mauves and peaches and tangerines and violets, and awaken after night had fallen. The ground would have cooled. The moon and stars would be out. I often lay still and whimsically wondered if I'd been asleep for an entire night and all of the next day. What had I missed? What if it had been several nights and days? Or several weeks? What if I'd missed graduation? What if I'd missed my life? What if everyone was dead and gone? What if I'd died long ago, too, and had only just come to notice it? To have let time pass without being able to give an account of it struck me as the worst fate imaginable. To have slept away one's life without knowing it . . .

I would jump up then, a little frightened, and occasionally even take hold of myself and feel my arms and shoulders, looking around to get my bearings. I often wanted to shout. *Here I am! Here I am!*

Because for all my troubles, I was so glad of it.

Before the first game of the season I went out to Sterns's place to invite him to come and watch me play. Mother drove a blue Volvo station wagon in those days, the only Volvo in Citrus at that time, as a matter of fact, and when she was out of town she allowed me to use it. Many of my friends had the much envied pickup trucks with enormous tires, but the Volvo station wagon suited my peculiar needs perfectly. It was stolid and responsible and tame, and each time I raced down the sand road to Reel Bait and Tackle at speeds often approaching seventy miles an hour—Poor Mother! Poor mothers everywhere!—it became possible, in spite of my fast driving, to imagine that my life was boring and suburban, the kind of life depicted in a television commercial, a safe and standard life without trials or adventures. I'd hold the steering wheel with both hands, elbows out, concentrating on the road with nerdish affability. Dusting off the dashboard from time to time, I attempted to make every movement dutiful and earnest. When I'd walk into Sterns's place acting like that, he'd take one look at me and grunt.

"Watch *you*. I *been* watching you for years. I'm tired of it."

"Come on."

"Are the cheerleaders still pretty?"

"Yep."

"Your girl still a cheerleader?"

"Yep."

"She sure cheers me up."

"So you'll come?"

"Maybe. I might be too busy being depressed."

Sterns had always been one for high lonesomes, but lately they'd been getting worse.

"The book?"

"You ask a lot of questions."

"Not about the book I don't. God forbid."

Sterns laughed. "I'll come to your game. Tell Lorri-Anne to do a herky for me. Oh, and one more thing. You need to start being a little more careful."

"What do you mean?"

He began twirling a heavy black curl behind his ear. He stared straight at me. As so often happened, his feet had twisted oddly, and it looked as if he might topple over.

"Your mother's on the warpath is what I mean. April came in here crying about it. I wasn't going to say anything to you, but I think I better. Your mother's worried about Leonard's drinking. And your mother can be a bit of a crusader. I don't mean anything bad in saying that. You know it as well as I do. Anyhow, apparently she went and talked to Leonard and they had an argument. I think it was pretty bad. I'm just saying things are a little tense right now and everybody needs to act right. So behave yourself. You understand me? Be sweet."

I nodded.

"Just play football, Roy. That'll do. Just play football and do whatever it is you do with Lorri-Anne."

THOUGH I HAD BEEN a talented running back all along, it was at this point that I came into my own. Had it not been for all the turmoil, and particularly the fact that there seemed to be nothing I could do about all the turmoil aside from making it worse, I likely would have had a very good final season anyway, but nothing remotely as exceptional as the season I actually had. I was never again to achieve such dominance. Nor would I ever again run as furiously, with such hunger. As good as former seasons had been, and as good as future seasons might be, it was in this season of my last year of high school that I came as close as I ever would to attaining Leonard's ideal.

From the very first game it was noticed that I had a new level of determination. People began to remark that Leonard's influence was clearly in evidence. No one, excepting Leonard himself, could have guessed how desperate and angry I really was, how after every snap I believed it would be better to die than to be brought down.

In our second game we played a team that was reputed to have one of the best linebackers in Florida. This was a big-league city team from Jacksonville, and we heard they had been making a lot of comments about our being rednecks and the like. The linebacker fellow, by way of preparing himself for the upcoming contest, I suppose, began to talk about how he would humiliate Roy Collier. Clancy and I had become accustomed to this sort of banter since that article about us had appeared in the sports magazine, but while Clancy used it as motivation and always fired back with his own caustic remarks, I never paid any attention because my playing had always been a something of a solipsistic affair.

I freely admit how unfortunate that was—football being a solipsistic affair, I mean—because of all sports, football is far and away the most team oriented. To take just the offense, for example, any of the eleven men on a team can ruin a play on *every play*. Any missed block can lead to mayhem. In other sports a botched assignment might lead to a victory for the other team, but a football player must always keep in mind that if he fails at his appointed task, someone could very well get hurt. Properly understood, this alone would be enough to explain why football binds its players together like no other sport. Along those same lines, one cannot underestimate the simple but profound fact that the offense *huddles* together while the defense looks on menacingly. Moreover, it is in these huddles, where one's hands are locked with one's teammates' to form a tight circle of refuge that will not give way to outside interference, that the team leader, the quarterback, crouched on one knee in the center of that circle, rallies everyone and gives him his next mission, after which the eleven players break from the huddle as one entity to make war against the opponents collected on the other side of the line of scrimmage.

Yet sadly all those admirable feelings were to some extent lost on me. I played in dreamy solitude, with private objectives and inducements. That is not to say I did not feel myself to be a member of the team, because even to this day when I think of my football career I am more likely to think of myself as a Citrus Wildcat than as anything else. And it certainly is not to suggest that I wouldn't have made sacrifices for the team. I made them regularly, with real pride and an undeniable sense of belonging. I am simply making it clear that when I was actually running downfield with the ball, the game became something other than a team sport for me, or a sport of any kind, for that matter. When I was running, it seemed I was running alone. In fact, once a play had been called and I had been handed the ball, I could not even be troubled to despise or be challenged by players on the other team, who were to me no more important a part of the game than the chalk marks on the field.

Clancy knew this very well. Because of it he would frequently tug at my face mask when we were huddled up. "Damnit, wake up, Roy," he'd say, which was always followed up by a desultory, "*Shit.*"

But the linebacker attenuated my solipsistic play for at least one game by claiming that Roy Collier was undoubtedly so countrified that he was probably shacking up one of his relatives, if not a farm animal. At least that is what he was reported to have said. It was Clancy who brought me this news. It turned out this linebacker was a cousin of Clancy's—an unliked cousin, at that, who was uppity around Clancy besides.

After learning of this remark I could not get it out of my mind. It was not, obviously, the sort of comment I could take lightly. For an entire week it remained a hectoring presence. I lay in bed every night and saw the linebacker cousin's demise quite clearly and anticipated it with extravagant impatience. So on the first snap of the game, when Clancy handed me the ball and I found that the hole over right guard had been filled by none other than that same uppity linebacker cousin, instead of sidestepping him I ran right at him, striking him as if to send him around the world and back again for a second beating. He gave way instantly.

We were fairly evenly matched physically, to tell the truth, but football is mostly a mental enterprise, no matter the level of competition, and it is especially so when players are young and unseasoned and much more susceptible to intimidation and various other emotional hazards. So what it came down to on that first encounter when the uppity linebacker and I collided was a question first and foremost of motivation. And since, as I have explained, I was playing for my life, while he was only playing for bragging rights, it wasn't very surprising that things didn't work out very well for him on that play or any other play of the night. I can still remember the sound he made when I hit him, the groan of shock as he was straightened up and driven backwards before landing on his back.

When my teammates rushed behind me into the end zone to celebrate that first touchdown, I was already jogging back to the sidelines, anxiously wanting our offense to take the field again. I couldn't hear the savory roar of the crowd, and my vision was strangely impaired. There seemed to be some confusion about something. Coach Taylor was addressing me, but he wasn't smiling or congratulating me as I might have expected. He seemed puzzled, then disturbed. Suddenly he reached toward my waist, and I jerked away from him.

"Give them the damned football, Roy! Damnit, have you gone crazy?"

Jacksonville's secondary turned out to be very, a facile and slightly facetious arrangement of bowling pins to be knocked down. Once Clancy's cousin had been turned into a deflated presence, the field was largely mine, and I ran four touchdowns that night. Clancy caught fire, too, and had one of his best games. We beat Jacksonville by fourteen points.

"You did it tonight," Leonard told me. "They'll be nervous about you from now on. Every defense you play, no matter what their coaches say, no matter what they tell themselves, no matter what, deep in their hearts there's gonna be a little bit of fear and doubt. And it ain't just 'cause of how hard you run. It's 'cause they won't understand *why* you run so hard. They won't understand you at all, Royce. And that'll scare 'em. Believe you me. You'll end up running so many damned touchdowns you'll get sick and tired of 'em."

Halfway through the season I'd rushed for almost eight hundred yards. Citrus High was undefeated. I could have rushed for even more yardage, but I had to share plays with Clancy, who was himself running and throwing beautifully. Photographers from newspapers around the state began to show up at our games. Clancy and I were being courted by college scouts every week. Old athletes never tire of boasting and dragging innocent bystanders back to browning record books—even our most committed cheerleader is now doubtless busy with her babies and thoroughly uninterested—but these achievements have been recalled because of something more than vanity. I pointed out that I had at last come close to Leonard's ideal, but it was not simply the intensity or the anger or the loneliness of my running that resembled the way Leonard played. It was also the sense that my running could prevent something bad from happening. I, too, was trying to get clear of the dark woods to make a rescue.

Sterns had said to just play football—what else could I do? I hoped that with enough success everything would work itself out. I never learned anything more about Mother's talk with Leonard, but I already had a good idea of how it went. I knew it didn't just concern whisky and brutish behavior. Whether Mother actually said so to Leonard's face or not, I knew it was about me and April, as well.

So when I looked into the stands and saw Mother and April and Leonard and Sterns cheering, and when, as happened twice that year, James Henderson showed up and his name was announced on the loudspeakers and he waved to the crowd from his seat next to Mother, I tried hard to believe we were entering a new phase in our lives, a happy one that I was in no small way making possible. I could well imagine them sitting in the bleachers of whatever university I attended and finally occupying box seats in one of the great professional stadiums, standing side by side, rooting me on for years to come. I conceived of my efforts as a down payment toward a future state of happiness. All of the things that I'd done wrong in my life, all of the bad decisions and selfish tricks I'd pulled, and even the sinister doings and intentions of my father, whatever they had been, were being washed away in the victorious tide of my playing.

After home games, friends and family members collected near the field, and I'd hug necks and shake hands and thank everyone for coming. If my running on the field had become a warped business, once the games were over I was as excitable as the next player and I daresay just as happy. April always placed herself at the fringe of these gatherings, careful to show deference to Mother, but when it came her turn she'd surge against me and throw her arms around me. Sometimes her hand would absently slip down my flank, lodging between hip pad and hip bone, grazing my bare skin and setting off sparks.

"Oh, Roy!" she'd say. "It's so pretty when you run!"

"Pretty? It ain't pretty. He runs like a damned freight train," Leonard always insisted.

"But gracefully. You cut and spin and off you go! I have to hold my breath every time you get the football."

"He runs right at people!" Leonard would growl.

"He runs *both* ways," Mother would point out, quite correctly.

During those too brief moments, when we were all together on the football field under the noisy, white-hot lights, with the thick smell of cleat-rutted earth and grass and the cheerleaders and dance corps girls and band members trotting around in Citrus High garnet and gold, it was impossible to imagine anything ever going wrong for us. And that was just the beginning of the night, after all. For once out of our respective uniforms Lorri-Anne and I would have our date: still Sonic, still cruising, and often parties down by the lake. Thanks to Mr. Little and the hip Harrises, who bought a video cassette recorder as soon as one became available, we could rent movies from Super Star Celebrity Video. Lorri-Anne demurely selected the films; I boldly acquiesced. Of course sometimes—sometimes!—somehow—somehow!—we would end up on a bucolic country lane, in the flatbed of Leonard's pickup truck beneath the teeming stars, tucked into a quilt made by my grandmother, laboring away after my sanity.

I've already expressed my preference for being out-of-doors, and the following vignette of young love is yet another example of why. One night when Mother was away in Washington I brought Lorri-Anne to the house. We had just begun cavorting about in a state of near undress in the library—that infernal strain of Lanier bookishness corrupted just about everything—when I heard a knock at the door. Lorri-Anne sprang from my lap as I sprang from Mother's favorite reading chair and then rushed to the window and saw April's Mustang. The front door opened suddenly. April called my name. There followed a long, terrible silence, after which I heard the door gently shut. I peered out my window from a slit between the curtains and watched April drive away. And then I realized that my khakis and Lorri-Anne's blue jeans and my shirt and her sweater had been abandoned only a few feet from the front door to fend for themselves. They stared at me helplessly, in a pile of shock and shame.

For the next few days it was all I could do to stay away from the trailer. I'd walk to the bend and then walk back home. I'd meander through the woods, approach the edge of April and Leonard's backyard and turn away.

Eventually April drove by the house to show me a new pair of silver sunglasses Leonard had bought her. They were silver, with rose-tinted lenses. The frames had been molded into hearts. She lifted them and looked me over. "Somebody's been up to the devil's business," she said.

"Me?" I said. I felt sick.

"Sneaking around my backyard. I've seen you. Should I leave some cookies out for you, scatter them out through the woods and lure you in like some wild animal?"

"Yeah. Sneaking gets me hungry," I said.

"You behave yourself," April said.

"That's who I always behave," I told her.

She made her hand into a claw as if to scratch me, then hit the gas and took off down the dirt road. I smiled and caught her looking in the rearview mirror and made a claw right back.

EIGHT

Only a few weeks after Lorri-Anne and I had played house in Mother's library, I walked into that very same library to discover Mother slumped and crying in that very same favorite reading chair, her hair disheveled, the collar of her blouse torn, her neck scratched.

"It's not her fault," she said. Her disrepair hardly concealed the fact that she was basking in what she considered a major triumph.

"What's not her fault?" I was trembling. "What? What's not her fault, Mother?"

"Don't yell. I don't need you jumping me after a night like tonight. That's the last thing I need."

"I didn't mean to yell," I said. "I'm sorry. What's happened?"

"This," she said, indicating her face and blouse. "This has happened."

"How?"

"Aren't you going to ask if I'm all right?"

"Of course, Mother. I'm asking."

"I'm fine," she said. "But I don't know how it happened. It was so unexpected. We got into a silly little argument and suddenly she just slapped me and started clawing me."

"April slapped you?" I said. "April clawed you?"

I thought of how April had slapped *me* and of her racing down the dirt road after having made a claw.

"I just tried to keep her off me. I don't know. She may have hurt herself. She flew into a rage. I'm not angry with her. I'm just embarrassed by the whole thing."

"Where was Leonard?"

"He'd gone to get beer. He can't drink wine. God forbid, not even for one night. I cooked you your favorite meal for a surprise, fried chicken and rice and milk gravy, and I invited April and Leonard to join us. When Leonard went to get the beer, April and I got into an argument. I just wanted to make sure Leonard wasn't hurting her. I have a right to ask her about that. But I guess I must have said the wrong thing, because she went *berserk*. She even threw my silver serving tray against the wall." Telling me this made her cry, and she took my hand and pressed her cheek against it. "I'm so sorry, Roy. I thought things were getting better, and then this. Will you please just sit with me for a minute? Please, just stay with me for a little while before you go rushing over there."

There was something disturbingly frank about Mother's expression. She seemed very vulnerable, tentatively searching my eyes for some sign of empathy from her only son, something every mother has a right to expect, after all. In my anger I tried to believe Mother was tricking me, though I knew better. I might well have left her there in that library had she not asked me a simple question that planted me in a soft leather club chair and lodged a cumbersome lump into my throat.

"You don't even really know how your father and I got married, do you?" she asked.

She looked at me and tried to smile.

"May I tell you? It has a lot to do with what happened here tonight. In fact, it has a lot to do with a lot of things in our lives."

"Yes, ma'am," I said. "I'm listening."

Mother sighed. "All right," she whispered, closing her eyes. She put her hand to her shoulder. "The situation with me and your father was never easy," she began. "You have to understand that. I don't want to romanticize things. It was difficult from the beginning, a constant struggle. As I've told you before, he was staying with James when we began to date, and at first everything was wonderful." Mother looked over, and my expression must have given her pause. "What's wrong?"

"Nothing."

"Yes, something's wrong," she said. "But I guess I don't blame you."

"Don't blame me for what?"

"For not liking your father. For hating him. I know you do. I know you do because Leonard has berated him in front of you all your life. And so has April in her own way. Don't think—"

"That's not true."

"Look," she said. "All I'm trying to say is that I understand how you might feel about your father. He didn't teach you to play football. He wasn't around to take you on your first hunting trip or to go fishing with you or to tell you about girls. I just wanted you to know it's normal to feel resentment toward him. I do, too, sometimes. It's normal. That's all I'm saying, all right?"

"All right."

She frowned and had a sip of wine. The grandfather clock in the living room began to chime.

"We never even had a real courtship," she continued. "Everywhere we went, April had to go along with us. I'm not putting her down, but having her tagging along with me and your father wasn't a lot of fun. You didn't know about that did you?"

I stared into the spines of her books and said nothing.

"Well, that's how it was. And wherever April went, Leonard went. That was the real problem. Sometimes the four of us would do something together, but it was always a flop because they were just kids. Leonard may have been my age, but believe me, he was an overgrown child. Your father tried to be nice by bringing along a bottle of wine for a picnic once and Leonard made a big production out of not drinking any of it. He just sat there sulking. Leonard wouldn't drink a single drop of alcohol in those days, if you can believe that. April was too young to drink, of course. But Leonard didn't have to make such a big deal out it. And plus they talked about the silliest things. It was like your father and I were baby-sitting."

"Why would April want to go with you?" My voice was severe, but Mother looked away and ignored it.

"Oh, lots of reasons," she said. "You'd be surprised." She stopped to finger the tear in her blouse for the umpteenth time, waiting for her words to sink in.

"So tell me," I said.

"I'm telling you. Just give me a chance."

She took her wine glass and stared at it thoughtfully. I believed she might begin to cry again and steeled myself against it. I was more than a little tired of periodically being told there was so much I didn't know and that I needed to know and would I please listen, only to find that an hour later I hadn't really learned very much at all, or at least that I hadn't learned what I was told I was going to learn. After years of such conversations, my line of defense was to pretend I didn't care if anybody ever told me anything or not.

"I was almost like a mother to April," Mother was saying sadly. "And I suppose over the years I allowed a pattern to establish itself. We were together almost constantly. Part of it was nothing more than simple habit. But that wasn't all there was to it. I'm going to tell you something I've never told you, Roy. Something important. And I don't want you to be angry with me or to take it the wrong way. And I certainly don't want you going back to April with it."

"Mother—"

"Just listen. April was very young at the time. In some ways, because of our circumstances, she was quite mature. But she was still very much a teenager and extremely impressionable. Tenderhearted people often are, and April is the kindest person in the world. In spite of what happened tonight, I know that April would never mean to harm anyone. April and I have had our troubles, but I care for her very much. I hope you realize that."

"Yes, ma'am."

"Anyway, what I'm trying to say is that April . . ." Mother closed her eyes. "April fell in love with your father."

A blistering feeling of revulsion spackled my chest and face. I turned on Mother with a vicious stare.

"You can deny it all you want, Roy. I know it's not easy for you to hear. And I know you don't want to believe it. The only reason I've told you is because I have to make you understand what's going on around here. Yes, Roy, April fell in love with your father. She was young and she'd never dated or had a boyfriend, really, because she always dreamed of some great romantic event, something spectacular. She's all or nothing, as you know. And when she feels something, she can't control herself. Well, she felt something for your father. It embarrassed your father sometimes. Not that he wasn't flattered or that he didn't find April attractive. But she was simply too young and her attentions made him nervous. And it made Leonard completely unpredictable."

She rolled her eyes and cringed slightly. I had not moved, though I felt at any moment I might leap up and do something to stop Mother from saying another word.

"Leonard has always been unsophisticated," she went on. "I'm not being cruel, it's just a fact. And unsophisticated people can be very single-minded and very, very determined. All Leonard ever thought about was April. April, April, April. She was his whole world. He was a complete fruit-loop over her. And when April fell in love with your father, Leonard completely flipped out, something I'll tell you about in a minute."

Mother poured herself more wine. I could hear my teeth grinding. She sat back and watched me and waited for me to look her way or to speak. When I did neither of those things she went on.

"We tried to keep away from them, your father and I, but you can't really hide in Citrus. When we tried to go off and be alone they would find us, or April would find us. It was terrible. Your father and I had to sneak around. And that made me feel guilty because I felt responsible for April. I'm sure that's been the cause of many of our troubles, to tell you the truth, the way I had to mother her. But I didn't have a choice. April was devastated by Mama's death. She'd wander off into the woods by herself, sometimes at night, and be gone for hours. Daddy and I couldn't stop her. She'd go for days without eating. I thought she was going to waste away. And Daddy, bless his heart, he was so hurt by Mama's death, he didn't know what to do. *I* had to clean the house. *I* had to cook. *I* had to take care of things. I was only fifteen when she died, Roy. That's a lot of responsibility. And naturally I'm sure I was overbearing sometimes and I'm sure April resented it and I'm not saying I blame her. But somebody had to do something, do you see?"

I said nothing.

"Well, whether you choose to believe it or not, that's just the way it was. And I'm sure when April saw that your father and I were in love, it seemed unfair, because I took care of her and was supposed to always be on her side. She believed your father was meant for her. But I had every right to him. He was my reward, Roy. I could have gone to college. James helped me apply. I applied to Vanderbilt and Emory and Virginia. My dream was to go to Virginia. I loved all the history and tradition. And I was accepted. I could have gone. Think what that means. Your father was supposed to go to Virginia, too. That's where your grandfather Collier went, and his brother. But the funny thing is, if *I'd* gone there, I never would have met your father. And if *he'd* gone there, he never would have met me. We were both made for Virginia, do you see? But neither of us got to go, and that's what allowed us to meet. Everything about your father and me made perfect sense. We were meant for each other. It's as if we found each other to compensate for all that we'd been through. You can scowl all you want, Roy."

She set her wine glass down angrily. "Go ahead. Scowl away. But the reason I couldn't go to college was because of April. And Daddy. Somebody had to stay and take care of them. April just wasn't capable. Daddy's health was deteriorating, and April wasn't even in high school yet. It wasn't fair. And that might help you to understand why April's behavior was so galling to me. I know she was young. And as for falling for your father, well, who wouldn't? I can certainly understand that. But he was meant for me. After all the sacrifices, there he was. Do you see why I couldn't tolerate April's tricks? Forgive and forget, yes, but from time to time you remember and it hurts."

She leaned back in her chair and said nothing more. When I looked over, our eyes met, but then she looked away.

"Because the thing is, I almost lost your father. April almost caused me to lose him. Your father and I were very much in love, but things got so bad around here, your father had to leave town. He just disappeared one day. He didn't even tell me good-bye. I thought it was over. I thought that I'd never see him again. I was so scared. But you have to know *why* your father left town. That's the important part. After all these years of thinking about what's happened, I believe what I'm going to tell you is where everything got off track. The whole disaster started when Leonard went off to boot camp."

She pressed her skirt flat against her thighs. "I don't hate Leonard, if that's what you think. It may seem like it sometimes, but I don't. I've never believed he and April should have married. That's no secret. She could have had a completely different life. And for *that,* for holding her back, I resent him. But there are things about Leonard that I respect. He was your age when he went to Vietnam. Everybody loved him. He was a country boy—shy, polite, always in church, naive, you know the kind. But when he got on that bus at the old bus station right off the square, right where Betty's Florals is now, and that bus headed out of town to take him off to boot camp, it was awful. A lot of people had shown up to see him off and show support for him. They had little American flags. Brother Glenn said a prayer for him. I'll never forget that day as long as I live. It all happened on a Saturday morning."

Mother lit a cigarette. "He'd signed up to go, you know. He wasn't drafted. He probably could have gotten out of it. He had scholarships all over the place, and he was an only child. His mama and daddy weren't in very good health, either. But he felt strongly about going, about doing his duty, and that's something I've always admired. Of course, after he and your father began to have their troubles, he wanted out of it, but it was too late. He was in too deep. He wanted to stay here to look after April because he believed your father had designs on her. He believed everybody had designs on April. Ask James Henderson about that sometime. Leonard used to pout whenever he was around James, and I think he may have even said something to him one time. Embarrassing. I mean, people loved Leonard because he was a football star, but Leonard's problem was, he couldn't live on the football field. And once you got him off the football field he was inept, and at his worst he could be a lot of trouble."

Mother shook her head. "Of *course* people liked to *flirt* with April. But everybody was not in love with her, for heaven's sake. That's exactly what Leonard thought, though, and so he went around town guarding her and defending her and scheming against rivals that never existed except in his own head. And when he realized your father was going to stay in Citrus, *he* wanted to stay in Citrus. But, like I say, it was too late by then.

"Your father knew that he had to have a talk with April, and he did. He tried to explain that she needed to tell Leonard how things were, that he didn't have a romantic interest in her. But did she do anything? Of course not. She didn't listen to a word your father said. I remember the day she came back from the talk. They'd gone for a drive, and then here she comes walking back down the road toward the house not thirty minutes later. She was crying and hysterical and she wouldn't talk to anybody. She locked herself in her room and wouldn't come out. Typical. Finally Daddy demanded that she let him in and she did, but she still wouldn't talk. April could get like that.

"In the meantime, Leonard was growing more obsessed. The closer it got to the day he would have to leave Citrus, the more frantic he became. Well, your father wasn't going anywhere. I mean, whether Leonard and

April would recognize the fact or not, we were deeply in love. So finally Leonard proposed to April. His mother and his father had built up a savings for him to have when he went away to play football in college. They were hardworking people. That money didn't come easily. When he decided to enlist it broke his mother's heart. But they believed in honor and he explained that it wouldn't be right for him to play football when other boys were over in Vietnam, so they supported him. And when he told them that he wanted to get married before he went overseas, that he wanted to marry April, they wanted that for him more than anything in the world. Oh, they loved April.

"Sometimes we would be over at Leonard's house playing when we were children and they were already matchmaking. You know how parents do. His mama would bring out biscuits and give April the first one and fawn over her. Or we'd be over there riding ponies. Mr. Collins kept horses for people in town. Some of those horses were pretty much forgotten about as soon as they'd been bought, so Mr. Collins got paid to feed them and we got to ride them. There were four or five nice horses, but only two ponies. The ponies had been birthday presents for the Haney girls, who talked about them all the time but hardly ever rode them. Well, we rode them. And since there were only two, two of us had to double up, and Mr. Collins would say that I looked like I could handle a pony on my own, which was meant to flatter me, and if I were a feminist I suppose I'd be thanking my lucky stars and praising Mr. Collins to high heavens for not treating me like a helpless little girl. But that's not how little girls feel about such things. Women, either, for that matter. I'm as independent as any woman, but that doesn't mean I don't know what's what. I knew very well what was going on. He was getting Leonard and April on the same pony so Leonard could gallop off with her and I could follow along behind and watch her holding on to him with her cheek pressed against his back. Believe it or not, even though it was Leonard she was holding on to, I envied her. Oh, they *loved* April. April was the perfect girl in their eyes.

"Anyway, when Leonard's mama and daddy realized he wasn't going to play football right away if ever, and that he was going overseas where he might be hurt or even killed, they wanted to do something special for him. He was their only son, their pride and joy—Leonard was everything to them. And so they took their savings and gave it to him so he could buy a ring for April. Because they figured that if he was going to be giving up college and preaching, maybe forever, he could at least have one dream come true. Especially since it might be the last dream he would ever have a chance to have. I mean, they told him April was too young and that *he* was too young for that matter. But the war was on and people do things in a hurry in situations like that. Leonard wanted April so badly. What could they do? They couldn't say no under those circumstances. It's very sad, really. It's always made me sad. Right up to this day."

Mother looked away suddenly. Something was wrong.

"What happened?"

She put out her cigarette. She shook her head and stood and wiped her eyes and looked at the fireplace.

"Can we build a fire first? I need to get out of these clothes. If you'll build a fire I'll hurry back and we can finish."

WHEN MOTHER SHUT the door to her bedroom I rushed into the kitchen to telephone April. No one answered. A second try only produced another lonely string of gurgling, hollow rings—a broken necklace spilling its sorrowful baubles—and so I went to the porch for firewood. When I returned, Mother was standing in her housecoat and slippers, finishing a cigarette.

"Make a big fire," she said. She hugged herself and twisted. "All those coaches keep calling. They're just mad for you, Roy."

"This spring it'll get pretty intense," I said.

"I'm so proud. I'm especially proud that Virginia and Princeton are interested. You'd be perfect at Virginia."

"It's going pretty well," I admitted. I returned to my seat, and she followed me. "So what happened to Leonard?"

"Yes, Leonard. Poor Leonard." She sat down. "Sometimes when I think I hate him, when I've just had enough, I think about what happened and I feel sorry for him all over again." She took out another cigarette and lit it. "I'm going to end up going through a whole pack tonight," she said. She exhaled with force and groaned softly. "Well, anyway, they went to get a ring. All three of them. They drove all the way to Mobile to buy it. And not with a check, either. Oh, no. With cash."

Mother looked at me seriously. "Cash they'd kept in a safe in their attic. I can only imagine how many times they went up those stairs and opened that safe and counted that money, just to make sure none of it had evaporated, just to remind themselves, when they were tired and maybe wanted something they couldn't afford because of all that saving, that they at least had something to show for all their work and doing without. They were saving for Leonard's future. Even when it was obvious he was going to get a scholarship and that he might make it as a professional football player, they kept saving. Mainly they were saving for him to go to seminary, or if not that at least some bible college. They felt all that saving was God's will, that it had a divine purpose. Because they believed that Leonard was called to be a great preacher. They thought he'd be famous. I mean, it's enough to break anyone's heart. Do you see what all that ring meant? It meant *everything.* That ring was about their only child, their son, who was giving up his dreams and their dreams to go and serve his country."

She inhaled and shook her head, then exhaled and continued to shake her head.

"And a few days before Leonard had to leave, sure enough, he proposed. He took April out by the lake, out on that old dock Mr. Haney built where y'all go fishing. Leonard got down on one knee and showed her that ring that had cost his father countless new shirts through the years and maybe a Sunday suit or two. Who knows how many little things Mr. Collins went without in order to build up that savings. It cost his mother new dresses and Bible commentaries and study books that she would've liked to have had. And Leonard never had any money growing up. He never had a tackle box like you have. He never had a tackle box period. In fact, Leonard never even had his own bicycle. I mean, he had one. But not that his mother and father got him. It was Sterns. Sterns gave him a bicycle. Sterns gave him things even then.

"If he'd asked for one his mama and daddy would've bought one, of course, but he joined up with their savings program right off. He never asked for anything. He was a member of the Collins Savings and Trust since before he could talk. So that savings cost *him,* too. It cost the whole family. Years of lean birthdays and lean Christmases. The fact is, that engagement ring was the most expensive ring in the world." Mother stared at me without pretence. She appeared as if she would finish the story even if I left the room and she were alone. "With Leonard going off to war, quite possibly going off to die, it cost more than all the diamonds in all the diamond mines put together. When he pulled that ring out and handed it to April, kneeling there on that dock, it was as good as saying: This is my life, not just a symbol of my life, but my very life, all the years of my life and all the work of it, and of my mama and daddy's lives, too, and all their work, crystalized, crushed like coal—all their years and my years and all our hard work and all the things we gave up, all of it added together until the pressure was great enough, and sacrifice and sweat and tears were heavy enough, to make this diamond. And I'm asking you to take it and make it worth all that effort. Because you mean that much to me. Because we'd do it all over again for you. Because—"

She stopped and lowered her head and began to cry.

"Mother?"

"Do you see, Roy?" she managed.

"Yes, ma'am. I see. It's okay."

"No, it's not. It's not okay at all. Because she turned him down."

"She what?"

"She turned him down!"

"But—"

"But *nothing.* She turned him down. He had to go off to war after she'd rejected him. They weren't engaged to be married until he came back."

I'd never heard anything that could have prepared me for this. Not from Leonard or April or Sterns or Henderson, not from anybody. There had been no hints or warnings. Yet as soon as I heard it I knew it was true.

"And do you know why? Would you like to know why? I'll tell you why. She turned him down because of your father. You always say you want to know what happened—*this is what happened!* April believed your father was in love with her and that they were going to be married. It wasn't true, obviously, and it wreaked havoc. Leonard was devastated. I still believe that's what led to his mama and daddy deteriorating the way they did. They were destroyed because of April turning him down and him having to bear that and go overseas and bear *that.* I'm not saying she should have said yes, not at her age—she *should* have said no. But it was why she said no that caused such problems. It was a terrible time. Citrus had become intolerable. For me and April and your father and Leonard and James it had become a nightmare. When April turned Leonard down it was like a bomb going off. Everybody knew about it. And when Leonard boarded that bus to go off to boot camp, people could hardly stand it. Mr. Collins was a burnt-up old farmer who'd never shed a tear in his life, the kind of man who could endure anything. And Leonard's mother was a very godly sort of person, even stronger than her husband. Or so we thought.

"Because when it came time for the bus to leave and Leonard hugged his mother, she just fell to pieces. She'd worn the nicest dress she had and she even put on a little rouge and lipstick. And she'd worn heels. I remember her tottering and feeling sorry for her because what was happening was killing her and she was having to endure it standing there fighting for balance in those damned heels that she didn't know how to wear." Mother brought her handkerchief to her mouth. "It must have been a hundred degrees with the sun beating down on them, no privacy, right there off the square with a crowd of people standing around, and it was killing her. When I think of that poor woman standing there in those heels watching her son get on that bus . . . Oh, Roy. Don't you see?

There's nothing like a mother's love for her son. When I think about her having to watch him get on that bus with that cheap lipstick and those heels . . . *Those heels!* Because she couldn't do anything for him. And all a mother wants to do is to make it right for her son. Mrs. Collins would have given her life a thousand times over to help Leonard, but she couldn't. She couldn't make April marry him and she couldn't make the war go away and she wouldn't argue against his honor—but that honor was killing her.

"She had to figure he might die. Being the kind of person he was. Being the kind of person she'd *reared him to be.* She must have figured that he'd insist on getting right into the middle of it and die over there thousands of miles from home, alone, heartbroken, for what? For what? Tell me for what? Don't you see that a mother can't take that? Don't you see she just can't bear it?"

"It's all right, Mother. It's all right. I love you."

"Do you?"

"Yes. It's going to be all right."

"Don't ever leave me, Roy. I don't mean don't ever leave home. I want you to see the world, as much of it as you can, but you know what I mean. Don't ever leave me."

"I'll never leave you."

"You promise?"

"I promise."

"I get afraid that you will. That somebody will say something, that you'll find something out and you'll leave me. I've made mistakes, Roy. I've made many of them. But that doesn't mean I don't love you. You're all I have."

"I won't leave you."

She nodded. I drew close and took her hand. Eventually she quit crying and sat back in her chair, wiping her eyes.

"We saw all of this from around the corner. We were hiding. Leonard told April he didn't want her to see him off. He told her to stay away from him. But she had to see him off. So we hid around the corner and watched.

Everyone had little American flags to wave, but when the bus started old man Haney told everybody to stop. 'Put those damned things down and show some respect,' he said. He didn't say it loudly. I'm not even sure he meant for anyone to hear him, but everyone looked up to him and I guess nobody wanted to wave those flags anyway. And then Leonard got on and rode away and later he got on a plane and flew away. And he fought and came home. That was what he promised his mother and that's what he did. He cracked the window on the bus and told her he'd come back. I suppose it would have taken God Himself to prevent him from returning."

Mother was crying again, steadily and quietly. She retrieved a cigarette and lit it and tried to take some strength from it, but she could not stop crying.

"Seeing Leonard go off like that pushed April over the edge. She blamed everything on herself. But, unfortunately, she also continued to believe that she and your father were meant to be. He would go to her and console her and I didn't have the heart to stop it. I felt so sorry for her. I worried she might kill herself. I was generous with your father, just as I've been generous with you. But that kind of generosity causes problems. People in town thought it was improper the way your father was always chasing around after April. They didn't really know what was going on. They got the wrong idea. And when they thought about Leonard being overseas, fighting for his country, it made them despise your father. The whole town turned against him.

"It wasn't your father's fault. It was April's fault. But that didn't stop people from blaming your father, and pretty soon there were rumors circulating that he was trying to seduce April. Let me tell you—that hurt. It was a cruel slap in my face. And the next thing you know your father wasn't invited anywhere anymore. People would hardly say hello to him. And so he left town, just disappeared without a trace, without telling anyone. Not even me. And why? Because of April. Because he was afraid if anyone knew where he was going, she'd find out and follow him. That's how bad she'd gotten. She was out of her mind. Once she'd told Leonard no, it became imperative for her that she and your father end up together. Your father didn't even say good-bye to me, Roy. At the end of the summer he just up and vanished."

"Vanished where?"

"I didn't know. I thought my whole life was over, that I'd never see him again. But then I decided to do something, to try to find him. Sometimes you have to do that. You just have to take action." She looked at me. "You can't always just let things happen the way they're happening. Sometimes you have to stop things. You can't be afraid. And I wasn't. I went all the way to South Carolina. Right by myself. That's where I figured he might have gone and that's where I went. And that's where I found him. But I found him by accident." She looked away. "With that girl. That girl I told you about."

"The girl in the motel room?"

"Yes, but I didn't realize that right away. Because remember, your father hadn't told me the real reason why he'd left South Carolina yet. I only knew what he'd told us in Ligget's. So I didn't know about the motel sweetheart or whatever you want to call her. I had no idea about that."

"Where'd you find them?"

"When I went to his hometown I asked around for the Colliers and got directions to their house."

Mother took out another cigarette. She struggled with the lighter, and I leaned forward and lit her cigarette for her.

"Thank you. So I had directions, but then I saw that girl."

"How did you know it was her?"

"No, no. I mean I pulled into a filling station and when I looked across the road your father was sitting in a restaurant. With that girl." She stopped.

"In a restaurant?"

"Yes, a diner. I wanted to run over to him, but who was this girl? I parked my car and slid down in the seat and watched them. And I felt sick. I mean, what if he'd been lying to me? What if he'd been just toying with me? After all the promises he'd made. After all we'd shared. . . . After . . ."

"Mother?"

"Sometimes, Roy . . ."

"You don't have to—"

"Well, he could be a bastard when he wanted to. Sometimes he could be . . ."

She wasn't talking to me anymore. She wasn't paying any attention to me. I waited.

"But those were hard times. He had his reasons. I couldn't blame him. But I couldn't just let him walk away, either. Sometimes you—" Mother stopped and looked at me.

"Anyway, they walked out of the restaurant, and the girl gave your father an envelope. It turned out she'd given him money. Your father said she wouldn't stop giving him money because that's how she could still feel connected to him." Mother arched her brows at this. "At any rate, he took the envelope, and she got in her car. And your father stood there for a minute, and then he headed down the street with his satchel. I didn't know what to do or what to say, so I just followed him. I was sort of numb. Somebody stopped and he got inside the car and then I started following them. And about an hour down the highway, coming up on the Georgia line, he got out and hitched another ride and I followed that one. I kept thinking he wasn't really in love with me since he'd gone to see that girl. But pretty soon the most amazing thing happened—I realized he was heading back to Citrus. Or at least that general direction, back toward Florida. And when I realized he was coming back to me, I couldn't just sit and watch him anymore."

"What did you do?"

"Well, he got dropped off at a motel." She paused once again. "Oh, Roy, I shouldn't tell you this. I shouldn't tell this about your own mother. I was just a different person back then." She smiled. "Anyway, after he checked in and went to his room, I knocked on the door and said, 'Room service.' And he said, 'Room service?' And I said, 'Aren't you hungry?' He never knew what hit him! It was the first time we'd ever had the chance to be alone. It wasn't exactly the Ritz, but I remember it so clearly. We were up on the third floor, and the room had a balcony that overlooked the pool. It was just a little pool with little gravel beds around it, but we were so deeply in love it may as well have been the Mediterranean. We could have stayed like that forever."

She clasped her hands and shrugged. "But we didn't, of course. We couldn't. We had to come back to Citrus because of Daddy and April. And then Leonard got hurt and came back from overseas. He came home right after you were born, at the end of January. And he was bitter because he couldn't play football anymore because of his injury and because he believed April agreed to marry him out of pity. Which she did. That's exactly what she did. I'll get to that in a minute. The point is, Leonard blamed everything, every single failure and disappointment, on one person: Sanders Royce Collier.

"He knew April had feelings for your father, but to preserve his pride he turned it around as if it was your father who was hung up on April. April did the same thing. Once she knew Sanders and I were going to get married, she acted as if he still had eyes for her and was always putting the moves on her. She was always having some sort of crisis. We all lived together in this house. Just think about that. April was in her room. Your father and I were in mine. And Daddy was in his. And when Daddy died . . . Are you going to listen or not? I'm not going to beg you."

"Go on."

"Well."

"Go on."

"Fine. When your grandfather died things got even worse. The three of us living in that house together and April always causing some scene. She was ruining our marriage. It was hard to be intimate, and right after you're married you need intimacy. And I was beginning to come along with you, don't forget that. I needed your father's attention, but that's not what I got. Because April was always threatening to run away and going off into the woods, and there went your father right behind her.

"All of which is why I was very happy to see Leonard come back home. I thought we might finally get a little peace. When he returned he got a hero's welcome. Sterns organized a parade and got the mayor to declare it Leonard Collins Day and had ticker tape, you name it. And Leonard wasted no time in proposing to April again, either. Once she'd accepted I thought it was just a matter of time before your father and I could have our freedom."

Mother took a deep breath and stabbed out the cigarette she'd hardly touched. "What I'm trying to say is, your father wasn't perfect. And April had driven him crazy. I don't know exactly what happened. Because there's your father's version, which is pretty credible. And then there's Leonard's version, which is about what you'd expect. And then there's April's version, which she has never bothered to tell anybody."

"Version of what?"

"Version of what. Of what happened between them. Things got funny after April and Leonard were engaged. She was gone a lot, picking out things for the wedding, and she'd come home late at night and it was like she was afraid to be around the house. One night we all had a bad fight and she took off walking to the Collinses'. Your father said he'd make sure she got there safely. But he came right back a few minutes later and said April had attacked him. His face was cut. And then *she* came running in screaming and crying and went straight to her room and locked the door. 'I slapped her, all right? I'm sorry. She told me to stop following her and when I tried to explain she went crazy on me.' That's what your father told me. He said she came on to him. When you're disturbed it can affect you sexually, and that's to say nothing of the fact that she was in love with your father."

Mother was looking into the fire. She twitched at the recollection of something.

"He admitted he might have lost control of himself a little. April tried to kiss him, and he admitted he kissed her back. But then he realized what he was doing and stopped. She kept on and he became angry and kind of blacked out with rage, which I've seen him do many a time. That's when he slapped her and told her to get away. And that's when she clawed his face. No, you listen to me. I know a side of April and Leonard that you don't. You should trust me enough to listen. I've told you many, many times that Leonard is dangerous and that you should be careful around him. I've told you over and over and over again. When you and April are running around like kids, fine, there may not be anything wrong with it, you're just having fun, but you don't know about Leonard and what it might cause him to do.

"Especially with him drinking so much. He has a bad temper and he *hated* your father. When he found out about your father and April and the fight they had, all hell broke loose. And he found out that very night. I guess she called him from her room. Your father and I were arguing ourselves when all of a sudden Leonard comes bursting in here. He got April and drove her to his mama and daddy's house. He didn't say one word. Not one word.

"But the very next day he made April give him the engagement ring and he drove to Mobile and sold it and took the money and bought that trailer. And within a few weeks he and April were married. They dropped all their wedding plans. The only people who came to the wedding were me and Brother Glenn and Leonard's mama and daddy and Sterns. Your father wasn't invited, of course.

"Then Leonard went down to the courthouse and got a deed and determined what part of our property belonged to April and what part belonged to me and your father, and he put that trailer right on the property line. He actually had the surveyors leave one of those little orange ribbons up to show it. And then he walked over here and threw the deed down in front of your father and told him that if he ever stepped foot on April's property without his permission he'd kill him. 'I'll fucking kill you like there's no tomorrow,' he said. I'd never heard Leonard curse before. *Ever*. The whole room was hot because of him. I'd never been that afraid in my life. He was trembling and clicking his teeth like he was fixing to explode. 'And one more thing,' he said, pointing at your father. 'Contrary to what you may have heard, I ain't gonna be no fucking preacher, either. So it'd be a pure pleasure to crack your goddamned fucking head wide fucking open if I was to catch you over there!' And that's not all. Oh, no. Of course not.

"After April and Leonard were married everything seemed to settle down, but it didn't last. Because what Leonard said bothered your father. It got to him. We'd argue about it. He'd say how April had caused it all, how she'd tried to seduce him. He began to despise her because she hadn't told the truth. Worse, she hadn't said anything, which made it seem like something really awful had happened. He would taunt her sometimes when she'd come over to look after you. And he wanted to know who did Leonard think he was, marking that line, and didn't that property belong to both me and April, and then he'd launch into one of his tirades about how he hated fences, how he was a no-fences type of person and that he didn't like boundaries, and so on and so forth. It wasn't long before he started going for walks and carrying that deed with him to walk off the perimeter of the property. He'd walk around the bend and stare at that ribbon, and sometimes Leonard would come out and stare right back at him. And that was on top of all the other troubles we were having. Because the truth is, your father was having difficulty adapting to married life. He liked to wander. Which was fine by me. I loved that about him. But he was going to have to be your father, too, after all."

Mother lit another cigarette. She drew on it and then held it away from her, staring at the curling trails of smoke.

"And then your father was walking through the woods late that night. And whoever it was . . ."

"What did Sheriff Porter say?"

"I've told you before. They checked around and couldn't find out anything. There were a lot of people who didn't like your father at the time. People were not overly helpful with the investigation, either. They believed your father got what he deserved. And there I was with you, just a child, and a husband that'd been murdered and nobody gave a damn. And I had to keep hearing talk about your father killing himself because of April or how if it wasn't a suicide it was an act of God. I had to hear all of it. And I had to swallow it down and keep it down. But it was worth it. It was worth it because you're worth it."

Mother leaned forward in her chair. She reached out but did not touch me.

"I want you to listen to me, Roy. Please just listen. If I wasn't always a typical mother in some areas, that's because I'm not a typical woman in some areas. I know I let you go off with April and I made you memorize poems and read things and I still make fun of your protein drinks and all that pumping iron. Maybe you see why now. Everything has been so complicated and confusing. And if it's complicating and confusing for me, that means it's complicated and confusing for April. And for Leonard. That's why I'm worried about you. He could get drunk one night and the least little thing could set him off. He could hurt you. He could hurt April. I wish she could just get away for a while. Even if it was only for a few weeks. It would be so nice for her."

"Get away where?"

"I don't know. Take a vacation. She's not holding up very well under all of this. I'm sure Leonard's getting very difficult to deal with. I happen to know they're not getting along. If she could get away and let everything cool down, I think it would be good for everybody involved. They're packed into that little trailer all the time. And you, too, you're over there half the time—it's too much. I'm not overreacting. You ought to know that now. All these little games could suddenly become very serious. Are you listening to me?"

"I'm listening."

"You'd better. Because you have to remember one thing, Roy. I've seen little games like this become serious once before. Don't think something couldn't go wrong again. Do you understand?"

"Yes, ma'am."

"Do you *really* understand? Understand how serious this is. How dangerous."

"Yes. But nothing's dangerous."

"Then you don't understand." She stared directly into my eyes. "Yes you do. I know you do. I can see it. You understand exactly what I'm saying. I won't make you admit it. I'm not interested in scoring points. I'm just interested in protecting you. And if you love me, and if you love April and even Leonard, you'll be more careful."

"Yes, ma'am."

"Because believe me, Roy—I *will* protect you. Whatever I have to do. That's something you never have to worry about. I may not have been able to protect your father, but I'll damn sure make certain nobody ever hurts you."

NINE

That night I crossed the line. I had not known there was a line to be crossed, but as I walked over to April and Leonard's I saw it clearly, drawn in blood or the thin remains of what once had been blood. At least that is how I imagined it. I imagined the little orange-colored ribbon wound around the pine stakes—imagined my father, standing on the other side of that ribbon, staring at it and then looking up to the trailer. Maybe he saw April pass in front of the kitchen window. Perhaps he stood just behind the bay tree in the backyard and watched her doing the dishes, observing her fine arms as she scrubbed, tracing the curve of her neck, her shoulders. . . .

She would have been just seventeen. I'd never really considered the fact that she'd finished high school as Leonard's wife, that she had a marriage certificate before she had a diploma. I suppose Mother took me to her graduation. But perhaps she preferred to have the diploma sent through the mail instead, and so it was deposited into the tin mailbox that sat atop the creosote-scented fence post out by the road. She may have held me in her lap and looked it over. She may have smiled and talked to me about it. And my father may have been nearby, watching us on the other side of the line, because I was where he most wanted to be in all the world.

As I looked toward that white double-wide that had cost all of us so much, it seemed to lurch and sway under the moonlight. I recalled Mother's fears that the trailer would one day come flying around the bend, and my own wishes that it might do exactly that, but now I realized it had long ago been grounded for good.

Howl wandered over, wagging his tail. He groaned and collapsed at my feet to search for fleas. All the lights were out, and I figured April and Leonard had gone to bed. That meant I wouldn't find out what had happened until morning. It also meant I wouldn't sleep that night. But as I walked around to the deck, I heard a match strike. Leonard's face appeared, fierce as a jack-o'-lantern's. "Do me a favor, Royce," he said. His voice startled me.

"Sir?"

"Said do me a favor. I don't stutter. Your ears don't hang over."

"I came to check on April," I said.

"Yeah. Bet you did." He pitched the match at me. "You the second team?"

"No, sir. Is she here?"

He tilted a fifth of Early Times. "You gonna do me a favor or am I gonna come down from this deck and kick the ever-living shit out of you?"

"What is it?"

"Come over here."

"What?"

"Don't be such a little pussy. I said come over here."

"All right. I'm here."

"I'm not going to hurt you, for Christ's sake. Have I ever laid a hand on you?"

"No, sir."

"You're always over here eating up my food and drinking up my damned Cokes and sometimes my beers and have I ever charged you for it? I said, *have-I-ever-charged—*"

"No, sir."

"And don't I always make a big production out of your games? Huh? And how many goddamned times have I woke up hungover and all I wanted in the world was a bowl of fucking Cheerios and some bacon and you've done eaten up the last bowl and fried the last strips of bacon and the goddamned sausage, too? No grits in the damned house because y'all go through grits and eggs like they was going out of style. How many?"

"A lot of times."

He chuckled harshly. "A goddamned lot of times is exactly right, partner." He took a long pull. "Now get your ass over here where I don't have to holler."

I walked onto the deck and stood in front of him. He weaved a little from the whisky, but his eyes were steady. "I've got a favor to ask you," he said, setting his cigarette on the lid to the grill. "Man to man."

"All right."

"I want you to go get April for me."

He handed me his flashlight, a ponderous aluminum tube that weighed over a pound. It was more like a searchlight than a flashlight, but the batteries were low and so the beam it cast was pale and didn't reach very far.

"Batteries have gone to shit, I know, but you'll do fine with it," he said. "I wouldn't never find her. You know all the hiding places. She wouldn't let me find her anyhow. And I ain't gonna be able to sleep until she's back home, neither. God I hate it when she wanders off like this." He grunted and peered into the woods. "So I'm trusting you to go get her for me. You can come over for breakfast in the morning if you want. Eat up all the fucking bacon, all right?"

"All right," I said.

"Get the fuck on, then."

When I walked into the yard he called out to me.

"Hey, Royce. Don't be long about it. Y'all can talk here just as well as there. I'm exhausted."

When I arrived at the lake I found the johnboat lying far up on the beach. The dock was empty. There was a clearing back in the woods, a sandy hill where April and I sometimes sat and talked. I thought she might have gone there. Walking toward it, I heard the bull call of an alligator, deep and thumping. The moon swathed the woods in a fay veil of spun light. The trees seemed spellbound by it, frozen. I drew closer to our spot and squatted in country fashion and sank into the night noises. Beneath the human vantage it became possible to see and hear with greater accuracy. I sent the faint yellow beam once around. "April," I said, just a whisper. I missed her. I waited for a moment, then began calling loudly.

"I'm over here," she said. "Keep that light off. You'll draw the mosquitoes."

I found her with the flashlight. "Turn it off," she repeated. "Here," she said, tossing me a can of repellent. "They're bad tonight. They'll eat you up." She sat against an ear tree, her hands resting on the ground. She wore one of her floral-print cotton dresses and her flat-toed cowboy boots. "Turn it off, Roy." She gathered the dress between her legs.

"Are you all right?"

"I'll be fine."

"What happened?"

"Nothing. It was stupid. We started acting like two little girls and then your mama decided to wring my neck. She's had a thing about my neck for some time now."

"Can I see?"

"Keep that light off. I don't feel like being stared at. It's just a scratch, anyway. I think I got her, too. Oh, Roy, let's not talk about it. Can we just sit here a minute?"

She wanted us to be quiet, but I was intensely lonely and craved something from her, just as I had craved something from her after she caught me and Lorri-Anne in Mother's library. I felt a kind of desperation caused by the fact that I was coming to believe that even if I played by the rules, nobody else would.

"I'm coming over there," I said. "I want to make sure you're all right."

"Just wait a minute, Roy. Can you wait?"

"I just want to make sure you're all right."

"Turn the light off," she said. "Please."

Her hair was wild. She looked like something born of the woods, something untamed. I had to be a little closer.

"Are you all right?"

"I'm fine."

"What happened?"

"Turn that off and I'll tell you."

I turned it off. I turned it on again. I could hardly stand the distance between us.

"Oh, baby. Please. Stop. Just stop."

"Just tell me."

"Roy."

"Tell me."

"Don't get upset. We had an argument. That's all. Come here."

"About what?"

"Whenever somebody disagrees with your mother they're automatically crazy. If you don't see it her way, she figures you're deranged. And sometimes she tells you so. And if you don't take her seriously she has to do something to get your attention. But she's your mother, and it's not right for you to make me talk about things I don't want to talk about." She held my hand in her lap, drawing my head to her shoulder. "Don't get upset, Roy. There's nothing to be upset about."

"I won't let anything happen to you," I said.

"I know you won't," she said. "I know I can depend on you. I always have."

"What's Mother trying to do, anyway?"

"Who knows? Who ever really knows?"

"She's trying to do something."

"She thinks Leonard's going to hurt me and she thinks I should go away for a while. After football season, maybe after Christmas. She thinks we need counseling."

"But why does she want *you* to go away? What about Leonard? Why shouldn't he go?"

"Oh, that would be fine with her. But nobody's going anywhere. Don't you worry. June is not going to get the satisfaction of marching us around. And she can say what she wants about Leonard, but at least he's never laid a hand on me. She can say what she wants, that's one thing Leonard's never done. And that's more than I can say . . ."

April released my hand. I waited. Our hearts beat and blended. The katydids began to shriek in the silence—thrown ticking streamers, slung rattlers, thick ratcheting webs of sound. . . . My hand slipped through the noisy gauze of night and landed on April's thigh. Thin hot skin, girlish pretty heat. . . .

April took my hand up again. She leaned into me. "Come on, baby. We'd better go."

We walked down by the lake. April washed her face, and I stooped beside her and washed mine, too.

"Julep's good for tears," she said. "You can't imagine how many of my tears are in here."

She cupped a handful of water and poured it over my hands. She smiled. "When you were little I tried to teach you to snap your toes. Snap. Snap. Snap. You never got the hang of it."

"I don't think it can be done," I said.

"No, probably not. You would have been the first. But I believed in you."

"Do you still?"

"Yes, I do. Very much."

SHORTLY BEFORE DAWN I opened my eyes and saw the barrel of a twelve gauge hanging perpendicular to the stock, dangling just over my nose as if to pilfer my breath as it drifted from my nostrils. Leonard was loading shells pleasantly. “Get a good night’s sleep?” He brought the barrel back hard, jacking it into place. “There’s some eggs over there. Some bacon, too. And coffee. I’m going to the bathroom and when I get back I want you and me to go out and have a talk. Maybe we’ll do some hunting. You game?” He kicked the couch and frowned. “Hurry up,” he said.

We drove around for a while, neither of us saying anything. Finally we turned into a pasture and got out of the truck. I followed him over to a hammock of cypress trees.

“What do you want to hunt?” he asked.

“Whatever you do.”

“That’s a good answer.” His hand came down on my neck like a meaty clap of thunder. “Why don’t you run out for a pass. Go on out about twenty yards.”

“There’s no football.”

“Shit. I knew I forgot something. Well, go on out anyway. I’ll see what kinda pattern you run.”

“No sir.”

“No sir?”

“I don’t want to go,” I said. “It’s not funny.”

“No, it’s really not funny at all, is it?”

He dug into the ground with the heel of his boot. He cleared his throat, spat in the hole and covered it back up. Then he pulled the shotgun up and fired into the air and stared at me through the fierce ringing in my ears and the heavy odor of gun powder. A sleek white egret took to the air. Cattle rumbled away in the distance.

“You’re dangerous, Roy.” He screwed his mouth up and sighed. “Because your mama’s dangerous. Now you might take offense at that—it’d be natural, and I wouldn’t blame you. But then again, I don’t really give a flying fuck through a rolling donut one way or the other right now. Because at this point I’d just as soon knock you on your goddamned ass as look at you. You *and* your mama. You know what your mama did last night?”

"Yes, sir. I think I do."

"Well, let me tell you. Because I walked in on part of it. June was all over April, slapping at her, clawing her, calling her a bitch, telling her that she'd been after Sanders and that now she was after you. I'm serious as a fucking heart attack, boy." He popped the spent shells and reloaded. "Goddamn, I been through this shit before," he said. "And you know what your mama was saying to April to get everything started? She claimed that I was going to hurt you and maybe hurt April and that she was worried about you and April 'cause I'm an old jealous redneck who never got over your daddy and that I was bound to get drunk one night and take it out on you. Told April that things would be a whole lot better if April got out of town for a while. Fuck," he said. He spat again. "Do you hear what I'm saying?"

"Yes, sir."

"She's already called some women's home. That damned home is for *battered* women, by the by. She kept on about it and April said she was leaving and then your mama grabbed her and told her she was so sick that she couldn't realize what was going on. Said that April—April, as in *my wife*—probably had feelings for you and was unintentionally drawn to you. April'd had enough and pushed her off, and then your mama went haywire." He gritted his teeth and grunted. "Hay-fucking-wire!" He swung the gun up and fired into the sky again. The sunlight made fiery halos around the blond hairs of his forearms. He removed his cap and wiped his head, and I remembered what Mother had told me about how he'd made the room intolerably hot and how red he was. Now he was doing it to the whole world, burning everything up.

"Know what else your mama surmised? She *sur-mized* that I'd been knocking April around." He laughed viciously. "I ain't never done that and I never will. But if I ever do take to doing any hitting, guess who's gonna be on the receiving end?" He poked his fingers into my chest and shoved me back a few steps. "Just take you a wild guess."

"I'll stop her," I said.

"Damn right you will, partner. But not the way you think. Not through no confrontation." Leonard shook his head and stared off into the hammock. "I ain't saying this is entirely your fault, either. Because it ain't. Your mama can't live in peace. She never has been able to, and when she married your daddy they aggravated one another perfectly. She likes things all shook up and so did he. But *I don't.* I like things calm and easy. And when I walk into y'all's living room and see April having to fight June off, it's all I can do to control myself. Now, it may not be entirely your fault, but you're the reason it's happening. You're what's got her so worked up. Just the fact that you didn't come home last night has probably got her going again already. Just look at last night, Roy. Why the fuck didn't you go home and sleep in your own bed? I mean shit, son."

"I'm sorry," I said.

"I don't want your apology. I want you to straighten this shit out. Bible says abstain from all appearance of evil, did you know that?"

"Yes, sir."

"Because what we're gonna work on is appearances. We got us a snafu, here, Roy. Situation normal all fucked up. But we're gonna normalize things fast. You're gonna straighten up and fly right. Be a part of the solution and not a part of the problem. Right now you're playing into something you don't even know the half of. You hear me?"

"Yes, sir."

"So from now on I want you to ask yourself one question whenever you think about doing something, all right?"

"Yes, sir."

"One and only one question: What would Leonard Collins think?" He looked at me. "It's that easy. It's the Leonard Collins test. And it's a damned good one. You want to go walking with April—what would Leonard Collins think? Want to tell your mama something—what would old Leonard think? Expecting to have to take a piss in the ditch, ask yourself one question—what would Uncle Leonard think? You stick to that program and you're gonna be right as rain. Stick to your own program and you're gonna suffer. And that ain't the worst part. Worst part is, April's gonna suffer. Do we have an understanding?"

"Yes, sir."

"You do that and pretty soon you'll be graduated and playing football for Florida or whatever and we'll be coming to watch you and everything'll be just fine. But we've got to get from here to there, from A to B. And we will. Peacefully, goddamnit."

By the time I got home Mother was gone. I'd forgotten that she had needed me to drive her to the airport. She'd left a note on the door: "You'll have to do without the car. I couldn't find you anywhere. I trust you're okay. I'll speak to you when I get to Washington."

I reached for the telephone to call Lorri-Anne.

TEN

A few weeks after the Leonard Collins test was implemented I walked down the fifty-yard line to the middle of the football field holding Lorri-Anne's hand. We stood beside Clancy and Lee Johnson, who were Homecoming King and Queen, along with other homecoming court members, as flashbulbs snapped throughout the stadium. Our retinue included the school photographer, the *Citrus Sentinel* photographer, Principal Donaldson and Assistant Principal Davidson.

We swiped at gnats and waved and pretended that certain of our swipes were waves as our names were called from the depths of some depthless sea while the grasses of that sea undulated in coral stands and clapped and basked under the white lights of that aquarium. I noticed we seemed to be tipping in an undertow of sorts, but Lorri-Anne held fast to my arm and staid me as our names continued fishtailing over our heads on salty currents of purest static. Suddenly, the band blasted into the Citrus High fight song, right over the last name of the last name called, causing an anemic trumpeter to faint while trying to hit a high C, surely the sharpest fang of that old fight song. None of which mattered, however, for as we walked from that field of legend—and that poor slumped trumpet player dreamed of glistening Cs as clear and bracing as glaciers—Lorri-Anne leaned in close and whispered that she loved me. "Don't worry a thing about it," she said. "I just wanted you to know."

When the game was over the homecoming court gathered for another round of photographs, after which a sports reporter from a nearby television station interviewed Clancy and me. The Citrus High Wildcats were ranked number one in the state in our division. In consideration of the beating we'd given the Jacksonville team earlier in the season, some writers had speculated that we could take any team from any division. Clancy, ordinarily an unbearable card on such occasions, became inexplicably serious in front of the camera, behaving as if he were being deposed. Once back in the locker room I couldn't resist teasing him about this, which provoked from him an obscene harangue about the many girls he would be having that night, an entirely too familiar response of his.

"You know what your problem is, Clance?"

"My dick's too big?"

"Ah, no. Your problem is you're going to end up being a prude."

"A what?"

"A prude. You'll keep talking shit and one day you'll wind up in a church service and see the light and go on to make everybody completely miserable."

"Not tonight I won't." Clancy laughed and performed a series of lewd gesticulations, which provoked a general uproar from our teammates. Of course, that wasn't the end of it. I remained to be dealt with. "You're a weird motherfucker, Roy," Clancy allowed. "I've always said it. Know what *I* hope? I hope *you* don't end up a *serial killer.* That's what I hope *you* don't end up."

I emerged from the locker room in khakis and a T-shirt, holding a gym bag containing a starched button-down, a blazer and a tie for later that night. All tresses and juicy jitters, Lorri-Anne wore a bright red dress of fancy frills. A flouncy coquettish curl flipped and flopped on her forehead while she waited on one foot and then the other in the parking lot with April and Mother and Leonard, who were sharing conspiratorial smiles. I approached with exuberant caution.

"What's so funny?"

April handed me the keys to the Mustang. "She's yours tonight," she said.

Mother pretended to be floored. It was clear she was attempting to rebound from her crusade against April with a ferocious show of solidarity. She insisted that I thank April repeatedly, as if April had never before let me drive her car. In fact, I'd driven the Mustang often, though this was to be my first date in it. Since I could never bring myself to neck or nibble in April's car, I'd always refused it, opting for Mother's Volvo station wagon or Leonard's pickup instead, both of which, regarding the making of romance, were much more convenient anyway.

"Is that what you're wearing?" Mother wanted to know.

"Oh, no, ma'am." I held up my gym bag. "I'm going to change later. We're going to Sonic."

"Well, drive safe," Mother said.

"Roy's all grown up," April said.

"Before we knew it," Mother replied.

"Oh, please," Leonard told them.

Lorri-Anne and I drove to Sonic, then I dropped her off at the gymnasium before heading out to Sterns's place. I'd promised Clancy I'd procure alcohol, and Sterns wouldn't give me any if Lorri-Anne came along.

"Breaker one-nine for the Bull Shipper. . . ." I listened to the voices that droned in slightly threatening tones in the crackling distance. "Breaker one-nine for the Bull Shipper. Bull Shipper?"

When I walked in, Sterns was finishing a beer.

"I tried to get you on the C.B."

"How exciting." Sterns crushed the can and laughed. "Fucking homecoming and you're on a C.B. Shit. You're a goober, Roy. Breaker on *that*."

"I thought you kept it on during weekends."

"Nope. I'm incommunicado at present. By the way, I saw that picture of your girl in the paper. Put together rather nicely. Little Miss Lorri-

Anne Harris." Sterns motioned for me to follow him into one of the back rooms where his liquor was stored. "You certainly don't deserve her, but I guess maybe even the very worst sort of people get lucky now and again."

"Especially the very worst sort of people," I told him.

He retrieved a pint of Jim Beam from a filing cabinet. There were books everywhere. He had even more books than Mother, although most of the ones I saw were paperbacks with food-stained, dog-eared pages. Even in back I could hear the gurgling live wells, a peaceful sound that put me in mind of magical bass boats filled with velvety feathery pillows, which since childhood had floated me from secluded lakes to secret swampy glades to safe sleep—when I wasn't killing off my father, that is.

"I remember when Leonard was Homecoming King. I was thinking about that today. Your mama made the court, too. She was queen and Leonard was king. Imagine that. I used to have a little crush on your mama. We sorta got along because we both read so much. I daresay I read more than she did, though. 'Course when you're fat, you got a lot of free time. I guess I had an advantage. Now you be careful with this," he said, handing me the pint. "How are you getting home from the dance, anyhow?"

"Lorri-Anne's going to drive me."

"Better be," he said. "By the way, Leonard came by before the game. He's awfully proud of you."

"I know."

"He really loves you, Roy."

"I love him, too. What's wrong?"

"What's wrong?" Sterns scratched his head. "Oh, I got it. Anybody ever tell you you're a son-of-a-bitch?"

"Yeah, you did."

"I did?"

"Yeah. A couple of times," I said. "A couple of times a week."

"Good." Sterns bit off a sliver of fingernail and wiped it on his pants.

He appeared even greasier than usual. Oily black swaths of hair drooped in exhaustion across his forehead. "I ever tell you you were ugly?"

"Yeah. You did that, too."

"Oh, okay. Guess that about covers it."

"What is it, Sterns?"

"Aw, hell. I just been reminiscing is all," he said. "Thinking about the old times. These are *your* old times, you know that?"

"I get that feeling."

"Well, they are. So enjoy them. Oh, by the way, I got a little something for you." He handed me an envelope. "Don't open it now. Open it later tonight after you're good and snockered."

"Is this one of those little love notes you write for April?"

"You're in a pretty elite club now."

"Is it something from the book?"

"No, no. This here's one of my orphans. Sometimes I write these sentences that don't have homes. They don't fit in the book but I like 'em. A lot of times I like 'em better than the sentences that go in the book. Hell, I got a drawer full of 'em upstairs. I saw this one and said, shit, this little fella ought to go to the dance with Roy." He nodded and arched his brows lewdly. "And wherever else you're going tonight."

"It's not dirty, is it?"

"Just get drunk and read the damned thing." Sterns extended his hand, and we shook. "I don't care what nobody tells me—you're a pretty good kid, Roy. And trust me, everything's gonna be fine. Everything passes, even trouble. I think you're on your way. The worst is already behind you."

I DECIDED I'D STOP by the trailer before going to the dance. After what Sterns had said I wanted to tell Leonard I appreciated the time he'd spent teaching me to play football. I'd told him many times before, of course, but this night was special, and he was a large part of why it was special.

The Mustang coasted heavily beneath a sky of friendly stars, the long silvery blue hood catching the road and devouring it. I checked the glove box and found April's cherry-flavored Chap Stick. I popped the cap and put some on. She had a fat package of bubble gum in there, too, and I took a piece. Her alligator hair clip lay beside a tube of lipstick, which I also lovingly inspected.

Racing past my house, the radio blaring, I began to feel of my biceps and shoulders. It was a terrible habit I'd taken up in junior high. During exams or lectures, while walking through the woods or reading a book, I'd reach for various muscles, flex them, and poke and prod to determine how they were coming along. As I say, an altogether unappealing habit. Another nasty trade I practiced was chewing my tongue. In combination, the muscle squeezing and tongue chewing created an aspect of extreme imbecility, and according to Mother I appeared as if my frontal lobe had been spiked. She especially loathed the muscle squeezing. "You look like you're checking for lice," she'd tell me.

When I pulled up to the trailer I thought I'd lure April and Leonard outside by turning up the radio. A favorite song had just come on, Merle Haggard's "Mama Tried." I shudder even now when I remember that that was the song playing.

Howl ambled over with his tail down. He looked me over and slowly walked away. He seemed ashamed of something. Then I saw the screen door. It lay in the middle of the yard, torn from its hinges. The frame was bent.

I turned the radio off and immediately noticed how quiet it was. The air seemed rinsed and bare. The chickens were gone. As I walked over, my pulse thickened.

"Anyone home?" I called. The front door was open, and I peeked inside.

The trailer had been ransacked. Cheerios littered the kitchen floor. The dinette chairs were upturned. A *Citrus Sentinel* had been torn to pieces and scattered. Leonard sat on the couch with a fifth of whisky wedged between his legs. April stood in the kitchen. When she saw me she looked away. They were oddly discreet, almost bashful.

"Happy Homecoming from the former king and queen," Leonard announced. "I was king my year. And April was queen her year."

"What happened?"

"We're having us a wild party in your honor," Leonard said.

April stared at me. "Leonard's drunk."

"Oh, yeah. That, too. You better run on to the dance, Roycey-Poycey."

"Are you all right?" I asked.

"Sure she's all right."

"I'm fine, Roy," April said.

"See, she's fine. So run along. Ain't you got you that fine piece waiting for you?"

"Leonard, stop it!"

"What, honey? I'm just talking about the poontang. Shit, I mean the Mustang. Y'all excuse me. English is my second language this evening." He took a pull. "Don't you get anything on them seats. April's real proud of that car. She never would let me get any in it and you ought not to be able to, neither."

"That's it," April said.

"'Course, that's just my opinion," Leonard continued.

"I'm leaving," April said.

"No, honey. Roy's already got him a date tonight. Y'all can't go out swimming every night."

"Stop it right now!" April insisted.

"Just calm the hell down. I'm only having a little fun."

"Are you all right?" I repeated.

Leonard's head jerked over. His eyes drifted past me before he brought them into focus. "I don't need you butting in here like you're gonna save the day, partner. I'll fix you up just like I did your daddy. You ain't nothing but his little look-alike anyhow. A little Sanders Collier."

"That's it! I warned you!" April shouted.

Leonard was still staring at me. "Get your perverted ass out of my fucking house. Trailer. Whatever the fuck I live in, get the fuck out of it."

"Come on, Roy," April said. "I'll walk you out. You need to get to the dance."

"He can walk his own ass out."

Leonard bobbed up and down on the couch a few times before gaining his feet. This embarrassed him. When April tried to walk past, he blocked her.

"Move," she said.

"You're staying here. I'm not having any more of this running off to talk with Roy."

"Move, Leonard. I mean it."

She tried to push him aside, but he shoved her back. It happened without warning and seemed to have surprised him. He was quick about it and forceful enough to knock her over the coffee table. She tumbled into a pile of *Bassmaster* magazines. Leonard cried out her name, but I was already on him.

"If you ever touch her again I'll kill you."

He flung me into the couch without even thinking about it. "I'm gonna finish you right now," he told me.

"Stop it!" April was standing, holding her mouth. "Stop it! I'm all right!"

When I saw the blood between her fingers . . . well, when I saw the blood between her fingers, that was that. I didn't think anything, taste anything, smell anything, hear anything or feel anything. There was no poignant prelude, no piquant epiphany, no amplified voice directing me like a puppet with electrified strings of rage. I saw April holding her mouth. I saw blood. I hit Leonard's jaw as hard as I could. I may have been screaming. I simply don't know. I only know I hit him. I can still feel it, in my gut first, then in my heart, then my chest, then my hand, and truthfully my head never caught up with those hard-charging valiants. For his part, Leonard groaned and stumbled back. I swung again, grazing his shoulder, after which he had me by the T-shirt.

Things speeded up at that point. I felt my feet leave the floor, felt the fabric of my shirt giving and tearing away. A low growl seemed to push me backward, and I was aware of my awkwardness and the ungrounded pounding of my flying heart. I heard something shatter and was pierced by a sharp, molten pain along my back. April shouted from a distance. *Voices of war in a funneling wartex. Laden cornucopias for ears. A landing pad of noisy blades of grass and glass. Shot down.* Leonard had thrown me through the window.

But then I was on my feet. By the time Leonard made it out of the trailer I was already coming for him. My pulse was stabbing, unquenchable, drowning everything but the need to get to Leonard, who seemed to move toward me in a tilting, implacable surge, a tree falling. Everything was clear and imminent, and I maneuvered in a rush of certainty: I was to hit and keep hitting and that was all.

April pounced on Leonard's back, but he sloughed her off and rumbled on. I threw my fist at him again—my hand seemed disconnected from my arm, like a numb, throbbing, expendable clump—and tagged him in the stomach. He bent over and vomited, but suddenly he was right back up and had landed a drunken blow that doubled me over. April shoved him so hard his head snapped back. I managed an uppercut through clenched teeth that made my fist roar. He cursed and reached for me and April reached for him, spinning, tragic dunces, groaning and shouting and jabbing. I tried to kick Leonard but slipped from my own momentum. When I got to my feet April stood between us.

"Stop it! Stop it right now!" she cried. She pushed Leonard again. "Stop it, do you hear?"

"I hear," he said. "I'm stopped." He dropped his head and looked around as if attempting to locate the ground, then stepped back, wiping his mouth.

"You've never laid a hand on me, Leonard," April said. "Never."

"I just wanted—"

"No matter how bad it got. I've always admired you more than anyone in the world. But you . . ."

Leonard's massive frame convulsed. He sounded like an engine that wouldn't turn over. He stood with his hands covering his face, then he turned and wandered around toward the back of the trailer where we could still hear him.

"Are you all right, Roy?" April's voice was still hard.

"I'd just like to go on to the dance," I said. I could feel the blood seeping through my shirt. I faced April to keep her from noticing, backing further into the darkness toward the Mustang. "It's getting late and they're waiting on me. Lorri-Anne'll be worried."

"You might have been cut. You probably were. Come here."

"Damnit, I'm fine. I just want to go to the Homecoming dance like everyone else. Why can't I do that? It's my last Homecoming. Why can't things be normal? I just want to be left alone. Is that too much to ask?"

April stopped walking toward me then. After what I'd said, there was no way for her to come one inch closer. I could still hear Leonard crying and knew I was soon to cry myself. I wanted to put my arms around April, to throw myself at her feet and bathe her toes with my tears and her ankles with kisses and offer her my exploded heart. I got into the car.

"Roy," April said. "I'm so sorry. I'm . . ." She started to say something more, then shook her head.

"I'll be all right," I told her.

She took a step back and then turned to go inside.

After putting the Mustang in reverse, where my world was, I saw a fragment of Leonard standing in the rearview mirror, waiting for me. He was drying his eyes slowly, twisting his fists against his sockets like a ruined child. "Roy," he called. He walked toward me, pressing his fingers to his cheek. Then he reached into his mouth to jiggle a tooth loose. It was a plump tobacco-stained molar. Slick with saliva and blood, it looked like something malignant just birthed from his mouth.

"Take it, Royce," he said, pitching the tooth at me. "You and your daddy and mama have taken just about everything else."

. . .

I HEADED OUTSIDE of town to Pete's truck stop to see how badly I'd been cut. Once inside the rest room I removed my torn T-shirt and ran cold water over it. I twisted around so I could see my back in the mirror. There were a few deep gashes, and I used the T-shirt to sop up blood. I needed stitches. I gripped the edge of the sink and leaned toward the mirror, staring at myself. I felt as though I would cry and became outraged. "She's not supposed to take care of you!" I shouted. "She's supposed to take care of Leonard, you son-of-a-bitch!"

My heart continued to surge recklessly. Awash in adrenalin, I kicked a metal trash can over and began stomping it. I stomped its lid and sides and the things that spilled out of it: an old purse, candy wrappers, a curling iron. I began to cry then and stared into the mirror again. I believed the fight was my fault and was fearful of what would happen if Mother found out, but I did not know what to do about it. I felt a nauseating sense of panic and self-loathing and had an overwhelming desire to hit myself, to make a fist and actually strike myself in the face. I might very well have done so had it not been for the bourbon. At that moment I glanced down and saw it in my gym bag.

I'd seen it done in those Westerns Leonard and I watched together. Bullet holes, arrow piercings, knife gouges and hatchet gorges were all doused with strong drink, followed by the obligatory wrenching of the face, the manly muffled howl and sometimes the optional eye-rolling loss of consciousness. It stood to reason that Jim Beam could easily handle the careless work of a trailer window. The blood had been nearly stanched anyway, and when I dabbed bourbon on the lacerations they tightened even further. After which this came to mind: How much better to apply the bourbon both ways, internally as well as externally. Given that my pain was dualistic, it seemed an excellent idea.

I'd never been able to drink any kind of hard liquor straight before, but that night it went down smoothly. After several swallows I decided I should get to the dance at once. I had initially wanted to get to the dance to prevent Lorri-Anne from sending out a search party to find me, something that would have involved Mother. Furthermore, finishing off the night as if nothing had happened was simply mandatory, dictated by many quiet and resilient codes of manhood. But after a few more pulls it was beginning to seem that I should get to the dance so that I might actually be *dancing.*

There is a peculiar hallucinatory glaze that nicely coats the consciousness of someone who has been in a fight and survived it and realized that the damage was not so bad, considering. What's more, when a generous layer of alcohol is applied to that glaze, beading it like raindrops, a person can suddenly become downright invincible. And, of course, people who feel invincible are precisely the sort to demand a dance floor and a large crowd.

After changing clothes I walked out to find old man Coggins staring at me.

"They tell me you did all right tonight, Roy."

"Yes, sir. I ran hell out of it."

Coggins was a stump of a man, well into his eighties, who liked to pass his hours at the truck stop drinking coffee and meeting up with truckers from all over the country. It was rumored that he inhabited a shack out by Lake Julep and owned a blunderbuss, which he used to fetch supper, though I'd never seen him anywhere near the lake.

He leaned in and took a whiff of my breath. "You drunk?"

"No, sir."

"What were you doing in the ladies' room?"

I turned around. "There's a curling iron in there."

"You'd better let me drive. I'm heading back to town anyway and I was gonna have to walk. I'm goddamned tired of walking. Seems like I walked right up out of my mama's belly and was just made to keep on doing it."

Coggins cranked the Mustang with the pedal all the way to the floorboard. The alarmed beast fired to life instantly, but Coggins continued to rev the engine anyway as if he were trying to start a stampede, which of course loosened one of the perennially loose fan belts.

"Belt's loose," Coggins informed me, barely audible over the shrieking. This struck me as about the funniest thing I'd ever heard. Coggins let off the gas. "Hell, boy, you lit up like a Christmas tree, ain't ya? Got any more?"

"No, sir," I said. I did *not* have any more, in point of fact. Most of the rest belonged to Clancy.

Once on the highway Coggins selected the choice middle lane visible only to drunks and the elderly. After a short while he did not seem to care for this special lane, however. He began speeding up as if to pass someone, though there wasn't another car in sight. I could not stop laughing. "You had you some rocket fuel." He braked suddenly for no reason and then sped off again. "Some of that pistane."

"Some of that what?"

"Pistane."

"Pistane?"

"Yeah. You had it. You got all the signs."

Whatever pistane was, I began to sneak quick pulls from the more recognizable Jim Beam, turning to the side of the road and ducking into my blazer. Presently, Coggins resembled a corpse with Coggins's head attached to it and very fast hands. "I evermore hate walking," he reminded me, reaching into the glove box. He came out with April's lipstick. "Oh, I'd kiss her right upside her mouth," he bellowed. He unscrewed the top. "Get her naked. Oh, my, you'd see me walking for that."

I snatched the lipstick from him. "That's enough."

Coggins was chuckling and hitting the brakes and the laughing gas. "Kiss it! Kiss it! Kiss it good!" he croaked. It seems I was dabbling with the lipstick.

When we got to Citrus High he parked and gave me the keys and walked away without saying a word. I suspected he may have possibly disappeared. I was considering this when Clancy approached and demanded the bottle.

"Aw, shit, Roy. You already drank most of it. And I told you to get vodka or gin, not this shit!" He stared at me in disgust. "Oh, fuck. What the fuck's the matter with your mouth?"

I NEVER MADE IT to the dance floor. One look at me and my lips convinced Lorri-Anne that I must be evacuated from the premises before I encountered an adult. She decided that we should walk to her house immediately, something that required no small amount of vigilence on her part as the sidewalk kept trying to reach up and slap me in the face.

But those squares were only being playful. The fight of that night was long gone by now. It seemed there would be no more ruminations or rude hurts and heartbeats. Nor would there be endless revisitations from the hedious bare-knuckled ogre that had presided over that brawl. He'd been banished for the moment, and I was simply wonderfully wounded and walking alongside my best girl drunk to the kneecaps. To say nothing of the fact that Miss Harris was mewling over me with each stride. I had been, I kept telling her, a very bad boy.

"I don't even want to know what you've been up to tonight," she said.

"I was with old man Coggins."

"See, I don't want to know."

When we got to her house she told her mother and father just what she knew: that we were both sorry, but that someone had somehow gotten his hands on some alcohol and had had too much of it and that this same person, whom she would not name, had already been tired from the game and might that poor rascally fellow be housed in the spare bedroom for the night? I was sitting on the couch, nodding in perfect agreement.

The Harrises were somewhat amused. Moreover, Lorri-Anne's forthrightness, and my willingness to comply with her forthrightness, struck them as a show of responsibility that should be rewarded. They wondered, in unison, if I would like to remove my blazer. I shook my head, probably too vigorously, and thought of the clots of blood that had been leaking from time to time. Mr. Harris said okay and eased me to the kitchen for a glass of sweet tea, while Mrs. Harris prepared my bed with extra quilts. I was instructed to call Mother. Mr. Harris left to afford me some privacy.

"Mother?"

"Roy? Where are you?"

"Have you heard?"

"Heard what?"

"*I'm drunk!*"

"Oh, god, Roy. Drunk where, at the dance?"

"No, ma'am. Lorri-Anne took me home. I'm at her house. I'm very sorry to be drunken at the moment."

"I'm sure you are. At least you're safe."

"Oh, yes, safe. Very safe. Yes, ma'am."

"All right. Well, good for Lorri-Anne. She's a smart girl. I'll come get you."

"No, ma'am. The Harrises have invited me to—" I hiccuped and started over. "The Harris's have—" And hiccuped again.

"I've got it. Here, let me talk to Elizabeth."

I called for Lorri-Anne's mother, who picked up the telephone in the living room. Lorri-Anne came into the kitchen a few minutes later and made me a pimento cheese sandwich and then another. I chewed like a famished zombie with a new set of false teeth and made *mmm-mmm* noises. My eyes closed. I suddenly saw a shy trail of limping hopkins: there on the trailer floor, burning like embers, were slices of my daily bread, red, blue, green, yellow, orange, jigsaw pieces of newsprint that together made a headline, then a spent Cheerio and a pallet of twinkling shards. . . .

Lorri-Anne stood in front of me, tapping her foot. "I wish I could convince myself you've been smooching on some girl or something like that. Something normal."

"No way."

"Of course not. Why was I not surprised to see you show up wearing lipstick?"

"Come here and I'll show you."

"In a minute."

"Come here."

"In a minute. You're already in trouble, buddy."

I beat my chest as those innocent cavemen who painted lovely murals on their dining-room walls have been accused of doing. The labrador puppy, Grover, now fully grown, pawed at the back door and begged admittance to the petting zoo. A downstairs television was gagged and put to sleep. Lights were snuffed. The front door locked. Unlocked. Reading glasses. Retrieved. Locked. Unlocked! Mrs. Harris's book. *Anything else,* we all wondered. No. Locked. Granddaddy and Grandmama will be here for dinner tomorrow. Leaking again. Roy is invited. Leonard with masking tape and cardboard and perhaps a pot of coffee. Do NOT take off your blazer. April angry, crying, angry, crying, alone, behind a castle wall, a burning moat. . . . Don't forget to turn out the cozy kitchen lights. Do take off Lorri-Anne's . . . An extra toothbrush has been provided. You're always welcome here. Get some sleep.

All of this taking place just behind my head in a wide, flattened world of technicolor sound.

And then those helpful Harrises went to bed, after which Lorri-Anne and I crept to the guest bedroom, which blissfully awaited us on the other side of the house, silly miles away from the upstairs master suite.

I was tucked in and promised a bedtime story, but the next thing I knew I'd willed my cramped fighting hand to the waist of Lorri-Anne's flannel pajama bottoms (whenever had she changed clothes?), yanked them down with my more capable non-fighting hand (how pleased it was to finally be called into a game as the starter), swooned to discover that Miss Harris had worn not a thing under those red bottoms with their funny little antique two buttoned hatch (the devil was certainly in *that* loving detail) and upon catching my boozy grateful breath promptly fell asleep just as my first ever I-love-you wobbled from my telltale lips toward Lorri-Anne's tender, patient ears.

Good night at last.

ELEVEN

But not good riddance. A night as eventful as that was bound to have far-reaching consequences. Come morning, for instance, with the Harrises conveniently gone to town, I awakened indecently hungover, riddled with cranky aches and pains and indiscreetly ravenous for Lorri-Anne's companionship. The first thing that entered my mind, of course, was the fight, and next I worried about its aftermath. But those were not the only things on my mind that morning, itself something of a triumph.

Having secured Lorri-Anne's attention—she peeked in the door and wagged her finger as if I were that often bad hound, Grover—I anticipated a resounding cure for my dissipation. But as soon as she saw my back we began an all-out struggle over whether or not I should go to the hospital.

"I can't," I insisted, and pressed further with an important distinction: "And *won't*."

"At least tell me what happened," she said, pulling her pajama bottoms back up and causing me to hiss.

"I don't know. I don't want to talk about it. Come here."

"No. Did it have to do with the lipstick?"

I'd forgotten about that. "No. No, that was Coggins."

"Old man Coggins put lipstick on you?"

"No, he drove me to the dance and kept hitting the brakes and speeding up and—"

"Never mind. What about your back?"

"I don't know. Will you come here?"

"No, I won't. And what do you mean you don't know? Look at how swollen your hand is. And you don't *know?* You were wearing lipstick. Your back is cut to ribbons. Do you even remember what you said to me last night?"

"Of course I do."

"What did it mean?"

"What do you mean what did it mean? It meant what I said."

"That's not what I'm talking about. I'm talking about before you said that. *That* was sweet. I'm talking about before that."

I looked at her blankly. I thought I'd passed out after "I love you," but now a bit of not passing out came to mind. I cringed and turned away. "I don't remember," I lied.

"You said the trailer attacked you, Roy. You said April told you to never step foot on her property again. You started crying, do you remember that?"

"No."

"You said there was a property line now and you weren't allowed to cross it. I've never heard anybody cry so hard in my life. I was worried sick about you. Then you begged me to sneak out and take you to the trailer. Does any of this ring a bell? You really upset me. You just kept crying and crying. And you woke Mama and Daddy up."

"Shit. What did they do?"

"I went to tell them you were upset because you were drunk and that everything was okay. By the time I got back down here all of a sudden you were mister lovey-dovey again. You were out of your mind, Roy. What happened?"

"Something went wrong."

"No *duh.*" Lorri-Anne winced and batted her impassioned eyes. "Oh, and what is this may I ask?" She reached over to her desk.

"Where'd you get that?"

"In your back pocket." She held the envelope just out of reach. "Where'd you get it?"

"From Sterns. Did you read it?"

"Yes. And it's just *par for the course,* considering."

She handed me the wrinkled envelope, and I took out the single sheet of paper. There was one typed line: "Every fancy word stands."

"What the hell is that supposed to mean?" Lorri-Anne demanded.

There really wasn't much of a need to go the hospital at that point. My back should have been stitched right away, but as the blood had already clotted I would have to live with a set of thick ugly scars instead of a set of thin ugly scars. Miraculously, I hadn't broken a finger, though one was jammed. A common splint would make me fit for football practice. Eventually Lorri-Anne relented in regard to the hospital on the condition that I at some point tell her what had happened. I consented and was led to her upstairs bathroom.

To a young man like myself who had never had any sisters, Lorri-Anne's bathroom was a mysterious sanctuary, especially on the morning in question. Mother and April were both rather utilitarian about beauty aids; consequently, their bathrooms never resonated for me the way Lorri-Anne's did. While Mother and April had nice perfumes and expensive French creams and wrinkle reducers, they were not great collectors of cosmetics otherwise. They had what they needed and nothing more. Lorri-Anne, on the other hand, had whole shelves of brightly colored vials and scents and sparkly things and all manner of potions. Mother's shower curtain? A respectable taupe. April's? A shade of forest green. Lorri-Anne's? A twilight canvas featuring a mauve winking moon hovering over a watery world of pastel rowboats loaded down with whiskery singing cats that crooned on their hind legs while open hymnals rested across their upturned forepaws.

And, of course, starry Lorri-Anne's mirror was fitted out with enough of those little round lights to please even a veteran actress. Miss Harris had, I swear, at least a million combs and brushes. Here was a teen-tinted wonderland where Lorri-Anne routinely pranced about in the nude on the white tile floor while anointing and beautifying herself.

Visions of her like that became very prominent in my mind as she dexterously nursed and doctored. She found some large bandages that made her eyes go wide and mouth say "perfect." I sat on the edge of the tub quietly, knowing full well that I was as far away from what had happened the night before and whatever might happen because of it as I was going to get. I tried to be very good, to make those moments last. At some point I told Lorri-Anne a little secret, and shortly she had been convinced that I needed an altogether different form of treatment. Those same pajama bottoms were slain for the third time in twenty-four hours. But no sooner had one of her lithe legs been swung up to the sink sweetly than the downstairs door opened and in marched those inconvenient Harrises with groceries.

One last thing happened before we bolted from that bathroom and I had to face April and Leonard and Mother and the fallout from the fight. It might just be true, for all I know or care, that old line about how every man puts his pants on the same way in the morning. But on that particular morning I was not in a man's world, and I saw that a woman has more than one way of putting her pants on. I had thought Lorri-Anne would dress as madly as a dervish once the Harrises opened the door, but instead she turned her back to me and bent over and reached for the little flannel pile rather—*rather!*—carelessly. Then with a sharply pointed nonchalance she pulled her pajama bottoms up in a kind of slow-motion shimmy. "That's just what you get for keeping secrets," she huffed, and shut the door.

MOTHER HAD TO GO TO Washington that next week and apparently knew nothing of what had happened between me and Leonard and April. I explained that I'd injured my finger in the game, a most plausible evasion. Mother had a look. “You’re a mess,” she said contentedly. I suppose the truth of the matter was, she found the news that I had become drunk with friends of my own age at a homecoming dance and spent the night at my girlfriend’s house to be the very picture of healthy youth. The entire episode actually relieved her.

Once Mother left, April dropped by, hugging me so tightly I could not keep from whimpering.

Her eyes widened immediately. “Turn around!”

I tried to get hold of her arms, but she slipped free and said, “Damnit,” and pushed me onto the bed. I’d earlier gathered myself and my worries and complaints onto a billowy cloud of Mother’s exotic fabrics—Irish linen and sateen cottons—and from a certain perspective the entire scene that followed possessed a Turkish flavor with April playing the sultan and I the helpless but willing slave. She was certainly very bossy that afternoon, and a tightly packed coil of submissiveness sprang loose somewhere inside me and left me boinging.

“Take off your shirt!”

“Really, April, I’m a little surprised at you.”

“Don’t be smart! Get it off now!”

“Just give me a minute. I hadn’t expected this.”

“If you don’t get your shirt off you can expect my fist upside your head.”

I complied. April had a look and let out a yelp. “Oh, Roy! Why didn’t you tell me? Turn over and lie down. Why didn’t you say something? *Turn over, I said!*” She peeled away the bandages. “I’m so angry with you. You should have let me take you to a hospital.”

She was caressing the spaces between the cuts, moaning in horrible pain over what was now for me titillating pain, whispering in husky agony, while I, of course, was bursting with ecstasy. It was a pity I hadn’t thought of getting myself thrown through a window long ago.

“You should have told me. *Leonard!* Wait ’til I tell him. Wait ’til I *show* him!”

She lay down beside me. Propped on her elbow, she began weaving my hair through her fingers.

"You know what he told me? He said he made sure he didn't hit you in the face. He actually said that."

"I guess he didn't."

"Oh, thank you so much, Leonard Collins! How considerate of you!"

"Is he hurt?"

"Yeah. You got him pretty good. His mouth's all swollen up. He talks funny." She was tracing the curve of my ear. She stopped. "We've got to tell June."

I turned on my side to face her. "I'm fine. It's not that big a deal."

"She has a right to know."

"About a few *scratches?* About *one bad night?* If she finds out it'll ruin the whole rest of my senior year. Is that what you want?"

"She's your mother."

"I know. And if it were serious I'd tell her. But it's not serious. I won't even miss a game. Come on."

"She'll find out one way or another."

"No she won't. April, please. It's my decision. You can't tell her. *Please.* Promise me. There's no telling what would happen if she found out. And *I'll* be the one to suffer. You've got to promise me."

"All right."

"Swear it."

"All right," she said.

I PLANNED TO SKIP school for the better part of that week and called Coach Taylor to tell him I thought I should take a day or two off from practice as well. I had no illusions it would be as simple as that, and sure enough Coach Taylor arrived at the house a few minutes after I called him that Monday morning. He had a look at my finger, which didn't impress him, but I added that I had succumbed to dysentery—an ailment for which there could be no examination—and that I needed to ward off dehydration. This did the trick. I was granted one day's reprieve.

I also gave Lorri-Anne a pre-school morning phone call. I informed her that she would be sainted if she could bring me a snack or at any rate something delicious. We had in the past occasionally absented ourselves from a class or two for nourishment. Loving on the lam, one might say, though "playing hooky for nooky" is how Clancy once memorably described such excursions. In my hour of pain and need I had little doubt Lorri-Anne would be given a pass in order to assist me.

"It's Monday. They're serving country-fried steak, so bring me two plates." The women of Citrus High's cafeteria deserved an immortal sonnet for some of the best home cooking in the world and for always giving me mountains for portions. "And extra collard greens and macaroni and cheese."

"All right."

"And some peanut butter wedges. Noreen gives me extra."

"Oh, everybody gives you extra everything, don't they?"

"Roy hopes so."

"Do *not* refer to yourself in the third person."

Next on my agenda was Leonard. I had been told he was to quit drinking for a while, but when I walked over to the trailer that afternoon he was sitting on the deck with a High Life and did not seem especially repentant. I walked right up to him, stopping just before our knees touched.

"Cut it out," he said.

"What's wrong with your mouth?"

"I guess I deserve this."

"Where's April?"

"Gone to town. Would you *please* back off."

I took a step back. "You forgot the rule," I said.

"I reckon I did. And I reckon I'm more sorry about it than you could ever imagine."

I handed him his tooth. "I found this in the glove box. I must have put it there."

"Finders keepers. They're making me a new one."

"I don't want it."

He threw it into the yard. "Maybe it'll choke one of them damned chickens." He stood slowly and groaned and felt of his stomach. "Shit fire I wished I hadn't gotten you so big. I'm damn near crippled up. Come on. I'm supposed to apologize to you and I'd rather do it in private."

When we arrived at the dock Leonard sat down with his feet hanging over the edge. I sat beside him. The sky was bright and clear, still holding out against the coming cold weather. As was often the case when I skipped school, everything appeared slightly unreal and forbidden, as if the world, knowing that I did not belong, had simply stopped moving as soon as I walked up. I couldn't conceive of catching anything, for instance. Though the temperature was in the high seventies and the lake's surface was taut and glassy, I imagined that all the bass were in rebellion and that the more pliable and understanding bream, which could ordinarily be enticed with nothing more than a small ball of white bread, had formed a conspiracy to resist truant fishermen. Even the cypresses turned away from me.

Leonard sat in silence, digging into his tobacco pouch. When he finished he handed me the pouch and placed his hands on his knees. We spat, eventually. Then he grunted to get things under way.

"Your mama know anything yet?"

"No, sir."

"Well, she will."

"She thinks I was hurt in the game."

"She'll figure it out. You watch. Shit. You just wait."

"I don't think she will," I said. "I didn't go to a doctor. How could she know?"

"She just will." He grimaced and shook his head. "There's no point in telling you how sorry I am about what happened. I never thought I'd end up like this. Never."

He stopped swinging his legs and held them out straight to stare at his boots. He wore blue jeans, a plaid shirt, the sleeves of which had been cut off at the shoulders, and a sleeveless hunting jacket. Unshaven, red-eyed, ponderous—but he suddenly seemed childish, his massive legs extended, his boots clicking together, waiting for recess to end or begin. For some reason on this secretive day I saw his wrinkles more clearly and his newest gray hairs and his ill-kempt sideburns and his growing belly. I saw how sad a thing our fight had been. But I also saw just how enormous he was and how easy it had been for him to hoist all two hundred and twenty-five pounds of me through a window.

His legs came back down to dangle. He put his hands into his jacket pockets. "You ever know your daddy proposed to April?"

At first I thought I had not heard him. I waited as if nothing had been said. But he looked right into my eyes, and he kept to my eyes until I broke away.

"I guess not," he said. "He was hot for April from the moment he laid eyes on her in Ligget's that day. It liked to have killed me and then one day your mama tells me that your daddy had come over to the house to call on April. Said that your daddy would *corrupt* April. Said your daddy had one thing on his mind. June always knew how to get people going. When she finished with me, I was ready to tear your daddy's damned head off."

Leonard looked out over the lake. I knew I was about to experience something much worse than our fight. I suppose he knew there was no way to prepare me for it and that we'd best just get it done.

"I think April made your daddy feel like a good person, if you want to know the truth. She didn't *make* him a good person, but she made him *feel* like one. He was just obsessed. Your daddy had a thing about innocence. I believe he was traveling around the country looking for a fairy tale to happen to him." Leonard spat. A bream struck the tobacco juice and swam away. "Damn if they won't hit anything," he said.

"He proposed to her?"

"Oh, yeah. I remember one time I asked him what his intentions were and what the hell was he doing. He wanted to know if April was my girl and I had to tell him that she wasn't. He just smiled and stared right smack at me. Your daddy could get up under your skin. Always acting superior. But he blew it with April. All them sarcastic comments. Always teasing her 'cause she wouldn't drink. Usually the only way he could see her was to be with me and your mama. April was too young to go out on her own. Sometimes your daddy would swing by and pick up April and your mama without me knowing about it. He was running around in Henderson's little Thunderbird. That's another thing that burned me up, 'cause I didn't have no car and he was always asking the girls to go for a ride. Hell, I couldn't compete with that shit. Damned Henderson. Typical politician. Always fucking up somebody's business." He grunted and spat. "I don't know. Henderson's helped me and April out a time or two. He's got his good side. But boy he's nosy. Watch out what you say around him."

"Why did he help my father?"

"Well, he gave him a place to stay and introduced him to people and made it easy for him to get around, is all. Just being neighborly, I reckon. Henderson was pretty well taken in by your father. But damn that little Thunderbird. You know that road out there by the Hilliards' place? Where everybody goes to park. Or used to. Y'all still?"

"Some," I said.

"Some, huh?" He chuckled. "Some. All right, well, one afternoon your daddy took April out there. He waited till June wasn't around and scooted over to y'all's house and told April it was an emergency and that he had to talk to her privately. Once he got her out there he told her he loved her and that she was old enough to love him back and that love didn't have to have a certain age. Shit like that. He tried to work up a spell on her. And the next thing he tries to kiss her. But he went about it wrong. 'Cause he did the one thing that was guaranteed to piss April off."

Leonard cleared his throat.

"I learned all of this on our honeymoon, by the way. Oh, yeah. How's that for a honeymoon, partner? We drove down to Panama City. She'd already damaged me pretty badly at that point, and I told her she ought to go ahead and tell me everything I didn't know so I wouldn't have to wonder or have somebody like your daddy hold it over my head. And she told me. April is not a good liar. I'm telling you, if your mama was to ask her about what happened between you and me, she'd tell her. Or she wouldn't say anything at all. But she wouldn't lie."

"She promised me she wouldn't tell Mother."

"Then she won't." Leonard nodded. "Anyhow. The second time I asked her to marry me, I kept asking her if she was in love with me, and she just kept saying how much she loved me. She never would say she was *in* love." He held up two fingers. "That's right. I asked her twice." Then he held up three fingers, smiling. "So she's been asked three times that I know of. That ain't too shabby, is it?"

I shook my head. He quit smiling.

"Anyhow, she told me about your daddy. She'd never even thought of being scared of a man before. But your daddy scared her. He provided new experiences for just about all of us, I reckon. April said he wanted to know why they couldn't just kiss. She told him that he was too old. Then she told him that they weren't even going steady, and that made him laugh."

Leonard clucked his tongue.

"That laugh was it. That was his big mistake. Because if there's one thing April will not stand for, it's somebody mocking somebody. June had already made her sick of that kind of thing. It was a sore spot for April. Your daddy had no way of knowing, but he was behaving in the one way that was sure to make April hate his guts. She said his eyeteeth looked like he was the devil. You don't have them eyeteeth he had. Be glad of it."

Leonard took a deep breath, and I waited for him to continue. He was staring across the lake still. I began to feel the sting of sweat beneath my bandages.

"You learned all this on your honeymoon?"

"Ain't that some shit? Story of my life. We sat by the pool and I'd get her them piña coladas and put suntan lotion on her and she'd drink 'em and eventually we got it all talked out. We even got around to having sex a few times. Shit. I don't know. It was a weird damned honeymoon. She just never loved me that way. And I reckon the truth is, I shouldn't never have married her."

I had tried to ignore Leonard's earlier comment about April not being able to say she was in love with him, but now that he had brought it back up I began to burn from shame. I couldn't face him.

"That's not true," I said.

"Yeah it is. She was meant for somebody a lot better than me."

"Don't say that."

"I *am* saying it. 'Cause it's the truth. Maybe I could've been what she needed if I hadn't gone off to the war and if I'd played football and gotten an education and then gone to seminary and whatnot. Maybe then we'd have been more evenly matched. But even that don't mean she would have been in love with me. And even if she had been, she was too young. The first time I asked her, mama and daddy told me I might want to wait, but then with me going off it seemed like I couldn't. They weren't about to stand in my way—hell, they'd have done anything for me. But I was wrong to ask her then and I was wrong to ask her when I came back. I *made* her marry me. It kills me, but that's exactly what I did. She felt so guilty about what happened to me after she turned me down—which she had every right to do—that she was determined to make up for it. And I knew it. And I asked her anyway. 'We're going to be like little kids,' she told me one time. 'It doesn't have to be an ordinary marriage.' That's what she told me. She was good to me, Roy. April's always been good to me. God almighty I love her. And what have I done? All these years?"

"She loves you. She said she admired you more than anyone in the world."

"That ain't the same thing and you know it. You know every bit of this down in your gut. And that's why I'd just as soon tell it straight out and be done with it. So you know that I know, too. And that I'm sorry."

"But you shouldn't be. You take care of her."

"Shit, Roy. Please."

"You protected her from my father."

"Yeah. That I did do. For the most part anyway. 'Cept—" He looked into the sky, then brought his head down and wiped his mouth. "Look, I don't want to get into everything, all right? I just want to explain why we got married. 'Course, in a way, protecting her *was* part of why we got married, to get her away from your daddy. He was sure after her, especially after what happened that time he took her out there by the Hilliards' and laughed at her. 'Cause when he finished laughing he tried to get over where she was and she hauled off and cracked the ever-living fuck out of him and said 'take me home now.' And then she kept away from him and that's what made him propose to her. Hell, it wasn't too long after I'd asked her myself."

"And you bought her a ring and everything?"

"Yep. Bought her a ring and everything. My mama and daddy helped me. Your mama tell you some of this?"

"Yes, sir."

"Yeah. That wasn't such a good time for any of us."

"What was it like, going away like that?"

"I just put my mind to becoming a soldier. I thought I'd be a hero and that would change April's mind about me. It was a long way from home. I just wish I could have been here to keep an eye on things, mainly. I don't like talking about the war, though. Not because of the war. The war was all right as wars go. I was only in one, so how would I know? Your daddy said it was going to be bad, and when I got over there I saw he was pretty much right." He put his hands in his pockets and frowned. "I reckon I got into some pretty tight spots a time or two. Truth was when I got hurt I was just glad they were gonna send me back home. They said I was gonna get the Purple Heart and all, but I just wanted to know if that meant I could go home. I didn't really know how bad I'd . . ."

I waited and felt Leonard was becoming lost, and I realized I'd pushed him to a place he hadn't wanted to go. "It's okay," I said.

He rubbed his head. "You ever seen your daddy's medal?"

"When I was little. Mother keeps it locked up."

"Yeah. He never would show it to me. But after I came back I realized how a thing like that can embarrass you sometimes."

"What happened after you came back?" I asked, hoping to draw him away from the injury that had kept him from football and so much else.

"Well, everything had done been decided. April had decided she was going to marry me, and your mama and your daddy was together and you'd just been born. Everything happened while I was gone. But what started the major problems was your daddy was still chasing April around. Everything was sour when I got back. The town had done turned against your daddy. Thank God. This is a good little old town."

"I know."

Leonard chuckled to himself. "I remember hitting your daddy one time before I left for boot camp. I just walked up to him and plastered him. He got up laughing. 'All right,' he said. 'I know why. Just don't do it again.' We even fought once after you'd come along. Tell you what. Your daddy had been in more than a few fights, South Carolina big shot or not. You don't laugh like that unless you've been there a time or two, you know what I mean?"

"I haven't learned that part yet."

He put his arm around my neck. "I ain't, neither, partner. You damn sure learned the first rule of a fight, though."

"What's that?"

"Throw the first punch. But you did what you had to do. I'm proud. I surely deserved it."

"Well . . ."

"Yeah. You heard me."

I blushed and looked away. "So when did my father propose?"

"Just to hear you say that makes me realize what a bunch of damned loonies we all were. We got started young, didn't we? The freak show of Citrus." He smacked his legs. "Damn. Well, to answer your question, he proposed after I was gone. It happened right out back of y'all's house. She said no, of course. He wanted to know why, and she told him it was because she didn't love him and besides that she didn't trust him. And then to try to work up another spell on her he starts to tell her some things about himself that nobody else knew. Or so he claimed. I guess it was to show her he was honest. But she still wouldn't marry him. Shit, she didn't even hardly know him. I mean April and June were both googly-eyed over him for a while 'cause he'd just shown up all mysterious one day, coming from all that money. And he was pretty, I guess. But marry him? Besides which I might point out that they wasn't even dating. What the fuck did he think? I ain't never figured your daddy out. Not even close. On top of everything else, he was a *strange* son-of-a-bitch. Yeah, I guess it's funny now."

"I'm sorry."

"No. It *is* funny. And it helps to laugh about it. Old Sanders. He was just a whole other breed of human being."

"What things did he tell her?"

"I don't exactly know. April never would talk about it, and I really didn't give too much of a shit, to tell the truth. It was some sob story, some sort of angling, I reckon. I imagine he'd have said anything at that point. But after that he avoided her for a while. I reckon he was embarrassed because he'd asked her to marry him. And then the town didn't like him, so that just added insult to injury. So he left. He didn't even say good-bye to nobody. He just took off one day for parts unknown. Damn if it ain't getting hot all of a sudden." Leonard pulled out his handkerchief and dabbed his face. "But your mama went after him. You've got to admire June. She gets what she wants. April told me your mama went straight to South Carolina, and when she comes back, guess who's sitting beside her? And then about two months later she was engaged to him. They said that they'd gotten engaged back in South Carolina but that they didn't want to tell anybody and had agreed to come back to Citrus and do it right, with your daddy asking your granddaddy and everything."

"She got pregnant before going up to South Carolina."

He looked over. "She tell you that?"

"No. But I've done the math. That's why she found him and that's what brought him back."

Leonard reached over and patted my shoulder.

"It doesn't bother me," I said.

"No reason why it should. There's no telling what happened between them. They were both very persuasive people. And another thing—I'm not saying your daddy was actually truly in love with April and that he didn't love your mama. April was just something he wanted, and if getting her meant marrying her, so be it. He was ruthless like that. Your mama, on the other hand, was a match for him. But there again, if it wasn't for you, I'd have to say that her hooking into him was about the worst mistake of her life. Don't get me wrong."

"I understand."

"She would have gone off to college. And that would've meant April would have gone off to college. And that would have meant me and April wouldn't have never gotten married. Of course, there's one bad thing. It would've meant Citrus wouldn't be undefeated this year."

"They got Clancy."

"Clancy ain't enough."

"April loves you."

"Well, maybe if I'd have become a preacher and won her heart somehow." Leonard wiped his face again. He laughed bitterly. "But I never had that chance."

"She loves you," I pleaded.

"Sure. What's not to love?"

The bandages were slipping down my back. The sweat was making the cuts sting terribly now, and I could think of nothing to say to make what Leonard was saying go away.

"Anyhow, when I got back from Vietnam I told April I wanted her to marry me and she said yes and right after that your daddy tried something with her again. He just couldn't help it. I come over to the house and there's your mama, with a brand new baby, and there's your daddy, running around after April. It burnt me up good. So I sold our engagement ring and got us that trailer and moved her in there. I'd kept that engagement ring since the first time I tried to give it to her. After April told me no I went and put it up in our safe. My mama couldn't bear for me to get rid of it. And when I went off to the war I thought about that ring every minute of every day, sitting in that safe by itself. And I knew that I was going to get back home somehow or the other and that ring would be right there waiting for me. But after everything turning out the way it did, I was sick and tired of that ring, to tell you the truth. From a diamond to a double-wide. For fuck's sake. I ought to write me a damned song." He spat mercilessly.

"I like the trailer," I said.

"I reckon so. You've passed most of your life over there."

"Why didn't y'all move into your mama and daddy's house after they died?"

"We should've. But every time I'd look at that old house it reminded me of all my mama and daddy had done for me and I couldn't stand to think of living in it. I wasn't a preacher. I wasn't a football player. And even though I'd married April, she wasn't really in love with me. So I sold it. Gave up church, too. Since I never really wanted to be a drunk, being a drunk didn't remind me of anything from my past. I guess you could say that was one occupation that was available to me. I guess you take what you can get sometimes."

He sighed and stood up and gave me a hand. We had a last look over the lake and then turned toward home.

"I just got away from all the old things," he continued as we headed through the woods. "Bought me a rig, starting trucking a little. Piddled. Listened to Henderson talk about investing our money. Pretended to understand it. Hunted. Shot the shit with Sterns. Made you into a football player. You took up a lot of my time, you know that?"

"Yes, sir. I appreciate it."

He stopped walking suddenly. "We're awful proud of you, Roy. We really are. You just don't know."

"I know."

"And we're both real sorry about what happened."

"It's nothing."

He took my hand and pulled me in for a hug. I hugged him back, and the pain our embrace caused made me feel a little better.

"You all right?"

"Yes, sir."

"Well, if there's anything on your mind, Roy. Anything. Or anything I can do for you. You just let me know, you hear?"

I stepped back, staring at the ground. I was going to ask him about my father's death. It seemed like a good time. But strangely, the next thing I knew, I had posed a question before I'd even really thought about it: "Why didn't you and April ever have children?" I asked.

Leonard narrowed his eyes. Then he looked away.

"It's none of my business," I said.

"No, that's all right."

"It's none of my business."

"I don't mind," he said. "I guess it's like I told you. April said we didn't have to have an ordinary marriage. She always said we could be like children ourselves. You were our child, I reckon." He smiled. "And now I've put you through our goddamned window. It don't never seem to stop, does it?"

He put his hands in his pockets, shrugged and turned away.

TWELVE

Leonard was right, of course—it never seemed to stop. All the dramatic tussles and intrigues. The convolutions and confrontations. The constant zigging and zagging between peace and paranoia. The relentless reverberations from missing facts and well-kept secrets. The ghosts, goblins and lore. The endless stories and the endless stories within those endless stories. With a mere flick of my wrist I could set that glowing globe spinning in Mother's darkened library and the entire world repeated itself to me over and over again.

And one naturally began to wonder, as I did, if every day brings yet another denouement, then what's a denouement good for? If one never seems to reach the end of anything but keeps returning over and over again to the same heart-wrenching struggles by way of the same nerve-rending stratagems, why go on? Why bother? Why not close the book, so to speak? But that was just the point. This was not a book that could be closed or put down.

Looking back, I suppose it was this very sense of circularity, the continuous cycles of false alarms, that prevented me from believing that something truly decisive had occurred, or from seeing, as Leonard and April so clearly saw, that real trouble had been set in motion the night I'd flown through the window of the trailer. I suppose I was simply purblind from all the activity. No doubt I believed that something minor might happen, but not anything that would significantly change our circumstances. I'd lived in fear of exactly such a turn of events for so many years, yet after the fight and Leonard's talk, it seemed as though all of the possibilities had been exhausted. I was at last confident everything was behind us. I could not be shipped off to boarding school, for instance. It was too late for that. And that was the main thing—it was just too late for *anything* drastic to happen.

It was already the middle of December. Citrus High had won the state championship for the second year in a row, and I'd come within a hundred yards of Leonard's rushing record. Yet all I could think of was the somber truth that I'd just finished my last season of football in Citrus.

With no more practices or games, I began to run every afternoon before dark. My runs, always circuitous affairs anyway, had now become mazes of indecision. The town was dressed out with lights and bows and Christmas greetings, and I rushed down one smoky street after another, trying to take in all of it before it was too late. I'd stall on twinkling corners, wanting to be on more than one road. Leaves were falling everywhere, and I'd chase after them. Doors seemed to always be slamming shut. I'd circle the square and find it wasn't enough, and so I'd have to go around once again. Slowing to a jog as I came up Main, I'd stare at the Confederate monument, the courthouse, the nativity scene and gentle Jesus; but no matter how carefully I watched, and no matter how many times I covered that ground, I could already feel my last Christmas fading away.

When I arrived at my house, the porch dotted with poinsettias, the tin roof tidily trimmed with tiny lights of green and red, I'd stop and catch my breath and eye it furiously as if to fix it and prevent if from dissolving, but after just a few seconds it would splinter into ragged halos. As I walked on toward the bend, the trailer would be throbbing in the wintery air, nearly every inch of it covered with lights of every conceivable color, a great bursting capsule of cheer that was, as soon as I came upon it, somehow hemorrhaging and vanishing in the distance. The brightly lit cross that rose from the back of the carport would suddenly dim. The handmade sign in the front yard reading HE'S THE REASON FOR THE SEASON! would shrink into a thin, shadowy cylinder around which the letters spooled for a moment and finally drained from sight altogether. Here was where I realized how hopeless all my running was. Almost halfway finished with my senior year, my world was going to change forever, no matter what I or anyone else may have wanted.

Which, again, is why I never saw what was coming. I was completely distracted by the fact that I'd soon be graduating. That dizzy circularity I've been describing was about to end.

Yet something horrible did occur before I graduated. And while this unfortunate event was made possible by my fight with Leonard, that was not what really caused it. Had I been a more careful observer at the time, I could have seen the seeds of destruction within one of the gifts I received that Christmas.

Clancy: Nothing.

Sterns: A subscription to the Great Books club.

Leonard: Shells (it was hunting season) and half of a stereo for college.

April: An Arbogast Mud Bug (we always exchanged lures for Christmas) and the other half of the stereo.

Henderson: A Brooks Brothers suit, navy.

Mother: A tuxedo by those same pricey brothers.

Lorri-Anne: A bound collection of football clippings and various photographs, cologne, and a peacoat.

The culprit was two down from the grand center of the list—the seemingly innocent tuxedo. A further hint was the card found in its swank, silky pocket which read:

Dear Roy,

I love you more than life. You're going to get to do all the things that I never got to do, and I want you to do them in style. I know your father would approve of this. I picked it out with both of you in mind—but don't worry, it's sized to fit you!

Please think of me when you're up at Virginia or Princeton or North Carolina. Please remember how much I love you.

Yours Ever,

Mother

It was all there for me to see, but I didn't see it. In fact, it would be long after New Years, when the college scouts and coaches began coming to Citrus regularly, before I would finally understand the sort of reach that slick tuxedo had.

At first the arrival of those recruiting teams seemed to have set the stage for some of the best times that Mother and I had ever had. Sitting in the living room, enjoying iced tea and finger sandwiches, Mother would ask about academics. "And what about literature?" she'd want to know.

"Oh, we have a very strong English department," they would inevitably answer. Every department of every school was, of course, "very strong" or "first rate."

"Is the approach modern?"

"We're right on the cutting edge," they'd happily reply.

"That's not good. I want Roy in an environment where literature is respected and taught rigorously."

The men would stare blankly and shift their feet, having no idea what to say. Mother considered herself to be even more outré than the so-called avant garde. It mattered little that the academy had never heard of her; she began to tool about her days flushed with the pride of a counter-revolutionary. The poor recruiters were her one chance to antagonize what she saw as a corrupt academic establishment, and although they were hardly fit combatants she couldn't afford to waste the opportunity. I suppose she was not exactly the sort of mother they were accustomed to finding on their missions, which should have given them fair warning about the kind of football player they were wooing.

Truth be known, though mystified, the recruiters and coaches were actually quite taken with Mother. While she couldn't resist getting her digs in now and again, she remained a charming and gracious hostess. She also enjoyed it immensely when people stopped her on the square to ask how things were going for me, perhaps feeling that my performance in the classroom and on the football field served to vindicate her and even my father. She picked over all the school catalogues and carefully took notes. When she was in Washington she'd telephone me whenever she came across some new piece of information.

But soon enough that tuxedo escaped from its closet and lifted an empty arm at me accusingly: Was I, or was I not, going to go to a school that would accommodate it and allow it to shine? A young man in those days certainly had occasion to wear tuxedos at an Ivy League school or at Mother's beloved Virginia or North Carolina. He would even—and perhaps especially—have occasion to wear one at Alabama, say, or at a bastion of tradition like Ole Miss. Yet for the most part, the competitive football programs were to be found at schools that were quickly losing all sense of identity. I didn't like that, but at the time I believed I had to consider football first and foremost. Or that was what I kept telling myself, at any rate.

I'd narrowed my short list to Florida and Florida State but continued to talk about Virginia and North Carolina to avoid confrontations with Mother. Both schools on my short list had one thing in common that ranked them most highly with me, a thing that had nothing whatsoever to do with football. They were both football powerhouses, to be sure, but there were many other powerhouses with spare rooms. They were both Florida schools, too, and while I possessed a defiant streak of nativism, that was not what was on my mind.

What those two schools had in common and what was of principal interest to me was that they were close to Citrus. I simply couldn't conceive of being very far from Citrus at that point in my life. When I thought about North Carolina or Virginia I shuddered, imagining unbearable loneliness. I wanted April and Leonard and Mother to be able to come to every home game; and I wanted to be able to visit them without difficulty. Furthermore, the idea of weeks passing without contact with April unnerved me. I feared I would return one day to find her changed. I feared that if too many weeks passed I would one day come home to discover she was quite simply my aunt.

When Mother finally realized that I had no intention of going to the sort of place where I could wear that Christmas tuxedo, that in fact I was dead set on going to a school that was close to Citrus—the one thing she feared most and for the reason she feared most—it became obvious that we had not come to our great crisis after all.

I FIRST REALIZED THIS after a visit from the head coach at the University of Florida. We were sitting at the breakfast table, sipping coffee, when he suddenly said, "I bet it would make your uncle proud if you became a Gator."

I shot my eyes over just in time to see Mother purse her lips. She said not a word, the worst outcome possible. The coach sensed that someone had goofed, but who could that be? He pursed *his* lips and half-reached for a non-existent visor.

When Mother and I were alone she stared me down into a chair and delivered a lengthy and altogether accurate account of the ways in which Florida was not the best sort of place for me to be. "We'll just have to see what Virginia and North Carolina have to offer," she said. "Or Princeton. I hope you haven't ruled out Princeton."

I'd thought that Mother and I had reached an informal agreement on the matter of Princeton, at least, but here was Princeton popping up again. And with that clever move she set me at a disadvantage, for producing Princeton allowed her to speak of Virginia and North Carolina as if she would *accept* my going to either of those schools though it would be a letdown for her if I did. Of course, if Virginia and North Carolina were only mildly tolerable distant cousins, that meant Florida and Florida State were out of the family completely. In fact, they were not even citizens of the little country Mother and I had founded and were now fighting over concerning my choice of schools. Nor would they be granted passports.

"Roy, we're getting down to business here. Where *are* you going?" she asked me a few days after Florida's head coach made his fatal remark.

"I want to play in the South."

"But where?"

"I want to play in the Southeastern Conference, Mother. That's always been my dream. Ever since I started playing."

It was true that the Southeastern Conference was my favorite, and as far as football was concerned it was ideal. But as I have been pointing out, football was not what was really at issue here. I knew it, and Mother knew it.

"So you're going to Florida to play for Leonard," she said finally. "Is that it? Just like that coach said. That coach who would forget about you in less than a minute if you didn't run touchdowns for him. No matter what's best for you, is that it?" She would not even use the coach's name.

"Maybe I'll go to Florida State."

When I mentioned Florida State to her, a wild and desperate look came into her eyes, as if she were witnessing some brutal crime that she was hopeless to stop, which, I suppose, was indeed something of the case so far as she was concerned.

"Well, I certainly wouldn't go to Florida State, I'll tell you that right now," she said. She shook her head. "Florida State? Why on earth would you want to do that?"

"Why not?"

"Florida State's right in our backyard. Don't you want to get away?"

Her voice was tremulous. It was also, for the first time that I had ever known, depleted of power. I can still hear those defeated and wasted words of hers, and I wish so badly that I could return to that breakfast table, where we seemed to have had most of these conversations, and take her hand and tell her that she was right and that of course I would go to Virginia or North Carolina.

"I mean, two hours. Two hours, Roy. What is that? It would be like going to high school again."

"I thought you might like me being so close."

"*Me? Me?*" she said, pointing to her chest. "Roy, are you serious? *Me?*" she reached for her necklace and held to it as if for life itself. "Not me. That would be selfish of me. I want you to get away from here. I want you to see something of the world. It would be very, *very* selfish for me to try to get you to go to Florida State. I want what's best for you. I would never try to hold you back."

She looked away. I knew she was thinking of April, thinking that April had convinced me to go to Florida State. (In fact, April had become fond of Alabama for some reason.)

"I plan to travel, Mother," I said. "Come on. I plan to see the world. We've talked about all this before."

"But I want you away from here *now*," she said. "*Now*. Not later. It's important. Why would you want to be so close? I just don't understand it. A normal boy your age should jump at the chance to get away from home."

"Tallahassee's away from home."

"No it's not! It's not, Roy!" she pleaded, gathering her fingers around her necklace again. "What if you . . . you could go anywhere. Anywhere. Some place we haven't even talked about. Like Oxford. In Mississippi, I mean. I have that writer friend there and . . ."

She stopped herself. She saw that I had made up my mind.

LIKE A FOOL, within a few days I'd convinced myself that everything was going to be all right. But a week later, when a delegation of coaches from Florida State showed up, I saw how bankrupt my thinking had been. Mother did not make finger sandwiches for these gentlemen, believing as she did that they were nothing more than a team of executioners. In fact, she would not even stay in the living room with us while we talked. Instead she wandered in from time to time to fetch a book or to look for something that kept disappearing on her.

She was straightening the coffee table when one of the coaches promised that if I chose Florida State he expected me to get heavy rotation my sophomore year and to start as a junior. "We'll probably take a look at red-shirting you," he explained.

Mother did not have to be told what that meant. She was at that point very well versed in football terminology. She looked up from the coffee table and stared the man directly in the eyes. "You're going to red-shirt him?"

"Maybe. It all depends."

"Hold him back a year?"

I was watching the coach, avoiding Mother's presence, wondering how I could stop the conversation from going any further. Suddenly he ducked his head and said, "Ma'am? Are you all right?"

When I looked over Mother had covered her eyes as if she were playing a game of peek-a-boo. Then her sobs caught voice and groaned out pitifully. The burst was so forceful and loud, it startled all of us.

"Mother?"

I reached out my hand, but it was too late.

"Red-shirt him then! Fine! Just do whatever you goddamned well please to him! Why don't you go ahead and kill him while you're at it! Just go ahead and kill him and get it over with!"

Like an aggrieved woman in a romance novel, Mother fled from the room, but that room was not a perishable parlor from a musty period piece, it was our living room, and neither was Mother's escape from that living room melodramatic—it was shaky, made with her last ounce of will, on weak legs. Something was knocked over, of course, some figurine or domestic artifact that has been blocked from memory. But there will never be any forgetting the blistered air left in her wake, nor the razorous ringlets of grief that trailed her as she ran down the hallway and out into the yard.

The coaches excused themselves, and I went to look for Mother. She was not to be found in the yard, nor out by the barn. I began walking around the house, listening for her. I walked into the woods, confident I could track her, but I could find no prints. After an hour the sun began to set, and I returned to find her sitting on the back porch, wrapped in her quilt.

"When you finish up five glorious years at Florida State, you can go to bible college and then come back to Citrus and take over for Brother Glenn out at Citrus Hills Church of God," she said. "I can hardly wait."

"Mother, please."

"Please nothing. I want you to listen to me. And I want you to listen to me good. If you don't start thinking straight you're going to throw away every opportunity you have. All the hard work we've done. All the things I've taught you. Everything. Right down the drain."

"I haven't forgotten anything."

"You're not like them, Roy. How many times do I have to go over this? And if you try to act like them you'll end up being miserable. But you won't discover that until it's too late, until you've wasted the best years of your life. You'll live out all their dreams—all the dreams they never lived out, all the things they wished Leonard had been able to do—and you'll regret it. I'm sorry Leonard's had a hard life. I really am. I'm sick about their whole situation and what all they've been through. But be that as it may, I will not let them destroy your prospects, your chance to live up to *your* potential and *your* dreams and *your* name. You're not a Collins. You're a Collier. There's a difference. A big difference. Damnit, Roy, what's wrong with you!"

"Mother—"

"No, you let me finish! How could you do this? How could you do this to us?"

She began to cry again then. I walked over and put my arm around her, but she took my hand away.

"I won't stand by while they destroy you, Roy. I know they don't mean to hurt you. They'd do anything for you. But they don't know any better. And you don't, either. But I do. I know better. And I'll do whatever I have to do to protect you." She stood. "Because I *am* your mother. I won't sit by and do nothing while you throw your life away. I just won't do it. I love you too much to let that happen."

She walked to her room, slamming the door behind her, and I heard the lock click into place.

MOTHER HAD KNOWN about the "trailer incident," as she would later refer to it, for quite some time. As a matter of fact, she'd learned about it within a few weeks of its occurrence. She didn't do anything at first, and I suppose she might never have done anything, or at any rate she might not have done anything involving me. She might well have decided to hold it over April's and Leonard's heads instead or to save it for a rainy day. But that was not what happened. It was not what happened because I chose to go to Florida State.

She learned about the "trailer incident," it turned out, through none other than James Henderson, who had learned of it through none other than April. I didn't know it at the time, but Henderson had maintained a strong connection with April all through the years. They spoke on the telephone regularly, even when Mother was in Washington, though Mother never knew of it. Henderson always carried something of a sputtering torch for April, though his connection to her was more various than that. For one thing, because he had befriended my father, he felt obligated to help April and Leonard. As I have already pointed out, he had for years made investments for them, arranging sweetheart deals that greatly increased their otherwise modest income. For another, Henderson was simply nosy, as Leonard had told me. He'd set himself up as the benevolent wizard of Citrus, a puppeteer who liked pulling strings from a distance, perhaps to prevent himself from becoming deracinated, that condition about which he and Mother forever warned me.

When I learned that he had betrayed April by telling Mother, the cagey nature of our relationship was cemented for good. Furthermore, while I was in my cooler moments glad that he and Mother had become so close, I was never comfortable with the fact that they were lovers. I'd suspected that this was the case sometime after entering high school but had ignored it and pretended they were simply close friends. When I did think about the real nature of their relationship, I couldn't understand why Henderson wouldn't marry Mother. In my mind he sometimes appeared as a lecherous old man who was getting what he shouldn't have been getting and from no less a person than my own mother. The truth of the matter, however, was that *Mother* was the one that refused to marry. Though my father was dead and buried, she remained deeply wedded to his name, to the idea of Sanders Royce Collier—so wedded to it, in fact, that not even a distinguished United States Congressman could divorce her from it.

So Henderson had always been right in the thick of things, operating just behind the scenes, a role that gave him pleasure. After homecoming night, however, I suppose he realized that his game of playing both ends against the middle was going to be costly. He learned of the fight because after Mother flew to Washington that next week, April called him to tell him to keep her there a little longer. He wanted to know why, and she told him, believing Henderson could be trusted. Perhaps under ordinary circumstances he could have been, but he was about to enter a situation he was not at all prepared for—he was about to try to pull something over on Mother.

Apparently when he asked Mother to stay longer, a familiar enough request coming from him, his much vaunted diplomatic skills utterly failed to carry the day. She immediately realized he was hiding something and became dramatic with her protests. A photograph frame and its plate of glass were shattered, and I suspect Henderson may have even been *roughed up* a little. Mother told him he didn't respect her and that under the circumstances they could not continue seeing each other. Upon hearing that, Henderson folded and told her about the "trailer incident." He might well have been able to bluff presidents and all the bought men of those presidents, but he was no match for Mother.

As soon as she came home she telephoned Sheriff Porter and Deputy Chiles and forced them to go out to the trailer. I was in school when all of this took place. She pretended to be hysterical—which is itself a form of hysteria, I know, but Mother had earned such subtle distinctions—

and so cowed everyone involved that Leonard admitted to what he had done to me and April. She said she was going to press charges, and Sheriff Porter dutifully took statements from April and Leonard. But when Sheriff Porter told Mother that he would have to talk to me, she decided not to press charges, after all, because she didn't want to get me involved.

She of course knew from the beginning that it would come to that and furthermore that she wouldn't actually press charges. But what she had accomplished was by no means insignificant. There was now a public record of Leonard's attacking me and of pitching me through a window and of his hurting April. There was now the possibility of reprisal. Mother finally had what she'd always wanted: leverage. And when it was at last certain beyond all doubt that I would be going to a Collins, instead of a Collier, kind of school, she used that leverage. She used it to the hilt.

PART THREE

THIRTEEN

A signing party was arranged for me and Clancy and several other teammates at the high school that coming March, but Mother made last-minute plans to go to Washington and told me she couldn't attend. What she did not say, but what was evident from the hasty way she packed and the grim expression on her face, was that what I was signing was nothing less than my death warrant.

"If I keep my grades up I ought to be in the running for a Rhodes Scholarship. With football and all," I told her.

She flung a jar of Ponds cold cream into her makeup kit. "Mm-huh."

"Oxford. Wouldn't that be great?"

"Oh damnit." After cleaning messy Ponds with a washrag and screwing its chilly top down tight, she looked up at me. "I didn't know they had a professional football team in Oxford," was all she said.

April and Leonard accompanied me to the cafeteria, where the celebration was held. Clancy had declared for Florida, and several newspapers apparently expected that we would become mortal enemies. DIXIE'S DYNAMIC DUO EXPLODES INTO RIVALRY! was our favorite headline. It wasn't much of a celebration, however. A banner made by our cheerleaders congratulated us with dancing capital letters and three enormous throbbing purple exclamation points, all of which, for some reason, was put into dubious quotation marks. There were reporters from all over the state and purple and yellow streamers because no one makes streamers of garnet and gold. For the same reason our balloons were simply white. A runt lectern had been placed in the center of two sadly decorated signing tables. The larger Donaldson, the lesser Davidson, Coach Taylor, and eventually all of the players were to take its narrow shoulders and answer questions.

When my turn came I could only mumble. I knew that with the coming seemingly effortless stroke of a pen I would be sealing several fates at once. Consequently, in all those photographs there stands next to a beaming beige quarterback a grayish presence so blanched and withdrawn it threatens to tarnish all the other brassy smiles, some refugee phantom from reform school—or worse, from Sans Albino—trying to impersonate a normal fellow.

Afterwards April and Leonard and I returned to the trailer. There was to have been a gathering there that included Clancy and Lorri-Anne and Mother and Sterns, but that agenda had fallen apart with Mother's abrupt departure.

I sat with Leonard on the deck while April changed clothes.

"You know you could have gone to any school you wanted to," he remarked. Suddenly he grew angry with Howl and sent him into the yard. "I mean, hell, I wanted you to go to Florida, especially with Clancy going and all, but I can see where Florida State's a better situation for you. They're gonna need a good back pretty soon. They've got a lot of seniors and juniors this year."

"I know."

"And April, she didn't care one way or the other. We wanted you to make your own decision. You and your mama."

"Of course. I made my own decision."

"That's what we wanted."

April walked out holding up three sparklers. She wore gray cotton sweatpants, her negligible J. C. Penney tennis shoes, a white tank top and a well-worn denim jacket. She seemed soft, bustling and girlish. It was an outfit she often wore when we went fishing.

We lit the sparklers and drank sweet tea and ate lemon ice-box pie and tried to talk about Tallahassee and my prospects, but in no time the conversation stalled, and Leonard suddenly shoved his plate to the center of the table. "There's something we got to talk about," he said.

"Not now. Not yet," April said.

"Honey."

April looked down. When Leonard started talking again, she reached across the table and took my hand.

"Some things have happened, Roy," Leonard began. "We haven't told you about them because we didn't want to mess anything up worse than we already have, but here lately we've been left with no choice but to tell you."

And so he told me about how Sheriff Porter and Deputy Chiles had come out to the trailer. He explained that when Mother knew I was going to sign with Florida State, she called him and said that he and April were ruining my life and that they'd better figure out a way to stop it.

"You remember how we started talking about North Carolina all the time, what a good school it is?" April asked.

I remembered but could not answer.

"And we always said—well, *April* had always said—how proud she'd be if you went up to a place like Princeton," Leonard reminded me. "And I told you straight out many times—*many* times—not to base your decision just on football, but to follow your heart. Or what you thought was best for you."

"And that's why we never told you about Sheriff Porter," April said.

"We weren't going to tell you about all that stuff 'cause we didn't want you to make a decision based on trying to keep peace around here," Leonard allowed. "That's not your job. I heard your mama out on North Carolina and Virginia and thought she made a lot of sense and I told her so and I told you so and of course you could've gone pro from one of them schools."

April squeezed my hand.

"But then your mama kicked into high gear." Leonard sighed. "I guess she realized there was nothing she could do that would make you change your mind unless she just flat out threatened you about us. But that wasn't what she wanted. She just wanted to make us—" He broke off. He wiped his mouth. "June's not—" He stopped again. "Your mama . . ." He couldn't go on.

"There are a few things Leonard and I have to take care of," April said. "Little things. That's all we're trying to tell you."

"What kind of little things?"

Leonard forced a laugh. "I've got to go to a drying-out clinic and take the old cure. Ain't really a big deal. Ain't really a bad idea, neither. Matter of fact, it's about exactly what I need, to tell the truth."

I looked at April.

"And I'm going to go out of town for a little while, too. A little vacation. I've been wanting one anyway."

"Like hell you are."

"Oh, Roy, it's such a minor thing. We just need to get you off to school right now."

"Well, I don't want to go off to school right now. I'm not going to school for another four months."

"You know what I mean."

"This is just the way it is," Leonard said. "It's all my fault, and unfortunately everybody's got to pay for it some. But it'll be over before you know it, and we'll all be better off for it."

"You wait 'til I talk to Mother," I said.

April came around the table and sat beside me.

"What?" I snapped.

"June's not feeling well, Roy. We've been talking with James Henderson about it. She's not doing well with you leaving, baby. She's not herself."

I jerked away. "That's a lie. Mother's fine. I don't care what Mr. Henderson told you. It's all part of some trick they've come up with."

"It's not a trick, Roy," Leonard said.

"Well, there's nothing wrong with Mother, I can tell you *that!*" I laughed scornfully, my heart in a reckless sprint now. "I can't believe y'all are falling for this. She's making a joke out of both of you."

April gently placed her hand on my forearm. "June's been seeing a doctor in Washington. A psychiatrist."

I pulled away from her a second time. "That's bullshit!"

"Roy, listen to me," April said. "We wouldn't even have told you, but we had to so you'll understand. So you'll help us and not try to fight what has to be done."

"I'm not helping anybody do anything. Y'all are the ones that are crazy."

"No one's said anything about crazy, baby. June's under a lot of pressure, that's all. And her doctor is worried—"

"There is no doctor."

"Roy. Please. She's under a lot of stress. We need to be strong for her."

Leonard nodded. "And besides which your mama's right anyhow. No woman worth her salt would let somebody throw her boy through a window. That's a plain fact. No wonder she's so upset. I *do* need to get some help."

"April doesn't need help."

"Well, your mama thinks . . ." Leonard paused. "Your mama thinks I've been—"

"And you just let her say that about you? And about April? You just let her say anything she wants?"

"Please, honey. Why not do this for her? This little bitty thing. I really wouldn't mind getting away for a while."

"How long?"

"Not long at all."

"How long, damnit?"

"A month," Leonard said.

April reached for me, but I had already gotten clear of the table.

"Mother's fine," I cried. "And y'all are going to regret this. Everybody's fine. To hell with you! To hell with everybody!"

I ran down the steps and on toward the house. I was going to tell Mother that she had to put an end to her terrible plan, that I would not allow it. I was going to insist that April, at any rate, be left alone. And I was going to make it clear to Mother how disgusted I was that she was pretending to be in some state of distress just to get people do what she wanted. And how sick it was to lie about seeing a psychiatrist and how sick Henderson was to go along with all this and that if she was going to go around doing those kinds of things maybe she *should* see a psychiatrist, and Henderson, too. I was going to tell her I would go to North Carolina if that's what it came down to and that I would go to Virginia or even Princeton if she would just come to her senses and admit to everyone that she was sorry for lying and getting Henderson to lie. I was going to say that I loved her and that I was sorry for not listening to her and that all I wanted for graduation was for everything to go back to the way it used to be. I raced up the little brick walkway and had just taken hold of the screen door when I realized that all the lights were out and the house was empty. I heard the tinkling of the chimes above my panted breath and with a stronger gust of wind all around me came the sound of glass delicately falling and shattering.

LEONARD LEFT WITHIN the week. The facility Mother had chosen for him was in Tallahassee, and I suppose that was her attempt to make Tallahassee as unpleasant a place for Leonard as she imagined it would be for her over the next four years. When confronted with this bit of news, which I took to be significant, Leonard's response was remarkably blasé. "Like I give a fuck" were his exact words.

April was to go to a counseling center in Pensacola that provided assistance for battered women and women who were in relationships with alcoholics, not to mention, I assumed, women who were in relationships with battering alcoholics, though the literature was mute on this point. Mother demanded that either April and Leonard *both* go to get help or she would press charges. She actually said this directly to me at one point, in a telephone conversation that was so upsetting, I dared not argue back. She said I had hurt her beyond all consolation and that I'd probably destroyed my life. She further claimed that *she* would not be the one to receive another call in the middle of the night from Sheriff Porter, this time one to notify her that Leonard had shot April to death.

"So I see they've dragged you into this?" she finally asked caustically.

"No, Mother. They were just going to disappear for a month without telling me. That was a hell of a plan."

"I wasn't making plans. I was doing what I had to do as a mother *and* as a sister. I could have taken Leonard straight to court. How would you have liked that?"

I was no longer responding to her at that point. I was thinking about the story of how Leonard rescued April from the noose. "Get dressed, you pervert," Mother had said. "Sick. You're *both* perverts."

Now Mother had both their necks in the noose, and April and Leonard realized she wouldn't hesitate to kick the chair out from under them if they refused to do exactly as she wished. Involving me in legal proceedings, she had explained to them, would be far less harmful than allowing things to grow worse and one day waking up to discover that Leonard had killed me or April or both of us. Whenever she believed it was necessary, Mother could always make some reference to my father's death, as if Leonard had had something to do with it. The day she told them of her plans she made such a reference. "I'm not being a fanatic," she said. "Don't think I've forgotten what happened to Sanders."

So there was no doubt that if they did not comply with Mother's wishes she'd press charges, especially given that my decision to go to a Collins kind of school had made her feel that she had nothing left to lose. In Mother's mind, April and Leonard had prevailed over her where I was concerned.

Not surprisingly, she was to remain in Washington until April and Leonard had departed. Because of this I was able to talk April into allowing me to drive her down to Pensacola. She regarded the event bravely, irreverently and with a smile.

When I walked over to the trailer she was packing an old-fashioned checkered suitcase she'd ordered from some fancy catalogue years earlier. Into this snazzy contraption she placed her clothes and her Dake's study Bible. Since it had turned warm, she wore one of her light cotton dresses. The thought of her being so appealingly attired disconcerted me, considering where we were going. I was instantly taken hostage by thoughts of sadistic orderlies in white uniforms, though I'd already learned that there were no men on the premises and the counselors were supposedly kind and wore blue jeans.

I still felt April was too vulnerable and bare. Already browning from the good weather, her legs seemed overly long, and they flooded the room with a ticklish humidity. Standing nearly on the tips of her toes to search the top shelf of her closet, from which one of Grandmother's old hatboxes tumbled onto my head to scold me, she exhibited the exuberant poise of someone who has spent years dancing. Her calves tightened and plump balls of muscle appeared. Then, facing me, she stomped her foot because she couldn't find a favorite blouse, sending siren tremors out from her thighs. Drumming her chest absently, her hand slipped further down, still drumming.

"It might get cold," I warned. "You might better take some heavier clothes."

"Yeah, you're probably right. Oh, and a bathing suit. They have a pool. I bet Leonard doesn't have a pool. You wait 'til I get back. I'll be brown as a berry." Her heart-shape sunglasses were perched atop her head. "Maybe I'll take this sweater," she said.

"I would."

"Why are you so spiffy, anyway?" she asked.

I shrugged and was embarrassed. I'd worn khakis and a blue blazer. I suppose I was reaching for some sort of authority to help me on our trip. It seemed we had entered into very adult territory, and I wanted to be dressed for it. Of course, there was also a measure of defiance in wearing something a little formal. For several long minutes I had even debated whether or not I should wear my father's cuff links, but in the end decided I'd better not take any of his things along.

"Well, you look handsome," April said, giving my sleeve a jerk. "And you're sweet to do this, Roy. To take me." She clicked her tongue. "Oh, I forgot that damned book."

Svelte, stellar April retrieved a paperback of fat, middling *Middlemarch* with an exhausted bookmark poking its weary head from the penultimate chapter. Had I been as good a detective as I was a football player, that cruel assignment alone, made two months before, should have tipped me off to Mother's intent to seek vengeance. No matter how bad things got between those Lanier girls, they continued handing out assignments to each other, but *Middlemarch* was too much. Mother herself hated the book. She once told me she refused to believe it had been written by a woman. It reeked of manhood's worst aspects, she claimed. When I later read it, I kind of liked it, but at the time all I knew of it was what Mother told me. And here was April, heading off to a counseling center, loaded down with *Middlemarch*. I suppose it's all right to now reveal that April never read that last chapter. In fact, I strongly suspect she did not even get as far as that leaning bookmark suggested. At any rate, that was the only assignment she never completed.

We collected her luggage and walked into the living room. Everything was in its proper place and quiet. The television, the coffee table, the issues of *Bassmaster,* the stalwart spines of the *National Geographic* magazines filling three shelves of the large bookcase, the sink and refrigerator, the photographs and photograph albums, the enormous gold family Bible, Our Daily Bread, the stereo . . . All of them had tilted their heads for a nap and become perfectly still, while the replaced living room window looked on as innocent as a newborn.

"At least this place will stay clean for longer than five minutes," April said. She shrugged.

"Where's Howl?"

"Howl's with Sterns, living it up. Sterns spoils dogs. But you have to feed the chickens." After a wink she tossed me the keys. "Come on."

Top down, radio off, we left in the dreamy sunlight of that dazzlingly dark day without saying very much, with me playing the witless chauffeur, assisting Mother in her schemes. Almost immediately April began fiddling with her boots, which brought her legs into unsettling angles of display. She was in her prime and knew it, and furthermore knew she could get away with anything fashionwise and that she might as well take advantage of it while she could. There would come a day when she could no longer wear a flimsy cotton dress that stopped well short of the middle of her thighs with a pair of weathered black cowboy boots. There would come a day when so many bracelets would weigh her down. But that day was still far off, and April would not surrender to it a moment too soon.

"I feel like I forgot something," she said.

"Where's your forty-five?"

"See. I knew I forgot something."

I gripped the knobby knuckles of that wide Mustang steering wheel and again thought of Mother. I remained certain she wasn't as distressed as everyone made her out to be, and I absolutely refused to believe she was seeing a psychiatrist.

"Did you see that hawk?"

"Huh?"

"There was a hawk back there."

"I missed it."

"Wonder where my nail file is."

Mother didn't need counseling, nor did she need to be coddled when she became abusive. The idea that April should submit to her plans was condescending to her *and* to April—April, who was just then stretching into the backseat with one hand clamped across her bottom to keep her dress in place and digging after a nail file with the other!

"I'll hold your dress down."

"You'll hold yourself down, Mister."

But then April was safely back in her seat, a bright white tongue of comfort.

"Should we turn on the radio?" She touched my arm. "It's such a pretty day."

"This isn't right," I said.

"It's honestly not that big a deal. When you come back to pick me up, maybe we'll go to the beach. We'll make it fun."

"Deal. Deal. That's the word you and Leonard keep using. Because this *is* a deal. A bad deal. It's a swindle."

"You're good with words. Mama was good with words."

"Leonard was enough. You should have—"

"But I didn't, all right? I didn't. Please let's not talk about it now."

"It's not right."

"Fine. It's not right. Please, Roy."

"It's not," I said. "Fuck it."

"See, you *are* good with words. Better than Mama, even. With a vocabulary like that, think what kind of a preacher you'd make."

"Fuck it."

"You need to be healed. A *major* healing."

"I thought that's what Mother needed."

SOMEWHERE PAST DE FUNIAK SPRINGS I saw a hitchhiker sitting beneath an overpass. He seemed to be giving the entire world a dirty look as he tamped a cigarette. Even from the interstate I determined that his eyes were accusatory and that he held everything in vast contempt. As I passed him he made an unfriendly gesture with his finger, and we were suddenly both locked in one of the great time-space conundrums of high-speed highway travel: those times when one gets caught in a moment with someone stationary and even though one may be reaching speeds of sixty or seventy miles an hour, that moment swells and swallows the swift traveler and the bound pedestrian in a bubble of unnerving intimacy. Then the bubble bursts, and the two briefly contained parties are slung apart to scratch their heads.

I looked to see if April had been watching, but she was reading a *New Yorker* article on alcohol abuse, *another* very pointed assignment that Mother had given her. April seemed quite taken with it.

"Any good?"

"Interesting. There's something else in here I read earlier about a scientist from Alabama who teaches at Harvard. He says the densest old-growth forests in the United States are in the South." She looked around. "Sometimes I could just drive and drive."

"You mean sit and sit while I drive and drive."

"Yeah. That's what I mean."

A few minutes later, as we approached another overpass, something occurred that none of us—not Mother nor I nor April nor Leonard nor Henderson—had anticipated. My father appeared.

I spotted him leaning against one of the concrete pylons of an overpass and slowed the car.

"Everything all right, baby?"

"Mm? Yeah. We were going too fast."

It was not uncommon for me to picture him doing this or that. I often walked him up Main Street or had him take a seat in Ligget's, or I saw him coming toward me in the distance down the old dirt road in front of our house. But this time my father's appearance, the image of him watching us drive by from his cool vantage just beyond the reach of the sun, was different. It seemed less a case of my conjuring him up than of his conjuring himself up, as if we had had an appointment that I had forgotten and he was nonetheless determined to keep. He startled me and seemed to know it and to take satisfaction in it. I saw his signet ring, his satchel, his mohair jacket, his ankle-length cashmere coat, his tailored wool trousers, his wing tips, his Egyptian-cotton button-down, the French cuffs, the silver cuff links—all raided from our house! He stared right at me with his turbulent blue eyes, smiling, certain of himself, as if he were ready for a night out on the town, nothing to it, nothing to it at all.

No matter his faults, I suddenly realized I couldn't conceive of my father consenting to take April to a women's home, not under *any* circumstances. He might stalk her, torment her, tease her, attack her and try to commit adultery with her, but I was about to do something that I couldn't imagine him doing. Perhaps that is why he shrugged disappointedly as we passed him by. I could almost hear him say, "Catch you around, Roy."

"Are you all right, Roy?"

"What? Yes, I'm fine."

"You're sweating up a storm." She leaned over. "And we're doing forty-five."

My father kept appearing after that. The shocking thing was, I had begun to feel empathy for him.

It occurred to me that not every wanderer wants to wander, and I wondered if my father had detested roaming and desired nothing more than to live out a settled life. And not just any settled life but that variety of life that is the most rooted and settled of all, the life of the farmer; or given my father's background and his love of grandeur, the life of the gentleman planter, rocking on his front porch every evening and staring out over his crops and progeny. What if he feared he couldn't settle down unless he was held down by something even more powerful than his drives? After all his traveling and wandering he'd finally found her, only to blow it. How would he be able to endure it if that hope lived less than a quarter of a mile away, just around the bend, past a property line on the other side of which he became a trespasser and a target?

Good god it was hot!

By the time we arrived at the women's home I'd become positively feverish. I parked the Mustang and stared up at the Victorian two-story, a revolting strumpet of latticework, lace and loopy pastels, where April was soon to be questioned day after day about her allegedly battering husband, Leonard Collins. I wiped my eyes. The penitentiary was still there.

April snapped her fingers in front of my face. "Earth to Roy. We're here. The shuttle has landed."

"Yeah," I said. "I guess it has."

"This place is kind of cute. It might not be so bad after all."

When we went inside a kindly but fatigued older woman asked us to take a seat in what looked to be an ordinary living room. "I'm Mrs.

Huntley, the assistant director," she said. "We're very informal here. Just relax and I'll go get the forms."

Mrs. Huntley possessed an automatic yet winning smile, which she'd probably earned the hard way, but upon handing April a clipboard she seemed concerned about me. "Can I get you some water?" she asked. Unsure of my status, she eyed me warily. She was a tall woman with an enormous bosom. Or something up there of impressive size. You could not see actual breasts; rather, more of a large rounded shelf that appeared battleworthy. She turned her self and her shelf toward me, and I cowered beneath all of her. Perhaps I was the younger, jealous, abusive husband. Flushed and streaked with perspiration, perhaps I was experiencing the onset of the DTs and would presently go into a tirade. "No water?"

"No, ma'am."

"This is my nephew, Roy," April said. "He's a big football star. He's going to play for Florida State next year. They gave him a full scholarship."

"That's wonderful." Mrs. Huntley rolled back on her heels and came forward with a comfortable giggle. "You're both so good-looking. So striking. Stern jaws." She made a stern face. "Like the models. Of course, most of them do drugs, which is cheating, which is very dangerous, I might add." She was actually shaking a finger at us! "Wonderful. Well, I'll be just down the hall. Let me know if you need anything." She gave us a thumbs-up and was gone.

I watched April looking over the forms. She kept her head down, filling them out very slowly. Peach potpourri lay in a bowl on a nearby table, along with a Gideon Bible. Though they had tried to create a homey atmosphere, the room still reeked of something stale, sanitized and administrative like a hospital or a school cafeteria. I imagined that behind the less than convincing façade we would discover a labyrinth of white walls and sickbeds with cold, metal railings.

Indeed, as I accustomed myself to the room I discovered various impostors. An exit sign. A handicap ramp beside a set of stairs. A television with a note that asked viewers not to abscond with the remote control, which was nowhere to be seen. A water cooler suffering from indigestion that belched from time to time. A gold plaque thanking Dr. and Mrs. So-and-So for their generosity.

Missing items? Family photographs. Leavings. Love.

April was rocking a little. A woman walked in and opened the blinds. The room brightened with swift afternoon sunlight. I saw that April's hands were trembling. "March thirty-first," she said softly. She wrote that dire date down.

Neither of us had had the stomach to comment on the cruel irony of which month it was that April would be missing. We knew only too well that we were losing our last chance to walk every day to visit our favorite blooms of wisteria. We were losing our last month of trips to Lake Julep during spawning season to catch sow bellies. We were losing the last leisurely explorations of that best and brightest time of year. Most horribly, April's first full day alone in that home for mistreated women would be that famous day of fools.

I looked down and saw tear stains on the forms. April wiped her face. "I'm almost finished. Just a minute," she said. She looked up and laughed nervously. "I'm just a little embarrassed. I think all this is finally hitting me."

I took her hand. "Come on."

"Come on, what?"

"Let's get out of here. Just for a minute."

April peered around that shifty room, which held its breath. "But, Roy . . ."

But she followed me.

I walked her back to the car, opened her door and let her in. Mrs. Huntley charged onto the faux porch. "Is everything all right?"

"Yes, ma'am," I said. "We just need a few minutes."

Mrs. Huntley pulled on her lip as we pulled out of the driveway.

"Maybe a little drive would be good," April said. "But you'll have to take me back in a few minutes."

"Sure. We need gas."

I pulled into a service station and began to pump while April walked inside to pay. When I finished she returned with the paper bag from which she removed a Yoo-Hoo for me and a light beer for herself and a pack of minty gum to be shared.

"I could use a beer," she explained. "Just one. I won't be having any for a while."

She drank, I drove, both of us steadily. When she finished her beer she turned her head away and began to cry in earnest, and I knew to let her be. After a few minutes she noticed that I was heading toward the interstate. She turned to me, still crying. "You have to take me back in a little bit," she reminded me.

"I know. Let's just drive for a while," I said softly.

She leaned against the door. "For a while," she whispered.

Soon she was fast asleep, and I gingerly removed my feet from the stirrups and kicked my spurs into the sides of that old Mustang and galloped her down Interstate 10 across the panhandle of Florida, the heaviness unclogging and breaking away into a marvelous mist with every mile.

FOURTEEN

A sweet purring. . . . A timid moan, almost of fright, the stifled gasp of a little girl who has snuck downstairs late Christmas Eve to discover there really *is* a Santa Claus. . . . A bite of an imaginary something, perhaps a sugar cookie, in what I hoped for April was a diaphanous dream of a sumptuous feast by Lake Julep's gilded shore beneath a sky of fair weather. . . . An entire dream word, garbled, lost in translation between dream worlds. . . .

Who would dare turn on the radio?

According to the scientist whose hometown we were heading in the general direction of while April napped, we were passing through some of the densest old-growth forests in the country, not to mention, according to my own observations, the densest collection of vulgar fast-food restaurants in the world. Another chronicler of road escapes and escapades enjoyed by star-crossed relations found something favorable about America's busy highway commerce, but those were the days when solitary dreamers built personal castles. By the time I had my opportunity to make a run for it, all the business was merely bad business and repetitive at that. To this day I remain extremely angry that my greatest flight of fancy has such dirty thumbprints around its edges.

Mercifully it wasn't long before the landscape painter in me had been drugged, while the still-life, sleepy-life and portrait painter had been given a supercharged multiple vitamin. I devoted one half of one canthus to the highway, while the total rest of me was devoted to April as she continued to slumber in the mulled comfort of that drowsy afternoon. Frazzled and exhausted, she hadn't slept much at all for over a week, and I watched her twitch as she chased speckled puppies and a sleek nephew across familiar fields. Then she suddenly shifted and opened her eyes behind the rosy shield of her sunglasses. Lazily wiping a rivulet of drool from the corner of her mouth, she promptly fell asleep again. A fine, healthful shade of crimson splashed her neck and chest and cheeks and the tender bonnets of her ears. A rosy crease the length and shape of an eyelash nictitated on the side of her knee. Her balmy palms with their dreamy rivulets were aflame, gushing, as was her dark hair which I stroked. It was hot as toast and silky with life. Fiery strands turned auburn. . . .

Soon we passed the exit for Loxley and then Montrose, and after a few minutes Mobile Bay came into view. As I drove onto the massive bridge April awakened and smacked my arm. "Oh, no! Oh, Roy!" She saw the blue bay, a barge loaded with black barrels and a sick swordfish of a sailboat, its rigid fin listing. Looking straight ahead she saw gleaming towers and a pebbled roof or two. "You've got to be kidding. *That's Mobile!* Mobile, *Alabama,* Roy!"

"I'll be. I think you're right."

Then the lights went out, and our moices veowed through a lung vibrating funnel of tun. My varm took another peating in the barkness. My bair was bulled. A screaming beauty tat text to me raving, but I wore I coulden tundertand one ward.

Finally we were clear again.

"Pull over!"

"You said we could drive for a while."

"To Mobile, Alabama? Pull over." She was thoroughly worked up, and about to thoroughly work me over. "Pull over this instant!"

"No." What else was there for me to say?

"No?"

"No."

"Did you just say no?"

"Yes."

"Don't you no me. Pull this car over right now. It's *my* car. *Pull-it-over!*"

"I can't."

"When June finds—"

"Does it ever matter what I want? Ever?"

"Don't get like that. Pull over."

I pulled under the bridge and onto an alabaster parking lot of crushed shells and other sea stories. Down by one of the piers a ramshackle restaurant propped itself on gimp pilings. It was storming over the bay. The sunlight had become silvery and thin, the sort of magical sunlight a lonely poet would have precede a first blind date with his one true love. Being civilized, I insisted we get something to eat before anything else, and as luck would have it April was not only furious but famished. We ordered fried shrimp po'boys and chili-cheese fries and sat outside at a picnic table. After a few bites, I went to a telephone and called Henderson. Collect. By the time he'd accepted charges April was walking over to find out what I was doing.

"Where in the hell are you?" Henderson wanted to know.

"Oh, hello. I'm with April."

"I know that. I called down there and found out she never checked in. Now, where are you?"

"I'm not going to let her go to that place. It's that simple."

"Where are you, Roy?"

"Put Mother on."

"No."

"Put my mother on the phone," I said.

"She's not here, goddamnit. What on earth do you think you're doing? Let me talk to April."

"I'll tell you what I'm doing—"

"Just let me talk to April," he interrupted. "She's not tied up in the trunk is she?"

"Don't start fantasizing."

"Put her on."

"And putting her in a trunk would be better than what you planned for her. She hasn't done anything wrong. Maybe Leonard messed up, fine, but April doesn't have to do this."

"What about your mother? Have you for one minute thought about her and what this will do to her?"

"Yes, sir, I have, and I don't think she really wants to do this. I don't think she's crazy, either. And I'll tell you something else, I'm getting tired of you and everybody else saying that shit about her."

"You don't know what you're talking about. No one's saying anything about your mother. The simple fact is, she could press charges and Leonard would almost certainly be found guilty and all of us would be humiliated, not to mention the legal costs all the way around or the fact that the rest of your school year would be ruined. Those are the facts, Roy. Your mother has good reason to be upset, by the way."

"And I have good reason for what I'm doing."

April tried to take the phone. "Roy, give it."

"I've got to go," I said to Henderson.

"You're a selfish young man, Roy," he told me. "You just want to gallivant off with—"

"Go to hell." I hung up the phone.

April's mouth was open. "Uh-uh." She shook her head. "Uhh-Uhh." She swiveled. "*Go to hell?* Hold on a minute. You just told James Henderson to go to hell? Is that right? Did I just hear this? Did I? This is unbelievable. I'm calling James back right now."

"Knock yourself out."

"And give me the keys right now."

"I'm going to finish eating."

"Give me the keys, Roy."

"I'll be right over here."

After a few minutes she walked back and took a seat. "This is some stunt you've pulled. I've never seen you like this. You've never been defiant like this."

The bay was still blooming with that wonderful storm. It was so dark, I could hardly imagine there was anything across the water. It seemed like nowhere to me. I tried to study the far side, but April raised a finger and drew me back.

"What if your Mother presses charges, Roy?"

"She won't press charges. She's going to be fine."

"How do you know?"

"Because I know. Mother'll be all worried about me now. She'll know it wasn't you, and she'll do whatever I tell her. And she *should* be worried about me. Because maybe I can't handle this. Maybe *I'm* the one who can't take it anymore. Maybe *you* can handle it. Maybe *Leonard* can, and *Henderson,* but *I can't.* I just can't do this. You can't make me."

April looked into my eyes. Our napkins blew away. She reached for the hem of her dress.

"I'm going to be gone soon anyway," I said. "I'll be gone and then everything will be fine. Then everybody can have the time of their lives in perfect peace."

"Don't cry on me, baby."

"Well, I'm sick and tired of all this crap."

"All right. I understand." She got up and walked over and stood behind me. She pulled my head against her stomach and stroked my hair and my cheeks. "I won't make you do this."

WE DROVE THROUGH Mississippi: Moss Point, Gautier, Ocean Springs, Biloxie, Gulfport, Long Beach, Pass Christian, Bay Saint Louis. . . .

"Where are we going?"

"It's a surprise."

"If you don't slow down we're going to get a surprise ticket, smart aleck."

"I'm sure the cops are after us anyway."

"We're not going to New Orleans, if that's what you think. Let's just get that clear right now. I'm putting my foot down."

"Go ahead."

"And if you do that, if you take us there, we're just going to have to turn right back around and come all the way back to Citrus. We're a good seven hours from home as it is. And you're the one who'll have to do all the driving."

"Fine."

"I have to go to the little girl's room. And I have to call Henderson to tell him I've been taken hostage."

"Now you're talking."

Once she returned the key to the rest room she walked over to a pay phone. She talked for a few minutes, curling a strand of hair, and then began nodding her head. "Oh, we're fine, June," I heard her say. "Of course. I know you love me. I love you, too. I know. No, I know, I understand." When I walked over, April said, sure, he's here now and handed me the phone.

"Mother?"

"Roy, are you all right?"

"Yes, ma'am. Are you angry?"

"No, no. I just think there's been a terrible misunderstanding. I just . . ." She paused. I tried to determine if she was crying but could only hear the faint sizzling of the connection. "I only meant for April to have an *opportunity* to get away. She didn't *have* to go. My god, why *would* she? She can do what she wants. She's a grown woman. I just did some research for her in case there was trouble between her and Leonard. She's my baby sister, Roy. All I wanted was to give her the chance to get some help if she needed it. Do you see? I don't know what made her think. . . . Well, anyway, I'm glad you're all right."

"Yes, ma'am. If you'd been there you wouldn't have let her stay. It's not what you thought it was."

"Of course not," she said. "I didn't say I wanted her there in the first place."

"I'm only doing what you would have done."

"Well, I'm glad you were there. I just want her to be happy. That's all I want. Are y'all okay?"

"Yes, ma'am. But I'm too tired to drive back and I think April is pretty worn out, too. We might have to pull in somewhere and spend the night."

"By all means. I don't want y'all driving after such a rough day. Do you need any money?"

"We're fine. I love you."

"Oh, honey, I love you, too. When you come home we're just going to have to try again and make things right so you can graduate. Leonard's going to be much better off. There's no reason why we can't be happy. I promise. I'll make sure of it."

"Yes, ma'am."

"Let me talk to April one more time."

April took the phone. She looked at me and looked away. "No, no. I have money. I promise. Oh, by the way, I liked the alcohol article." She smiled. "We love you, too. We'll call tomorrow. Good-bye." She hung up the phone, then curled her lip like Elvis. "Well," she said.

"Well, what?"

"She said we should spend the night somewhere and enjoy ourselves and have a big supper." April looked at me. "What did she say to you?"

"That we were all going to be happy. She said she's going to make sure of it."

"Is that good news or bad news?"

"You tell me."

A middle-aged couple pulled up in an ancient beetle-like black Oldsmobile just then. I remember this minor quarter note in our impromptu roadside quartet—a darling dot or two to form an alluring adagio moment in an otherwise very fast-paced concerto—because the exceedingly white-haired woman, who was thin, tight-lipped and elegant, with intense almond-shape eyes, drove up cautiously while her husband stared directly at me and April with a disturbing amount of interest. We both felt a little on the spot, the way primitives reportedly do when someone is siphoning their souls through a camera or a tape recorder. The man smiled—the Oldsmobile braked, regurgitating something from its tail pipe—got out and continued to examine us cheerfully, the wrinkles around his eyes as lively as sea spray. He wore a white derby hat, failing socks—what calves he had!—boyish shorts, a V-neck sweater and a cotton shirt, the collar of which was behaving badly and tormenting his ears. April laughed, and he laughed back, his eyes pure and electric. He had a large head and a nice tan. He waved. We waved. We all chuckled. Then he walked inside the service station.

His curious, mischievous presence made us happy somehow, although I didn't want to admit it at the time. He and his wife were our bon voyage party, I suppose.

"What a cute little man."

"He was weird."

"Oh, Roy. He was sweet. And his wife was so pretty."

"He was up to something."

"Well, you would know." April took my arm and jumped up and down like a child begging for candy. I was nearly dissocketed by her joy. "Hey, I've got it! Why don't we go back to Mobile. We can stay over in Fairhope. It's so beautiful there. I'd love for you to see Fairhope."

When we turned toward the Mustang we saw a small bluish butterfly centered at the top of its windshield. It fanned once, very slowly. Then it fanned again. It looked as if it were attempting to lift the car off the ground and fly away with it. At last the little thing gave up and took to the air empty-handed, herking and jerking in large loops toward the Oldsmobile, and my suspicious disposition snidely remarked that the old fellow would certainly capture the beautiful blue creature and pin it to some horrible collection, just as he had been trying to bracket April and me into something or other.

But we resisted brackets and all such existential roadblocks that fine day. We had been given wings and freedom and moderately priced gasoline and marching orders from Mother and a special pixie powder with which to crush poshlust to dust, leaving only a coastal daisy chain of dear hopkins.

"Eastward ho, James!" April called, grabbing a blanket and a pillow from the trunk and crawling into the backseat. She said good-bye to the service station and the funny man, who had come out in time to give us an energetic send-off. After nestling and cozying and settling, she watched me from behind those sweetheart shades while chewing a fingernail. "I'm keeping an eye on you," she warned the delirious driver. "We better be going in the right direction."

"Yes, ma'am," I said. "We are."

LATE THAT AFTERNOON we crossed into Louisiana.

"This is all I'm saying." April sat up. "I'd better not see the bridge to New Orleans." She removed her sunglasses. Her face seemed nude without them. A touch of lace from her bra had crept from beneath her dress. She straightened herself. "What time is it?"

"Almost six."

She gave the rearview mirror a mean look, which it faithfully passed along to me. The sun had darkened her further, giving her just a touch of a burn. She stretched and yawned. She rubbed her arms. She was coming to life in the backseat, establishing herself again, and the force of her made me look away.

"I know that's not a bridge."

"Of course not."

"Have you ever been to New Orleans?"

"Nope."

"Leonard took me once. We danced all night. Actually, I danced around him. He's not much of a dancer. Did you have a hotel in mind, reservations, money?"

"As a matter of fact, I took a little from my savings."

"No you didn't."

"Yes I did. It's my money. It's my account. And it's my business. Hey, why are you coming up here?"

She crawled over the seat and plopped down heavily. Then she reached for my wallet. Deft pickpocket that she was, I never had a chance.

"You're really something. You're just walking around with this kind of money waiting to get mugged. Oh, and by the way, if you were just going to be taking me to Pensacola, why did you need this?"

"You never know."

We hummed over bayou tree tops, tin roofs and fishermen, across Lake Pontchartrain, where a sign directed us to the French Quarter. I had no idea where I was going, and April remained wickedly silent. Soon we were bumping along brick streets slick from a recent rain. There were enormous, mustachioed men pushing enormous, glistening hot dogs on wheels and shaggy banana trees behind mysterious courtyard walls. The smell of stale beer struck a sour gong in what was otherwise a steamy symphony of exotic scents. Loudly dressed people gathered at babbling corners. A bearded old man in a boater waved at us, then turned toward a dark corridor. Three bow-tied black children tap-danced for a pickled crowd. A raggedy man in a soiled three-piece suit accosted himself and was ruthlessly reprimanded by himself for it. There was iron everywhere, and everything was beautifully aged; even the vibrant colors of the buildings seemed to be of some vintage pigment made in an old country that had long ago turned its back on time.

We drove down Canal Street and came to the river and parked. The Mississippi stunned me. I could hardly believe its size, its deceptive docility. It was such a large, sleeping thing, a brown sluggard carrying limbs and trash and boats on its back. I had read of its terrible currents, of its epic flooding, but on that glorious day, as April held my hand and pointed to tugs and trees, it was nothing more or less than our burly pet.

After another thirty minutes of driving I eventually found a fancy-looking hotel off Bourbon Street and made what Mother referred to as an executive decision. "I'm making an executive decision," I announced.

I pulled into the small driveway, and the valet walked over and took my keys while a grizzled elderly bellman, still cackling from the last joke he'd told, opened April's door. Without giving me so much as a look, April walked right into the lobby.

"You got your hands full," the bellman told me.

"That's my aunt."

"Whatever you want to call her, you got your hands full. God bless you and amen on that."

I walked up to the reception desk. "Here you are, room three forty-two," a woman was saying.

"That's a room with a balcony, right? It's my nephew's first time in New Orleans."

"Third-floor balcony, directly over the state flag." She paused and bit her lip. "Oh, hold on a second." She typed something and began speaking again. "Here's something just down the hall. It's a corner room with a balcony. It's a better view."

"Perfect," said April. She saw me reaching for my pocket. "No, no, no. This is my treat. It's an early graduation present. And I'm buying dinner, too."

"No, you're not."

"We'll see."

We stared around the lobby, two breathless bumpkins bedazzled by all the brass and marble. After a few minutes we were handed a self-important skeleton key (these were the days before soulless plastic cards) and given directions to our room. At the elevator April said, "Shoot," and sent me back for a second key in case we lost the first.

The woman at the front desk was on the telephone. She looked at me and raised a forefinger banded with red rubber. "A man came by earlier asking about you," she said. "He looked a lot like you, as a matter of fact, but he was older. Yeah. He said not to worry, that he'd find you later." She listened, nodding. She looked at me tensely. "Oh, I bet he knows exactly whose side you're on. You'd better be careful." She hung up. "May I help you?"

The accommodations were, as far as I knew, sublime, but in those days I hadn't seen very much of the world. I gawked at and caressed the antiques of the proud suite April had obtained for us, and like a rustic who has never seen indoor plumbing I tried the faucets and flushed the toilet. Still warming to my character, I picked up one of the tiny milled bars of soap and said, "Hey, look, baby soap!" April called me over. We eased open thick velvet curtains and French doors and tittered onto the balcony, where we basked in our view of the street. Presently April shrieked and ran inside and threw herself on the bed. I followed and leaped onto the other bed and began jumping. Both of us were bouncing when the old bellman knocked on the door.

After he deposited April's bags I walked into the hallway to tip him and to ask where we should have supper. His hair had been straightened and combed back. His face was flat, the color of a worn penny with black freckles. "That's quite a rare specimen of a woman in there," he said through dry lips. He parted with his words carefully, punctuating everything with convincing smacks. "The good Lord don't manage that but every once in a while."

Galatoire's was the restaurant he suggested, which pleased me because I'd heard Mother mention it many times. After explaining how to get there he actually clicked his heels together and offered a burlesque salute. "Carry on, young man," he said.

April was showering when I returned. I went to the balcony and after a few minutes heard the blow drier. When I walked back inside she was barefoot, wearing one of her little black dresses.

"You expected to use that at a home for battered women?"

"This?" She shut the loud-mouthed thing off.

"No, that dress."

"You never know."

She fired a gun made from her fingers, then finished drying her hair.

Next she walked over and strapped on a pair of heels and examined her legs in the mirror.

"You kick ass," I told her gallantly.

She felt of her ass! "You're the ass kicker."

"I guess we can both kick a little ass when we have to."

"You better believe it." She pointed to her hair. "Up or down?"

"Up."

She saw to that while I washed my face. When I walked out she gave a last glance at her earrings and spun toward me. "Ready, Freddy!" she said. "Ready, Roy!" I responded, stiff-arming foppish Frederick right out of the picture. That done, I opened the door, and we headed for storied streets of trinkets and treasures, or so a waxy brochure described it.

Since I'd never eaten oysters our first stop was an oyster bar where April ordered a dozen and two beers. The idea that teenage drinking was the greatest evil in the universe had not yet occurred to the good people of New Orleans, and all through the night we were grateful for the fact. When the tin plate of oysters arrived, April passed me a Proustian inhalation of nasal dynamite, namely a dipping sauce she'd concocted with horseradish, cocktail sauce *and* hot sauce. She said it was the absolute thing to do.

I found my first oysters to be quite excellent, though after three I feared they might lead to unpredictable gastric consequences and left them to their barnacled beds, where they hardly had time to count ten sheep before April reached over and forked them straight to her mouth.

Next she wanted a piña colada. We turned down Bourbon Street and spotted a place that served frozen drinks and then stopped at a corner bar to listen to a soul band.

"How do you sashay, anyhow?" the friendly dunce nephew wondered aloud.

"Come on. You'll see."

We found a beer stand and imbibed as the French Quarter glittered tipsily in the strangely agitated orange dusk. We discovered a shop of antiquated maps and charted courses through time. As evening arrived I noticed that the streets and buildings were becoming more aggressive with their tricks and special effects. A newspaper crawled in a trance from a forbidding doorstep and begged about my ankle until I kicked the damn thing. A pretty woman and a paunchy man exchanged glances and whispers and envelopes. Musics mingled. Pigeons scattered. A pair of stockinged legs belonging to a manikin swung out over our heads. The sun was gone but not the sharp twilight. We were not alone, only anonymous. Nightfall created conspiracies of pleasure behind every corner.

I was smiling at something April said when I spotted a shadowy figure smirking with a cigarette down a dark alley across the street. My waltzing heart skipped a beat, and I grabbed April's hand and rushed over, but as we drew closer the man became a smudged pipe venting steam.

"What was it?"

"I just wanted to try this other side," the gullible dunce nephew explained.

Mad laughter somewhere. Things awakening. April had my hand. She led me.

"We'd better get to the restaurant."

"Yes."

"Isn't this wonderful, Roy?"

"No one knows us here."

"I know."

"We could be anybody.

"We could be famous."

"I'm starting to think we might be famous."

"All right, we're famous. We're very, very, very famous. You're a famous football player and I'm a famous actress."

We'd expected something intimate and were rather intimidated when we walked past the curtains of the anteroom directly into the glare of glamorous Galatoire's. The giant dining area was a stage of brazen mirrors and bold lights where everyone could easily look at everyone else and did. From the moment we stepped inside I constantly had to ward off the unwanted glances of male patrons. A pair of lascivious eyes would alight somewhere on April's frame like two fat flies, and the only way to remove them was to swat them back with the nettled whips of my own addled irises. I could not have cared less that these fellows hailed from some of New Orleans's most prestigious families, nor that they cheekily thought of Galatoire's as an unpretentious little supper club where one might still a rumbling stomach with trout almondine and a stiff drink. I did not care that they were exceptionally well dressed and traveled and spoken, either. I just wished they would go away and that an understanding waiter would dim the lights.

But after a second glass of wine arrived it no longer seemed necessary to be quite so vigilant.

"A toast," April was saying. "To you."

"To *you*."

"To us."

April reached across the table and took my thumb. Thirty-nine wanton eyes bore down on us (one of the rogues wore a patch), but April squeezed, then patted, then petted.

"You have so much heart, Roy. You're young and you don't know yet how rare that is. I'm just so proud of the way you've grown up. I'm proud of who you are." She stared at me until her eyes went soft and finally she smiled. "Good thing you got dressed up to carry your old aunt to the nuthouse."

"We deserve this," I told her.

"One day we'll look back on all this and laugh," April promised. "You just keep getting knocked around, don't you?"

"If you're knocked around, I'm knocked around. I don't think that will ever change."

Who could possibly care what they served us or what our waiter's name was or about the strong cologne he wore or the condition of his skin, or about the lanky, balding gentleman next to us doctoring his ice cream with bourbon? Someone had several glasses of champagne sent to our table—perhaps the owl-eyed man with the beard, sitting at the table with the kind-looking physician who had intoxicated his ice cream—and I felt nothing but gratitude.

We went dancing afterwards. April had taught me how to dip a woman long ago (Leonard had taught me how to dip tobacco during that same long ago), instructing me in the importance of moving with quick authority, of dropping the female body down firmly, head almost to the floor, pausing, then pulling up with great force. If it isn't a little dangerous, April explained, it's no good at all. I soon learned that when this maneuver was executed correctly, it excited a woman so thoroughly that she experienced a thrilling moment of embarrassment. I'd sometimes walk over to Mother, catch her unawares and throw down on her. When I'd rip her up close to me, she always let out a little gasp. "Do it again," she'd say. And April, too: "Oh, my. Do it again. Okay, ready," she'd demand, becoming limber. "One more time!" Lorri-Anne would plead, her pleats rippling. I was ever their man for the job.

I dipped April more than a few times that night in New Orleans. The name of that particular bar has been sealed in a silk-lined box in memory's safest and plushest vault (likewise the name and exact location of our hotel, to say nothing of that imperishable room number just down the hall from 342) but not what we did there. We danced closely, recklessly. We danced until we were sweating and clinging. We danced until there was a crowd and applause, and my feet became wheels and my legs wings and my mind a merry-go-round and April everything.

She took my hand again and led me down streets of brick and bliss. She leaned into me and gripped my arm tightly, her body tense with energy. We talked of what it would be like to have a place in New Orleans. Perhaps I would play for the Saints someday. A barker promised us a fully nude show to end all shows if we would only step right up.

"Would you live down here or in the Garden District?"

"What's the Garden District?"

"Oh, Roy. With the big oaks and the streetcars. They have huge mansions. We'll go tomorrow. You *have* to see the Garden District." She took my hand. "I have a surprise for you. Turn right here. You have to go here."

We went there. Two women were playing piano before slanted mirrors that licked up their fingers along with the keys, which rose in staccato bursts to catch at those fingers. The audience watched on in a cavernous room. Rocky Top Tennessee. Bill Dance! Two tall glasses of something reddish paraded past us, did a double take and returned to our table.

"Here you are. What a striking couple you two make."

"Why, thank you. This is my nephew, Roy."

They talked. I observed April's mouth. Her fingers found my knee. I sat back. Somewhere in that sickeningly sweet drink was a real troublemaker.

"Scoot over next to me."

I did and put my arm around her, and she captured and kissed my dangling hand.

"These blizzards are pretty strong," I ventured.

"Hurricanes!"

"Hurricanes, then."

Soon we were off to a garden patio where we grew feverish by a watery fire percolating hellish colors. April smoothed my excited lapels. The night sky sagged opulently, a limpid indigo illusion behind fluttering eyelashes of black leaves. There went the surgeon and his bearded friend on foot. There veered the middle-aged couple on a magic carpet with an enchanted key to room 342. (Hunting us again perhaps.) There bounced a brontosaurus with a mug of beer. Here come the daredevil cherubs!

"I believe I'm a little drunk," said April.

"I'm . . . *Yes!*"

"Let's have another hurricane."

"You think?"

"I think."

I was going after those hurricanes when in the corner of that seething patio, just beyond the flicker of a frightened gas lamp, there came a familiar laugh. I tried to follow the derisive thing, but a bulky group of conventioneers slowed me down. I bumped through and finally beyond them and spied a sinister cloud of fresh smoke on the street. When I got to it I looked around and heard a live recording of that laugh again. I knocked into a trio of mink shawls and kept moving. There it was, turning a corner. I rounded that corner, but to my right was that same alley from earlier and that same smudged pipe again, this time steamless. I took out my skeleton key. I thought of the woman at the front desk and replaced her with a woman who for all practical purposes could have been an exact duplicate of the original—only an artist would have noticed the difference—and she said: *A man who looks just like you . . . very much like you . . . but is older . . . is older, right . . . was by . . . had dropped by . . . will see you . . . will see you around . . . catch you around . . . will find you!*

I tapped my timepiece of short-term memory, but its arms were drunkenly swimming in a stormy potion of potent red liquid. I tapped again. It ticked and tocked and then performed a sluggish backstroke. I bumped into that trio of mink shawls once more and apologized. I kept moving, but had there not been an ankle-length gray coat standing against a blank wall?

I ran back, turning the corner on a thin dime, but the trail had gone cold. Now the street was clogged with bullies and more conventioneers. A group of clowns who were passing out religious tracts had surrounded a guilty Baptist on a bender. And I was drunk, a drunk in a farce who had forgotten his drinks—a farce of a farce. I was an actor running around in what I'd thought was a romantic thriller with noir edges when in fact I was playing the dummy's part in a low comedy of mental errors. I went back to the bar.

"Where have you been?"

"I thought . . . I had to go to the bathroom. Here's yours."

"I missed you."

"I missed you, too. Have you ever had pistane?"

There beside the wet flames, April began attacking her knee. "What did you say?"

I sat next to her. "Pistane."

"Pistane?"

"Pistane."

"Please stop saying it! Pistane!"

"Pistane."

"Stop it! I beg you!"

"Coggins told me about it."

"Bad Coggins. Pistane. Come here."

"Where?"

"Closer."

We mixed drinks and carried on with one very lucky straw, having dropped the unfortunate other.

"I don't know what I ever would have done without you, Roy."

"You don't have to ever do without me, April."

She put her head on my shoulder, burned a brand there. She settled in, branding. I touched her cheek, wove my throbbing hand through her wild hair. Pink-eared, a touch copper-topped, the hurt and happiness of watching her never stopped for a moment but just kept going. Her hand reached for my lapel again, then my dimple, then my nose. What those fingers so carefully skipped over trembled.

"Should we just move down here?"

"Yes."

"We could bring the trailer."

"Perfect."

"That way we wouldn't have to pack."

"I'll be a lawyer."

"Be a pediatrician."

"Okay, a pediatrician."

"And take care of me."

"Always."

"Wear a stethoscope." She put one around my neck. "And those cute little green outfits. Say ah."

"Ah."

"Say I think I better take April to bed."

"I think I better take April to bed."

"You know what I mean."

"You know what I mean."

When we arrived at the hotel a puff of smoke hovered before the glass doors, and I almost fell for it. But how could I with April pulling me past a smiling new bellman and a leering valet into an almost empty lobby? Nevertheless, I did have a quick look around as we awaited the elevator. I noted a pounding heart, a WET FLOOR sign, a pool of soapy marble, two fingers tucked into the back of my pants, two o'clock in the morning, a man where the woman had been at the front desk, a muffled bell, parting doors, April against me, what floor, up or down?

Up. Out. Onward. But I smelled smoke again. A door slammed down the hall. Lingering smoke. I was going to say something about this when an outraged cotton puppet sprang upside down from the front pocket of my pants to demand justice. "I robbed you, see how easy?" April held the money. "Rich guy, huh?" She wrinkled her nose. "Good-looking rich guy is all you are. Well, no thanks, Mister."

I pushed the buck teeth of our gold key into its slot and slurred sesame. The room was crisp and cool in the way that hotel rooms always seem to be crisp and cool. The darkness fluttered. The bathroom light came on. I sat smiling while April brushed her teeth and washed her face. I stood in a breathless haze when she walked out. I think I must have pointed.

Tank top, boxers.

"Can you believe I forgot to pack pajamas?"

"Those are mine."

"I washed these for you months ago. If you're gonna leave them for that long they're mine."

"No, they're mine."

I was at her, but she giggled by. Not quite. I seized a stranded wrist. She fought like a fish. I fished like a champion. As I reeled she tried to dive, to run, to jump from the water, to throw the hook with squeals and twists and shakes, but I wouldn't let her go, so finally she played dead. When I brought her near she revived and broke from the boat and splashed into the bed. Hands above her head, wrists crossed. "Got you," she said. Her words were heavy. One knee up, one splayed. Her tank top bid farewell to my boxers, and their parting produced a belly button and a stretch of taut skin. Her eyes closed. Her head turned to the side. "I'm sleepy. Turn out that light."

Anything to please her. I turned out the light and walked over to the French doors leading to the balcony. I again smelled smoke and figured it was my clothes. I threw my blazer to the floor and began unbuttoning my shirt, staring at April. Her eyes were bright in that burning abyss. I unbuckled my belt. There was some difficulty with the zipper, and April beat her poor pillow as a result.

"Some strip show!"

"Damnit!"

At last I coaxed that zipper into being my partner and then sat down and pulled off my shoes and pitched my socks at April, who screamed as if she were fifteen. I went to my bed and lay on my side as if I were thirty-five.

"I'm getting my clothes back," I said.

"Oh no you're not."

The room stirred with the hushed light from the street. April slowly emerged on the bed, first her tank top, then her boxers, then the rest of her, a rapt teenybopper chewing a fingernail, staring at me, splayed knee still splayed, up knee now down.

"Yes I am."

I got up. She didn't move. I sat beside her.

"Yes I am."

"No."

The boxers had slipped down her hips a little. I was breathing in swoons and moans. She made not a sound, but her stomach quivered and sucked in when I placed a finger on it. I encircled her navel, drowning.

"Roy."

I leaped up to a rib.

"Roy. You're about to get into trouble."

"I'm just playing."

I crawled down to a lower rib and careened along its curve and came to a soft shoal of hip and then a firm bone.

"Roy."

I nudged the boxers. She grabbed my hand. I said no; she said no. We attempted to laugh. We tried no again. No good, no nothing. So my hand slapped her hand, and her hand slapped back, and then my hand took her hand and placed it above her head where lay its lifelong bunk mate.

"Roy. Come on." She caught her breath. I caught her breath.

We exhaled, spinning. "Roy. Roy. Baby, listen."

But my fingers had found the gaping waistband of my boxers once more. "These don't fit." Her tank top was not in good shape, either. Nor her hair. Nor her breathing. Stunning wreck.

"Baby, please. Please."

I put my fingers to her lips to quench her voice. She drank them softly and pulled me down to her. And the tears she cried in that sudden burst still fall now. They will fall every day until she is gone and until I am gone. Then they will fall in some other world. Limp as a ragdoll, brokenly calling my name, she sat back up, and I gathered her funny elbows and her hot face and all the tears I could find. I gathered her up as she banged fragile fists into my chest, and I told her it would be all right. And the oddly sad thing was that what I had been saying to her all those years had proven to be far more true than I could have ever imagined—I was not my father, after all, and I would never, ever fail April.

FIFTEEN

April told me that Sterns had become depressed and decided to close the bait and tackle for a few days. She said I should go see him.

When I pulled up I realized for the first time that his place was in serious decline. I'd always thought the two-story house possessed a sort of ramshackle charm, but with the lights out, with a rusted CLOSED sign hanging on the door, it seemed merely dilapidated. Even the pecan trees, which had formerly provided such generous shade, appeared tattered. I'd somehow never noticed the rows of bullet holes that warring woodpeckers had made in their trunks, nor that some of their branches were sickly. The neighboring oaks and cedars and pines seemed lackluster, as well, and the blades of grass beneath them were wilted.

Adding to this decay was an exhausted bitch nursing her pups under the front porch. "Hey, girl," I called. Her tail thumped twice before she shut her eyes. When I dropped to my knees to reach for her, Sterns came to the door.

"Some of them aren't even hers," he said. "I don't know where the other mama is. She's run off or got hit one. They both just showed up here with their litters a couple of days ago. Howl acted like a big shot for 'em. I tell you what, people think I'm the gee-dee humane society. Now I've got another ten puppies to find homes for."

"They're wearing her out," I said.

"Yeah, ain't they? Come on in."

Sterns turned on a small lamp and pulled a chair over for me. It didn't look as if he had been getting much sleep. He hadn't shaved or bathed, apparently. He stank. It didn't appear he'd changed clothes in a while, either. He almost seemed flyspecked.

"April told me what happened with you two when she came by to pick up Howl," he said. He walked into the back room and returned with two tall-boy beers. "James Henderson called me to see if I knew where y'all were. Boy, was he hot as hell." Sterns was laughing. "Here," he said, handing me a beer and taking a seat. "You deserve it."

"There was never any choice in it."

"Choice or not."

"You would have done the same."

"I'd do anything for her. Do anything for Leonard, too. Anything," he said firmly, his face suddenly grave. "You love somebody enough, sometimes you have to step out into uncharted territory."

"I guess that's what I was in. I just did what I had to do."

Sterns stared at me as if I'd said something demanding without knowing the consequences. I felt ridiculous.

"It was a lot of fun," I said finally.

"Sounds like y'all had a big time." Sterns began to peer out one of the windows.

"What's the matter?"

"I just can't seem to sit down anymore." He stood as if to prove it. "I'm having trouble staying in any one place for more than a minute tops. I guess what happened just reminded me of all the old times. Seems like no matter what, sometimes you're going to catch it."

He began wandering around the bait and tackle, touching the surfaces of things with troubled reverence, as if the world were presently to disappear and he had just this last chance to savor it but was discovering that the grief was already too much.

"I can't write for some reason, either. Hell of it is, I never wrote to get published anyhow. This book I been working on all these years was for April and Leonard. I was going to have it bound up by one of those vanity presses and make a gift of it when I finished. I hoped to have it done by their twenty-fifth anniversary. Which is coming up. You'll just be getting started in the pros by then. We could have us a celebration."

"We will," I said.

"Yeah. But I can't pull it together. The words are clumsy, and even when I'm writing well, I start thinking about what I'm trying to write about and what I've written seems slicker than shit. The better the writing, the bigger the lies, and bad writing is the most terrible lie of all and not worth reading besides. It's hopeless. It's impossible. I'm not equal to it. I never was, but now I realize it and it's unbearable. I really want to do something for them. For all of us. But hell, I can't do shit."

"It's just writer's block," I said. "You'll get over it."

The bitch pressed her nose against the screen door and nudged it. Sterns went behind the counter and retrieved a can of dog food. "She never whines. I bought her some of the good stuff to fatten her up. Canned is like caviar to a dog."

I peeked into one of the live wells. Several dead shiners floated on top, already rancid and bloated, their fins gone to a glutinous mush, their eyes bulging and drained of color. The rest hovered near the bottom as far away from the sky of swollen white bellies and descending scales as they could manage.

Sterns returned and saw me.

"Seems like all the chickens are coming home to roost," he said. "And here I am utterly defenseless. 'Cause I defended myself—and April and Leonard and even your mama—with that book. All the things that went wrong. All the things that might've been. That was what the book was for. To make up for it. And that's why when I can't work I feel so worthless. Hell, what am I thinking, trying to write a damned book anyhow? Answer me that."

"Come on, Sterns," I said.

"Just let me talk, Roy. I'm sorry it has to be you, but it does. You happen to be available."

After returning to his recliner with a Rebel top-water plug he'd taken from his discount bin, Sterns sat with his legs spread and began spinning its propeller. "That's a nice sound, ain't it?"

"Yeah."

"Soothing. Prrr. Prrr. Lookit here." He hung one of the prongs from one of the treble hooks on his ear. "You think we could market this to the punk rockers?"

"It might be a good idea."

He drank, and wiped his mouth. "Shit," he hissed. "The only real question is, why do I keep going?" He waited for it to sink in. "That's the question. Hell, it's a constant decision against suicide every waking moment."

"Sterns."

"I'm not saying I'd do that. This is just a particularly bad spell. Up all night staring at a single spot on the wall and only able to sleep a few hours in the afternoon. Tired all the time, but whenever I lie down a jolt of pain hits me and I try to write again. But I can't come up with a damned thing that fits anywhere anymore. I can't even write my little sentences."

"I like those."

"Me, too. I like to read 'em like they're something out of a fortune cookie. They just come out of nowhere. But they please me for some reason."

He sat back heavily. I stared at the floor.

"Shit, would you slap me next time I go on like that?"

"I'm happy to listen."

"I think I just been alone for too long. Maybe that's all it is. Stir-crazy. If I don't open the store back up I'll end up jabbering like Coggins."

"Coggins scares me."

"Now, he's a creepy old thing. Just pops up places. Anywhere. Everywhere. And he ain't even got a car."

"I'd like to see some of the book sometime," I said.

"Shit. Wouldn't that be nice." Sterns stood. "Tell you what. Maybe one of these days after you get settled up at school, maybe I'll send you a page or two. When are you leaving, anyhow?"

"July."

"Bittersweet, ain't it?"

"Yeah. Bittersweet."

"Actually, that ain't true. It's just bitter. Then later on, if you're lucky and you start having a good time, you'll look back and add the sweet. 'Course, I never got around to that part."

There was something I wanted to tell Sterns, but I felt somehow I shouldn't. We stared at each other.

"I know that look," he said. "What's bothering you?"

"I just wanted to say thanks, I guess."

"For what?"

"For everything."

"Hell, Roy. Don't get weepy on me."

"No, I mean, Leonard. . . ."

"Leonard *what*?"

"Leonard's been like a father to me and . . . in a way . . . you—"

Sterns cut me off. "Stop it," he said. He was almost angry. "Don't say that." He frowned and looked down, tapping his fingers on the wooden counter, shaking his head.

"I just meant—"

He cut me off again. "I know what you meant. And I appreciate it." He tried to smile. "I guess I just don't want to bear any responsibility for you being such a motherfucker."

"I know what you mean."

"Good. Hey, you want to take care of one of my orphans?"

"I'd be honored."

Sterns went upstairs. When he came back down he seemed genuinely cheered. "I picked this one out just for you. It tickles hell out of me." He handed me an envelope. "You know the rules. Don't look at it until later. It's bad luck to open it now."

I walked down the road and couldn't resist having a look, so I took out the sheet of paper and opened it: "Repeat." That's all it said.

APRIL AND I FISHED every afternoon and almost every night and some mornings before school. In the mornings we used top-water baits, which rattled and chortled as we worked them through the cattails and lily pads and cypresses. Julep was often placid and misty, and the only sound would be the noises of our lures until an explosive strike. No one I know of has ever gotten used to the thrill of a strike. It claims the blood every time.

On the weekends we bought shiners and fished lazily all day, sometimes from the boat, sometimes from the dock, taking frequent swimming breaks and repairing to various states of undress to soak up the sun. We swam by sunlight and moonlight. We climbed into the branches of our old tree friends and made oaths. We waited for Leonard's call every night and pretended to be happy for him. April killed three water moccasins—sombitches.

Lorri-Anne and I drifted apart during those weeks. She never protested or pressured, never demanded my time, though she surely had a right to it. I could hardly say a thing to anybody anyway, sometimes not even to April. We passed many silent hours, commenting only on the fact that yet another day had passed.

When Leonard came back from Tallahassee he'd lost a few pounds and said he'd never felt better. The doctor he was assigned to was serious about church and had made him promise to start attending services, something Leonard was eager to do. I noticed that Leonard had picked up little tricks concerning his drinking. Once he'd had a beer or two he'd go for a big glass of water. He'd learned to drink whisky very slowly, and he usually only drank it on weekends. He started working out with weights and even running. Within a few weeks he'd lost fifteen pounds. The first Sunday he showed up at church Brother Glenn made a big production of his return, and several members of the congregation testified that they had been interceding for him all through the years. Leonard was deeply gratified and told me that it seemed strange to him that he'd held himself away from such happiness for so long.

What a loving haven Citrus Hills Church of God was. Even a wretch like me got special treatment. The Sunday before I graduated Brother Glenn called me down front and presented me with a Dake's study Bible with my name embossed on the cover in gold. He had everyone come forward and lay hands on me and pray for my future. I can still hear the intense whispers of those prayers, the occasional shouts. Sometimes I can almost feel the warm hands pressing against me and buoying me up. Finally Brother Glenn gave me a blessing and said Jesus would be with me and told me to go forth in the name of the Lord. I vowed I would.

That May I graduated.

At our graduation party Lorri-Anne informed me she'd decided to go to Alabama. I thought it would be nice to follow her and sneak into the Kappa Delta house—she was, she claimed, destined to be a Kappa Delta—and make love to her on the sly. She made me promise to visit, and I said that I would, though neither of us believed it was likely.

"Don't get lost up there," she warned. She tapped my head. "You think too much."

"I do?"

"Yes. And you need constant sugar to keep it from happening."

"Constant sugar, huh?"

"Oh, you know," she said, working a husky drawl, wiping a tear. "Sugar, Roy. Don't act like you don't know sugar."

AFTER GRADUATION I found it difficult to be around anyone for very long and took to wandering the countryside alone. The magnolias were blooming. Bold cones the color of cream sprouted almost overnight, and toward the end of May the petals began to unfold in decadent repose. Lush, tenderly curled, they resembled great pearly scoops of ice cream. The bigger trees seemed to have hundreds of flowers, and from a distance it appeared that the slick, dark green leaves, with their veined lime bellies, were surrendering spectacular bursts of white fire. When the lightning bugs began to spark, there was no describing it, just quiet wonder.

The aroma was lovely, and I'd bend branches down and stand transfixed, pushing the flowers against my nose and peeling petals away to keep in my pockets. Soon they would begin to fall to the ground, indecent and helpless. They'd turn a honeyish taupe, becoming dusty and rubbery. Finally they'd fold into themselves, making slender browning scrolls the texture of thin supple leather. Then they'd vanish to earth, and it would be time for me to go.

THE DAY BEFORE I left for Tallahassee, April and I had a last fishing trip. We sat for nearly an hour working a rise in the middle of the lake, casting listlessly. It was only ten or twelve feet deep, and the curdled sandy bottom was inviting. I longed to dive in and feel the clean white grains beneath my toes and to dig for mussels. It was one of our favorite places to swim. On hot days we'd jump in and take a seat on the lake's floor. The temperature down there was at least ten degrees cooler than at the surface. We'd see who could sit the longest. We'd laugh and pretend to drink coffee. Pass the milk, please. Would you care for a biscuit? Oh, could you hand me the butter. *Roy,* April always told me, was a fun word to holler underwater.

I grew frustrated, and my casting became erratic and angry. Soon enough I looked down to find an enormous tangle and recalled the first time I fished with shiners, when Sterns had spooked me because of his intimacy with April and how I wondered if my father had ever fished with her.

"You've got a snag," April said.

"Yeah."

"Do you want me to fix it for old times' sake?"

"Yeah."

"Hold on. I'm coming."

"I don't want to go," I told her.

"I know," she said. "But *I* want you to. You don't have to give up any of this. . . ." She swept her hand and took in Lake Julep and the countryside. "You don't have to give up Citrus or how you've grown up. But take your future, too. Take all of it: the part you've already lived and the part you're going to live. I want everything for you, Roy. And you're ready for it. You're more ready for it than you know."

The following day we all gathered in front of the house. I wore seersucker trousers, white bucks and a white button-down at Mother's request. The true-blue Mustang was packed and waiting. April and Mother and Leonard had given it to me for college.

"Please don't ever wear sandals," Mother teased. "It would kill me to know you were slouching around in sandals."

Leonard gave me a bear hug. "Give 'em hell, Royce."

"We're so proud," Mother said. "Call as soon as you get there." She touched my cheek. "Your mother loves you," she said.

When I went to April she took my hand, all of her fingers curling and pressing into my palm as her nails dug in with a frantic, piercing kiss. I backed away and couldn't say good-bye. I got into the car and drove around the bend, past the trailer and Leonard's truck and his rig and barking Howl, past the fields and farms and rolling hills, and on to the main highway. From there I took Interstate 10. When it was too much, when I thought I would turn around and go back, I'd open my hand and stare at the marks April had made there, at the little incisions from her fingernails, her painful kisses. And I would tell myself to keep going, that it was the only way to help her. To help Mother and Leonard and even Sterns, to help any of them, I had to keep going.

SIXTEEN

We started two-a-days. We wore shorts and shoulder pads and helmets. When we weren't running, working through drills or weight training, we were watching game films; but mostly we were on the field, where I fidgeted with my face mask, trying to ward off the hornets of memory that followed me everywhere.

I'd return to my room exhausted, only to lie in bed night after night until three or four in the morning, waking at seven with a rush of pain, my heart pounding away. I called Citrus every day, but the conversations were depressing, and I began to dread them. Sometimes April would cry, sometimes Mother would cry, sometimes Leonard would complain about all the crying, but their feelings seemed like feelings invented for my benefit, while my own were genuine. When they were enthusiastic it hurt even worse. April's attempts to fortify me were simply appalling. She sounded almost matronly.

Mother wrote once or twice a week. I'd read her letters over and over again, concentrating on any news about April and trying to determine Mother's state of mind, which I had for the most part concluded was steady.

Dearest Roy,

I love and miss you more than you could ever know. Leonard and April came by the other day for supper. She was cleaning out her freezer and found a bunch of fish that you two had caught. We thawed them out and fried them and had them with grits and hush puppies, but we couldn't stop thinking about you and finally poor April broke down and then we all did, even Leonard. April and I are getting along better than we ever have before. I have to admit she's the reason. She's really tried to reach out to me, and it makes me ashamed of all that's happened. I just wish she weren't so fragile. We can't wait for the first game. James might fly down for it. Wouldn't that be fun?

By the way, I asked James to get a list of books to counter any trendy literary criticism you might encounter. I do hope you'll major in literature. Anyway, you remember "Dover Beach." Well, James says you should get some of Matthew Arnold's essays. He also says you should try Ruskin and Pater and Baudelaire and Poe. I'm going to read them, too. We'll read them together.

We're all very proud of you or else we couldn't stand the separation. I have to be strong for April. She's not taking it very well. I suppose you were her child, too, in a way. God bless you, my dear. Oh, one more thing, you left your tuxedo. Don't worry, I'll bring it when we come for the game.

Yours always,

Mother.

Since the campus was empty I began to take long drives during the evenings. Wheeling away into the hills of Tallahassee, whenever I came across a promising stretch of pasture I'd pull over and lean against the hood of the Mustang and watch the lightning bugs wafting about with the ease of gentle music. Afterwards I'd drive to a truck stop off I-10 to get a bite to eat. The one I began to frequent was small, with only a few tables and a menu of fried chicken, catfish and potato logs, but I could sit and stare at the interstate and remember my weekend with April. When the big rigs rolled by I thought of Leonard, too. The idea that people were going places and doing things made me feel better.

There were other truck stops, most of them massive, with bright signs that shot fifty feet into the air. These newer places had fresh food and clean tables, but there were too many people in them to afford any consolation. I preferred the lonely truck stop I'd found. The man who managed it was kind and allowed me to keep to myself. There was a carousel of bumper stickers that always tickled a grin out of me. One sticker read "We Don't Give a Damn How You Do It Up North!" Another read "Southern By The Grace of God!" A third—my favorite—read "If Your Heart's Not In Dixie, Get Your Ass Out!"

The man who ran the place wore gold-rimmed spectacles and comported himself with gentle dignity. He had a kempt beard and sharp eyes. Sitting in an easy chair behind the counter, he read books and magazines, dabbing his thumb on his tongue every now and again before turning a page. I started going every night. During the first week we hardly spoke.

"You sure like that highway," he said finally.

"Yes, sir."

"I do, too. I can watch it for hours."

He walked over and introduced himself. His hands were even bigger than Leonard's, thick black vices with fleshy palms. He clamped down approvingly. "I already know you are," he said. "Royce Collier. You were one of our top recruits this year." He placed a magazine about Florida State football on the table and pointed to my photograph. "Used to play myself. Fullback. I'm a season ticket holder now. I recognized you when you came in last week. Guess you're having trouble sleeping."

"Yes, sir."

"A beer might help. Just one to knock the edge off. I'd be happy to buy you one. If anybody comes in just slide it under the table. I'm pretty good friends with the law." He smiled. "By the way, they tell me you're pretty good for a white boy."

Bobby Lester gave me a beer or two every night. He often gave me sleeping pills as well. I'd sip beer and think of the lightning bugs among the oaks and cypresses surrounding Lake Julep and sometimes walk outside to the pay phone to call April. The conversations were almost always variations on a humiliating theme:

"Just talk to me like you used to."

"What do you mean, Roy? I am talking like I used to."

"No you're not."

"Roy."

"No you're not. You know you're not."

"Roy."

"April."

"Oh, baby. You'll feel better when the rest of the kids get there."

"Sure. That'll be great."

"Come on, darling."

"Forget it. I've got to go."

WHEN WE BEGAN to practice full contact I walked onto the field with a tremendous sense of relief. The hitting would at least be familiar to me. After twenty minutes of scrimmaging, I was called in. Players on the defensive squad began to taunt me just as they taunted every rookie who makes his first appearance, but I managed to take it personally. The line cleared a sizeable hole, and I went at it confidently, but from somewhere—I never saw him, never even sensed his presence—a linebacker cracked me like a sledgehammer, knocking me dizzy.

"Got to get to the hole faster, Collier," the running back coach called. "These are linebackers. They don't move around in wheelchairs like they do in high school. They come like trains."

Suddenly I spotted the great head coach. He stared at me behind his assassin's shades. His hangdog jowls, which sagged under the best of circumstances, seemed unusually heavy. He fiddled with his mouth, then turned away.

I was taken out of the rotation to stand on the sidelines, where I picked the hot mulch that had once been grass from my face mask. The running back coach walked over, scratching his crotch nonchalantly, and then used that same busy hand to grab my face mask. He pulled my head close to his. "Got to hit that hole, Collier," he whispered. "Disregard everything but tearing at that hole, you hear?" He pushed me away. "We know you're mean, Roy. We've watched you play. Riot-Roy. You better get to rioting. 'Cause you ain't been giving us shit out here. You're out in the wild blue yonder, running with the damned clouds."

When I went in again they sent me up the middle. I was angry and wanted everyone to leave me alone. There was no hole this time—another irate linebacker had shucked a pulled guard like so much corn—but I burst through with a roar and drove on and gained ten yards.

The head coach picked up his electrified megaphone. "Roy Collier?"

"Yes, sir." Now the grass smelled fruity and sweet, just as it always did after a good run.

"You like to hit, son?"

"Yes, sir."

"Good. Keep it up."

I quickly realized these were to be the only untroubled minutes of my existence for a long while, the only minutes that did not have to be endured, discrete moments of peace in which I knew exactly what to do and what was required of me: to run as hard as I could and to try to knock people down if they got in my way. Being a rookie, I was the one who was most often knocked down, but at least the task at hand remained clear. Day after day my ranking improved, and my reputation was established, the same reputation as the old one—quiet, shy, aloof, a hard hitter and a hard worker.

IN LATE AUGUST the other students began to arrive. Being from sleepy Citrus, I'd never seen so many girls in one place in my life. The groves and halls, which had been quiet and respectful, were suddenly palpitating with chatter. The simplest maneuvers became complicated. Stooping to tie a shoelace, for instance, formerly a mindless and solitary activity, now had to be accomplished while delectable female legs rubbed and jointed about my ears. Walking had also become difficult. I tried to avert my eyes as I threaded the campus, but I was often stopped dead in my tracks by some girl who would smile and then go on her way. These college girls seemed so carefree and leggy!

Not surprisingly, my response was to retreat and become more lonely and miserable than ever. That first week of school there was a pep rally and bonfire. It should have been a wonderful experience, but I was having trouble crediting experiences that could not be shared with April. Furthermore, she was to arrive in just a few days for the opening game, a thought that for some reason no longer sat well with me.

When I saw her—the morning before the game, she and Mother and Leonard and Henderson came to my dorm room—I was a little shocked to discover she was not quite like the image of her I'd carried with me each day to the practice field and to the weight room and each evening through the bucolic pastures and back roads and on to Bobby Lester's. Having known and adored her all my life, how was it possible that I could have failed to see this aspect of her? She looked older but more confident. She was even better-looking than I had supposed, though in a more womanly way. I had always thought she could have enrolled in Citrus High and no one would have thought a thing about it, but when she walked into my small dorm room and rushed to put her arms around me I saw that I had been wrong. Furthermore, when I tried to remember how it was that I'd been imagining her all those years, I couldn't seem to come up with anything solid and instead was harassed by fleeting visions of various girls I'd noticed over the course of the last week. By comparison, April almost looked to be a woman I'd never seen before, in a fetching dress Henderson had bought for her in New York.

"James went down to SoHo to get it," Mother explained. "One of those fancy boutiques. And the purse. And the sunglasses and shoes. I adore it. Doesn't she look great?"

April pulled down her sunglasses and winked at me. "Are you ready, Roy?" she drawled, teasing me. "We're expecting at least three touchdowns."

"I'll be sitting on the bench."

"Well, you'd better get off it."

A thin strip of black mesh had been woven around the middle of her dress, just above her navel. Later that day I could see it even from the sidelines. I stared and sucked on my mouthpiece. Smell of smoke and burning sulfur. Flood of tears. Good god, would the stupid game never end?

April and I were alone once during that weekend. Mother had gone to use the rest room, and Leonard and Henderson were poking around campus. As soon as they were gone I did the one thing I'd sworn I wouldn't do—I started crying. April hurried over and took me into her arms. "Oh, baby," she said. I wanted to plead with her, to beg her, but as I stood there, stiff in her tender arms, I realized I did not even know what to beg her for.

THAT SUNDAY NIGHT I drove out to Bobby Lester's and accepted a beer. Though Sterns hadn't come to the game, he'd sent me a letter. The paper had been folded over and over again, like a note from grade school.

Dear Roy,

I'm still struggling with the book. There's a lot of crap in it and in some places it's even worse than that. Granted, I believe there's some good passages, too, but the sheer number of pages—750 total—is beginning to overwhelm me. I figure nearly a third of that is shit, and I'm losing heart. All those bad pages and bad lines are clotting up the book and crowding out the good stuff. Sometimes I begin to imagine those bad pages are growing day by day, taking over the good pages and infesting them with bad writing. I guess I'm afraid to find out just how many pages are really awful. What if it's more like half? Or three-quarters? What if I found out ninety percent of it was no good? I don't think I could live with that. It would be like looking back over your life and finding out that most of it had been a waste of time.

And it gets worse. Some of the pages are merely notes. I was always supposed to go back and replace the notes with real writing, but I never got around to it and as the years passed I just kept moving forward, leaving all those uncompleted pages behind. I had plans to get a great many good pages written, to build up a little momentum, and then go back and finish off the ones that were mostly notes, but it never seemed like the right time. I never felt I had enough good pages or enough momentum. Sometimes I suspect that days—maybe even years—of my life are just notes like those notes in the book.

The funny thing is I've always been nostalgic to a flaw. I've always wanted to return to this or that point in time, to relive certain moments. Repeat! Yet with the book, where I've been afforded precisely that opportunity, I've fled as fast as I could. I think it must be a form of cowardice.

Anyway, this is a long, confused way of asking if maybe you'd read over some of the book. It was supposed to be about all of us, but it's beginning to remind me of me, and I truly hate that.

Yr. Obd. Srvt.,

Sterns Reel

As playful fate would have it, I received a postcard from eloquent Clancy the next day.

Punk,

Your days are numbered.

Clance.

P.S. You wouldn't believe all the women!

Sterns sent about thirty pages the following week. He explained they were foundational and had helped him properly conceive of his story. Much of the writing was historical, and he thought it might interest me. There were exceptional portraits of April and Mother and Leonard and my grandparents. I read with growing excitement. In no time I'd finished, yet April was only twelve years old. I groaned and reached for the telephone.

"Sterns."

"Yello."

"It's incredible!"

"Roy? That you?"

"Hell yes, it's me. This stuff is great. Send me more."

"You really like it?"

"Yes. I want more."

"Well, the part you've read was the easy part. Most of it doesn't even belong in the book. Anybody could have written it."

"That's not true."

"There's some things that happen later that I can't seem to get right. I'm stuck over a few things. I like experimental stuff. Loosely linked vignettes and whatnot. You know, stuff that's atmospheric. But with this, I feel I ought to stick to some kind of chronology. Not minute by minute necessarily, but you know. I guess I feel a need to document everything."

"Just send me some more."

I BECAME SO INSPIRED by his writing I tried to write a little myself. I'd tackle a few pages, and a few pages would arrive from Sterns. Soon it felt as if we were working on the same story from different angles and points in time. It made me less homesick and more confident that Citrus and Mother and Leonard and April were still there, just as I remembered them. After much pleading Sterns finally sent me a portion of the actual book. He insisted I tell him what I really thought no matter the verdict. I took the pages out to Bobby's.

For a few minutes I sat in my customary booth at the back of the truck stop, staring at the manila envelope, relishing my anticipation. Then, slowly, I opened the envelope and withdrew the pages. I intended to straighten them before I began reading, but my eyes pounced on the first sentence.

I often imagine Sanders Royce Collier coming into town that long ago Christmas Eve when the world seemed to tilt from its axis and a nightmare confusion of weather advanced upon Citrus. A cold front had descended from the north, bringing industrial hues and unforgiving temperatures, while at the same time the remains of a hurricane suddenly moved inland. Some have said the air had a faintly brackish odor, as if one were standing in a coastal town.

By four o'clock the hinterlands of the county had vanished in furious darkness, and it felt in your bones that some apocalypse had begun its devouring work from the four corners of the earth. Now, at last, the pestilence and plague-weather had surrounded Citrus, the last town left in the entire world, on the day before Christmas—and there he stood, a stranger come in from the void.

His eyes were livid, a hazardous shade of sulfuric blue, burning up everything before him. In his wake came laughter. His very presence was pungent, like the striking of a match. You would imagine trailing somewhere behind him was a ghost limousine with a ghost chauffeur, and he'd walked ahead to make a game of his arrival. Slumming. Slumming into our lives wearing tailored trousers and a fancy coat.

James Henderson was there. . . .

I looked up from that first page in an exhilarated state of shock. I couldn't imagine anything less doing service to the event of my father's arrival. And behind his arrival, behind the words describing it, I could feel Sterns himself: corpulent, heavy-footed, asweat, glowering, troubled. It was clear that Sterns knew quite a lot about my father. I consumed every word, mumbling and chewing my tongue.

"You really like it?"

"Yes, yes. You've got to send more."

"You *really* like it? Don't cut me any shit."

"I love it. I can't wait for more."

I was glad to assure him. Of course, I kept wondering if I would be in the next installment. I furthermore wondered how Sterns handled Mother and my father getting together. I wondered how he would handle Leonard's going off to war and all the other stories I'd been told. I wondered what he knew about my father's death. I wanted more descriptions of April and my father, too. I wanted to know if Sterns thought *I* had sulfuric blue eyes and a brooding presence. I wanted to see if he wrote about how he'd once despised me and hated April's concern for me. How honest would Sterns be? How much would he tell? I believed he would tell all of it and that was why it had taken him so long.

In the meantime I continued writing. I wrote to be closer to April, to make her familiar again. When I called her on the telephone her voice sounded nothing at all like the voice I was writing for her. She was solid and strong in my writing. She wasn't fading away. She was good to me. She was the way I remembered her and a little like I'd always wanted her to be, while the voice on the telephone sounded like a lie.

I TRIED TO CALL Sterns a few times to tell him about my writing, but he'd quit answering the telephone. Leonard told me he'd closed the bait and tackle down again for a few weeks, and I supposed he was trying to finish up his book. But on a rainy Monday morning in October I received a telephone call from April. Sterns was dead.

SEVENTEEN

Sterns had released his shiners into Lake Julep. He'd set his crickets free and found homes for all his stray dogs. He'd called Brother Glenn. "Jesus loves me," he said. It turned out Brother Glenn had grown accustomed to getting calls like that from Sterns and thought nothing of it. "He's crazy about you, Sterns," he replied. "Just as I am," Sterns continued, quoting the hymn. "Just as you are," Brother Glenn assured him. Sterns said he'd always thought so.

He'd left several drafts of highly specific instructions pertaining to every aspect of his death. He'd forbidden a viewing. He didn't want April or Leonard to be the ones to find him, so he called Sheriff Porter and walked out back of the bait and tackle and used his thirty-eight. He'd meant to be helpful, of course, but the extent to which he'd prepared everything was profoundly upsetting. April and Leonard went to see him privately at the funeral home. He looked cleaner than he had in months.

More than a hundred people turned out for the funeral. The line of headlights curled once around the square and on out to the highway, where they appeared to float along like gaseous disks. The day had turned hot. As we headed out of town cars pulled over all along the side of the road as passersby stopped and shut off their engines in Sterns's honor.

There were six pallbearers. Aside from Leonard and me and Henderson, the others were various friends from Citrus, men who came to Sterns for his bait and beer and companionship. He'd asked that old man Coggins be a pallbearer in one of his notes, but Coggins was too slight, and when we lifted the casket from the hearse his side veered and other men had to rush forward to prevent it from crashing to the ground.

We slowly began walking toward the hill where my father was buried, under the same ferocious sun that had shown up for his death and maybe for all the deaths in the little country cemetery. For a moment it seemed we wouldn't make it. Some of the men were actually groaning aloud. Leonard's neck bulged. I tried to take as much of the load as I could, but the weight kept shifting, and we stumbled along. Thunderclouds were building several miles away, but the air was still and humid. We were sweating through our shirts, sweating so thoroughly that it didn't matter any longer. We crossed a swarm of gnats and choked them down.

We placed the casket onto a canvas sling, suspending it over the grave. The funeral director turned a crank and lowered it into the hole in accordance with Sterns's request.

From my seat in the front row of metal folding chairs I turned to take in the familiar faces. Citrus was there for Sterns. I would later come to know funerals where the only people in attendance were a few family members and business associates, men and women who had died far from home and could not attract a crowd, much less a decent group of mourners. I've tried to imagine the terrible isolation that must have tolled so heavily upon the bereaved in those cases but have never been able to do it. Once, driving past a vast and elaborately manicured cemetery just off a highway, I spotted ten or fifteen strangers pitifully huddled about a hole in the ground and realized that the only funeral in the little cemetery of my home that had not been well attended was my father's.

I stood between Mother and April with my arms around them. Henderson and Leonard were behind us. At some point during Brother Glenn's message April broke away and walked to the far side of the grave, where she stood alone with sprigs of fern and cypress she'd collected and a brown paper grocery sack that had somehow escaped my notice. Brother Glenn glanced at her, then continued nervously, halting now and again to be sure she was all right. When he finished, a soloist from Citrus Hills began "Amazing Grace."

The first breezes from the storm reached us during the song, and April's silky black dress clung to her. I remember her complaining and worrying about its not being somber enough, but Leonard and I assured her that Sterns would have approved. The thought of going to purchase something for Stern's funeral devastated her, and she hadn't been able to do it. She'd tried to make the plunging neckline of the dress more circumspect by tying its lace drawstrings into a tight knot at her throat, but now, with the wind blowing over our heads and over the casket and the grave and against April, the dress was coming to life. It wrapped around her legs and danced and twisted behind her, the sunlight piercing the fabric.

April didn't care anymore. She stood straight, staring intently. I noticed she was too near the edge of the great hole where Sterns was to be buried, weaving and tilting toward it unreliably. I wanted to go to her and cover her and pull her to safety. Everyone stared at her. When the song ended Brother Glenn asked us to bow our heads, but no one did. He paused. He looked at April. She had knelt down and tossed the sprigs of cypress and fern onto the casket. She opened the paper sack and reached inside and for a moment just kept her hand there. Then she whispered something and held the bag over the grave and turned it upside down. Thin strips of paper tumbled out like confetti. Sterns's orphans. A few blew back up against April and she caught at them frantically, but they twirled and spun and fled her grasping fingers. Finally she dropped her hands and let them take flight. She looked up at me and smiled as if she were embarrassed and then began to cry. I took a step forward but felt a hand close down on my shoulder, firmly holding me in place. It was Leonard's.

Mother opened our house after the funeral. Since Sterns had frequented a variety of churches in Citrus, there were a variety of churchgoers and pastors and so a wide variety of food. Each and every ladies' auxiliary had prepared a covered dish to add to mother's table. The women from First Baptist brought fried chicken and macaroni and cheese; the women from Second Baptist, fried chicken and collards. The Episcopalians arrived with finger sandwiches and Key lime pie, Sterns's favorite. The women of Citrus Hills Church of God brought barbecued ribs and potato salad and more fried chicken, and the Presbyterians, a honey-baked ham.

An old black man who belonged to no church whatsoever showed up with a mason jar of whisky and claimed to be the only person Sterns had ever really felt comfortable around. He grew angry and burst into tears. "What we gone do now, huh? Y'all don't care! Nobody but God and Ripley Tucker give a shit!" he hollered, jamming his thumb into his chest.

I found Leonard on the back porch. He'd pulled his chair off to the side and was staring out into the yard.

"Sure are a lot of people," I said.

"Yeah. Sure are."

"It's hard to believe it's true."

"It's hard to believe anything," he said.

"You couldn't find his mother I don't guess."

"No. Apparently she's off in Europe somewhere. People in New Orleans said she sort of disappeared a few months back on account of her spiritual well-being or some such malarky. They claimed Sterns had been to see her before she left and that he was the only one who knew where she was. He left you his paintings and books, by the way. He left me and April the house and the land. I guess we were just about his only family.

He left you that book he was working on, too." Leonard took his fist and struck his thigh. He let out a low moan. "Oh, God!" He hit himself again. "I believe I better be alone, Roy. April's back there in the yard somewhere, back behind the canning shed. She wants to talk to you." When I started to get up he grabbed my wrist. "Sterns did the best he could," he said.

"I know." I stared at Leonard. "What is it?"

"I just want you to know we all did the best we could."

I found April pumping water and running it over her head and neck. "Hey," she said. "I just got tired of being in there." She smiled and wiped her face with a towel. "June did me a favor by keeping this old pump primed all these years. I walked out here and thought I would cry when I saw it."

"Are you all right?"

"No," she said. "I'm not anywhere close to all right. I'm not even in the same vicinity."

"Me, either."

She wrung her hair out and continued drying herself with the towel. "Go tell June I'm taking you out to Sterns's place." She looked up at me. "I already told her I was going to. Go tell her I'm taking you now. Go on."

Leonard was no longer on the back porch when I returned. I walked into the house and found Mother in the living room. When she saw me she excused herself from the group of people she was talking to and motioned me to follow her to her room. She closed the door behind us and then sat on the bed.

"Are you going with April?"

"Yes, ma'am. She wants to have a look around the bait and tackle, I guess. Sterns left me his paintings. And the book."

Mother nodded. "I know," she said. She began to cry. "I want you to go."

I took her hand and put my arm around her. "Are you all right?"

"I just love you," she said. "I've always wanted what was best for you. But sometimes I didn't know what that was." She smiled at me gently. "I want you to go with April. That's what I want. Just remember I love you."

STERNS'S COLLECTION OF the latest rods and reels, once a source of endless fascination for me, appeared dated and ready for an old black-and-white photograph. His lures and plastic worms had become mute and gray. The Rebel top-water plug from the discount bin lay in the middle of the counter. It looked like something that had died and no one had thought to close its pained, pale blue eyes. I wondered if Sterns had left it there, and then I knew he had.

April squeezed my hand. "Come on," she said, guiding me upstairs.

If Reel Bait and Tackle was a reflection of the way Sterns actually looked, his inner sanctum provided a glimpse of the way he wished to conceive of himself. The decor was sleek and stylish. The odors of bait and tackle and beer and tobacco gave way to a slightly perfumed scent. Small tables and candelabras lined the walls, which were painted a rich crimson. There were three rooms with floor-to-ceiling bookcases. In the center of each room sat a simple table and a club chair. In one room there was a planter's desk and racks for some of Sterns's maps.

April led me from room to room without comment. I looked around in astonishment. "I had no idea," I said.

"Very few people knew about this. That's the way Sterns wanted it."

"Have you ever been up here before?

"A few times. Sterns was very private about it."

"It's beautiful."

"It is. It's Sterns. This is how I think of Sterns."

April sighed, stepping out of her shoes. She undid her drawstring and rubbed her chest. She looked as if she'd just come home from a ball and was a little drunk and careless and a little hungover, as well.

"He never liked to go anywhere, but he'd read magazines and talk to antiques dealers—he dialed up the world. He thought that was eccentric. I guess it was. He'd have things shipped to Citrus from all over. 'It won't go in the trailer, Sterns,' we'd tell him. You know how he was." She laughed. "Then he'd threaten to buy us a house."

"When did you come up here?"

"Different times," she said. "Come on. He wanted you to see his paintings."

Sterns had made a fine studio of a corner room. Art books were stacked around a cot that sat under a large window. Old paint was everywhere. Though some of the paintings had been framed, none of them hung on the walls. Rather they were set against the walls, on the floor. The room was dusty. Unlike the other rooms it very much felt like a room that belonged to a person who had recently died. "Look at these first. He was just getting started when he did these."

The first painting was of April as a young girl sitting beside my grandfather. It was decently executed but lacked vitality. The next was a pointillist field at twilight, the sort of pretty but trite work found in beach houses. The third was a fetching image of April reclining on the old dock down by the lake. She had one leg up and one flat and used her arms to cover her breasts. "I did *not* pose for that," she remarked.

The next group was of Citrus landmarks. I saw the bleached square under the glare of the noon sun. The colors were rich and true, and the buildings, though carefully drawn, seemed to shimmer and grasp for personality. It was nearly Citrus. "These are good," I said. The next was of the courthouse at daybreak. A small canvas revealed the corner of Main Street and Second Avenue at dusk. A streetlight danced in a cool breeze. There was another of the square, its sidewalks filled with people: Mr. Haney and Mother and April and even Henderson. I'd passed over to a large painting of First Baptist when suddenly I noticed a dark speck off to the side of the square. My eyes jerked back. An ill-formed figure stood in the alley beside Citrus Savings. I reached out and felt of the speck that was, now that I focused on it, more of a specter. Its face was smudged of lineament. Its hands were overly large, cupped around a lighter's flame. I looked at the next painting. It was of Ligget's. The sidewalks were full of talk and movement, except for that same figure who was now fixed in a shadow. I looked over yet another painting of the square and couldn't find the figure until April pointed to the abandoned second floor of the hardware store. It was clearly my father, staring down upon the town with his blue eyes. Behind him, in the darkness of that cavernous room, gray wedges fluttered like dirty wings of ash.

He appeared in every painting after that. Sterns drew him with increasing clarity and terror. He haunted the square, brooded around street corners, stood malignantly in empty parking lots. He was just as I'd always imagined him, in some of the very places I'd imagined him. He was just as I'd seen him on I-10 and on the streets of the French Quarter. Here was Sanders Royce Collier, the reason Sterns had had to stop painting altogether.

"He shouldn't have quit."

"I've got something else to show you," April told me.

We walked into Sterns's bedroom. His king-size bed—still sadly tousled from a last night of insomnia—sat squarely and strangely in the middle of the room. Old lamps stood in the corners and before each one a tiny French chair faced the bed.

"He always thought of himself as delicate and small," April explained.

"Is this his mother?" I reached for a photograph on Sterns's chest of drawers.

"Yes. She's a pretty lady. And that's his daddy."

April disappeared into a walk-in closet and returned with a tall, messy stack of typing paper. It was the book Sterns had been working on. Sitting beside me on the bed, she handed me a note Sterns had written her. "Go ahead. I want you to read it."

Dearest April,

I know there's only supposed to be one suicide note, but I keep forgetting things, so this here is the second. Typical of me, right? Anyway, give Roy the letter I wrote for him before giving him the book. If you just give him the whole manuscript to read by himself he might not come to that part of the story for, what, maybe years from now if ever? If you can I'd like for you to be there to explain things.

When I think about you and Roy and Leonard reading this book, it makes me want to burn it. I couldn't bear the thing. It seemed horrid, an embarrassment. But what if it wasn't? And anyway, it's a tribute, whether well done or otherwise—a richly deserved tribute, I might add. I have no right to destroy it. Yet I couldn't complete it and it tormented me. We may both be heavy and larded up, but the book has a few good pages here and there. Who knows, maybe Roy will edit it one day and finish it up.

Anyway, please don't blame yourself. I said that in the other note and I'm beginning to worry about it more and more. Dearest April. This is unkind and selfish and I wouldn't do it if I could possibly avoid it. I love you and Leonard so. Don't think of me this way.

Yours ever,
Sterns

"Here's the letter," April said.

I reached into my pocket and gave her my handkerchief.

"I'll go in the other room to give you a little privacy. Just call me when you're ready. I really don't know what to say about this, Roy. June asked us not to tell you certain things. She insisted, really. Sometimes she threatened us when she thought we were going to tell you. She threatened to send you away to school or to sell the house and move away herself. And it seemed that we had no right to tell you if she didn't want us to. To be honest, we didn't much want to talk about it anyway." She touched my hand. "I guess Sterns forced the issue. He wanted you to know. He needed to explain everything to you. You'll see why, you'll . . ."

"It's all right."

"So maybe you just read."

"I'll read," I said. "Don't go far."

She hugged me tightly. "I won't. I'll be in the next room."

Dear Roy,

I wanted to write a book about all of us and that meant including what I'm going to reveal to you. I started wanting to write such a book many years ago, when you were still a child. I've shared some of that writing with you. Now I'm giving you the rest of it. You can read the book when you have time, but what I've put together here is the heart of the matter. It's one of the things that set me to writing. There is so much that April and Leonard would have told you long ago if they could have. Don't be offended that old Sterns is the one to crash the party. But, as you'll see, I have the right to.

You know how much I think of April and how protective I feel about her. I never fell in love with her the way so many of the boys did. She'd always been too kind for me to fall in love with. Does that sound strange? It does to me and I don't think I can explain it, except to say that I've always felt April was my best friend and I've always been in love with the idea of April and Leonard being together. I also might add that whenever I imagined marrying someone I cooked up a bookish little slut who used bad language. But that's another story.

Anyhow, after you were born I began to sort of watch over April. She and Leonard had married under less than perfect circumstances. How much of that she wants to go into I'll leave up to her, but the fact is their early years together were trying. I'll put it this way: Leonard quit looking out for her, something that broke my heart. And someone else took the job up in his place—your daddy. And when I noticed this one day—I saw your daddy following her through the square and following her on home from a distance—it concerned me. Or maybe the truth was it just pissed me off. I've never made a secret of the fact that I never cared for your daddy. Whatever he was up to, I couldn't believe it was good.

You were around a lot. She took you everywhere and I always thought you looked like a little idiot monkey, hanging on her like some senseless animal. As you know, I didn't think much of you until you were older and could speak up for yourself.

So it was you and your daddy and April—you hanging all over her and him sneaking around and watching her like he wanted to be hanging all over her. To be clear about it, your daddy didn't take out after her every waking minute, but he nosed around enough for people to notice. I think it's safe to say your daddy had lost his balance at that point. He'd come to Citrus playing the part of the big shot, but he'd been rattled, and his stylish veneer had begun to wear thin. He would get into fights occasionally, something that was not at all a part of the Sanders Collier mystique he'd cultivated. He became profane. He began to seem common.

Since he was following April, I felt someone should follow him. The first time I followed them the result was dismal. She hadn't gotten very far from the square when they got into an argument. April kept telling him to leave her alone, and I couldn't hear what he was saying. Finally she left and he turned back and after passing me—I was tucked behind a tree—he saw me.

"What are you doing?" he asked.

"Nothing," I said. "To hell with you."

"What did you say?"

"I said nothing. Leave us alone."

"Oh, yeah. I've been hearing that." He began to walk away, but then he stopped. "By the way, you'd better find a bigger tree next time."

That really seemed to tickle him.

At any rate, since he kept following her, I kept following her. Whenever he'd catch me, it seemed to delight him.

"Howdy, Sterns."

"Fuck you."

"Sure. I've heard that one too. Have a good day."

That sort of shit. So after two or three more attempts, I got out of the detective business. Your daddy had me beat.

But then Leonard came in one day talking about how April had been going without eating, fasting and praying, you know how she does sometimes. He said that on Wednesdays she'd come home from church late at night and then head right back out to go walking and that she would be gone for hours. The first few times he went with her, trying to talk her out of staying out so late by herself, especially since she always went into the woods, but she said she was fine and that she wanted to be alone. They fought pretty badly about it. Eventually he just gave up. He told me he felt like he didn't have the right to stop her.

She always went to the same place—those woods behind the old house where Leonard grew up. I never liked those woods. That's old growth out there. It's creepy as hell. When Leonard told me where she was going and when she was going there, I was so disturbed I asked him if I could keep an eye on her for him. "When you get caught, make sure you tell her I didn't put you up to it," was all he said.

I'd go early and find a spot and wait for her. I carried my rifle with me, my hunting rifle, a thirty aught six. It may sound fanciful, but it made me feel like I was some sort of bodyguard hired to protect April. Anyhow, those woods bothered me so much I couldn't stand to be without a gun.

I know April would have caught me hiding out there right away except she was so upset. The first time I was out there I'd been waiting for about an hour when I heard this awful moaning. It terrified me. It almost didn't sound human. But then I knew it was the most human sound I'd ever heard in my life. It was April.

I'd never heard grief like that before. And I never forgot it. I just had no idea how unhappy she was until that night. I had to sit there clinching my teeth, forcing myself to keep quiet and to keep still, but it was all I could do not to run to her. I actually felt sick inside, sick and almost dizzy. To hear or see anyone like that would be awful, but for it to be April, who was always so happy and enthusiastic, I could hardly stand it. Even more than what I'm about to explain to you, hearing her like that, completely unhinged with pain—well, it never left me.

Every Wednesday night after that it was the same. I felt guilty about being there, about hearing her and watching her. She walked in little circles for a while and then just fell to the ground, praying, crying—I don't know, just hurting. It was a horrible violation of her privacy for me to be there, but I couldn't stop. I'd watch her and begin to tear apart and I swore that I'd find a way to make it up to her and to give her a little happiness.

But then one night there was no crying. There was arguing. She came walking up and someone was with her. I saw a flashlight. That alone was strange. April sometimes carried a flashlight, but she rarely used it. One voice was April's, and pretty quickly I realized the other voice was your daddy's. There was a full moon and I could see them pretty clearly. Your daddy was drunk. He kept putting that flashlight on April and she kept telling him to stop. He was ranting about how he'd told April everything and how she'd rejected him and then how she'd done nothing to stop Leonard. He turned the flashlight on again. Said he wanted to see her better. She told him to turn it off. On and off, on and off. Finally he said she'd made a fool of him. He kept saying he'd told her the truth and why didn't she believe him. She said she did believe him and she told him to go away and then he grabbed her. I started to move toward them when for some reason I hesitated. Why? The truth is I was simply too curious to step forward and stop them. I wanted to know what the hell he was talking about and what was going to happen. I'm not proud of that, but don't worry, it only gets worse.

She pulled away and told him to go home. He blocked her again and said that she had to admit that she loved him. She pushed him and told him to stop it. "You're married. To my sister. You have no business being out here," she said. He started to cry.

This shocked me. He was the kind you would think had never shed a tear in his life, but he began to cry hard. He said he'd been tricked. He said it wasn't his fault. He wanted to know if she'd ever told anybody what he'd told her. He kept on about that, asking if she'd told Leonard, if she'd told June. You told June, didn't you? Didn't you? She began to walk away and he started after her again. He was still crying, but it had turned into a pretty fierce crying and he ran her down and they fell to the ground.

At that point they were only about ten or fifteen yards beyond me. I didn't move. I waited. You can't view my actions with any more disgust than I do, so don't bother trying. And I'll tell you the worst of it—there's no doubt in my mind that I again hesitated just to see what would happen, and worst of all, because I wondered if perhaps April felt something for your father. That is an ugly comment and an ugly thought, but life is like that, Roy, and even the best people can find themselves under the sway of something truly hideous.

April wasn't, but it turns out I was. Let me explain. It's so easy to explain everything without any fear now that I'm going away. Going away helps when it comes to writing, too, by the way, though I suppose it's not a very useful method unless you just intend to write one book. Sorry to sound so cavalier—oh, hell, why am I apologizing?

Your daddy was still begging. He said he loved her and she was saying she would hurt him and he wanted to know how she could and she said get away or you'll find out. And that's what snapped me out of it. Because I was right there with him—I realized it then, I was crawling along the ground with him, believing that when you desired someone more than anything in the world it simply could not be possible that that person did not feel the same way or at least share something of that attraction. That's a man's view, Roy. Male narcissism at its most dangerous. And it is utter bullshit.

So it was me—me and your daddy—going after her. It's sick, I acknowledge that. Nevertheless, it's true.

But her voice snapped me out of the trance I was in. There was just enough distance between me and her voice to prevent corruption. If I'd been right up on her like your daddy I wouldn't have heard her correctly. I would've heard love and desire and whatever else I wanted to hear. Being a third party, being those few feet away, I heard a young woman telling your daddy to get the hell back and meaning it. She kicked him in the face. Hard. He reached for her and they struggled. I couldn't say anything. He'd spun her around so that she lay on her back with the top of her head pointed in my direction, and he was grabbing at her dress, trying to get ahold of her. But it wasn't happening the way it happens in a movie. She wasn't giving up and she wasn't being meek, she was fighting him, thrashing around and telling him she'd kill him. Threatening him! And meaning it!

I think at that point your daddy had gone too far and it was simply a matter of wills, his against hers. At that point it was as if he had to subdue her to save face. Whatever it was he'd told her was of a nature that he couldn't live knowing she knew it and yet didn't love him. I believe he was trying to get that back or to make it so that she did in fact love him. That's what I've come to believe through the years at any rate.

My shame is in knowing that I watched for so long and was thrilled by it. I use the word thrilled, because at this juncture in my life—at the end of my life, on my way to meet my Maker—I figure I'd better not decorate the truth in the least regard. No, I don't mean I wanted to see April being attacked. And I'm far from certain your daddy knew what he was doing at all. I'm just saying he couldn't stop fighting if she was still fighting, and I couldn't stop watching in any case. I've apologized to April a thousand times and it's never made me feel any better. I've written about it over and over, and that's never done much good either. Sometimes you learn something about yourself, and you find it's hard to live with it. That's what happened to me. And to your father. I don't think he was happy about what was happening at all. I still get chills when I think about what he was saying all this time: Stop it! Stop it! I love you! Stop it! As if April were the one attacking him.

All of this occurred in a matter of seconds, by the way. I'm making it sound dragged out but it wasn't. And in one of those seconds I realized I hated your father more than anything in the world. I also realized how much I hated myself. It was easy to hate your father, and I saw it was just as easy to hate myself. I wanted to rid the earth of both of us. I guess getting rid of your father was the more urgent business, so I sighted the rifle in and fired. I wasn't trying to kill him. I wasn't trying to not kill him either. I just aimed for the middle. It blew him back and he didn't move and April was screaming. She rushed over and felt for a pulse but of course there wasn't one. "Oh, June," she said. "Oh, June." She took my hand and said I had to call the hospital. I got sick and said she had to go with me but she yelled at me and said for me to go, and so I ran back to where I'd parked my truck and raced to my place and called and then I drove right back out to those old woods again.

When I walked up April had pulled your father's head into her lap. She was rocking and moaning. "Come on, Sanders," she was saying, rubbing his head. "We've got to go see Roy. Come on. I believe you. I do." She looked up at me, crying. "Pray for him, Sterns. Please pray for him."

I did, Roy. I really did. As hard as I could.

Lolly Porter came pulling up and then the ambulance and April was telling them to hurry. Her dress was torn and she was dirty and Lolly tried to talk to her but she kept saying to hurry and finally he asked me to take her back to my place and that he'd see about Leonard and your mother and everything else.

A few days later Judge Lindsey and Lolly Porter met with us in private chambers and decided there would be no trial. April told your mama what happened, but your mama flew off the handle and said it was a lie, that it was Leonard and that she was going to get to the bottom of it. But of course she never did anything. She knew better. As a matter of fact, your mama herself asked Judge Lindsey to let everything be. She did that privately, and I didn't learn of it for years.

Your mama and me had always gotten along. Like I've told you, she'd been a real friend to me when I was growing up and I always admired her grit and her style. But after that, we were through. I never had a conversation with her again. She was never rude to me, though. Whenever we ran into each other we'd nod and say hello or whatever. As you can imagine, after what happened, neither one of us was comfortable being together anymore. But I always respected her, especially considering what took place. Now you know why I was so hard on you whenever I knew you were giving her fits. Your mama's had a lot to deal with.

There were only a few people who ever learned what happened, to my knowledge. Judge Lindsey, Lolly Porter, Deputy Chiles, myself, April, your mama and Leonard and Henderson. Most people assumed Leonard had done it and felt your daddy had it coming. Some even thought it was your mama or April. There were all sorts of rumors, but I don't think anyone ever thought it was me unless someone told them straight out.

But it was me. And now I've disappeared on you without giving you the chance to hit me or whatever it is you want to do. I can only hope you understand that I really didn't have any choice. Your father could have taken that rifle from me without any problem if I'd given him the opportunity. I have no doubt that he'd worked himself up to the point where he would not have allowed me to take him back to town at gunpoint. There would have been a struggle and I would have lost and then who knows what might have happened. Maybe nothing. Maybe not. That's what torments me. I've never even come close to getting over his death, but the fact remains I'm glad I was there that night.

As you grew older, I came to admire you. I won't take an apologetic tone, as I know this would aggravate you and you would realize it wasn't genuine. I like to think that despite that pile of poor writing in front of you and the fact that I've made a cowardly exit, you will in time come to understand my actions. I also hope you realize how much I think of you. You've made all of us—me and Leonard and April and your mama and Henderson and the whole town and I'm betting even your daddy—so proud. Because you've survived, Roy. Hell, son, you've survived beautifully.

Yr. Obt. Srvt.,
Sterns Reel

EIGHTEEN

I didn't feel like returning to the house, and April suggested we go to the lake. Even though the afternoon had by now darkened with storm clouds and the smell of rain was in the wind, when we came to the dock she said she wanted to go out in the boat, anyway.

She took my coat, and I loosened my tie and unbuttoned my shirt. She walked to the middle bench and sat and faced me, propping her elbows on her knees. "Take us far out," she said. "Don't use the motor. Just paddle."

April stared across the lake, and I knew she didn't feel like talking yet. As I rowed I recalled how I once told her I wanted to be with God and my grandmother and grandfather when I died, but that I couldn't stomach streets paved with gold nor could I abide city mansions of whatever size, no matter how jeweled. This was much on my mind, as Brother Glenn had just finished a sermon on Heaven. His news of a celestial city utterly depressed me.

I wanted to be able to fish. The disciples were fishermen and frequently camped on the shores of Galilee. Jesus performed a miracle to help them catch fish and even cooked fish over an open fire. And then to hear that after I died I was *going to a city*. How could I have been so eternally betrayed?

When I complained about this to April, she smiled and told me that I wouldn't spend eternity in Heaven, but on earth, a new earth with fresh streams and brand-new lakes and thirty-pound bass and no mosquitoes or sand spurs. Heaven was merely a waiting room. "Can I swim underwater for an hour and then fly around?" I asked. She kissed my cheek. "Can I run as fast as a cheetah?" She didn't see why not. "Can we sing as much as we want and climb trees and fall down and not get hurt and bounce back up into the branches?" We could sing, she allowed. "Will there be snakes?" She didn't believe that at all. If there were snakes, she explained, there would have to be shotguns.

"Did you know the Haneys have sold off about two hundred acres to some developer?" April suddenly asked. She motioned and pointed. "It's way over on the other side. Around both bends, over where all the summer cottages are. They're going to have a fancy subdivision. They're bringing a new furniture plant to Citrus and something else. I don't know what. We've never had a subdivision in Citrus. Old man Haney said they'd rather sell now, when they can control how they build, than to have the property sold off when they won't have any say in it. I guess that means when he's dead. Of course, a lot of his prettiest land is in some foundation he and Henderson dreamed up. It can never be developed. I don't think he trusts his daughters very much. I wouldn't. Anyway, there are all sorts of rules the developers have to follow. They're not supposed to cut down a lot of trees to build the houses, for one thing. But I don't know."

"Maybe that's the best thing, then," I said.

April's lips began to tremble. "Sterns said everything would change."

Strong gusts were striking the far side of the lake, tearing into the trees and bending them. We could hear the winds before we felt them. I dug the oar in deep. It was difficult to keep straight and almost impossible to gain any momentum. We would edge forward a few inches, yet before the next stroke the wind would drive us back. A johnboat is not an easy craft to maneuver with an oar even under the best of circumstances, but I would not relent because of April, and when a lull arrived, I put my head down and took us far out over the lake.

"I think we're about to get drenched," I said. The air was becoming heavier.

"We'll be all right."

She motioned for me to share the middle bench with her. "He left us some orphans. He wanted some to go with him, but he wanted you and me to have some." She smiled. She took my hand. "Joint custody."

I wrapped my arm around her. "I'm sorry," I said.

"Sorry for what?"

"For what my father did. I always figured something like that happened."

She put her head on my shoulder. "I think that when it didn't work out the way your daddy wanted it to, he believed I'd made some judgment about him, about his soul. Especially considering what he told me about himself. Because he *did* want to start over, to make himself over. But whatever he wanted to become, he wasn't there yet. Oh, I don't know. I was so young, Roy. Everything was happening so fast."

"What did my father tell you, anyway?" I asked.

April took a deep breath. The wind had picked up again, and we were spinning toward the shore. "We're going back. I don't want to go back."

"All right," I said.

I had to return to my seat to keep us steady. Propped on her palms, her legs outstretched, April pressed the soles of her feet to mine and began pushing against me.

"Just keep us out here. Keep us out here as long as you can."

"I will," I promised.

She wiped her eyes. "Sterns took me back to his place after that night. He called Leonard and drew a bath for me. He was terrified about what had happened, but he took care of me. Once I got into the warm water I felt better. I made Leonard go to the hospital to check on June, and when he came back Sterns told him I was in the bathroom and he came up, and after a while I said I thought I could get out and talk to Sheriff Porter. So I put on a bathrobe and went downstairs and told him everything. After he left Sterns said for us to come back upstairs and have a drink with him. He was so scared. While I was in the bathroom I heard him ask Leonard if he thought Sanders was dead. Sterns didn't want your father to be dead. He was hoping he was somehow still alive even though he knew better."

April hugged herself. She looked all around the lake as if seeing it for the first time.

"I remember sitting between them on the bed. I wanted them to be around me, like when you're little and you want all your stuffed animals around you to make sure you're safe. Poor Leonard. He said he didn't know what he would have done if I'd been hurt and that he hadn't been a good husband and now he hated himself for letting me go off by myself. Then he started telling Sterns how much he loved him and appreciated him, how he could never thank him enough. And Sterns told him that it was all right, that he just wanted us to be happy. What could he do to make us happy was what Sterns wanted to know. That was all he wanted to know. That was all Sterns ever wanted to know. What could he do? What could he do, Roy? He'd do anything. Anything at all if we'd just tell him. He'd buy us anything. He'd send us on a trip around the world. What, what? What did we want? He'd get it. He'd arrange it. Why don't you two go for a second honeymoon and have a baby, he said. Why don't you? It would be the prettiest baby in the world. He said he'd teach our baby to paint and to be an actor and Leonard could teach him football, and if it was a girl, if it was a girl she'd be the prettiest girl and if it was a boy—"

"April—"

"But we couldn't because Leonard got hurt when he went to fight. He got hurt and we couldn't. We tried. I tried to love Leonard so hard it would work no matter what, but it wouldn't. And then Leonard didn't want to try anymore. He didn't want to touch me. He said he didn't deserve me and that he'd ruined my life. And I told him, I told him—*that's not true!* And I tried to love him but he wouldn't let me. He blamed himself. But it was *my fault!* It was *my fault* he went over and got hurt. *It was all my fault.* All of it. June, too. All she went through was my fault. And Leonard never getting to play football, never getting to be a preacher, never getting to have children. It was my fault! *Everything!* Oh, Roy, we couldn't—"

"I've got you," I said, stepping toward her. "I've got you."

I held her and let her cry while we drifted into an old cypress a few feet from shore. I heard the distant patter of rain. There was no thunder. There was only rain. Even the winds died down as we waited for the cool drops to cross Lake Julep and find us.

NINETEEN

Of the many capital chats Henderson and I had, the one that stands out was our last. It was occasioned by a trip I'd made back to Citrus. Clancy and some of my other buddies were in town having an informal reunion, and I'd flown home from Washington to join them. Mother had gone shopping on one of those mornings, and I took to wandering about the house. Perhaps knowing I was a year away from finishing college created an urge to have a good look at everything. Whatever the case, that stubborn sense of privacy I had all my life cultivated began to give way. I found myself snooping around Mother's room, something I'd never done while growing up. I kept telling myself to stop, to leave . . . *to search faster*. In no time I had unlocked and gone into her closet. Though repulsed by my behavior, I kept digging. At last, in a change purse buried beneath Mother's sweaters on a cedar shelf, I found a small key. Even before I examined it I knew what it was for.

When I returned to Washington late Monday afternoon I wrote Henderson a note and placed it in an envelope. It was an odd thing to do since I intended on being there when he read it and could have just as well told him what it was I wanted him to know, but I suppose I was again reaching for something formal by way of defense, just as I had when I wore the blazer and khakis and bucks the day I drove April to Pensacola. I was prepared to hand it to him right away, but that evening when he came home he said he had something important to tell me. He was fussy and excitable, loosening and tightening his tie, patting me on the back nervously, walking around the rooms of his old brownstone while muttering to himself and checking his pocket watch. I had no choice but to wait for him to tell me whatever it was he had to tell me.

He insisted on playing the bartender that night, pouring me a bourbon and water of such strength it earned one of his most charming sobriquets. "Be warned," he said merrily. "This one's a real doozy." He handed me my doozy and had a seat with a contented sigh. We touched glasses and drank. "Oh, look, they've just lit the monuments." He saw I wasn't looking. He had another long pull and grunted. "You really don't like it here, do you?"

"This city depresses me."

"The nation's capital and it depresses you," he said, rolling his eyes.

"I thought you would go in for Greek city-states, with populations of no more than twenty thousand, isn't that right? Isn't that what Aristotle said? Not this bureaucratic empire."

"I reckon you've learned something between games."

"No, sir. Mother had it all worked out for me before I ever left for college. I'm an agrarian. She told me. She made sure of it. Just like my father."

Henderson smiled ruthlessly. "You're a smart-ass is what you are."

"You said you had something to tell me."

"As a matter of fact, I do. Something important." He picked at his trousers, then frowned. "But stop flexing your muscles every time you take a drink. It's appalling. Every time you bring that glass to your mouth you make your bicep pop up like you're in one of those body-building contests."

"All right. Just tell me."

"Well, give me a little time."

"I think I already know."

"What do you mean you already know?" Henderson narrowed his eyes and cursed under his breath. "Did she tell you? She said she was going to wait and let me talk to you first."

"She didn't exactly tell me, but I figured it out. You have my permission."

"You little . . ." He growled. "I wasn't going to ask for your permission. I just wanted to be formal about it. You're the man of the house, after all."

"And you have my blessing."

"Oh, thanks, a lot. Here I am running around like a teen suitor who's prepping to ask his sweetheart's father for her hand in marriage, and look at you, sitting there playing Charles Atlas and already knowing everything and spoiling everything. I even wore white linen today. Kept everything very traditional. You can be a real killjoy, Roy."

"Have you set a date?"

"Yes. As soon as you finish football this fall. God forbid we do anything to interrupt your football career."

"Well, I'm glad it's finally happening. Congratulations."

We touched glasses again and began to laugh.

"By the way, for your information, I wanted to get married a long time ago but your mother wouldn't. You didn't help matters, either, young man." He pointed at me. "There was always something stirring down in Citrus that kept your mother busy. And then of course *Sanders.* I guess she never wanted to be married to me while you were growing up because she didn't want to confuse you. You were *Sanders Collier's* son. End of story. I wasn't to interfere with that for one minute."

"Yes, sir. She kept things simple."

Henderson chuckled dryly. "Listen, your mother would have done anything for you."

"I know that." I looked at him. I didn't want to ruin his announcement about the coming engagement, but I couldn't wait any longer. "I have something I want to talk to you about, too," I said. "About my father and keeping things simple."

"Oh, yes. Our favorite subject." He grinned and had another sip of his drink. "Now that we're going to be family I guess we can get everything out in the open. Of course, I think we've covered just about everything already, haven't we?"

"No, sir. Not everything."

I stood and removed the envelope from my pocket and handed it to him.

"What's this?"

"Here, I'll freshen our drinks."

I heard him tearing the seal behind my back. "You're an odd duck," he said. "This must be one of your tricks." Then he went silent.

I opened the satchel yesterday. There was a pocket that had been sewn shut and I cut it open and found the bronze star and the letter from the president. I'm going to see the Colliers right away. I want you to call them for me. But I want you to explain everything first. I've said nothing to mother.

When I turned around Henderson's eyes were glistening. The letter rested on his lap. One of his hands had been balled into a fragile fist that hung from the edge of his armrest. He stared at me pitifully.

"I'm going before school starts," I told him.

"You can't, Roy," he said softly.

"Well, I am. With or without your help."

"You can't go see the Colliers. I'm sorry. Sit down."

"Why not?"

"I'm going to tell you. Sit down."

I gave him his drink and returned to my chair. He began reading the note again, rubbing his head.

"My god," he whispered. "So no one ever told you."

"Told me *what?*" I asked harshly.

Henderson looked up at me with a pained expression. He winced and focused and then turned to the window.

"It's hard to believe. All these years. I always just assumed . . ." He shook his head. His hands were trembling. "Of course, who *would* tell you? April and your mother were the only ones who knew, aside from me. I thought after a while it might get out, but now that I think of it, April wouldn't tell anyone because she promised not to and your mother . . . your mother . . ." His eyes were drawn back to the letter. "I suppose it might as well be me. I suppose it makes sense in a way." He shook his head again. "Oh, Roy. Where do I begin?"

"How about who does the Bronze Star belong to?"

"To your father."

"But that's not him."

"Yes. It's him."

"No it's not. I saw it. It's not him."

Henderson said nothing. He simply looked on with a blunt compassion I found unbearable. After a few seconds he folded my note and put it back into the envelope and placed it on the table between us.

"It turns out your father had a secret, Roy," he began, still keeping his glassy eyes on the envelope. "He told April about it. She was the only person he ever told. Your mother had to learn his secret the hard way. She had to learn it the hard way twice, actually. The first time through April. April told her because she knew your mother was falling for your father and she felt your mother had a right to know the truth about him. So I reckon April broke her promise that one time. For your mother's sake. The second time your mother learned your father's secret firsthand, you might say. But it was too late by then. At that point, she was already in too deep because of . . ."

"Because of what?"

"I'd better back up."

"Because of me."

"Did April never mention any of this to you?"

"I knew my father told her something she wasn't supposed to tell anybody. I figured it was some lie he'd made up."

"Well, it wasn't. It was the one time he told the truth."

"So what did he tell her?"

"Who he was. William Cane. The name on the letter of commendation. That was his given name. I'm sorry, Roy. . . ."

My heart tightened and burned. I wanted to stand but could only glare at Henderson with my jaw clenched.

"Sanders Royce Collier was a name your father took on. He took it on legally. He changed his name is what I'm trying to say. I'm terribly sorry, Roy. I had no idea—"

"So there are no Colliers?" I shook my head and attempted to laugh. I wanted to call Henderson a liar, to point my finger at him and take him on, but I kept sitting there smirking, growing strangely ashamed. "My *name* was made up? And my *father?* All of it was just *made up,* is that what you're telling me? And Mother *knew it?*"

"It's more complicated than that. I know this is hard."

I stood then. I felt as if I wouldn't be able to get out of the room, but I did. I walked to the bathroom and locked the door.

WHEN I RETURNED Henderson was standing by the window. He came over and touched my arm. "Roy," he said.

"Who are the fucking Colliers? *Are* there any? *Besides me?*"

"Let's sit down. Come on." He guided me over, and after we sat he reached into his pocket and leaned toward me. "Here."

"Just go on. Just tell me."

"Here."

I took his handkerchief.

"The answer is yes," he said, sitting back. "Yes, there are Colliers. Yes, they're from South Carolina. Yes, they're wealthy and all that. And they *knew* your father. But they're not kin to you. There was even a Sanders Royce Collier. He served in Vietnam with your father. But *your* father was from Okeechobee, Florida, not South Carolina. He was the son of the foreman of a cattle ranch. His father, your *real* granddaddy, was an alcoholic. . . . Roy?"

"Please."

"All right." He sat back. "Your father got into some trouble when he was young, that's what started it. He stabbed a man with a straight razor, and the judge told him he had a choice: He could either go to prison or he could go into the military. I talked to the judge once. This was years ago when I was checking up on your father. I'd been suspicious from the beginning, and after he was killed I had a little investigating done. I tracked him back to his real name and his real hometown. The judge said your father was smart as hell and mean as hell and kind of a pretty boy, but he felt like your father had the potential to amount to something with a little guidance, which is why he didn't send him directly to prison. I tried to tell your mother all this one time, but she accused me of conspiring with April, and I thought, *Why in the hell, now that Sanders is dead and gone, why am I doing this to this poor woman who has suffered more than enough already?* There didn't seem to be a good reason. There wasn't a good reason at the time, was there?"

He looked over as if waiting for an answer. I stared back, clutching his handkerchief.

"Well, anyhow, what she said about April made me think April knew something, too. And one day I was talking with April and we both sort of realized that we both knew the truth about Sanders. It turned out everything he'd told April aligned with everything I'd learned. April knew a lot more than I did, of course. I'd just gotten the skeleton—she'd been given the flesh and blood. In a way, when I learned the whole thing from April, I had to admire him. For better *and* for worse, your father was an extraordinary man, Roy."

"Just tell me what happened."

"Well, he went into the military and got sent overseas, is what happened, and that's where he met the real Sanders Royce Collier. *This* Sanders *was* from a pretty illustrious family. He took your father on as something of a little brother. Told him all about his life and what it had been like growing up in South Carolina. He started to teach him the social graces. Taught him about clothes and women. Your father had told him about how his daddy used to beat him—which was true, from what I gathered from that judge—and how he really didn't have a family of his own, how he was all alone, which was also true. His mother died when he was just a little boy, and he never had any brothers or sisters. It was just him and his daddy, and like I say, they didn't really get along.

"So the real Sanders Collier told your father he'd help him. Noblesse oblige, you might say. He told your father he'd lend him some money once they came back home. He explained that he could get the G.I. Bill and go to school and that he could stay in South Carolina as long as he wanted as his guest. Meanwhile, he'd written to his mother and father telling them all about Sanders—your father, I mean—and they wrote back and of course they were more than willing to help. Your father had had it pretty rough, after all. April said she asked Sanders if the beatings happened when his daddy was drunk and he said he didn't need to be drunk to beat on him, he did it just as well and just as often when he was sober. Your father deserved some help."

Henderson sighed. "But the plan got fouled up. It got fouled up because the real Sanders Collier died. He was shot in combat. That's how your father won the Bronze Star. He dragged the real Sanders Collier out of a very bad situation. There are no two ways about it—your father risked his life and saved Sanders Collier's life. Unfortunately Sanders Collier only lived a few more weeks. And when his parents learned what your father had done, they begged him to stay with them as soon as he'd finished his tour of duty.

"He was a hero to them. Hell, he *was* a hero. He was on the run from some hot spot when the Collier boy got gunned down. There was heavy fire, and their situation had deteriorated to the point where it was every man for himself. But your father shot his way back and carried that Collier boy right out of there. That *is* uncommon bravery and valor, just like that letter says. Whatever else may be true of your father, whatever else I've told you about him, that much is true, too.

"Anyhow, quite naturally, the Collier family wanted any contact with their son they could get, and that meant contact with your father. They became very attached to him. And they could think of no finer way of honoring their son's memory than to help your father out since he'd put his life on the line for their son and had been his closest friend overseas.

They let your father live with them, bought him clothes and gave him spending money, you name it. For a while, it must have seemed perfect. But then the sister. Oh, boy. Your father and the Collier boy's sister began to fall for each other."

"Was that the girl he got caught with in the motel?"

Henderson eyed me carefully. "What did your mother say about her?"

"That she was someone my father had dated, a high school sweetheart. That there'd been a scene in a motel involving my grandfather Collier. That he'd . . ." I turned away. "I don't know. What happened?"

"Well, she *was* a high school sweetheart. Principally because she was *still in high school.* And they did get caught in a motel. But it wasn't any grandfather Collier who caught them. It was the girl's father, Mr. Collier."

Henderson waited to see if I would look over. When I didn't, he continued. "The father took it about as well as could be expected, I suppose. He wasn't angry, just disappointed. He and his wife had clung to your father like a second son. They doted on him and even made big plans for him to go to school. Oh, they had high hopes for your father. And according to April, your father had high hopes for himself, as well. He'd never been loved like that before. No one had ever gathered him in and mended him and told him he could make something of his life. Besides all of which he was awfully gratified to be pleasing those Colliers, to be mending *them* and giving *them* a little relief. But then the sister."

Henderson took a drink and cleared his throat. "Maybe if their daughter had been a little older or if she and Sanders had courted with their clothes on . . . who knows? From what I learned I'd have to say they weren't necessarily against them being together. If your father could have been a little more decorous it might have been fine. It wasn't as if they thought your father wasn't good enough. But when Mr. Collier caught them together, that was a little much to ask him to bear. He told your father he'd have to move along. He even gave him a few thousand dollars of traveling money. That was a heck of a lot of money back then. He didn't feel hostility toward your father. He was actually sad that Sanders had to go. But the party was over.

"Except it turned out the girl was pretty hooked on your father. She'd wire him money whenever he was short. She wired him money right up until he died as a matter of fact. The Colliers allowed her to do it. As long as Sanders was away from South Carolina, they wanted the best for him. One thing they didn't know was that she begged him to run off with her, to elope. And that's another thing to your father's credit—he wouldn't, even though he wanted to. He wouldn't, out of respect for the Colliers. He told April that he'd wanted to prove he was worthy of their love. That he'd go away just as they'd requested, and maybe if he went away for a while and became successful and then came back, they'd be proud of him and he and the Collier girl could be married after all."

"The sister was the girl Mother found him with when she followed him to South Carolina," I said.

Henderson nodded. "Yes, that was the sister. After your father's situation with April blew up in his face, he kind of got wild, chasing April around all the time. People didn't like it one bit, and at some point I guess he knew he needed to get out of town. He was having a hard time behaving like Sanders Royce Collier. He was starting to act like William Cane. So he went back to South Carolina to see the girl."

"Did Mr. Collier ever catch them and come at them with a crowbar?"

"*Mr. Collier?* Heavens no! What a crazy idea. That was . . ." Henderson's mouth slowly closed. He shut his eyes and rubbed his head. "That was your Mother," he said softly.

"She was going to tell him that she was pregnant with me. That's why she followed him up there."

"I don't know exactly what happened, so don't ask. I know she spotted them in a diner and followed them to the motel. And then she pried the door open—or maybe they'd just left the door unlocked, I don't know—but at any rate she had a crowbar and apparently she broke the place up pretty badly. It was in that motel room that she learned the truth the second time the hard way. Because when your mother asked who the girl was and heard her say her last name, Collier, your mother thought Sanders had run off and got married and there she was, pregnant with you. And then the girl says no, she's Sanders's sister, and well, my god, who knows what your mother thought then? I reckon all three of them came unglued at that point. They were on the third floor and a chair and a lamp ended up in the pool, I'll tell you that. It sounds comical, but I've never been able to laugh about it. Not once. More importantly, neither has your mother."

Henderson groaned quietly. He cupped his hand to his forehead as if taking a measurement.

"She's told me things about finding them but always on the worst occasions, when she would be hysterical and it would be two in the morning and you were out being a bassmaster with April. I never knew what to think. I know it was bad enough that the owner of the motel called the police and they were arrested."

"Arrested?"

"Oh, yes. But not the girl. They let her go. They didn't even call the Colliers. I think they saw her as a victim of the whole debacle. What a mess. I had to call the man who owned the motel and talk him out of pressing charges. Do you know who called me? Your father. He begged me to help get them out of trouble. I promised the owner we'd pay for everything and talked to the police and to your mother to calm her down. I hate to think of your mother going through all that. She was awfully young, and she'd believed everything your father had told her. When April came to her with what Sanders had said, it must have seemed like the most ridiculous story in the world." He sighed. "I don't know. Maybe not. Maybe what April told her seemed like the truth the first time your mother heard it. And maybe the fact that he'd gone to April to reveal it seemed like the truth, too."

I folded Henderson's handkerchief and set it on the table next to the letter. I felt that as long as I didn't look into his eyes I could ask him anything, and that I should.

"Did the Colliers ever find out he'd changed his name to theirs?"

"Oh, I don't think so. Perhaps it would have flattered them. You've got to hand it to your father, he'd concocted quite a transformation. Between Sanders and June, you're bound to have one hell of an imagination. You ought to be able to make up anything out of thin air. Just get your accents right. The little things always give you away. Your father never did have the South Carolina accent down. But he had the name. Perfectly legal. And he had those lovely initials: SRC."

"Except the letter from the president."

"Yes. Except that letter."

"Did you ever talk to the family?"

"Sure. After I talked to April I called to tell them your father had died. They were upset about it. They said they would have come to the funeral if they'd known. That's when they told me they'd thought of him as a sort of second son. I sometimes wonder what might have happened if the real Sanders Royce Collier had lived. What if he'd had the opportunity to teach your father and to make sure your father and his sister didn't get out of hand. Because your father was a quick study. He just needed more work and more time. But before he knew it, he was left to his own devices again.

"Just think about it—your father might well have ended up at the University of Virginia. That's where the other Sanders had gone. After your father had served his country like he did and with the whole Collier clan behind him, why, hell, it very well could have happened. And if your mother had gone to Virginia, which she would have, she might have met your father anyway. Under those circumstances they could have made quite a pair. Even if he hadn't shown up that Christmas Eve, you might have come along anyway." Henderson tilted his head back. "Maybe you were inevitable, Roy."

"Maybe."

"Well, inevitable or not, there's one thing you must always remember—your mother did the best she could. I can just guess some of what she's told you over the years because she's told me the same, as if I didn't know different. But you have to understand that your father's death was a critical turning point for your mother because she had so much riding on who he was. Maybe she'd made a mistake by marrying him, but since he was dead it was possible to believe everything had been just fine. He was available to anybody who came along and needed an alibi or a justification or a sense of importance, anything, you name it. Don't tell me you never gave him a little work from time to time. He may have been willful and stubborn before he died, but afterwards he became downright pliable, didn't he? And as far as your mother was concerned, if you couldn't have a father, you could at least have a heritage. You were going to have a prestigious heritage, by god, and with your father out of the way it was entirely possible.

"The ironic thing about all this is that your father was hot and heavy to found something prestigious himself. He never wanted to be rich or famous or powerful. Not one bit. He wanted to look good and to be a damned *patriarch,* for god's sake. He told me so more than once. He wanted to start his *own* line of Colliers. I say ironic because he wasn't altogether excited about having a child, as you well know. And because he was by nature a drifter. Not a happy drifter but the kind who's being pursued by something. Well, you put all that together and then realize that he founded something after all—by dying and letting your mother take over the patriarchy for him. She was better at it anyway. Talk about insurance, your father left one hell of a nest egg."

"And Mother was always worried I wouldn't draw down on it."

"That and she knew it was all a fabrication and couldn't come to grips with it. Everything she ever felt for you was filtered and refracted through God only knows how many lenses and mirrors—her guilt about April, her jealousy about April, her admiration for Leonard, her contempt for Leonard, her feelings for your father, that South Carolina trip. She looked at you through a kaleidoscope, Roy. A horrifying one. And the little shapes and colors just kept shifting around as the world turned, and she had to look harder and harder to make sense of it. That just happens to be the human condition, of course, but for your mother, I suppose, the pieces moved faster than for other people. The colors were darker, too."

Henderson took a long drink and rested the glass against his stomach. "But how she loved you. And when she saw what she'd been doing to you she was terrified. The first thing she wanted to do was to tell you the truth, but she thought she was too late and that someone had already told you and that you'd lost your respect for her. That someone was April, of course. And it nearly killed your mother to realize that your father had told everything to April in the first place, never mind what happened between April and your father, another thing that nearly killed your mother. Because if she hadn't dragged Sanders back from South Carolina that whole business might not have happened. You have no idea how guilty your mother felt about that, which was one of the reasons she gave April such freedom with you. That along with the fact that April and Leonard couldn't have a child of their own, which made you something of a gift, a peace offering."

Henderson shrugged. He took a deep breath and held his head back.

"Your mother would sometimes tell me April did a better job with you than she did. She believed it, too. She almost felt like she didn't have a right to you. And we'd sit here, right in this very room, having a good time, when all of a sudden everything would hit her. I tried to console her, but I didn't know what to do. Finally I'd have to call April. Because for all the tension between them, April was the only one she ever really trusted. And April said the same thing every time: 'Come home, June. We miss you. We need you.' And then your mother would pull herself together and go back home to Citrus."

"She was a good mother," I said.

Henderson looked over at me, surprised. His eyes glassed over again, and I handed him his handkerchief.

"She was a good mother," I repeated.

We stared at each other, and then Henderson nodded his head and smiled. "I guess things didn't turn out so bad, did they, Roy? The Sanders Royce Collier ideal wasn't such a bad one, after all. Your mother just wanted the same thing for you that your father had wanted for himself—to be strong and honest and dependable and to have a little style. What the hell's wrong with that? Your father didn't get very far with his plans and there were parts of his plans that were just phony, granted. And perhaps your mother pursued those same plans in ways that weren't always best, and I know it's hurt you plenty, but I daresay it's benefited you as well. And I'll tell you something else. The William Cane story is inspiring in its own right, don't you think?"

"Yes, sir. I do."

"You know, I've always thought about that Christmas Eve from our perspective. I've told you a thousand times. I always think about the moment *before* we saw him. The square all dressed up for Christmas. Those two storms coming on. Everything so dark all of a sudden. And June and April just a couple of girls sitting at a soda fountain, wondering what Santy Clause was bringing them. Our lives were before us. All the possibilities. And then, in a flash, all those possibilities are gone. Your father has arrived.

"But your father had dreams, too, as you now know. I've said some rough things about your father in the past. I always thought you already knew everything. One minute you feel you've been too hard on Sanders, and the next you think you weren't nearly hard enough. I guess the one thing he never counted on was April. He went for broke for her. Laid all his cards down. What a hand he had. He'd been attempting a brilliant bluff, but telling the truth was by far the trickier and riskier proposition. Coming clean was the best your father could do. I can only imagine what it took for him to do it. And I can only imagine what it felt like when it didn't work. The wonder is, he never got rid of that damned satchel. He never destroyed the evidence. But I guess it was evidence of courage, too, not just lies." Henderson touched his chin thoughtfully. "Speaking of which, did you sew that flap shut after you opened it?"

"No, sir. I finally gave William Cane his freedom. He'd been a prisoner of war long enough."

"Yes, I suppose he had." Henderson chuckled and then looked at me nervously. When he saw me smiling he allowed himself to laugh freely. "You liberated him from a P.O.W. pocket. I reckon in a way you've liberated all of us."

He stood and weaved a little. "Damnit if I'm not good and pickled.

But I'll have one more. I'm a congressman. The last thing in the world you want is for me to go to work tomorrow." He took my glass without asking. "Whatever became of your little high school sweetheart, by the way?"

"She's fine, I guess."

"She was a real spark plug. Passionate. You don't find a woman like that very often. She really loved you. And I'm here to tell you, in case you haven't figured it out, that you're not by a long shot easy to love."

"I had no idea."

Henderson pushed the tongs to the side of the ice bucket, digging in with his bare hands. When he returned, he handed me a doozy and stared at me intently.

"Are you all right, Roy?"

"I think so."

"I think you are, too." Henderson patted my shoulders, then took his seat and crossed his legs. "My lord, and now you're about to graduate. One more year. Seems like just the other day I was picking out that dress for April for your game. You remember that?"

"I remember that dress."

"Damn right you do. Who wouldn't? Boy, your mother was really trying to get into the swing of things to make up for lost time. She wanted to become the biggest Florida State booster ever. Being June that didn't mean some tacky football sweatshirt or a cap. Oh, no. That meant something fashionable. And expensive. First thing she did was send me traipsing off to Barney's to get you suited up some more. Do you know what you cost? Take a guess?"

Henderson motioned with his drink, sloshing bourbon over the sides of the glass.

"More than you're worth is the right answer. As if you were going to have the chance to wear those clothes anyway. Anyhow, your mother wanted a new dress for that first game. I had reason to be in New York, so I went to Saks Fifth Avenue. I was long distance over the telephone with your mother and the saleswoman went and picked up on the same line across the way. It was like we were air-traffic controllers. God amighty. But we got her set up. Did she ever look pretty."

"She did."

"And we decided April should have some sexy little number to wear, so I headed to one of those boutiques in SoHo and poked around and found just the place. I recognized it instantly. It was the window where, when I looked through it, I saw a good-looking blonde salesgirl smiling back at me. Well, she goes digging around and says she's got just the ticket. I wasn't much impressed at first. A two-thousand-dollar shift is how I thought of the thing until I saw April wearing it. It was nothing more than that, a damned slip, a piece of black cloth with two spaghetti straps. But my god, once she had it on, it was revelatory."

"And you got her those sunglasses and shoes."

"And that little purse! Don't you *dare* forget *that.* That damned purse cost nearly three hundred dollars and it was no bigger than a postcard. But it was like living out a little dream, shopping for them. It almost sounds like we were having fun back then, doesn't it?"

"I suppose it does."

"Well, hell. We *were* having fun, Roy."

"I guess we were."

"Until poor Sterns." Henderson snapped his fingers. "That reminds me of something I've been meaning to ask you for a long time. Did you ever finish that book he was working on?"

"Every word. I read it right away."

"I figured. Did you learn anything?"

"Yes, sir."

"For instance?"

"What to do with myself."

Henderson squinted and cocked his head. Then he said: "Oh, no! Don't tell me! *You're going to write a book!*"

I began to laugh. "I didn't say that."

"I should have known. I reckon you've been perfectly prepared for it. And it's your revenge for being kept in the dark for so long. You rascal.

You'd damn well better not make me look bad. While you're at it, make it so that I never switched parties. I regret that." He looked at me excitedly. "Oh, I bet you do, though—I bet right at the very end you'll really stick it to me."

"I didn't say I was going to write anything."

"Haven't you heard that books are dying out anyway? There aren't going to be readers much longer, they say."

"That's all right by me."

Henderson seemed proud.

"That's right. I reckon a book like what you have in mind doesn't get written for any reason like that." He sighed. "Just please tell me it's going to be fiction. Tell me you won't do one of those confessional numbers."

"I wouldn't do that."

"You'll have to change all the names, of course."

"There's been enough of that already."

"You'd better change mine!"

"All right."

"So what will happen to your name? Will you make yourself a Cane? Or will you reverse the whole thing and make Collier the original last name and Cane the assumed name? Or something different altogether?"

"You'll just have to see."

"I suppose there's one name that can't ever be changed, though."

"Yes, sir."

"Is that what you're going to call it? That's what I'd call it. It couldn't very well be called anything else, could it?"

Henderson looked at me tenderly and nodded his head.

"Well, Roy, long may she live." He raised his glass. "To April."

EPILOGUE

Henderson had always been right about a great many things, but writing a book wasn't what had been on my mind after reading Sterns's manuscript. Furthermore, once I'd learned the truth about my father during that final capital chat, I was more certain than ever that what I had to do was "survive beautifully," as Sterns so nicely put it.

When I went upstairs to the guest room that night and closed the curtains and got into bed, I didn't feel betrayed or burdened or wronged as I might have expected. More than anything else I felt gratitude. I believed that Mother and Henderson and Sterns and Leonard and April and even my father had invested a great deal in me. My heritage, as Mother would have it, may have been complicated, and it may have possessed some aspects better abandoned, but that did not make it any less mine, nor did that mean it was any less nourishing or fruitful. Just as Henderson had suggested, between Sanders Collier and William Cane, there was all the room in the world for me if I had the courage for it.

Some changes weren't long in coming. After graduating from college I was drafted by the New Orleans Saints, but it proved to be a deeply dispiriting endeavor. The fact of the matter was, football no longer seemed necessary, and since it had never been a game in my mind, once it lost its necessity, it lost its power. After my second season on the bench I called it quits.

One night the following spring I was fishing with April when I stopped casting and began to peer into the empty spaces between the stars that so troubled Pascal, the very spaces I'd come to feel were something of my own. "I'm going to go to seminary," I announced.

"When did you decide this?"

"Just now. Or maybe it was a long time ago. I don't know, maybe it was inevitable."

Henderson pushed me to become Episcopal and promised to arrange everything. "If you don't become Episcopal, it will kill your mother," he said. "Though let me tell you," he added gravely, "I don't have the slightest idea *why* you're doing it. I think you'd make a rotten preacher."

About that same time Henderson gave a hundred acres of land to Leonard and April. It was a gift, he said, from himself and Mother. Twenty acres fronted Lake Julep. They built a two-story house with wrap-around porches and a tin roof, though they kept the trailer, which remains on the other side of that fated property line to this day. They built a dock, too, and Leonard bought April a bass boat that sparkles. Whenever I'd come home from Sewanee for a break from my studies, Mother and I, and sometimes Henderson if he was around, would drive over and sit with Leonard and April and Howl and watch the sun drop behind the cypresses and oaks across the lake. Mother had started school herself and would eventually graduate with honors from the University of Virginia. "Well, one of us *had* to do it," she said when she handed me her diploma.

My own academic experience proved more troubling. Intense readings and coffee-wired evenings led to severe depressions and fantastic binges. I'd come to after a sordid weekend and notice that I'd drained several fifths of bourbon. Perfectly innocent books had been tossed at glowering lamps, and opened beer cans and tins of food littered the distressed apartment. It seemed quite odd and not a little terrifying to have arrived at seminary only to become more unsettled.

During one of those weekends Lorri-Anne looked me up and knocked on my door. She peered into the apartment aghast but said nothing.

"Aren't you married yet?" I asked.

"No, and obviously you aren't, either," she said, pushing past me and shaking her head at the mess.

She was in graduate school in psychology at the University of Florida. She'd run into Clancy—who was still playing football and, just as I predicted, had started a ministry for wayward teens—and he'd told her where to find me. "He thinks you're doing fine just because you're in seminary."

"I am fine."

"No, you're not."

"I don't have constant sugar," I said.

"Well, that's *your* fault."

Naturally I decided to continue my abasement until I had a doctorate of theology. My dissertation, available only in the darkest basements of the most indiscriminate libraries, was titled *Edenic Insights: Postlapsarian Glimpses of Paradise*.

When I graduated I was sent across Mobile Bay to Point Clear, Alabama, a few miles from the Florida–Alabama state line. A small congregation meets there in a quaint antebellum church made of simple white planks of wood and filled with simple wooden pews. Mother took one look and adored it. They continue to use the 1928 edition of the Book of Common Prayer, and the bishop thought I'd fit right in, though it just so happened I was the only person he could locate who evinced any enthusiasm for the position. Most of the parishioners are well up in years and utterly unimpressed with fads and new theologies. They appreciate sermons about Heaven and a world made new, subjects I am well equipped to deal with.

For a long year I lived alone in perfectly named Fairhope, but the following autumn Lorri-Anne drove through that old tunnel and across that trusty bridge that she had not allowed me to burn, and the first thing out of my mouth was, "Would you marry me?" Soon we had two sons, Leonard and Royce, Jr., and later Sterns, an angel of a daughter who could dance on the head of a pin if she pleased or wriggle into anyone's heart.

We summer in Citrus, of course. We Christmas in Citrus, too. We're there for spring breaks and fishing weekends, as well. I'm afraid it's become popular, just as Sterns warned. All the playful otters have vanished. The alligators are going fast, and there aren't as many fish. We tell the children of how the lake was once open and wild and how there were only a few houses. "And a Coggins," my daughter insists. "And Sterns." Yes, I tell her, there once was a Coggins and Sterns.

I'm proud to report that Lorri-Anne has convinced Mother and April to become more elaborate with their beautifying techniques. They get manicures and pedicures and facials and scout out skin creams to keep them youthful. They attend culinary seminars together. Leonard and I take the boys hunting, and we've put them on a training program that includes protein shakes, sprints and workouts. April and I take the children into the woods to climb all our favorite trees. There are assignments galore. After much protest, April finally admitted she needed reading glasses, and Lorri-Anne, a smart spectacle wearer of many years, met her in Mobile, where they spent a ridiculous sum of money. We still go fishing together, April and I, though as often as not Sternsy or one or both of the boys will come along. Whenever we sneak off by ourselves we talk about my sermons or the weather or Sterns or even my father, but sometimes we just sit quietly. Occasionally we may be seen passing notes like a couple of flirts. Orphans.

I realize I've been very fortunate, but every now and then the bliss seems to break my heart. Whenever I feel one of my strange tremors coming on I'll head to my study, which overlooks Mobile Bay, and bring out Sterns's manuscript from the bottom drawer of my desk. It's full of Latinate rambles, endless digressions and indulgent cul-de-sacs, but that's just the kind of thing that suits me. All the stylistic tics and antics are simply the heavings that precede a lost child's lonely tears. And the detours down avenues of alliteration are only wistful wanderings after the jingles and jangles of old nursery rhymes, the search for the beloved mnemonic devices that polka-dot the playground of one's past. I read around and around.

Sometimes I take it a page at a time, sometimes a year at a time. It's all there for me, a sourcebook written by a suicide who killed my father. There's no telling where I'll land. It might be that long-ago Christmas Eve when my father is walking up Main Street as a nightmare confusion of weather advances upon Citrus. It could simply be a dappled sunlit day, and April is toting me down the dirt road while I clutch a lime green Christ's-words-in-red-letters New Testament. Perhaps Mother and Leonard are on the fifty-yard line being named king and queen of Citrus High. Or Leonard is running a touchdown. Or I'm running a touchdown. April is cheering. I hide behind trees with Sterns. I take rides in Henderson's Thunderbird. I watch Leonard throwing the football to himself. I dive into Julep's midnight waters. Now and again I flip a page just in time to catch a young man taking a pint of whisky into the night for a dance he'll never get to. My line gets tangled. *Every fancy word stands. Repeat.*

After a while the pages always become fuzzy, though, and I find myself staring out over the bay in a stupor. My hands twitch. My heart trembles. I try to see all the way across to the spot where April and I had po'boys so long ago. I imagine us sitting on those wooden benches. She gives me a look over her sweetheart shades and tries to keep her dress down. Then we get into that true-blue Mustang, which I still drive. Or sometimes I simply close my eyes and picture Lake Julep and the lone dock. She stands there waiting. Everything is blooming—the magnolia and wisteria and dogwood all at once. Lightning bugs flit across an expanse of twilight sky. A perfect place full of hopkins, and I'm going there with a foamy crown of No More Tears. I've walked down to the shore yearning to do just that many times, wanting to go to all the old fresh places again as if for the first time. Of course, the only way to do it would be to walk on water.

Don't think I haven't tried.

ACKNOWLEDGMENTS

I have depended on the kindness and support of friends throughout my writing career. Fortunately, I've been gifted with friends in abundance. Here are just a few of them—with apologies to those not mentioned—in no particular order:

Dear Jessica Perkins for her joy and steadfast devotion. Jack and Lela Perkins for so many good times. Tim Griffin, a Federal Reserve of enthusiam. Jay Nordlinger, who saw *April* when she was just a baby. Alison Nichols for repeated rescues. Kyle Jackson for the same. Julie Rose for her wonderful intelligence, unfailing generosity and for believing in my work early on. Duncan Murrell for savvy exertions on *April*'s behalf. Kathy Pories, *April*'s new friend. All the others who have worked hard for *April* at Algonquin. Amy Williams, of ICM, for putting on the brass knucles and Ron Bernstein, also at ICM, for escorting *April* safely around wild Hollywood. David Kuo. Jimmy Cundiff. Kathan Dearman who remembers how it all began. Greg Vaughan, kind brother. Jay Oglesby, my reliable comrade of many years, who never flinched from telling me to stay the course. Scott P. Jones, my oldest chum, with whom so many dreams have been shared and realized. Last are all those in my beloved Jackson, Mississippi, who helped make a happy home for me and *April:* Fenian's, sweet, dark Martin's, where one finds Wade, Pam, Robert and the legendary Beaux Miller. My enablers at Bravo. Geronimo Rex, the band. Tim and Ed for securing the perimeter. Thomas Morrison and all fellow members of the Blue Tongue club. John Evans and my pals at Lemuria. Lida and Gregg Caraway. Kevin Broughton. The inimitable, talented Bob Kelly. The hardest working man in the friendship business, "Super" Dave Myers. Dean Vonkrull, from whom I learned so much. Mac, fine neighbor. And Sid Scott, who knows very well—and who lived to the fullest—the exasperating splendor of 945 Bellevue Place, where so many great things began.